MYSTERY

Cooper, Natasha
Bloody roses

20.00
1/93

Bloody Roses

Bloody Roses

NATASHA COOPER

CROWN PUBLISHERS, INC.

NEW YORK

Published by Crown Publishers, Inc., 201 East 50th Street, New York,
New York 10022. Member of the Crown Publishing Group.
Random House, Inc. New York, Toronto, London, Sydney, Auckland

Originally published in Great Britain by Simon & Schuster, Ltd., in 1992

CROWN is a trademark of Crown Publishers, Inc.

Manufactured in the United States of America

LIBRARY OF CONGRESS CATALOGING-IN-PUBLICATION DATA
Cooper, Natasha.
Bloody roses / Natasha Cooper.—1st American ed.
p.   cm.
I. Title.
PR6073.R47B58   1993   92-30328
823'.914—dc20   CIP
ISBN 0-517-59022-0

10 9 8 7 6 5 4 3 2 1

First American Edition

For
Sheila and James Turner

Author's Note

All the characters, institutions, organizations, companies and partnerships mentioned in this novel are wholly imaginary and have no connection with any in the real world. As far as I know there has never been a murder in a London merchant bank. Long may that happy state continue!

Prologue

SHE died as the knife sliced through her trachea. It had already severed the left carotid artery and blood had spurted all over her desk. The offer document she had been checking was covered in blood and so was the Yellow Book that lay beside it. There were horizontal splashes across the flickering screen of her computer and across the long yellow silk dress that hung against the grey partition to her left. Even the roses, which had been pure white, were pied with crimson streaks.

As she died, she fell, pulling the keyboard of her computer with her. The hem of her slim, knee-length skirt caught on the edge of the chair and so she hung with her head bumping on the floor and her legs sprawled over the arm of the chair. The knife had taken her life and all her dignity, too. She was a thing by then, ugly and frightening.

Chapter 1

WILLOW lay with only a sheet covering her. The bed was hard and high, uncomfortable and yet so suitable to the big empty room with its tiled floor and few pieces of massive antique furniture that she forgave it. She had propped her pillows against the heavy walnut bedhead so that she could look out through the window at the hillside opposite.

The day had been hot and the walls and red-tiled floors of the old house were still warm to the touch. But the grey-green olive trees outside looked as though they were made of icy foil in the moonlight. The leaves moved in the slight wind, changing from white to silver to grey and back to white again. She envied their coolness.

Something whined in Willow's ear. She brushed the fly away and then wiped the sweat from each eyebrow in turn with her forefinger. Lying still, she waited for proof that the poison tablet on its little plastic heater could really kill.

Detaching her attention from the mosquito's possible and longed-for death for a moment, she looked sideways at the sleeping figure beside her. Tom slept on his back, without a sound, his chest hardly moving as he breathed, as though not only his mind but even his reflexes had been relaxed by the long, slow days in the sun.

They had both been tired when they arrived at the old farmhouse on the borders of Tuscany and Umbria, but Willow had satisfied her urgent need of sleep more quickly than Tom. They spent their days idling beside the swimming pool, which seemed incongruously modern and sparkling among the bent olive trees, the rough grass and the few tall cypress spires of the so-called garden. Their simple meals consisted of pasta, vegetables, *prosciutto crudo* or salami and fruit, and they drank the thin local wine.

Occasionally one or other of them would murmur about driving into Perugia or up to Arezzo for the day, but they rarely stirred from the house and garden. They swam sometimes, and made love often in the hot darkness of their shuttered bedroom, and felt a million miles away from London and the books and bodies that filled their working lives. Tom never talked of his manifold anxieties about cases he had left unfinished, and Willow ignored the complexities of her London existence, in which she lived not only as Willow King, a civil servant taking a six-month sabbatical, but also as 'Cressida Woodruffe', a bestselling romantic novelist.

Sleep began to dissolve the edges of Willow's mind as she contemplated the leisurely journey across Europe that she and Tom had made to the glorious landscape of low, curved, golden hills and dark cypresses. Thinking of the easily pleasant days they had spent together, she slid down the bed, idly watching the scene in the window change from silver trees to dark-blue, star-speckled sky. Her eyelids closed and reddened pictures of the olive trees formed inside them.

Her eyes opened as the silence of the room registered in her mind and made its edges firm again. A slight, satisfied smile twitched at the corners of her mouth as she thought of the mosquito's death. Once more her concentration faded and her eyelids began to droop. Her hot limbs felt heavy as they pressed downwards against the unyielding mattress.

A new buzzing disturbed her heavy fall into darkness and pulled her back with a jerk. The sound came again, then stopped, sounded once more. Understanding it at last, Willow put one damp, languid hand on the bedside table and reached for the telephone receiver.

When it was comfortably resting half on her bare shoulder and half on the coarse white pillow, she said carefully:

'*Pronto?*'

'Willow, is that you?'

There was a rawness in the urgent English voice that made her concentrate at once. Abandoning her minimal Italian, she said:

'Yes. Richard? You sound very odd. What's the trouble? It's the middle of the night.'

'I've been arrested.'

'What?'

Willow sat up, the sheet falling away from her naked body. There was some movement beside her but she did not feel it.

'They think I murdered a woman in the office. Christ, Willow, I need help.'

'Don't panic,' she said, sounding businesslike enough to make Tom sit up too.

He could not resist watching her as she sat in the moonlight, oblivious of him and of herself. She looked wonderful with her dark-red hair flowing about her pale body, which the sun was never allowed to colour. All the angularity that had once distorted it had gone. She was still slim but there was a new grace about her as though she had become used· to herself and knew how to move with her body instead of against it.

'Have you got a lawyer?' Willow's voice was serious.

'No, that's the point. The only ones I know deal with mergers and acquisitions, and sometimes fraud. They've no experience of this sort of thing. I need a criminal lawyer.

You've been involved with murder cases. Tell me who to get.'

'I'll have to think, Richard; I . . .'

'This is my one telephone call. You're the only person I can think of who can recommend the best man.'

'I will. Calm down and tell me what happened.'

'Her throat was cut. I found her.'

Richard's voice sounded choked and the horror in it worried Willow far more than the ludicrous news that he was suspected of murder. Knowing he was unlikely to get bail, Willow tried to think what she could do to help.

'Where are you? I'll get someone to you as soon as I can.'

'The King William Street police station. Willow –'

'Quiet. Don't worry. This can be sorted out. Don't say anything to them. Make them give you tea or something and hold on until someone gets there.'

'Willow, I've . . . I've got to go.'

'I won't abandon you. You'll be all right. Hang on.'

There was a click on the line and Willow was left clutching the receiver, her mind empty of everything except Richard's horror. A large, warm hand closed on her wrist and she started.

'Willow?'

Tom's reassuring voice sounded confident beside her in the half-darkness. He rolled over, took the telephone receiver out of her hand and leaned still further to replace it on its cradle.

'What's happened?' he asked as he propped himself up against banked-up pillows.

Willow's pale-green eyes looked dazed as she tried to focus on his familiar face, darkened by the sun and the whiteness of the pillows to a rich tan.

'Richard Crescent has been arrested for murder,' she said slowly. 'There's been some mistake, but I've got to find him a lawyer.'

'The miracles of modern telephones,' said Tom with a

note of caustic in his voice that made Willow's eyes sharpen and her lips thin. It was odd how easy it was to forget that he was a policeman.

'In the old days a suspect would never have been able to ring beyond London, let alone Tuscany.' Watching her face, Tom added: 'Don't look like that; I'm not taking this lightly.'

Willow switched on the lamp and saw from the hardness in his dark eyes that he was telling the exact truth.

'Murder is never a joke,' he went on. 'What happened?'

Willow told him what little she knew, adding: 'I must find him the best lawyer. What a good thing you're here, Tom. Who should I get?'

'Do you think he did it?' he asked, ignoring the ease with which she seemed to have forgotten he was her lover in her need for his police experience.

Willow got out of bed and walked away. Coming to the foot of the bed to stand with her hands gripping the bedstead, she looked at Tom.

'How can you even ask that?'

'Come on, Willow,' said Tom gently. 'I hardly know the man; that's why I asked you. You do know him. And it's important: different talents are desirable in lawyers acting for the innocent and the guilty. I can't recommend anyone unless I know which is more likely.'

'Richard Crescent could not kill anyone,' said Willow, enunciating each syllable as though she were swearing an oath in court.

'Good. Then I'd suggest a man called Martin Roylandson of Tithe, Kingdome. He's excellent and very quick to protect the innocent.'

'In other words, loathed by the police,' said Willow sharply because she was suddenly afraid of what Tom represented.

He shook his head, running both hands through his thick, dark hair. 'The last thing the police want to do is go miles down the road of getting together a case against an innocent person. Come back to bed, Will?'

'You don't really believe that's always true, do you? After everything we've learned recently about the fitting-up and the doctoring of evidence.' She pushed her hair away from her hot, damp face and then shook her head, trying to speak more kindly.

'I can't come back to bed. I must get hold of this man. I don't suppose you've got your address book with you?'

'Try Directory Enquiries,' Tom suggested. 'Or would you rather I did it for you?'

Willow closed her eyes for a moment. The question was typical of him; he would never bother to play games just because someone had snapped at him, and he would always help if he could. Knowing that, she could not take advantage of his offer. She shook her head and reached for a towel to wrap round her body and went downstairs to find an Italian telephone directory. Twenty minutes later she was still trying to get hold of the London Directory Enquiries.

Tom appeared, also wearing a towel, and silently handed her a mug of tea. Regretting the things she had said and the way she had said them, she waited until he had put the mug down beside the telephone and then took his hand and held it against her cheek. With his other hand he stroked her head.

'I know it's bloody for you,' he said quietly, 'to be so far away and unable to help. But if he is innocent he'll be all right. He may well not get bail—this sounds like a pretty brutal killing—and imprisonment will be frightening for him and humiliating, but it won't kill him.'

Willow put the telephone down on her knee and turned in her chair to look up at Tom.

'It's the fear and the humiliation that make me so sorry for him; it's not that he and I . . . I'm not still . . . He's just a friend these days.'

'I know,' said Tom seriously, and then added with a glinting smile that she knew well: 'After all, you're here with me.'

'*Pronto,*' she said, having seized the squawking telephone. 'No: British Directory Enquiries.'

An incomprehensible flow of Italian made her shake her head and put the telephone back in unbearable frustration. Languages had never been among her talents and she knew that Tom's did not include Italian. She picked up her address book again and flipped through the pages. Half a minute later she had dialled a number and was waiting while it rang in a small Kensington house.

'Hello?' said a gentle, sleepy voice just in time to stop Willow giving up in despair.

'Emma, is that you? It's Cressida here. I'm sorry to ring so late, but I need your help badly.'

'Cressida! Golly! I mean, of course. What can I do? I thought you were in Italy.'

'I am. That's why I need you. Richard Crescent has been arrested for murder.' There was a gasp and Willow remembered, too late, that Emma Gnatche had always had a schoolgirl crush on Richard.

'I have to get a lawyer to go to the police station to act for him,' Willow said briskly, because it was too late to wrap up the announcement in some acceptable euphemism. 'Tom has recommended one called Martin Roylandson of Tithe, Kingdome, but I simply cannot find out how to get his home telephone number from here. Emma, will you take over?'

'Yes,' she said at once.

Willow remembered with relief that, although Emma was only a year out of school and still planning to go to university, she had spent several months working for a Member of Parliament and was said to be a reasonably competent secretary. She could be relied on to find the lawyer.

'I'll get him somehow and go and see Richard, too, if they'll let me,' Emma went on.

'I knew I could count on you, Emma. Will you keep me posted?'

Willow read the telephone number of the farmhouse and then, having listened to renewed assurances from Emma, she rang off.

'Tom,' she said, sitting staring at the telephone, 'I don't think I'll be able to sleep. You go back to bed and I'll sit and brood for a while.'

Instead of obeying he picked up her mug of tea and his own.

'Don't be a clot. I'm not leaving you to sit through this alone. Come and drink your tea outside. It'll be blissfully cool.'

With unnatural obedience, Willow stood up and followed him out through the heavy oak doors to sit at the long, grey marble table and drink her English tea.

The cicadas shrilled and crackled and small bats swooped down to pick flies off the surface of the blue swimming pool. As a cloud shut out the moon, Willow asked Tom what would be happening to Richard. Quietly he explained the details of police procedure, describing the sort of cell in which Richard would be spending the night and what would happen to him the following day.

Two hours later they went back to bed and eventually even Willow slept.

The next morning Willow could hardly bear to leave the house, even to breakfast at the table under the vines, in case Emma should telephone. Tom persuaded her that if they left the shutters open the telephone's discreet buzz would reach as far as the terrace.

The heat was already drying the dew from the grass round the pool and burning the thin white mist from the valley as they shared a pot of strong coffee and toasted rolls spread with fig jam. Willow looked across to the terraces of olive trees with regret. The holiday, on which she had embarked with such reservations and yet found to be so satisfying, was over. Tom had proved to be the most undemanding and at the same time most stimulating companion she had ever known. To Willow's surprise neither their isolation from the rest of the world nor their unwonted proximity had troubled her.

But Richard Crescent was in a police cell, afraid and facing a murder charge. Even though he had yielded his place in her life to Tom many months ago, Richard mattered to Willow and she could not sit by and watch him suffer.

Tom sat, drinking the bitter dregs of his coffee and watching her across the marble table. Some sun flickered through the vine-leaf canopy and fell on her face. She was so intent on her thoughts that her eyelids never blinked even when a small spider lowered itself on an invisible filament just in front of her face. Tom leaned across to remove it to a safer distance.

'What?'

'Only a spider, Will. It's absurd to say "don't worry", but Richard won't benefit from your misery.'

Willow was too intelligent to protest at that piece of common sense and an appreciative smile did relax her lips for a moment.

'I know. But it helps me to worry about him.'

There was a short laugh from Tom and he leaned across the table to touch her hand lightly. 'I've always thought it strange that someone who has lived a double life like yours for so long should be so honest,' he said and then stood up. 'I've got an errand to do this morning in Siena; I assume you won't want to come, too?'

Willow shook her red head. 'I must stay and wait for the telephone.'

'Okay. But don't forget that you can hear it out here just as well as indoors. You might as well benefit from the fresh air while you can. I'll be back as soon as I can. Keep yourself together.'

With his usual unhurried ease of movement, Tom collected his car keys, money, sunglasses and battered panama and drove away. Willow carried the breakfast dishes into the kitchen to await the attention of Paola, the daily maid, and brewed another pot of coffee to drink on the terrace.

It was half past eleven before the telephone rang, and there was still no sign of Tom's return. Willow dropped the book she had been pretending to read and ran into the sparsely furnished drawing room to seize the telephone.

'Emma?' she said.

'Yes.' There was a gasp in Emma's voice and a roughness that suggested she was working hard to control herself. All at once Willow felt calm and in charge. Pulling a pad of paper and a pencil towards her, she said:

'Did you get the solicitor?'

'Yes, after quite a lot of trouble. He was a bit reluctant to go out in the middle of the night, but I did manage to persuade him and he's just rung with news. Oh, Cressida!'

'Tell me.'

'He's been accused of cutting the throat of a woman called Sarah Allfarthing, who worked at the bank.'

'But why, Emma?' Willow's voice was sharp once more. 'How could anybody imagine Richard doing something like that?'

'Apparently he was found, covered in her blood, beside the body. And there was no one else at the bank except for the security men on the door and a man in the computer room downstairs, who couldn't have done it.'

'I don't believe that,' said Willow at once. 'From all Richard's said, there are always people there practically all night. It's part of their Battle-of-Britain fantasies to work ludicrous hours.'

A small flying creature landed on her bare arm and she swotted it angrily, slapping her own flesh hard enough to make her wince.

'Not last Friday,' came the rueful answer. 'It was the bank's annual summer dinner dance. Everyone had gone. Richard was due to be there, too, but he'd just flown back from Japan and was late.'

Willow thought for a few seconds, absent-mindedly stroking the reddening patch on her arm.

'There's obviously some other explanation. You and I both know that he couldn't have done it. Hang on to that. Do you know who is handling the case for the police?'

'A woman called Jane Moreby, Chief Inspector Moreby.'

'Thank heavens it's a woman,' said Willow without thinking. 'Give me Mr Roylandson's office number and I'll ring him up tomorrow.'

Emma dictated the telephone number and added: 'Aren't you coming back? Richard needs you. They let me see him when I took him some clothes this morning and he's desperate.'

Willow thought of Tom and his enthusiasm for their long-awaited holiday. All possibility of pleasure in it had been destroyed for her by Richard's predicament, but she could not force Tom back to London early. And yet the thought of Richard's anguish pulled at her, like barbed wire catching on loose knitting. Immensely competent in her civil-service work, highly successful in her life of fantasy, Willow found that the business of caring about other people, on which she had embarked only in the last year or so, was proving endlessly difficult.

'I'll come back as soon as I can,' she said at last. 'Please ring me whenever there's news.'

'All right,' said Emma with noticeable coldness just before she rang off.

Paola appeared in the doorway, plump and bustling, to ask Willow something in Italian. She shook her head. After much sign language it became clear that Paola wanted to know whether to prepare lunch.

'Si. Grazie, Paola,' Willow managed to say.

Tom drove up on to the gravel sweep a little later and came round the house to find Willow sitting at the table once more. He held out a flimsy, red-covered folder.

'It's the first flight with a spare seat: tomorrow morning from Pisa.'

'Oh, Tom. I . . .'

'Never mind. I went to buy you a cordless telephone so that at least you could lie by the pool while you waited, but halfway to Siena I realized that you'd have to go back and so I bought the ticket instead.'

'Won't you mind doing that long drive back on your own?'

Tom shook his head and then grinned. 'Your sitting beside me in a state of suppressed hysteria would make it much more difficult.'

'That's playing dirty,' said Willow with a grimace. But when she took the ticket from him she was much kinder.

Later that afternoon, as they were lying side by side at the edge of the swimming pool with Tom's body in full sunlight and Willow's in the heavy shade of a canvas awning, she asked him about Chief Inspector Jane Moreby.

'You'd like her,' he said, propping himself up on one elbow. His shaggy eyebrows contracted over his broken nose. 'Is she handling Richard's case?'

'According to Emma Gnatche.'

There was a silence that filled Willow with foreboding until Tom said again:

'You'd like her. She's remarkably intelligent and thoroughly sensible. I'd be surprised if . . .'

Willow looked at him, the recent trust and affection fighting with the coldness that had always been her refuge.

'You sound as though you think she must be right about Richard,' she said at last.

'Occasionally she does let her prejudices get the better of her reason,' he answered slowly. 'But then that is true of us all. I'd be surprised if she were ever badly wrong. There must be a reason, Will.'

He looked down into Willow's face and she saw that his eyes were hard.

'The only consolation I can offer you is that she is far too sensible to get things badly wrong. If you are right and there is some evidence that Crescent is innocent, she will be easily convinced by it.'

'That doesn't sound as comforting as it ought,' said Willow slowly.

'No.'

Chapter 2

'MISS Woodruffe, if you really wish to help Mr Crescent, I suggest that you write him cheery letters and send him one of your books to read,' said Martin Roylandson.

'And knit socks and perhaps bake a rabbit pie,' Willow answered tartly. She was in a state of such anxiety that her powerlessness to do anything for Richard was causing her acute distress, which as usual took the form of.anger rather than tears.

If it had not been for Tom's recommendation of Roylandson, Willow would have taken an instant dislike to him and tried to find someone else to represent Richard. The solicitor was a short, stout man with pale-red hair that looked so dry that she expected a shower of dandruff to fall out of it whenever he moved. Like his mincing manner and his virtually rimless round spectacles, the unattractive hair made her think he must be both old-fashioned and unintelligent.

He was wearing a pinstriped suit of a particularly dark blue cloth and across his rounded waistcoat hung a gold watch chain, as though he wanted to be thought an old man. In fact he could not have been more than fifty, if as much.

It shocked her that she could be so swayed by something as silly as a man's physical appearance, but she found it hard to believe that anyone who looked as he did could be both perceptive and hard enough to fight Richard's case as it should be fought.

'The patronage was unintentional,' he said in answer to her small outburst. He bowed slightly as he spoke, but there was no snowstorm of white flakes from his head. Willow accepted the apology.

'I have had a certain amount of experience of murder cases,' she said, forbearing to remind the solicitor that she was paying his bill and therefore planned to force him to accept her help, 'and fully intend to do what I can to get Richard out of prison. It would seem sensible as well as economical of effort if we were to cooperate.'

'Very well.' There was resignation as well as a certain grudging respect in Roylandson's high, dry voice. 'What is it that you wish to do?'

'Discover enough to prove that Richard did not commit the murder.' Willow's pale-green eyes narrowed into the first hint of a smile that morning. 'To do so, I need to know exactly what it is the police have on him.'

Pushing his spectacles further up his inadequate nose, the solicitor grimaced as though he disliked her use of slang, but he pulled forward a file and read out the précis he had made of the police evidence against his client. Willow listened in fierce concentration to a more detailed account of the scene Emma had described to her over the telephone.

'And where was the blood?' she asked at one moment.

'Everywhere.' The solicitor's dry, red eyebrows twitched. 'His hands, his face, his shirt front, his trousers, his coat, his shoes . . .'

'But that sounds as though he'd rolled in it. It's absurd.'

'The severing of carotid arteries tends to produce a considerable quantity of blood, as does similar damage to the smaller vessels in the neck. Besides, my client was in the process of moving the cadaver when he was disturbed.'

Roylandson pursed his lips in distaste, whether at the thought of the bloody mess or Richard himself, Willow could not decide.

'Have you got photographs of Richard and the scene of the crime?' she asked as calmly as though she did not even know him.

'Not yet. But I shall have them in due course. The police have promised to send a set of prints.'

'And Richard was really the only person in the building? How can they be sure that she hadn't been killed earlier when there were more people around?'

'The last people who are known to have left the corporate finance department went at seven fifteen. The condition of the blood suggests that Mrs Allfarthing must have died only a short time before the body was discovered, a suggestion that is confirmed by the short-circuiting of her computer only minutes before the man from the computer room found them.'

'Short-circuiting? I don't understand.'

'The blood that dripped from Mrs Allfarthing's severed neck into the keyboard of her computer caused the electricity to short-circuit. The time at which that happened is recorded on the monitors in the basement computer room.'

'Then perhaps she did not die at once,' suggested Willow. 'She might have been only wounded and then slowly bled to death.'

Roylandson visibly controlled himself. In a voice even more precise than usual, he said:

'When the trachea is severed, death is apt to be instantaneous. Besides that does not alter the time at which the computer went down.'

'Oh, yes. Silly of me,' Willow murmured more to herself than to him. She knew that she would have to study the police photographs for which she had asked, but the very idea of them sickened her. 'But you were going to tell me about the inhabitants of the office.'

'Apart from Mr Stephen Draycott from the basement and

the janitors at the door, everyone else was at the dance. They were all required to identify themselves at the door to prevent gate-crashers and each employee and his or her companion was ticked off the list as they entered.'

'Surely the murderer could have done that to establish an alibi and returned to the bank surreptitiously,' said Willow, surprised that Roylandson should not have seen that himself. 'Climbing out of a lavatory window or something.'

'That would seem possible, but they would have had to enter the bank building by the front door, since all the others had already been locked from the inside, and so pass the two janitors, who have reported that no one except my client entered the bank after half past seven when the doors are locked. As you can imagine, I have nothing with which to defend my client except his statement that the woman was dead when he entered his office. There really is nothing that you can do, Miss Woodruffe.'

Roylandson straightened his right arm and admired the plain gold cufflink that glowed chastely against his faintly striped shirt.

'I refuse to believe that. Richard is the least violent of men, and he —'

'Ah, now we come to a most unfortunate piece of corroborative evidence for the police.' The solicitor pushed himself further back into his leather chair and looked over Willow's head to a set of dingy grey-and-white architectural prints that were supposed to enliven the cream-coloured wall opposite his desk.

'Yes?' Willow's face was cold and her voice was one that many of her junior civil servants would have recognized.

'Yes. At a meeting three days before the incident, Mr Crescent was seen by several witnesses to take hold of the victim by her shoulders and shake her. He was said by more than one of the witnesses to have been in a violent rage.'

Willow's face was blank with a mixture of shock and stubborn disbelief.

'I must speak to Richard himself,' she said, getting out of her chair and pacing up and down the solicitor's tidy room.

'You will find that he won't deny that he shook her,' said Mr Roylandson, taking off his spectacles and laying them on his desk precisely equidistant between his telephone and the wire tray that held his incoming letters.

'Nevertheless I must see him,' said Willow, finding herself infected by Roylandson's pompous phraseology and clear articulation. 'Will you please arrange it for this afternoon? You can presumably identify me as one of your temporary clerks.'

'That may be difficult.' Willow looked up and was disconcerted by the sight of a prim face suffused with laughter. 'I've never had a clerk – temporary or otherwise – who dressed at Yves Saint Laurent.'

After a moment in which she was too surprised to speak, Willow looked down at her plain suit and then smiled with equal amusement. There was also relief in her face.

'I'm quite used to disguising myself,' she said, thinking of the ill-dressed, severely coiffured spinster she had been before she had invented Cressida Woodruffe. Until she had taken her six-month sabbatical from the civil service, she had turned herself back into that much-despised figure for the three days every week that she had worked as an assistant secretary at the Department of Old-Age Pensions.

Leaving behind not only her expensive clothes but also the luxury of her Belgravia flat, she would return to the small flat in Clapham that she had bought when she had first been promoted to principal. It was only ten minutes' walk away from the dull modern tower block that housed the department, and the mortgage that she was still paying was well within the means of a part-time assistant secretary. But it was damp and depressing.

Her growing confidence in herself and the life she had built with Cressida's royalties had begun to persuade her of the absurdity of retreating to Clapham every week and she had decided to try life without the civil service. Too cautious to resign before she knew what it would be like, she had told her establishments officer more of the lies she had always used to conceal her days as Cressida Woodruffe and been given six months of unpaid compassionate leave.

'And I have plenty of other clothes,' she added with a smile.

'I see. Then perhaps we've both been guilty of judging by appearances.'

Willow met his eyes and thought that she saw the ghost of a very different man looking out of them: a man of wit and intelligence and all the sharpness she could have wanted. She could not imagine why he assumed such an absurd part and made himself appear so foolish, but since she had played her own, not dissimilar, games for years she was prepared to believe that he had a reason.

Martin Roylandson reached for the telephone and made an appointment to see Richard at the prison at half past two that afternoon.

'What about suicide?' Willow asked as he put down the telephone receiver. 'That sounds the most likely alternative explanation.'

'Suicide will undoubtedly be our best defence, but it is nevertheless going to be difficult to prove.'

Willow raised her eyebrows.

'There was no suicide note. The police checked all the desks in the department and all the wastepaper bins in case it could have been misplaced, and there was nothing.'

'Presumably not everyone leaves a note,' Willow suggested, not convincing even herself.

'I cannot recall hearing of any woman who could bear to take leave of this life without leaving an essay in explanation.'

Willow's lips tightened. Roylandson allowed himself to smile at her expression.

'In addition to that, the nature of the wound suggests it was not self-inflicted. Very few suicides have the resolution to kill themselves that way without several unsuccessful cuts. There was only one slash across Mrs Allfarthing's throat.'

'I see.'

'There is also the condition of the victim's scalp, which apparently suggests that her head was held back with enough savagery to pull some of the hairs out of her head.'

All Willow's frustrations and anxieties were taken over by a single surge of sympathy for the dead woman. The imagination that allowed Cressida Woodruffe to capture the interest of hundreds of thousands of readers across the world made it impossible for her not to understand something of the pain and terror Sarah Allfarthing must have suffered before she died.

Somehow Willow buried the sensations deep enough to allow her to thank Roylandson and get her out of his office. She went straight back to her large flat in Chesham Place intending to change out of the green suit into something less obviously expensive. Her housekeeper, who had promised to look into the flat every few days while Willow was on holiday, came into the tiny, polished hall just as she was shutting the door behind her.

'I saw that you were back, Miss Woodruffe. Is everything all right?'

'I'm afraid not,' said Willow and, as gently as possible, told her housekeeper what had happened.

The shock in Mrs Rusham's eyes and the uncharacteristic quiver in her voice made Willow urge her to sit down.

'No. I'm perfectly all right,' she said, drawing herself up to her full height of five foot three inches. 'But how is Mr Lawrence-Crescent?'

Mrs Rusham, whose devotion to him was of such long standing that it would probably not change even if he were to admit to murder, was almost the only person who ever used Richard's full surname.

'I know very little yet.' Willow wanted to be kind, but she had nothing reassuring to say. 'I shall be seeing him this afternoon and things ought to be clearer by then. I must change. Do you think you could manage some kind of lunch by half past twelve?'

'Certainly, Miss Woodruffe. Perhaps this is the moment to tell you that I've made no arrangements for the next two weeks and I should like to work as normal.'

'Are you sure? I know how inconvenient my return must be to you.'

'I am perfectly certain. No inconvenience could possibly matter compared with what may be happening to Mr Lawrence-Crescent.' She gasped, recovered herself and retreated to the kitchen. Willow watched her go, and then shrugged and turned into her bedroom.

It was a big, light room, decorated in cool ivories and grey-greens with small touches of pink to set off a frivolous eighteenth-century painting of a French *fête champêtre* she had bought a few years earlier. There was an Irish lace counterpane on the bed, and on the pink-clothed circular tables at each side were French porcelain lamps, new books and matching cream-ware vases filled with identical arrangements of dark ivy and pale-pink roses. There were ivy and roses printed on the pale chintz curtains that hung in heavy swags at the windows.

Willow, who usually spent a few minutes admiring the room each time she went into it, ignored all the possessions and arrangements that she had chosen with such care over the past nine years. She did not even notice the newly arranged flowers as she went to fling open the doors of one of her big wardrobes.

There were lots of designer suits and dresses hanging there, each one swathed in a linen bag to keep the dust and moths away, but she pushed them aside and found a plain, relatively inexpensive navy-blue linen suit, which a solicitor's clerk might well have worn. Choosing a blue-and-white-striped shirt and a pair of low-heeled black court shoes, Willow dressed and then made up her face again with no mascara and a much paler lipstick. With her hair tied back into a simple knot, she looked quite different from the rich, elegant woman who had been sitting in the solicitor's office. Her nose looked bigger without the counterweight of blackened eyelashes and her eyes much paler. When she had taken out the big gold earrings she had been wearing, her transformation was almost complete.

She went to a small safe hidden at the back of the wardrobe, in which she kept some of her jewellery and all the official documents that confirmed her life as Willow King. Taking out a pair of pale-rimmed, unfashionable spectacles, she slipped them into her handbag.

When she walked into the small dining room at precisely half past twelve, Willow saw Mrs Rusham looking at her in some surprise and said with a self-conscious smile:

'Do you think this is suitable dress for a police cell?'

The housekeeper's face cleared at once.

'Yes, indeed,' she said and placed in front of Willow a delicately arranged salad of grilled goat's cheese with rocket and radicchio.

There was a chilled bottle of San Pellegrino mineral water and a new loaf of olive bread, which Mrs Rusham had baked that morning. She retired to the kitchen and Willow ate, making a list of all the things that she wanted to ask Richard. It would be frustrating to leave him and realize too late that there was one vital question unanswered.

The questions all seemed irrelevant when she found herself face to face with Richard across the grey plastic-coated table in the stuffy green prison interview room. She had known that he would look tired and distressed, but she had not imagined anything like the defeat or the desperation she saw in his grey-blue eyes. He had not shaved and as he sat slumped in his chair, running his long fingers through his greasy hair again and again, she saw that the nails were cracked and dirty. There were bags under his eyes and the eyes themselves were red with sleeplessness and pain. But they looked straight at her and never slid away as he answered her questions, and that alone gave Willow some comfort.

With the solicitor at her side, she asked Richard to tell her precisely what happened when he arrived at the office from Tokyo on the night of the murder. In a voice as hard and expressionless as the sound of a machine, Richard told his story.

'I got to the office at about ten past eight. There'd been an appalling snarl-up on the M4 so that the drive from Heathrow took twice as long as it ought,' he said, scratching the side of his nose.

'Why didn't you take the tube?'

'I had two enormously heavy pilot cases of documents,' he said, shrugging and transferring the scratching finger to his ear. 'I'd done a damn good deal for the client and I was bloody tired. Oh, God!' he said and stopped scratching so that he could cover his face.

Willow laid one long white hand on his shoulder.

'Come on, Richard. We haven't all that long. If I'm to help, I must get through these questions.'

'Sorry,' he said, pulling up his head and straightening his shoulders with a visible effort. 'After all the scandals of the last few years I'd sort of accustomed myself to the thought that I might one day be a witness in a fraud trial, but this has thrown me completely.'

'I know.' There was real sympathy in Willow's voice, but it grew brisker as she went on: 'So, you decided against the tube, although you knew that it would be quicker than a cab.'

'That's right.' Richard took a deep breath. 'I staggered up the steps at the bank, let Bert (one of the security men on the evening shift that week) open the main doors for me, because of the two bags, and he summoned the lift. I got in, went up to the fourth floor, got out . . . Do you really need this much detail?'

'Absolutely.'

'Fine.' Richard rubbed his eyes. 'Then I walked across to the doors to Corporate Finance. I had to put down the bag in my right hand then in order to punch in the code that opens the doors.'

'Punch in?'

'Yes,' he said, sounding impatient. 'The doors are electronically operated. There's a keypad to the right of them. We all have to use the code to get the doors open.'

'I see. Thanks. Then?'

'Then I picked up the case again, walked through, kicked the door shut with my foot, and walked round to my cubbyhole. There seemed to be no one else in the place. It's hardly ever like that. I had been going to change in the bog, but since I was alone I dumped the bags of documents and dropped my trousers.'

That was the first time Willow had heard Richard use the crude slang of his schooldays. She let it pass without comment.

'Where was your dinner jacket?'

'Hanging on the edge of the partition. I'd left it there in the cleaner's bag before I went to Tokyo, because I knew I might not have time to go home to change.'

'Why not? Wouldn't it have been better to go straight home?'

'Oh, God!' said Richard again. 'Don't you think I wish I had? But the documents in those cases were highly secret. I couldn't risk it. I knew I'd have to get them back to the bank before the weekend. My flat just isn't secure enough. I –'

'All right, Richard. Forget about the papers. What happened? You'd just changed when I interrupted.'

'N'yah,' he muttered, taking hold of his wits again. 'My tie caused the usual trouble, but I'd got it done and just realized that my hands were filthy. So I dashed out to the bog, after all, washed, combed my hair and was just about to leave the building, when I noticed I'd left my wallet in the pocket of my suit. So I had to go back, you see, into Corporate Finance. As I was shutting the doors behind me, I heard something, some slight sound, and so I called out.'

'What did you say?'

'Oh, I can't remember.' The impatience was back in his tired, hoarse voice. 'I suppose I called out something like

"Hello! I thought everyone had gone." But no one answered me and so I went round to the other side of the office and then I saw it.'

He broke off again and covered his face, but he was not quick enough to hide the mixture of terror and disgust in his eyes. Willow waited, all her attention on the humbled figure of her one-time lover, asking herself why he was quite so distraught. Shock and sympathy for the dead woman and dislike of the blood would all be readily understandable, but Richard was displaying something more than all those.

Martin Roylandson had been sitting absolutely still and silent throughout the interview and she had forgotten that he was there.

'Richard,' she said, more gently than she had ever spoken to him in the old days, 'try to tell me.'

He raised his head and she was distressed to see tears hanging clumsily about his eyelashes and sliding down the sides of his strong nose.

'Did you like her?' Willow asked slowly, moving her tongue gingerly, almost as though she were tasting some unfamiliar and disconcerting food. She had been thinking for forty-eight hours about his troubles, but it had not occurred to her that bereavement might have been one of them.

'Christ!' he burst out and banged his clenched fists on the table.

Willow flinched, but Roylandson sat like a rock.

'Of course I bloody did! Sarah was . . . She lit up the office.'

'I hadn't realized. I'm so sorry.' Willow knew it was not the moment to remind Richard of the things he used to say to her about women bankers. Loosely translated into the sort of schoolboy slang he had started to use, they might have been summed up as 'if God had meant women to work in Corporate Finance, he would have given them willies'. She also suppressed for the moment her questions about the meeting at which Richard had shaken his paragon.

'Tell me what you saw.'

Richard gulped, uncurled his hands and laid them in his lap.

'She was lying sort of suspended from her chair. Her skirt was hooked over it somehow, so that her head was hanging down. Oh, God! Willow, must I?'

'Yes.'

'It was hanging, you see, because of the cut, and the veins in her neck were like bloody rubber tubes. She must have knocked over her keyboard. There was blood all over the desk, and there were flowers, too – roses, I think – all mashed and bloody. She was still bleeding.'

He broke off and looked at Willow, silently pleading with her to let him off. She could not.

'What did you do?'

'I knew she couldn't be dead, because bodies don't bleed after the heart stops pumping. I've read that thousands of times in detective stories. Of course she looked dead with that great slash across her throat, but I thought by some miracle she couldn't be, and so I tried to straighten her up. She felt warm still. But she was too heavy and ungainly. I'd never realized how heavy she might be, she was so slender and . . .' He took out a grubby handkerchief from his trouser pocket, wiped his eyes and then blew his nose.

'Anyway,' he said, beginning to sound slightly more like himself, 'I tripped as I was lifting her and she fell right off the chair then and I realized that despite the blood she must be dead. I was trying to hold her head up with one hand while I switched on her speaker phone with the other and punched in 999. When they answered I told them what had happened and they said they'd send people. Then they asked if I could see a weapon.'

Willow took a leather-backed pad out of her handbag and wrote herself a note.

'Was there one?'

'Yes. It was obvious, because it was covered in blood. A paperknife, but wickedly sharp. They asked what it looked like, you see, and so I picked it up. That's why my finger-prints are all over it.'

'Did you tell them that?'

'Of course I did.' Richard sounded thoroughly in charge, but his shoulders sagged again as he went on: 'But they clearly didn't believe me. Before they got to us, Steve Draycott – one of the computer boffins – came steaming in demanding to know who was buggering about with the computers.'

'Why?'

'Apparently the blood – or the water from the flowers, or both – had short-circuited the electrics in Sarah's keyboard and it had shown up on his monitor in the basement.'

Willow wrote herself another note.

'And then they arrested you?'

'After a bit. They wouldn't even let me wash. I was lugged back to the police station and they took away my clothes and scraped out the blood and fluff from under my fingernails and took all kinds of swabs. And all the time Sarah was lying there in the morgue, and . . . Christ! It was unspeakable.'

'I see.'

'Do you? No one could imagine what it was like who wasn't there. Willow, you must get me out of here. No one else can.'

'Hush, Richard. I'll do my best.' Willow pushed back her chair as though to get up. His panic horrified her even as she sympathized with it. 'Will you tell me one more thing?'

Richard simply nodded as he stuffed the handkerchief back in his trouser pocket.

'If you were so fond of her, why did you shake her? I've been told that you took hold of both her shoulders – in public – and shook her until her teeth rattled.'

Richard got out of his dark-green plastic chair and stood with his back against the wall. Willow thought that he looked as though he were posing for police photographs.

With his haggard face and his dirty hair standing on end he looked hunted and dangerous, almost like a criminal on the run. She had a sudden, frighteningly disloyal surge of doubt, which she suppressed at once.

Looking round the room, she thought that it was completely unlike the Dickensian gaol that she had been imagining, and yet Richard's terror of it was easy to understand.

'It was so stupid,' he said, sighing. 'I was at the end of my tether; we've been appallingly busy for months and that was at the end of a thirty-hour negotiation. Everything had been agreed at last and we were waiting for the lawyers to complete the final documents for signing so that we could all go to bed, and Sarah started a most ill-advised conversation with one of the American lawyers. It so frightened him that they refused to sign.'

Martin Roylandson, who had clearly not asked Richard for any details, sat up straighter and pushed his little bottom further back into the plastic chair.

'What did she say?' asked Willow, ignoring him. She was curious about anything to do with Sarah Allfarthing.

'It was a very complicated deal involving lots of small family companies, all of whom had to sell to the Yanks if the deal was to work at all. She told Bob Stonewall (one of the American lawyers) that when she was at the Revenue at the beginning of her career she had heard a story in which most members of a family had wanted to sell their company but one had refused.'

Richard shook his head and came back to stand with his hands on the back of his chair. Stooping, he looked across the table at Willow.

'I'm so hellishly tired,' he said. 'Must I tell you now?'

'Not if you can't bear it; but why not sit down?'

Richard obeyed and after a few moments seemed to gather together the remains of his strength.

'According to Sarah's story, the rest of the family pretended that the recalcitrant aunt was dead, got probate on her estate and voted on her behalf to sell,' he said with a curious mixture of boredom and residual anger in his grey face. 'It was enough to put the wind up the Americans and our whole labyrinthine deal was called off until the various firms produced the relevant death certificates to prove that they had the right to vote the shares.'

Willow made more notes before looking up.

'It sounds bizarre,' she said. 'How could they have got probate without a death certificate? D'you think Sarah was making the story up?'

'No. You don't need a death certificate to get probate. But what on earth does all this matter now? Sarah's dead.' His voice sounded harsh as well as defeated.

'It probably doesn't matter at all,' said Willow, still trying to be comforting. 'But since your violence to Sarah on that occasion has given the police confidence that you must have killed her, we need to know all the exonerating details there are. That's all.'

'The most exonerating thing I can think about it is that despite her spanner in the works, the deal was signed two days later. The only costs were several thousand in extra interest for the various firms whose sales did not go through on the appointed day, but that was no skin off my nose. I suppose we lost a little of our American clients' confidence, but it wasn't the end of the world.'

Wondering whether the clichés made Richard feel safer, Willow smiled at him and said: 'We'll leave you alone now. Keep –'

'Smiling?' Richard suggested with a faint echo of his old, sardonic self gleaming through the horror. 'Do my best, Willow.'

'And I'll do mine. I'll be back as soon as I've got anything to report. Mr Roylandson will keep us in touch.'

She stood up, walked round the thin-topped table and kissed Richard's stubbly cheek, hiding her distaste from him, but not from Roylandson.

'By the way,' she said as the two of them reached the door, 'who do you think did it?'

Richard shrugged and the whites of his eyes reddened again. 'I can't imagine. There wasn't anybody else there. It must have happened while I was in the bog, but there wasn't anybody else there. There wasn't. And there wasn't enough time.'

The rising note of hysteria in his voice made Willow force her voice to sound almost syrupy. 'Perhaps she killed herself,' she suggested, having been clinging to that possibility for some time.

Richard shrugged and shook his head. 'She had too much guts for that,' he said, his voice calming as his mind started to work again. 'Like you, Willow. You'd never do yourself in, would you?'

Willow thought of the various times in her life when she had hated herself and everything that surrounded her. Then she shook her head. 'No, I don't think I would. But there's no reason to think she was like me.'

'Yes, she was,' said Richard. 'I've often thought so. Oh, not on the surface: her manner was quite different and so was her sense of humour; but there were definite similarities.' He raised his eyes and there was a faint smile in them. 'I've always thought that's why I liked her so much.'

Willow could not say anything.

'But it wasn't only me. Everyone liked her. Everyone did.'

'Are you sure? Somebody must have been afraid of her, at least.'

'I can't think who,' he said, tears welling in his eyes again. 'I'm sure she never did anyone an injury. It must have been a mistake, but I've been racking my brains and I can't see how they did it or who.'

'Then she must have killed herself, Richard.'

'She wouldn't have,' he insisted. 'She was incredibly strong in herself. She'd never let herself get so desperate, and even if she was, she'd never do it like that and she'd have left a note. She was far too bright and kind – and aware of other people's feelings – to make such a mess. She was . . . Oh, God!'

Willow watched him in useless sympathy while Roylandson knocked on the door. A warder took Richard away. As soon as the other two were outside the prison, the lawyer said in real curiosity:

'Why did he call you Willow?'

She stopped, both feet in a puddle of old muddy rainwater that she did not even notice. Usually as careful to protect her double identity as her expensive shoes, she had not even considered it in the face of Richard's distress.

'Oh, it's just a pet name he used to use,' she said, clumsily trying to sound lightly amused. 'Something to do with my being tall, I suppose. I'm so accustomed to it, I never even noticed. You must have been awfully surprised.'

'Slightly,' he admitted, sounding even more old-maidish than usual. 'But not quite so surprised as I was by all your questions. How did you suppose they would help?'

'Anything that happened to Sarah Allfarthing in the last week of her life must be relevant to who killed her.' Willow's eyes were cold and her voice severe, but they appeared to have no chastening effect on the solicitor.

'The only thing that could possibly help my client is the discovery that there was someone else in the building when Mrs Allfarthing died,' he said; 'someone who had access to the Corporate Finance Department and knew the code number of the doors.'

Willow achieved a smile that she hoped was as patronizing as his voice had been. 'Knowing that Richard Crescent is innocent,' she said slowly, 'I am seeking the reason for the woman's death that will identify her killer. When I have done that, I can work out how the murder was effected.'

'I think you are oversanguine.'

'Rather like poor old Richard,' said Willow, clinging to flippancy in an attempt to hide her doubts.

Roylandson's pursed lips suggested that he did not share her taste in word games. They parted in mutual dislike that was only slightly tempered by their shared intention to get Richard out of the hands of the police.

Chapter 3

*A*s SHE travelled back to Belgravia in a taxi, Willow tried to think of some acceptable reason she could have given the solicitor for her determination to believe in Richard's innocence. She could not think of anything convincing. During the previous eight months she had met and spoken to – and even quite liked – two apparently gentle men who had turned out to be killers. If they could have successfully hidden their murderousness, then perhaps anyone could.

Despite the heaviness of the air, Willow shivered. The taxi was an old one and it smelled of stale cigarette smoke. She decided that it was the smell that was making her feel sick.

All she could use for comfort was the fact that, unlike either of the two murderers, Richard was successful in his work, had plenty of faithful friends, and had shown no signs of inadequacy in any area of his life. He disliked freely expressed emotion, but since that was something Willow shared with him she found it natural.

With her mind on ways of proving him innocent, she handed the taxi driver a note and told him to keep the change, hardly aware of what she was doing until he said:

'That was twenty quid you gave me, love.'

'What? Oh, thank you. Well, just give me ten back.'

She took the money from his callused hands and turned away, not seeing his puzzled expression. Nothing in her appearance or voice had led him to expect such a cavalier attitude to money, and in normal circumstances it would have been quite foreign to her. She could be both generous and extravagant, but she had been afraid of poverty for too long ever to take money for granted. She knew the exact price and value of the things she bought, just as she knew to the last percentage point how much her carefully invested royalties were earning for her.

The taxi drove off as she was fumbling in her handbag for her front-door key. Once she was inside the door, she remembered Mrs Rusham's shock at the sight of her clerkly disguise and took off her spectacles. In the middle of all the drama of Richard's imprisonment it seemed important to keep her own life well within its accustomed routines. Mrs Rusham had never seen her employer wearing glasses and Willow did not want her to do so then. She folded them into their case and took out the small plastic contraption that held her contact lenses. One of them refused to settle on her eyeball and she had to fish out a hand-mirror so that she could find out where it was and push it into place.

Blinking, and a little red-eyed, but looking more like Cressida than Willow King, she climbed the stairs and opened her own front door. She was surprised to hear voices coming from the kitchen. Never in the years since she had first employed Mrs Rusham had the housekeeper entertained her own friends in the flat.

Curious and a little affronted, Willow walked into the kitchen to be faced with the familiar small figure of Emma Gnatche sitting on the edge of the table, swinging her legs. Willow relaxed.

'Hello,' she said.

Emma slid off the table at once and came to stand in front of Willow, looking even younger than usual in a pair of skin-tight yellow leggings and a loosely knitted yellow-and-white cotton sweater. The clothes would have looked no more than trendy if she had not also been wearing her usual black velvet hairband and pearls. The combination was really extremely odd, thought Willow, as odd as the blush that was rising in Emma's face.

'What's the matter? You look as though you thought I was about to hit you,' said Willow. 'I'm really glad to see you and extremely grateful that you were there to help Richard when I rang you from Italy.'

'No, but it's a bit thick to invade your flat like this. 'Specially after being rather rude to you on the telephone on Sunday. It's just that Mrs Rusham told me you were back when I rang her this morning, and she and I both wanted to know how things were going and I hoped you wouldn't mind too much if I came to talk to her while we were waiting for you. Is that all right?'

'I don't mind at all.' Willow smiled slightly at Emma's breathless explanation. 'Mrs Rusham, what about a pot of tea? I think we could do with some.'

'Certainly, Miss Woodruffe,' she said, smoothing her voluminous white overall down over her thighs and sounding controlled and distant. 'The sandwiches are ready. I shall bring a tray to the drawing room in a moment.'

'Would you? That's splendid. Come along, Emma.'

'She's awfully worried, you know,' Emma whispered. 'Couldn't we all have tea together in the kitchen so that she can hear everything too?'

Willow smiled slightly at the reproach as the two of them walked into the drawing room, which she had had decorated in yellow and white as though to match Emma's eccentric clothes.

'The only way to comfort Mrs Rusham,' said Willow drily as she took off her severe jacket and sank into the thick down cushions of one of the matching sofas, 'is to allow her to keep up her terrific standards – and her dignity. She'd hate us to have tea in the kitchen. Wait until you see the tea tray.' She pulled the pins out of her hair and ran her fingers through it until it looked much more like Cressida's usual style.

Only a few minutes later the drawing-room door opened and Mrs Rusham appeared with a heavy-looking antique mahogany tray. She placed it carefully on a low table in front of Willow's sofa and departed.

'You see,' said Willow, gesturing to the plates of delicate sandwiches and little cakes and the highly polished silver teapot. Sharing the tray with them were a silver milk jug, a plate of thinly cut slices of lemon and some dark-blue-and-gold Minton china. It all looked perfectly suitable in that room with its French chintz curtains, the golden eighteenth-century secretaire and card tables, and the group of delicate, sunny watercolours; but it seemed absurdly luxurious in comparison with the unpleasant idea of Richard's cell.

'Yes,' said Emma. 'I do. I could never match her standards. Will you tell me how he is?'

'Not well.' Willow poured out the tea, handed Emma one cup and added a slice of lemon to her own. 'I hadn't realized he was so fond of the dead woman. It complicates things.'

'Why?' Emma's pretty pink-and-white face was creased into a study in perplexity.

When they had first met, Willow had found Emma's appearance and occasionally idiotic manner almost as irritating as the family background, connections and money that had given her a confidence she had not earned. Unfairly Willow had assumed that it was also undeserved, but as she came to know Emma, she discovered that the girl was both intelligent and sensible. She was also much more genuinely warm than Willow had suspected and slowly her irritation and unacknowledged jealousy had given way to a kind of amused affection.

'Because it means that Richard is much less aware of what Sarah Allfarthing might have done to annoy someone into killing her. He apparently thinks she was perfect (apart from once annoying him in a meeting) and so he can't give us any clues about who might have slit her throat.'

Emma shivered. Then she shook herself like a young horse blowing and dancing under summer trees and took a deep breath.

'Will you let me help?'

'Help? I don't understand.'

'I know that you're going to try to find the murderer and I want to help. I'm sure I could. I've told Mrs Tothill that I won't be able to go on working at her catering business and so I'm free until term starts. Please let me help. I can type and do shorthand and run errands – and I'm quite bright. Really I am.'

Willow grinned, looking much more human than usual.

'I know you are, Emma. And I'm sure you would be an enormous help, but you ought to be concentrating on getting yourself to university.'

'That's not as important as Richard's safety,' she said, displaying the unlikely stubbornness that Willow had noticed once or twice before. Willow was torn between wanting the help that Emma could undoubtedly give her and fearing the proximity involved. It was one thing to share the secrets of her past and her double life with Tom Worth; quite another to let Emma know of the reality that lay behind the façade of wealth and certainty that Cressida Woodruffe provided.

'Nothing is as important as Richard's safety.' Emma's voice held not only confidence but also authority. Willow reluctantly bowed before it.

'Very well. After all, I did once tell you that I'd willingly employ you as a research assistant. I can hardly refuse you now. How much was Mrs Tothill paying you?'

Emma put down her expensive cup with an audible snap, which made Willow wince. From where she was sitting it did not look as though the cup was damaged and she relaxed.

'How can you think I would take money from you for

helping save Richard?' Emma said. 'You must think I'm the most selfish pig in the world.'

Willow shook her head, her red hair flying about her face.

'Good. That's settled. Now, what do you want me to do first?'

Willow had hardly thought about her own next moves, let alone what she could ask someone else to do, but she was too experienced an administrator to fumble.

'The most important thing is to find out all we can about the dead woman, what she did at the bank, how she behaved, and what the others thought about her,' she said, adding as she sat up: 'Just a second!'

Emma was fiddling in the round pink-and-blue basket that did duty as a handbag, and she looked up at the sharpness of Willow's tone.

'I'll be back in a moment.'

Willow left her and went into the small writing room, where she picked up the telephone, punched in the number of Richard's bank and asked to speak to Jeremy Stedington. Willow had never met him, but she could well remember Richard telling her that Stedington was the director for whom he did most of his deals and for whom he had the most respect.

'Who's calling, please?' said the receptionist.

'Cressida Woodruffe.'

'Oh!' came an involuntary gasp. 'Sorry. I'll put you through.'

A moment later a richly confident voice said: 'Jeremy Stedington.'

'Hello, Mr Stedington, we haven't met, but –'

'You're a friend of poor old Richard Crescent. I know. He's often boasted about knowing you.'

Willow, mentally brushing aside that comment as she had done with the receptionist's excitement, did not notice Mr Stedington's amusement.

'I'm trying to help him and I wondered whether we could

meet,' she said. 'There are some things I badly need to ask you.'

'He certainly needs help, poor bugger, though whether a romantic novelist . . . Sorry. When would you like to meet?'

'Are you busy later this afternoon? Have you got a deal on?'

There was a short laugh. 'I can see Richard's trained you well,' he said, making Willow frown involuntarily. 'No. No deals at the moment. Let's meet at half past five. There's a champagne bar just round the corner from here. Not many of us drink champagne since the recession started . . .'

'I know it. I'll be there,' she said. 'How will I recognize you?'

'Tall, dark, pinstriped, *Financial Times*.'

'Goodness,' said Willow with ill-timed frivolity. 'That'll be perfectly easy then. There can't be anyone else in the City who looks like that.'

'Don't you worry.' Despite the short laugh, the voice was grim. 'I'll know who you are. See you later.'

'Sorry about that, Emma,' said Willow a few moments later. 'I just thought of someone I had to talk to.'

'That's all right. I'd better not take up any more of your time. I'll report as soon as I've found anything. That was a delicious tea. Thank you very much. May I go and thank Mrs Rusham?'

'But you haven't had any of her cakes,' said Willow.

'Mustn't. Far too fattening. The sandwiches were brill. Promise to ring me as soon as you need me for anything?'

'I promise. Thank you, Emma. Between us we'll sort it all out.'

Emma suddenly gave her a brilliant smile. 'Now you're back, I think we might.'

'Off with you,' said Willow with a laugh, 'before you make me overconfident.'

When Emma had gone, Willow pushed off her shoes and swung her long legs up on to the sofa. With her back propped against the cushioned arm, she reached out for her plate and took a small nut-meringue confection. She ate it, noticing the sweetness and the crunch with part of her mind while the rest was listing the things she could usefully do to establish Richard's innocence.

The appointment with his director required yet another change of clothes and as she was searching through her wardrobe for the perfect thing to wear a little later, Willow could not help thinking that she had made her life ludicrously complicated with its secrets. It was a relief to be done with the civil service for six months at least.

Eventually she chose a plain dark-blue silk dress, which she lightened with a long string of pearls she had bought herself just before she went to Tuscany. The combination looked sober enough for a City bar, but expensive enough for a successful romantic novelist. She had not had time to have her hair or nails done since she got back from Italy but she thought that they would just pass muster. When she made up her face, she added enough mascara to give her eyes drama and disguise their paleness.

Stedington leaped to his feet when she walked into the dark bar, and waved with considerable enthusiasm. Willow walked slowly towards his table, thinking how odd it was that two pinstriped suits could look so different. Where Martin Roylandson's had expressed fussiness and an extraordinary attachment to tradition, Jeremy Stedington's was assertive and almost flamboyant. The contrast could have been created only by the width of the stripes and the cut of the jackets, and yet it was immense.

Reaching the banker's table, Willow shook hands with him. There was an ice bucket beside his chair with a bottle of Pol Roger in it waiting to be opened. Willow, who had planned to whisk him discreetly away for their talk, looked quickly round the dark room and saw that very few of the tables were occupied.

'That's why I suggested half past five,' said Stedington.

'The boys don't usually get here for at least another hour. That'll give us time to polish off the bottle and sort out what you need from me.'

'It's handy to know that you'll understand me even without words,' said Willow cheerfully. 'But I thought you said that none of you drank champagne any more.'

Stedington laughed. Although there was some amusement in his face, there was bitterness too, but he ignored her gibe.

'Just as handy as knowing that you're a lot brighter than your books would suggest,' he said, competently opening the bottle and pouring the foaming wine into the waiting glasses. 'Here's to a successful liberation of poor old Richard.'

'That sounds as though you think he's innocent.'

'Don't you?' said Jeremy Stedington, apparently outraged. Willow, feeling slightly cheered, had not quite decided what to say when Stedington went on: 'You can't believe he'd slit a woman's throat, any woman's?'

'I don't, in fact. But that sounds as though you think he would be capable of killing a man.'

'Slightly more capable of it, I suppose. But I'd take a lot of persuading even of that,' said Stedington, drinking some of his wine as though it were cider.

'But he did shake her,' said Willow, frowning, 'and I'd have thought that in itself completely foreign to the Richard I thought I knew.'

Stedington nodded. 'He did, but I don't think it's particularly significant. He'd been on the go for thirty hours without a break, and so had she. She was so tired that she made a stupid mistake that could have jeopardized a huge deal and a relationship Richard has spent years building with one of our most important American clients. In those exceptional circumstances, he did grab her shoulders. But whatever you may have heard, it was over in a few seconds. He did no damage, and she got over it pretty quickly. She was fond of him.'

Willow drank some of the dry, biscuity champagne, letting the sharp little bubbles burst against her palate.

'He'd been working very hard in Japan, too,' she said, thinking back to Richard's ravaged face and damp eyes. 'What if he came back, found her alone, and she annoyed him again? What if she taunted him about something, or told him she'd stolen one of his British clients? Wouldn't that have made him angry?'

'Possibly. But not enough to make him any angrier than I am at this moment and, tempted though I might be, I'm not about to clock you over the head with this bottle.'

Looking into his dark face, Willow realized that, however jocular Stedington's words, he was speaking the basic truth. She had made him very angry indeed. While she was choosing what to say next, he went on:

'From all that Richard has told me I thought you were a friend of his. Still.' The last word seemed to express a horribly cynical acceptance of treachery, which surprised Willow.

'I am,' she said, a little shaken by his bitterness. 'And I'm glad to find that you are too – and unmoved by my devil's advocacy. I'm here because I want to prove who did it, knowing that it couldn't have been Richard. Will you help?'

The taut shoulders in their dark pinstripes relaxed slightly and a faint smile turned the thin, straight lips into a curly smile of some charm. But Willow got the distinct impression that the banker was reserving judgement about her.

'What is it that you think you could do?'

Reminding herself that Stedington knew her only as a romantic novelist, Willow tried to think how to persuade him of her credentials without taking him further into her confidence than he had any right to be.

'It's not something I want talked about,' she said slowly, 'but before I wrote novels I built up a career in administration and I have had a certain amount of experience in investigating things. I am quite capable of uncovering anything there is to find that will exonerate Richard.'

'I see,' said Stedington, with amusement overtaking his reservation. 'And what do you want from me?'

'An excuse to be in the bank for a few days asking questions of all and sundry. Richard always talked about you as though you were completely trustworthy and so I thought you'd be the best person to approach.'

Stedington turned his champagne flute round and round between his well-manicured fingers.

'Thank you. It's a good idea, but a bit tricky,' he said, looking down at the golden dregs in the glass, 'because so much of what we do has to be secret.'

'I'm actually pretty discreet,' said Willow. It seemed ironic that the only way to convince him of that might be to betray her own secrets.

Jeremy Stedington looked up, his dark eyes reflecting pinpoints of glitter from the spotlights over the long brass-and-mahogany bar.

'There is one possibility. Did your administrative career teach you anything about management training, or could you mug it up in time?'

'I do know a bit.' Willow thought of the innumerable civil-service courses she had attended and taught. 'Why?'

'We, that is the directors, have been talking for some time about training needs and since Richard's outburst the pace of talks has speeded up. It's become very clear that we need to do something about stress management at least, and most people in the bank know we're planning to call in advisers.'

Willow laughed. 'Yes, I've heard from Richard that none of you are taught anything. You just appear from university and, being good chaps, pick up the job as you do it. Isn't that right?'

'Not quite. Most of the Corporate Financiers are lawyers or accountants first. But I suppose it's pretty much like that.'

He refilled their glasses and looked across the small round mahogany table with a rueful smile.

'We burned our fingers a bit a year or two ago with a training course, and so . . .'

'What happened?' Seeing reluctance in his face, Willow added in a reasonable voice: 'If I'm to be a convincing training assessor, I'll need to know all the background.'

'I suppose so. We rather fell for a bit of slick salesmanship and brought in a couple of men who persuaded us they could sort out all our management problems and teach the boys to be better negotiators and better users of human resources by sorting out their own problems.'

'Sounds excellent,' said Willow when she had swallowed another mouthful of champagne.

'What we hadn't grasped was that during the course the boys had to lie about on the floor with blankets and piles of cushions and pretend to be born again.'

Stedington spoke with such embarrassment and outrage that Willow put back her head and laughed. She could not help it.

'That sounds like a version of rebirthing. I don't know that I approve of it myself, but lots of people think it solves all psychological and emotional difficulties.'

'But what in God's name has it got to do with being a good negotiator?'

'Don't ask me. I'm a bad advocate for any of those psycho-circuses, because I cannot make myself believe that efficiency at work is affected by birth traumas or the tentacles of childhood emotions. But I do believe in the benefits of more straightforward training. It saves such a lot of time and wear and tear if people are taught instead of having to learn by making mistakes.'

'It really does sound as though you could pass yourself off as the right sort of person,' said Stedington, looking hard at Willow as she sat, faintly smiling at him. 'Will you let me talk to the chief executive? He's unshakable on Richard's innocence, too.'

'Excellent. Will you ring me when you've done it?'

The sound of self-satisfied, rollicking voices at the door made Willow look up.

'It seems that your boys are arriving; we'd better depart.'

Stedington looked at the new arrivals.

'None of that lot are ours, but you're right. They won't be long.' He poured the last of the wine into their glasses and raised his own. 'To Richard!'

Willow echoed his toast and they downed their wine. At the street door, Jeremy Stedington half turned and looked her up and down.

'There is only one snag.'

'Yes?'

'You can't possibly persuade anyone you're from a training consultancy if you appear like that and call yourself Cressida Woodruffe. Even if the boys don't read your books, they'll all have heard of you. And the secretaries would pretty soon tell them if they hadn't.'

'I'm quite good at disguise,' said Willow, lifting the wavy mass of thick red hair in both hands and twisting it into her civil service pleat. 'A pair of spectacles, different make-up and a suit and I'd convince anyone.'

'What will we call you?'

Willow pretended to think and did her best to ignore the increasing absurdity of her disguises.

'How about King? Willow King?'

Stedington pushed open the door, laughing.

'King's all right, but no one would ever believe Willow. It's the most ridiculous name I've ever heard.'

Taken aback, because no one had ever said that to her before, Willow said rather sharply that they could either call her Ann (which was her middle name) or simply Miss King.

'Very well, Miss King,' said Stedington, holding out his hand. 'I'll telephone you when I've some news. What's your number?'

She dictated her telephone number and then spent the journey back to Belgravia trying not to think of what might be going through Richard's mind as he waited in his cell. Only the prospect of talking to Tom helped to suppress her anxiety, but when she tried to reach him the telephone let her down. At first she got nothing but a recorded message telling her that all lines from London were busy, and later nothing but a busy signal.

As she gave up trying to talk to him, Willow told herself how much she wanted Tom's advice. Only when she went to bed alone did she admit that it was the man himself she missed so badly.

Chapter 4

*T*HE next morning Willow woke at six o'clock, her normal Tuesday time, and got straight out of bed. It was not until she had reached automatically for her noncommittal jeans and sweater that her mind sharpened enough to remember her sabbatical from the civil service. She had no need to go to Clapham.

There seemed little point in returning to bed so she put away the jeans, bathed and dressed in a pair of comfortable Issey Miyake trousers and a loose grey-and-cream silk shirt. As she sat brushing her hair, she thought of trying once more to ring Tom in Italy, but the unfairness of waking him so early stopped her.

It was not until she was making herself a pot of coffee that she realized her subconscious had been working better than the upper layer of her mind. If she were to impersonate Miss King the training consultant, she would need some of her civil-service suits and they were all hanging in the painted whitewood wardrobe in her Clapham flat.

Three-quarters of an hour later she was unlocking the door of the first-floor flat off Abbeville Road. Assaulted by a smell of damp and dust as she opened the door, she felt depressed and rather silly. Her well-established charade seemed grossly inappropriate when she thought of the horrible reality of Richard's predicament. Reminding herself that she had successfully identified two murderers while frolicking from one life to another, and that there was nothing inherently wicked about the way she lived out her fantasies, Willow stalked into her bedroom and flung open the window. Even street dust, petrol fumes and carbon monoxide would be preferable to the damp, foetid stuffiness of the flat.

Then she laid out on the bed the suits and blouses she had worn as Willow King. Made of mixed wool and polyester or linen and viscose in various shades of grey and beige, they had been bought in chain stores over the years and they looked skimpy and bedraggled. Staring down at them, Willow looked back at the loneliness and emotional poverty of the life that they represented.

That life had led directly to her meeting Richard. Although she had moved on, he had been the first person to whom she had been at all close. For a long time he had been the only one to whom she had revealed anything of herself beyond the brains, coldness and reserve that had made her both so successful and so unpopular at DOAP. Willow had always denied that she had loved Richard in anything but the most straightforward physical sense, but in that moment she acknowledged that there had been a different kind of love as well.

In what she now realized had been a real struggle to free herself from a life she had hated and become the person she had been meant to be, Richard had played an important part and played it with great tact and discretion. Without him and the bridge he had offered her between the two lives, she might never have been able to let herself love Tom Worth and, as she was beginning to understand if not to acknowledge, that ability to love was of immense importance.

'I must get him out of there,' she said aloud, thinking that it was simply not possible for Richard to have done what the police believed.

The doubts of the previous day seemed absurd when she thought of the times she had spent with Richard. She tried to pull herself together and concentrate on collecting enough evidence to prove that he was the man she had always thought him.

The clothes laid out like corpses on her bed looked useless after all. Anyone retained as a consultant by a successful merchant bank would need much better – and more expensive – suits than those. She picked up all the skirts and jackets and returned them to the wardrobe.

Something in her shouted that she ought to be piling them into black dustbin bags and throwing them away, but the habits of her northern childhood had been too strongly inculcated in her to allow such waste. And she was still not certain whether or not she would return to DOAP at the end of her six months. When she had decided that, she could deal with the clothes. Skimpy and ill-made though they were, someone might have a use for them, even if it were only the local primary school wanting jumble or dressing-up clothes.

In a mood of unusual humility Willow shut the windows, locked up the flat again and took a bus back to Cressida's side of the river, where she set about buying enough clothes suitable to a successful training consultant to see her through the next week.

When she had hung up the resulting suits, better made and more flamboyant than Willow's though more Thatcher-ite than Cressida's, and put away the appropriate shirts, tights and shoes, she made an appointment with a Sloane Street hairdresser whom she had never patronized.

As she shut her bedroom door behind her, she found herself face to face with Mrs Rusham. The housekeeper's face had lost all the vulnerability of the previous day and had hardened into its customary expression of dis-approval.

'I was not certain whether you would be requiring breakfast, Miss Woodruffe, since it's a Tuesday,' she said.

'Life is not as simple as it once was, Mrs Rusham,' said Willow. 'I shall be here full-time from now until we get Mr Crescent out of prison.'

'May I say how very pleased I am to hear it?' A slight relaxation loosened Mrs Rusham's tight mouth. 'I shall bring your coffee to the dining room.'

'Isn't it a bit late for breakfast?' asked Willow, feeling as though she had been up and busy for most of the morning. She looked down at her watch and saw that it was still only half past ten. 'Well, perhaps not.'

Obediently she walked through to the small, sunny room beside the kitchen and sat down at the oval table. A few minutes later Mrs Rusham carried in a tray with Willow's customary large cup of cappuccino. There were also some prettily arranged slices of sweet melon interspersed with iced mint leaves and a rack of hot, thin toast.

'Would you like a baked egg? I have no fish or bacon prepared.'

'This looks wonderful. I don't think I'll need an egg.'

The doorbell rang before Mrs Rusham could say any more and she left the room to answer it. Willow leaned back in her chair, with a newspaper in one hand and her coffee in the other.

'Is it all right if I come in?'

At the sound of Emma Gnatche's voice Willow put down her newspaper and made herself smile. The knowledge that she had brought the invasion on herself by involving Emma in Richard's predicament did not make it feel any less intrusive. No one, not even Tom, appeared in Willow's flat without at least a telephoned warning, and she disliked Emma's dropping-in intensely.

'Yes, but do ask Mrs Rusham for another cup of coffee.'

'She said she'd bring one, actually,' said Emma, coming to sit down at the table and dumping her multicoloured basket at her feet. She took out a ring-bound shorthand notebook and flipped back the cover in a businesslike manner.

'They're a funny lot at that bank,' Emma said, looking up.

'Really?' Willow knew that she sounded abrupt, but she could not help it.

'Yes,' said Emma just as Mrs Rusham brought in her coffee and another plate of fanned melon slices.

When she had gone, Emma stirred a teaspoonful of sugar into her coffee and drank some.

'I wonder if I'll ever make enough to live like this,' she said, gazing round the room, which Willow had turned into an octagon with open-fronted cupboards built across each corner to hold her glorious collections of glass, china and Georgian silver.

A window filled the space between two of the angled cupboards, the door another, the original white marble fireplace a third and an unusually delicate Chippendale sideboard the last. The walls and insides of the cupboards had been painted with a subtle rosy-lavender colour dragged over a cream ground and the curtains were of billowing taffeta that gleamed in the sunlight and looked as though it were made of finely beaten silver. The whole effect was quite unlike the stuffy, portrait-filled, roast-meat-scented dining rooms of Emma's youth, and belonged to a different world from the austerely ugly Newcastle house in which Willow had spent her hard-working, emotionless childhood.

'It is fun,' Willow admitted. 'But you sound as though you've discovered something about Richard's bank. How?'

Emma pushed her blond hair behind her ears with both hands, showing off the pearl earrings she never seemed to remove. 'One of Richard's chaps occasionally takes me out to dinner and so I rang him up yesterday and suggested it myself,' she said, looking a trifle shocked at herself.

'Good for you!' Willow felt the first stirrings of amusement and waited to hear what Emma had come to tell her.

'Well, anyway, we went out and he didn't need much urging to talk about poor Richard.' Emma ate a piece of melon, almost driving Willow to snap out her impatience.

'Does he believe that Richard could have killed her?'

'He didn't say,' said Emma, adding after a moment's thought: 'But I suspect he thinks it is possible. He seemed to find Richard quite frightening.'

'Richard?' Willow's voice echoed Emma's tone of surprise. Emma nodded.

'Apparently Richard is an unforgiving slavedriver.' Emma looked at Willow from under her darkened eyelashes, her cheeks growing pink. 'James thinks that he was in love with Sarah Allfarthing, too, and desperately jealous of the others who took her fancy.'

'He told me himself that he thought she was wonderful,' said Willow slowly, 'but I don't believe that whatever he felt for her could have led to murderous jealousy. Who are the others?'

'Well, nearly all of them, but mostly the chief executive,' said Emma, running one pink fingernail down the notes in her book. 'He's called Robert Biggleigh-Clart – the boys call him Biggles.'

'Typical!'

'And someone called William Beeking, who's junior to Richard. He's a bit of a spotter.'

'A what?' Willow put down her coffee cup and stared at Emma's face, which was lit by a consciously mischievous smile.

'A spotter,' she repeated kindly. 'It's what the boys call people who are a bit thick, or not frightfully successful or glamorous.'

'Oh.' Willow was interested, as always by peculiar words or usages. 'Does it derive from acne?'

Emma put back her head and laughed. Her thick blond hair fell down behind her head like a well-conditioned lion's mane.

'Abs'y not. It's short for train spotter.'

'Oh,' said Willow inadequately. 'Well, did your sneering informant tell you why everyone thought Sarah Allfarthing was so marvellous?'

Emma shook her head, her face sobering. 'No. He did say she was very glamorous and fun to be with when she wasn't involved in a tough deal; but that was all.'

'I see. And was there anyone who hated Sarah?'

'Only one of the secretaries in the department,' said Emma. She picked up the big cup and drank some more coffee. 'Apparently she is a real thicko and –'

'Another spotter?'

'No. Only boys can be spotters,' said Emma earnestly. 'But apparently Mrs Allfarthing used to lose her temper quite often with Tracy and she got so fed up she's leaving the bank.' Emma picked up the small silver knife and fork again and went on eating her melon.

'Because of the murder?'

'No. She gave in her notice just before it and everyone heaved a collective sigh of relief.'

Willow fetched a notebook of her own and started to make a list under the encouraging heading 'Suspects'.

'Did you discover anything about the meeting that Sarah messed up for Richard?'

'Absolutely,' said Emma, pronouncing all four syllables for once. 'James was full of the story: it seemed to give him a frisson even though she's dead now.' Emma put down her fork, looking sick. She added slowly, as though she were working it out as she spoke: 'I think he was a bit frightened of Sarah, too, although he talked about her glamour and the fun and all the rest of it; and I think he rather liked the idea of shaking her himself.'

'I can believe it,' said Willow, who had suffered for years from the punitive impulses of her frightened colleagues at DOAP and could well imagine those that Sarah had aroused. She felt a stirring of identification with the dead woman and shuddered. 'What about the British client whose deal she almost ruined?'

'He was the owner of a medium-sized cutting-tool factory. It makes scissors, garden tools and penknives, razors and all that sort of thing. He's called Ronald Hopecastle.'

'I'll have to talk to him,' said Willow, adding his name to her short list and then those of the two apparently besotted merchant bankers. 'And of course her family. Emma, did your banker tell you anything about them?'

'Mrs Allfarthing's? No. I did ask James, but all he knew is that she is well and truly married. I mean, not divorced or anything. Still living with her husband and a daughter who's just left school.'

Knowing from what Martin Roylandson had told her that Sarah Allfarthing had been only a year older than she was, Willow was astonished that she should have a child that old. It was possible, of course, but strange. Looking across the breakfast table at the intent face of Emma Gnatche, who was eighteen, Willow realized for the first time that she was old enough to be Emma's mother. It was a peculiarly disconcerting thought.

'Right,' she said with a crispness designed to get rid of the odd distaste she felt. Looking at her watch, she then drained her coffee cup. 'I've got to go out now. Can you see what you can find out about her family and her past career? It's possible that I'll be working at the bank for a bit, and –'

'Undercover?' Emma's blue eyes were gleaming. 'Well done.'

'Thank you. If it does come off, I can look into the meeting and who else might have been damaged by Sarah's indiscretions.'

'But, Cressida!' Emma's face suggested that she had seen some enormous obstacle. 'James will recognize you.'

Willow looked so blank that Emma tried to explain.

'Don't you remember? We both met him at that dinner of Richard's last spring. James Montholme. The boy who's been telling me all this.'

'Oh, damn! Yes, I do remember, but I'm sure we can get round it somehow. Emma, I must go now. We can talk later, but I've an appointment to have all my hair cut off in an attempt to lessen the likelihood of recognition.'

'That's quite a sacrifice,' said Emma, with obvious admiration. 'I hope Richard won't be cross. He's always talked about how wonderful your hair is.'

'Tough!' Willow's protest was robust. She was not prepared to explain to Emma that she was seeking a middle way for herself as much as trying to further the investigation.

Emma got up, pushed her notebook and pencil back into her basket and waited while Willow fetched a jacket. Together they walked out into Sloane Street and parted at the door of the hairdresser's.

Having watched Emma walk off towards the buses that would take her back to Kensington, her pink-and-blue basket swinging from her shoulder, Willow took a deep breath and went into the calm black-and-white interior.

She was taken away to have her hair washed and then offered a padded chair in front of an unforgivingly well-lit mirror. An apprentice teased out the inevitable tangles with a hard comb and then yielded his place to a casually dressed woman whose smile held more than a hint of amusement.

'I love doing this,' she said, picking up her scissors. 'How short would you like it?'

'Not exactly short,' said Willow warily. She watched the scissors flash as they caught the light from an overhead spot. 'A compromise length.'

She felt a thick crunch as the scissor blades closed over the first handful of hair and winced, admitting for the first time that she had used her long red tresses as a western version of a yashmak. Feeling that more and more of her hidden selves were being revealed, she watched her hair being levelled off at about an inch below the point of her jaw.

'How's that for length?'

'It wouldn't be much good if I said it was too short, would

it?' There was some civil-service asperity in Willow's voice, but the hairdresser grinned.

'Don't worry. It'll look quite different when I've shaped it.'

Willow shut her eyes and felt the gentle, efficient hands complete their work of snipping, brushing, moussing, drying and brushing once more.

'There! How's that?'

Willow opened her eyes and smiled at herself. The luxuriant curls had gone and in their place was a slightly tousled but shining helmet.

'It makes you look younger.' The hairdresser held up a hand mirror so that Willow could inspect the back of her head.

'D'you know, I think you're right,' she said, turning her head one way and then the other. 'But my earrings are all wrong.'

'That's a good excuse to buy some more,' said the hairdresser with a hint of asperity herself. Then she looked more closely and added: 'Or to have them reset. I hadn't noticed that they were real.'

Willow met her eyes in the mirror and nodded. It was peculiarly restful, she thought, to have her hair cut without being treated to the ritual, meaningless flirtation her usual male hairdresser handed out to his women customers as part of his service.

'Shall we be seeing you again?'

'Very probably,' said Willow, pushing back the black padded chair. 'I think I like it quite a lot.'

'It suits you and it's less exaggerated than all those curls.'

Willow smiled suddenly, not her usual smile of amused observation but something much warmer and more revealing.

'I'll be back,' she said and went off to pay her bill.

She walked briskly back to Chesham Place to hear from Mrs Rusham that Mr Stedington had telephoned from the bank. Willow thanked her and went into her writing room, where a pile of dusty typescript reminded her that she had promised to send a full synopsis of a new novel to her agent at least a month ago. Telling herself that she would be able to polish it off in no time once she had got Richard out of prison, Willow ignored her notes for the book and picked up the telephone.

Jeremy Stedington told her that the chief executive had agreed to their plan for getting her into the bank and invited her to a meeting in his office at half past five. Checking that she had plenty of time, Willow agreed to the appointment and went to dress herself up as Miss King, the training consultant, in one of the two new suits.

It sat well on her tall figure, its long, collarless green jacket and straight black knee-length skirt looking both elegant and businesslike. For that first meeting she wore it without a shirt and was amazed at the length of her neck, newly revealed by the short hair.

She made up her face carefully to disguise the size of her nose and the paleness of her eyes, changed her earrings for a pair of large gold knots, slipped a big pad of lined paper into the leather briefcase in which she took her novels to her agent and publisher, and went downstairs to hail a taxi.

At the bank she gave her name to one of the two security guards and was politely asked to wait in the reception area for Mr Stedington. She had hardly had time to settle herself in one of the angular but comfortable dark-red chairs in the plant-filled waiting area before he appeared.

'I think I've persuaded Robert Biggleigh-Clart of the sense of our proposition,' he said as he held open the lift doors for Willow, 'and I'm hoping we can get him to agree to an immediate start.'

'Why shouldn't he?' asked Willow, immediately suspicious. Biggleigh-Clart was after all a potential suspect. Stedington flushed slightly.

'I suppose because I don't know enough about what you called your administrative career to persuade him that you'll be able to do any good, and he's reluctant to let a stranger into the bank.'

'I see. How do you suggest I tackle him? I don't think a c.v. is quite appropriate in this case.'

'I suspect once he's talking to you, he'll see the point of letting you in, but there will be one or two parameters to sort out.'

Trained as a mathematician, Willow always disliked the sloppy misuse of technical words like 'parameter', but she smiled at Stedington and decided to ignore his ignorance.

He took her up to the top floor of the tower, where, despite the modernity of the building, the chief executive's office had been decorated to look like an eighteenth-century library. Nothing could disguise the plate-glass window, which gave on to a spectacular view over the City towards the river, but the other walls were covered with mahogany bookshelves ranged above low built-in cupboards. His desk was a large flat-topped affair, from which all signs of modern office life had been banished. There was a telephone on a discreet side table, but it must have been the only room in the entire building that held no computer screen of any kind. To add to the illusion, there was a set of library steps and even a pair of antique globes.

As they walked into the room, the sound of their footsteps absorbed in the velvet pile of the pale-grey Wilton carpet, a man rose from behind the desk. The smoothest-looking person Willow had ever seen in the flesh, he could not have been much more than forty-eight or so. He was of middle height, his hair looked as though it never moved independently of his head, and his complexion was absolutely clear and perfectly matt, as though he never sweated at all. His suit was of bird's-eye worsted of such perfect cut that it seemed hardly real.

Walking round the desk, he held out his right hand. Willow saw that his nails were not only clean but also neatly filed, with the cuticles kept under impressive control. She shook his hand, thinking of the things she had heard and read about him in the five years he had been in charge of the bank.

The most impressive – or sinister – was that he was adored by the upper echelons of both the main political parties. Those of the Labour rank and file who were aware of his existence distrusted his apparently effortless success, his enormous salary and his glamorous life, but he had so efficiently assisted their front-bench colleagues in their attempts to build up a coherent economic policy that would keep the financial institutions from panic that they would have done almost anything for him.

One of Willow's principal informants had told her that various junior members of the bank resented the fact that their chief executive paid so little attention to the bank's own work, although they were glad enough that his circumspection had kept them out of all the scandals of the last few years. In fact, by his shrewd political manoeuvring he had probably done more to ensure their continuing employment than any of their own marathon negotiating sessions or last-minute dashes to New York to save their deals.

'It is good of you to come and see us, Miss King,' he said as he shook her hand, adding with a smile of great charm: 'I understand from Jeremy that that is what you would prefer to be called.'

'It seems sensible,' Willow answered, watching him closely. He seemed to be entirely genuine, but she was not prepared to trust anyone in the bank without good evidence and was quite ready to consider the possibility that he might be the kind of man who so firmly believed in each part he played that it seemed real even to him while he was playing it.

'I'm glad that you share my conviction of Richard's innocence,' she went on, 'although I understand that you are reluctant to let me try to prove it.'

'Hardly reluctant,' he said, turning to his subordinate with a frosty expression in his eyes. He turned back to

Willow, again smiling. 'But I remain to be convinced that the upheaval you might cause in Corporate Finance would be outweighed by anything you could discover here. Have you any particular talents or experience in detection?'

Willow said nothing for a moment. It was a fair question.

'I have no specifically appropriate qualifications,' she admitted, 'but I can tell you in confidence that I was involved in the unmasking of a murderer a few months ago. If you need a referee, you could always speak to the policeman in charge of that investigation. I'm afraid that he is on holiday in Tuscany at the moment, but I could give you his number there.'

'Thank you,' said the chief executive, holding out his hand. 'That is reassuring.'

Surprised, because she had assumed that he would accept her assurance, Willow scribbled the number of the villa on a piece of paper with Tom's name and rank, adding:

'I've given you his office number in London, too, because it's sometimes impossible to get through to Italy. He's due back at the weekend. Now, can you tell me why you believe so strongly in Richard's innocence?'

'Naturally I will,' he said, ushering her towards a group of chairs and sofas beside the astral globe, 'but I'll deal with this first. Jeremy, will you see to drinks?'

'Yes, indeed. Miss King, what will you have?' He opened one of the cupboards beneath the bookshelves, while Robert Biggleigh-Clart left the office.

'Is that Vichy water? If so, I'd love some.'

Stedington smiled at her as though admiring both her abstemiousness and her taste in mineral water. He mixed himself some weak whisky and soda and settled down to entertain her until Biggleigh-Clart returned.

He was back in a remarkably short time, saying: 'That seems quite satisfactory, Miss King. Now –'

'May I ask how you got through to Italy so quickly?' asked Willow with a smile. 'It always takes me ages.'

Biggleigh-Clart smiled too.

'I didn't. I spoke to Chief Inspector Worth's superior, who appeared to know enough about you to confirm your claim about the investigation you assisted. May I welcome you formally to the bank and say that I shall do all I can to help in your search?'

'Thank you.' Willow sounded wary. She wondered whom Biggleigh-Clart had talked to at Scotland Yard and what on earth he had said.

'Now,' he said when he was sipping a different brand of chilled water, 'I think that you should start tomorrow. Jeremy's idea of your apparently studying the training needs of the Corporate Finance Department seems ideal, but to make it realistic you will have to do something to convince the staff of your *bona fides*.'

'That ought not to be a problem,' said Willow crisply. 'I'm pretty well briefed about techniques of stress management, the development of skills and the deployment of human resources.'

'I'm delighted to hear it, although I do wonder why,' said Biggleigh-Clart.

Willow ignored his interpolation. She felt that she had done quite enough to persuade him of her credentials.

'Human resources may be the most important, because I shall have to talk to the secretarial staff as well as the bankers.'

'Yes,' said Biggleigh-Clart, drawing out the word so that it sounded doubtful yet acquiescent.

'I suspect you're thinking about Tracy, but I'm quite experienced enough to disregard her malice, and her very interest in Mrs Allfarthing will probably make her a useful witness.'

Jeremy Stedington started to laugh and then turned the sound into a cough that he soothed with a draught of whisky.

'May I say that you are not quite as I had expected?' Robert Biggleigh-Clart shook his elegant spectacles a little way down his splendidly straight nose and looked at Willow over the top of them. 'And rather better informed.'

'You may say whatever you want,' she answered directly, 'particularly when it's as flattering as that. May I in turn
put in a request?'

Biggleigh-Clart nodded and pushed the spectacles back
up over his brown eyes again.

'There is a young man on Richard's staff whom I once
met and who would probably recognize me as Cressida
Woodruffe. His name is James Montholme. Is there any
possibility that you could get him out of the way for a few
days?'

The two bankers looked at one another.

'He is well used to secrecy,' said Stedington. 'They all are.'

'Chinese walls and all that,' said Willow, wondering for
the first time why imaginary barriers should be oriental.
'Yes, I know, but I do think it's important that as few people
as possible know who I am.'

'We could always send him over to New York on
a diplomatic mission to Richard's clients,' suggested
Biggleigh-Clart. 'We ought to do something in any case,
and he'd go like a shot. His last departmental report suggested that he's slightly short of international experience.'

'Is he . . . weighty enough, d'you think?' Stedington's
brows touched over his nose as he frowned.

'I think it ought to be all right. After all, Richard will be
flying out himself pretty soon, unless the worst happens
and . . .' Biggleigh-Clart broke off, leaving the other two to
finish the sentence off in their own minds. Neither had any
difficulty.

'Is Montholme still here?'

Jeremy Stedington got out of his deep leather chair and
pushed open the door to the secretary's office.

'You will be discreet, won't you?' said Biggleigh-Clart,
taking advantage of his subordinate's absence. 'The whole
staff, particularly in that department, is in a state of in-
describable tension since the tragedy. I'd hate – even in
my enthusiasm for proving Richard's innocence – to cause
an uproar.'

Willow crossed one long leg over the other. 'My enthusiasm for getting Richard out overrides everything else,' she said carefully, 'but I do recognize that yours may not. I won't knowingly jeopardize your profitable business or worry your staff.'

'Thank you. I can see why Richard has such respect for you.' He bowed before her and she saw how easy it would be to succumb to his charming technique.

'Montholme will come up to see you at half past six,' said Stedington as he returned.

'But,' said Willow, putting out a restraining hand to stop the conversation running away before she had finished, 'you must not rely on me to conceal anything I find if it would help Richard. Obviously it would suit you best if I could prove that Mrs Allfarthing was indeed murdered and that her killer had nothing to do with the bank. But that does seem unlikely.'

Robert Biggleigh-Clart said nothing. From above and behind Willow's head, Jeremy Stedington's voice said:

'That is fair, Robert. Whatever she finds out, it'll be better than having Richard convicted unjustly.'

The chief executive looked up towards his junior. There was no discernible expression on his face.

'Provided that what she finds out is true,' he said coolly after a significant pause.

'It will be,' said Willow with equal chilliness.

'Very well. But if you do start to cause trouble I will stop you at once, without the slightest compunction. Any kind of trouble. You do understand that, don't you?'

'Yes.' Willow saw the ruthlessness that she had always known must lie beneath the charm. 'I don't like it, but I certainly understand.'

'Splendid,' said Stedington with such patent relief in his voice that it was clear to the others that he had felt like a nut held between the two arms of a pair of nutcrackers. 'Then all we have to decide is Miss King's access.'

'I beg your pardon?' she said, turning the politeness into a question.

'Most of our work is secret,' said Robert Biggleigh-Clart, crossing his own legs and revealing three inches of navy-blue sock above his hand-made tasselled loafers, which were decorated with the kind of perforations usually seen on heavy brogues.

Suddenly Willow could not suppress a smile. She remembered Tom Worth's telling her that he had once worn a pair of similar shoes when visiting his father, who had looked at them in disgust and muttered about 'poove's galoshes'.

'Miss King?'

'My apologies, Mr Biggleigh-Clart. I had had a sudden thought. You were telling me that your work is secret. I'm fully aware of the exigencies of the Financial Services Act and the dangers of insider trading. I can safely promise you that I won't reveal anything I learn of your proposed mergers and takeovers.'

'Or use the information on your own account?'

For a moment Willow looked puzzled but then she smiled.

'You mean, gamble on the Stock Exchange on the basis of information I'd learned here? I can safely promise that too. My pension, my Peps and my investment trusts are all equity-based, but that's as far as I'm prepared to go. The rest is merely earning decent interest in various accounts. I am not prepared to put the whole of my funds through an organization that decides their value on the basis of English cricketers' test scores.'

'I beg your pardon?' The smooth Mr Biggleigh-Clart seemed as puzzled as Willow had done earlier.

'Richard told me one evening a few years ago that the market had leaped up several points when one of our batsmen made a century. I am not prepared to have my money at the mercy of that kind of irrelevance.'

'I see. Well, I shall have to rely on your discretion,' said

Mr Biggleigh-Clart, watching her as though she were a peculiarly dim-witted foreigner. 'But I must lay down some restrictions. You will obviously have to question members of the Corporate Finance Department, but I cannot have you sitting in on any of their meetings with clients, for example.'

'Oh, but I must.' Willow's protest was instant and heartfelt. 'For one thing, if my cover is that I'm to report on your training needs after the scene Richard made in his meeting, then I shall have to see how your people work in meetings.'

Jeremy Stedington handed his chief a list. 'I asked Annabel for those, Robert. They might help your decision.'

Biggleigh-Clart rose and took a Mont Blanc pen from the top drawer of his desk, crossing out some of the names on the list. When he had finished he screwed the top on the pen and put it away, reread the list and then handed it back to Jeremy.

'She may sit in on any meetings to do with those clients: none of the others.' He turned to Willow as she sat, confident and impassive, where he had left her. 'It's not that I don't trust you, but I have to protect the confidentiality of certain deals.'

He looked at the slender Piaget watch on his hairless wrist and then held out his right hand again. Willow got to her feet and shook it once more.

'I must go now,' he said. 'But I look forward to our meeting again, and to hearing of your progress. Thank you for coming.'

Aware that she had no power to force him to answer questions then or at any other time, Willow accepted the dismissal. Jeremy Stedington took her back down in the lift. About halfway down, he said:

'Please don't misunderstand him.'

Willow looked straight at the banker and saw in his eyes a worried affection that she had not expected.

'He seemed perfectly fair,' she said. 'And I can quite understand his wanting to keep me well controlled.'

Stedington laughed.

'That wasn't quite what I meant,' he said as the lift doors were sucked open with a surge of compressed air. Putting his finger on the button that would keep them apart, he went on: 'He looks utterly unfeeling and wholly selfish, doesn't he? But he's not. Did you know that he goes regularly to two south London prisons to teach the illiterate prisoners to read?'

'How very unexpected!'

'I know. But I know just what a charming steamroller he can appear, and I'd hate you to misjudge him.'

'You must like him a lot,' said Willow, efficiently hiding her bounding curiosity.

'I've got a lot of time for him. He and his wife have been remarkably decent to me just recently when I've . . . er . . . needed it. I owe him more than simply opening your eyes a bit.'

'All right. Thank you, Jeremy.' Willow's mind filed the information of his strong allegiance. 'I'll see you in the morning. Is nine o'clock too late?'

'I'd make it a bit later still. Give them a chance to get the letters distributed and the secretaries working. I'll have a visitor's pass waiting for you. We can't give you the code for the Corporate Finance Department doors, but one of the receptionists will ring up when you arrive. Then just push the bell when you get to the fourth floor. Someone will always let you in. Good night.'

They shook hands just as a voice called: 'Hold the lift, Jeremy.'

Willow looked round and saw a slight, fair-haired man carrying a briefcase run towards them. Stedington put his finger back on the button that held open the doors and nodded to the breathless newcomer.

'Evening, James. May I introduce Miss King, who will be assessing our training needs over the next couple of weeks. This is James Certes of Blenkort & Wilson, solicitors.'

Willow held out her hand, losing interest in the man as soon as Jeremy pointed out that he did not belong to the bank.

Chapter 5

*I*N defiance of Jeremy Stedington's suggestion – which had seemed too much of an order for her liking – Willow reached the bank well before nine the following morning. She wanted to know as much as possible about the organization and its staff, and that included both the morning and evening rush hour.

Sitting in an inconspicuous chair in the reception area with a newspaper in front of her, she watched the staff as they came through the double glass doors. There had clearly been many people already at work by the time she arrived, but she saw plenty more. At nine o'clock the three receptionists arrived, dressed in identical suits in the company's dark red. Having discovered that Willow did not need their assistance and that she had a right to be sitting where she was, they busied themselves with laying out the day's newspapers and periodicals on the tables, moving the stiffly arranged flowers to positions where they would not get in the way, switching on their computer screens and settling themselves behind the long, curving grey-and-dark-red reception desk.

Willow had noticed that they, like everyone else, had

waved their passes at the two security guards. No one's card was scrutinized and no one was challenged. Some greeted the guards by name and were greeted in return, but others simply hurried through, running for lift doors that were already closing. By half past nine the stream had dwindled to a few obviously senior men, who strolled in through the doors to the salutes of the guards. Each of them carried the muddily pink *Financial Times*, but none of them had a briefcase, and none bothered to show his pass.

At last Willow folded up her own newspaper, put it into her own briefcase and asked one of the receptionists to warn Jeremy Stedington that she was on her way up. With all her senses alert she made her way to the fourth floor, walked out of the lift as Richard had done on the night of the murder and stopped in front of the electronically locked doors.

Just as he had said, there was a keypad to the right with an ordinary-looking bell underneath it. She pressed the bell and waited. After a moment the doors swung open and she found herself face to face with Jeremy Stedington. That morning he was dressed in an unstriped dark-grey suit that looked utterly conventional until he turned suddenly, making the jacket blow open. Willow saw with amusement that it was lined with scarlet paisley-patterned silk. His crisp white shirt had narrow red lines on it to match and his tie was neatly patterned with diagonal rows of scarlet frogs on a dark-green background.

'Come on in, Miss King.' Willow admired the lack of complicity or even amusement in his deep voice and stepped across the threshhold.

Immediately in front of her were two pale-grey desks facing each other and at right angles to the door. There was a tousled blond woman in her early twenties at the right-hand desk and a darker, tidier one tapping away at the keyboard of a businesslike word processor opposite her.

'Come and meet the girls,' said Stedington. 'This is Tracy Blank and the one who can't tear herself away from her work is Maggie Blake. Girls, this is Miss King who has come to assess the training needs of the department. She'll be in and out of the office over the next week or so.'

Willow was interested to see that the second secretary's eyes were reddened and that she looked as though she had not slept. Tracy, on the other hand, seemed positively alert with curiosity.

'Perhaps I could have a word with you both, later?' Willow said gently, in deference to Maggie's obvious unhappiness. Both secretaries nodded. Maggie returned to her typing at once.

'You'll obviously need a desk,' Steddington was saying as he led Willow away to the left, 'and we wondered whether you'd mind taking over one that was used by a colleague of ours who died recently.'

'Not at all,' said Willow, hoping that she sounded convincingly casual. As they rounded the dark-red felt screen behind the secretaries' desks, she saw a row of grey carrels, each one divided from its neighbours by similar screens. Between the screens there was a fitted desk, about four feet wide, containing a small computer screen and keyboard, a speaker telephone, shelves of books and piles of paper. Each desk was provided with a remarkably comfortable tilting, swivelling chair, upholstered in the ubiquitous dark red.

It was easy to see which miniature office had belonged to Sarah Allfarthing. The chair was obviously new and there was a section of the anthracite-coloured carpet that was less scuffed than the rest.

Willow stopped, remembering Richard's horrifyingly vivid description of Sarah's body. She started as she felt a hand on her elbow.

'Are you sure you don't mind? It's all new. The police took away absolutely everything that was on the desk when she died.'

Willow gathered herself together, reminding herself that she was a fearless investigator, and smiled at Jeremy Steddington over her shoulder.

'I'm fine. It was a momentary distaste.' She walked forwards and put her briefcase down on the desk with a snap, noticing that there was an unused stapler already there beside a new roll of Sellotape on a flimsy plastic stand, a box of paperclips and a handful of pencils.

Jeremy introduced Willow to all the other members of the department and explained that she would be working there for at least the next week, observing them as they worked, asking them questions and ultimately writing a report on a possible training schedule. Then he took her through a pair of unlocked doors at the far end of the long room.

'Our offices are here,' he explained, pushing open one door.

'Our?'

'The directors. There are six of us. I'll take you and introduce you in a moment, but I wanted a word first. I hope you really don't mind about Sarah's desk. The thing is: the boys are all rather jumpy and I thought it would be good for them if they got used to seeing someone working there. Take a bit of the ghostliness away.'

'Good idea. I just hope that the ones who were fond of her won't resent me – like Maggie, for instance.'

'I'm sure she won't. She's a thoroughly sensible creature.' There was enough stress on the pronoun to make Willow remember Emma Gnatche's reported description of Tracy.

'Now, before I take you to meet the other directors, is there anything you want from me?' Stedington sat down in a larger version of the swivelling, tilting chairs in the main office and leaned back, his hands clasped behind his head and his arms and legs spread wide.

'Yes,' said Willow, trying to ignore what she had read of body language. She wondered how much Jeremy knew about pheromones and whether he understood that his subconscious was urging him to send her signals of dominance or attraction through his sweat glands. 'I'd like a list of all the people who left the building on the night of the murder after the main rush. Can you get that for me?'

'I can try, but it may not be complete. We don't clock on and off here, you know.' He straightened his chair and picked up a pen to write himself a note.

'No, I know. I watched this morning. But I also saw that most people arrived in a bunch and then there were stragglers. I assume it's the same in the evening. The security men ought to be able to remember whether there were any people who went out alone, later than the rest. And I'd also like a list of everyone who attended the dance. Is that possible?'

'Surely. We had problems with gate-crashers one year and so everyone had to bring his invitation this time and be ticked off on arrival. I can get you a copy of the list easily.'

'Wonderful. Then I think I'd better get back to my new desk and start sorting myself out.'

'Leaving the other directors until later?'

'Yes, please,' said Willow with a smile. 'I do want to talk to Mr Biggleigh-Clart, though. Can you arrange it?'

Stedington shrugged. 'All I'd be able to do would be talk to Annabel – his secretary. Why don't you ring her direct? The number will be in your office directory: a dark-red booklet. Or send her a message through the computer system. Will you be able to work Sarah's computer?'

'I expect I'll cope with it.'

'May I take you out to lunch later?' Stedington seemed to think that he might have sounded unhelpful and needed to make amends.

Willow shook her head. 'I think I'd rather prowl about and listen. But it was kind of you to suggest it.'

She turned away and went back to her desk, where she immediately switched on the computer screen. As it flickered into life she searched the grey bookshelf for the manual that ought to be there. It did not take her very long to find out how to work the electronic-mail system and discover that without a password she could not bring up on the screen any of the messages that had been sent to Sarah Allfarthing in the last few days before she died.

Taking the dark-red booklet off the shelf in front of her, Willow found Jeremy's extension number and got through to his office.

'Do you know the password for this machine?' she asked.

'You don't need a password to operate it. If you're having problems, ask Maggie. She'll help.' Stedington sounded thoroughly irritable.

Willow patiently – and very quietly – explained why she wanted the password and eventually Stedington agreed to try to get hold of it for her. Frustrated, Willow typed in her own message to Annabel, the chief executive's secretary, requesting a meeting. When she pressed the buttons to send the message the machine offered an elaborate ritual for creating a new password, which she completed. She then spent half an hour roughing out headings for her training report in order to put enough into the computer to establish her alibi at the bank.

Towards the end of the morning she had mastered the graphics facility of the computer and drawn up a series of impressive-looking charts with lists of multiple-choice questions to be addressed to each category of staff. Each of the four possible answers to the first question led on to the next layer of questions and eventually to a neatly boxed recommendation for training. Once the charts had been completed, Willow would be able to present the bank with an easily read analysis of the staff's existing skills and the areas in which they needed more expertise.

She walked round the thick screen to talk to the secretaries to find out how to print her lists and charts in sufficient numbers to distribute around the Corporate Finance Department.

'Maggie,' she started. The girl looked up with a professionally helpful smile that only made her look more miserable. 'I wonder whether we could fix a time when you might not be too busy so that we can talk.'

The helpfulness was diluted by a slightly harassed frown.

'I've got a huge report to finish, actually. I'm staying late tonight. I don't think –'

'That's fine. It doesn't have to be today. When you can see a short gap, why not pop round to my cubbyhole?'

'Oh, if that's all right, of course I will.' She was already laying her fingers back on the keys as she finished speaking.

Willow agreed with Stedington's assessment of her attitude and turned to the other secretary.

'Tracy, isn't it?'

'Yes. I'm not too busy to talk at all.'

'Excellent. Then perhaps you could help me with these.' Willow explained what she needed and Tracy showed her where both the printers and the photocopiers were housed. While one of the machines was spitting out a pile of questionnaires, Willow said:

'You have been helpful, Tracy. Have you got plans for lunchtime, or could I take you out? We could have a chat over a drink somewhere.'

The girl looked rather surprised but after a moment she picked a piece of sticky mascara off one of her eyelashes and said, shrugging:

'Okay. That'd be great. One o'clock?'

Willow looked at her slim watch and noticed with a sinking feeling that she had not changed Cressida's gold Cartier for Willow's more utilitarian watch. For the first time in her life she hoped that anyone who noticed it would think that it was a fake.

'It's twenty to one now; why don't we go off as soon as the printing has been done? It's work, after all.'

Nothing loath, Tracy picked up the pile of paper as soon as the machine had stopped, removed her key card from it and escorted Willow back to her desk. Having collected their handbags, they left the building and went, at Tracy's suggestion, to a cocktail bar she liked. There she asked for a cheeseburger and chips and a sickly-sounding mixture of amaretto, coconut cream, grenadine and gin. Willow suppressed any comment and ordered a spritzer and a smoked-fish salad for herself.

As soon as the drinks were brought to their table, she said: 'I know that you're leaving the bank, Tracy, and I expect that because of that you can give me some very useful help.'

Tracy removed her lips from the bent and highly decorated straw that protruded from her viscous drink. 'Why's that?' she asked, looking stubborn.

'One of the things that executive staff often lack,' said Willow smiling brightly, 'is the art of delegation and proper use of support staff. From what I've seen at the bank, I think it is possible that you and Maggie have to put up with a lot of frustrations.'

'Sometimes.' Tracy applied herself to the straw once more.

Willow watched her, noticing the narrow, peaky-looking face, the exaggeratedly long brown leather jacket that looked so incongruous over the short skirt and white, high-heeled shoes. Willow tried to imagine herself as Tracy in order to think of ways to break through her obstructive shortness. Eventually, with a mixture of flattery and artificial sympathy culled from the dimly remembered complaints of her own typists at DOAP, she managed to find a key to Tracy's dissatisfactions. Then the only difficulty was to control the flow and pick out from it something that might be useful.

Among other things, Willow learned that although all the corporate financiers were difficult and demanding and unreasonable in the way they used secretarial time, Sarah Allfarthing had been the worst; that Maggie had always sucked up to her and received unfairly favourable treatment; that Tracy couldn't wait to leave the bank and had a far better job lined up with a firm of solicitors called Blenkort & Wilson; and that among the things she had done that had made Mrs Allfarthing angry was sending some confidential documents in an envelope addressed to the wrong recipient.

Willow sat listening to the outpouring and felt her sympathy for the murdered woman growing with almost every word. She watched Tracy in amazement as she reached the end of her puddinglike cocktail and sat up straight again, twirling the paper parasol between her fingers.

'I had heard that Mrs Allfarthing was a particularly popular woman,' Willow said. 'Would you like another drink?'

'Well, I wouldn't mind. Like I said, Maggie liked her, but I thought she was really awful. I shouldn't say so now she's dead and I'm really sorry about that. I am. Really. But I never wanted to work for a woman. They're always worst. I get on fine with all the men, but she just liked finding fault. I don't know what they all saw in her.'

Willow signalled to the waitress, who stopped chatting to her friend behind the bar and came to take the order. When she had gone, Willow turned back to Tracy.

'I don't quite understand. What did who see in her?'

'All the men; they were all in love with her. Or else pretending to be.'

'All of them?' Willow's smile and mocking voice made Tracy's sharp little face flush.

'Most. They all took her out to lunch and gave her presents and flowers. Roses. Bloody roses arrived twice a week.' Tracy spread out her hands and pointed to two fading marks. 'I used to hurt myself doing her horrible flowers.'

'How irritating for you. Who sent the roses?'

'It could have been any of them: even Mr B himself. She called him "Mr Big". Or it could have been Bill Beeking. D'you know? He was always going through her diary and her wastepaper basket when she was out.'

'Why on earth?' Willow was too interested to take much notice of the relish in Tracy's face.

'To see who else she was having lunch with, of course. She really played them off against each other, you see.

Drove them mad, in my opinion. I think that's what happened to poor Richard Crescent.'

Willow took a draught of her cool drink to calm herself.

'Do you mean that you think he killed her?' she enquired.

'Well, it stands to reason, doesn't it? The police know he did it and he was all covered in blood, after all. They say that his fingers were actually dripping with it, as though he'd – you know – felt about in her cut throat.'

Willow felt sick. Tracy seemed to notice nothing amiss. She picked up her second drink and took a good suck at the straw.

'She was asking for it, if you ask me,' she went on when she had freed her lips. 'I wasn't surprised that something happened even if I didn't ever suspect that he'd kill her: all that flirting to make him jealous and then spoiling his deal like that. She asked for it.'

Before Willow could protest, the waitress returned with their food. Willow picked at the minute piece of smoked salmon that lay in the middle of her salad, rejected the large, oily slab of orange smoked mackerel and tried to eat the lettuce and cucumber that filled the rest of the plate.

'She wasn't so clever either, for all the airs she gave herself,' said Tracy, breaking the silence.

She took the top bun off her burger, added a large splutter of tomato ketchup from a squeezable bottle and put the bun back.

'She was always losing and forgetting things,' she said as soon as she had swallowed her mouthful. 'I sometimes used to think she'd forget her own name.'

'What can you mean?' Willow drank some of her mouth-puckering white wine and was relieved that it had been diluted with soda water.

'Well! For a start she often couldn't remember the combination of her briefcase locks. They all get them, you see, after they've been at the bank for four years. Black leather briefcases with those programmable locks. They decide on the lock numbers themselves, and she chose 987654, because she always used a series of numbers like that for anything where she needed to remember a code, but even so she couldn't always remember which number she started the series with. She was always having to ask Maggie or me. And I once caught her kicking at the doors, you know, because she'd forgotten the code that opens them. And once she even had her cash card swallowed by the bank because she couldn't get her own pin number right. And then she carried on as though she was the brain of Britain. I mean!'

Willow listened, unable to imagine the efficient, clever, admired banker that Richard had described having such trouble with code numbers. If it were true there must be an explanation, but none occurred to Willow. Perhaps Sarah's mind had always been too full of other things to remember all the different codes she needed; or perhaps her forgetting them had been some kind of psychological resistance to, or defence against, the extraordinary world in which she had worked. After sitting in silence for a few minutes, staring unseeing at Tracy's face, Willow asked another question that set the girl talking again.

It was well after half past two before they returned to the bank, by which time Willow had had her fill of Tracy Blank and firmly sympathized with the dead woman's reputed impatience with her. How a girl of such limited intelligence and such obvious laziness had avoided being sacked, Willow could not understand. But Tracy had been useful.

She had made it quite clear that Sarah Allfarthing had enjoyed the attentions of her male colleagues, allowed them to take her out to extravagant restaurants for lunch and to give her flowers and presents. It sounded as though Emma had been right in suggesting that the main applicants for Sarah's favours had been young Mr Beeking, a bachelor who had been at the bank a year less than Sarah herself, and the chief executive, whose wife, according to Tracy, was a skinny, spendthrift socialite who had no time for him.

That afternoon Willow made a point of watching Tracy work and discovered that she was in fact a perfectly efficient and quite quick typist. If her work were confined to typing and photocopying it would have no scope for devastating mistakes and she might well be an adequately useful member of the department.

Walking back to her miniature office, Willow began to think that what Tracy lacked might be imagination more than actual intelligence. She clearly found it impossible to put herself in anyone else's position or to think of the consequences of what she or anyone else might say, but that was something she shared with numberless people of considerable intelligence.

Pushing aside her analysis of Tracy's character for the moment, Willow worked on her ideas for executive training for a while and then sat, trying to sort out the questions she would have to ask to get at the truth of what had happened on Friday evening. The buzzing of the telephone interrupted her and she answered it to find the chief executive's secretary offering her a meeting at nine fifteen the following morning.

'Thank you,' said Willow at once. 'That would be splendid.'

Putting the receiver back, she fell to wondering whether Jeremy Stedington had been one of Sarah Allfarthing's many suitors. Willow got the chance to ask him herself that evening when he came round to her carrel at six o'clock to give her the list of people whom the security men could remember having left the building late on the evening of the dance.

He handed it to her, saying: 'I'm afraid it won't be much help. These two chaps will be on morning duty for the next two weeks and so if you need to ask anything, you'll get them between half past seven and noon. The dance list will be sent down in the morning. How did you get on with young Tracy? I saw you taking her out.'

'Did you?' Willow pushed back her chair, enjoying the

smoothness of its casters after the elderly and less comfortable chair she had had at DOAP, and put the list into her briefcase. 'Have you got a minute?'

'Plenty. As I said, all my deals are held up at the moment. Come into the office.'

Willow followed his tall figure past the carrels where shirt-sleeved men were telephoning, tapping figures into their computers, sweating over proofs of offer documents, reading the cricket scores off their Reuter's screens or telling each other hair-raising jokes.

'What was she really like?' asked Willow when they were alone in Jeremy's office.

'Sarah?' said Jeremy, opening a cupboard and taking out a pair of glasses. 'You will have a glass of wine, won't you?'

'Thank you.'

'She was in her early forties,' he said, removing the cork from a bottle of 1982 Château Le Grolet with neat-fingered efficiency, 'very good-looking, quite good at her job, good company, not at all what we'd been afraid of.'

'What was that?'

Stedington grinned at Willow over his dark-grey shoulder as he poured out the wine. He put down the bottle and brought her a glassful.

'She was the first woman in Corporate Finance here and most of the boys were afraid she'd be a ballbreaker – or a siren. But she wasn't either of those.'

'Glad to hear it,' Willow muttered into her drink. Then she looked up. 'Everyone talks of her with respect and affection – except for Tracy that is – and yet someone hated her enough to kill her. How do you explain that if she was really such a paragon?'

Stedington took a deep swallow of wine. He looked at Willow rather as though she were a traffic warden writing a ticket for his car: resentful, slightly ashamed and therefore angry.

'Of course she wasn't a paragon,' he said sharply. 'No one working here could be. The job needs other talents.' He

83

gave a short, sharp laugh. 'She was ruthless and ambitious – like the rest of us – but that doesn't make her murder excusable.'

There was genuine fury in his eyes and Willow hastily told him that she considered no murder was excusable unless in self-defence.

'Clearly there was no question of that here.'

'No,' Willow agreed. 'But what about suicide? That does seem to be the most likely explanation given all the locked doors.'

Stedington thought for a while.

'I can't see it myself,' he said at last. 'She was so sensible.'

'So everyone tells me, but what if something happened to threaten her? She had a demanding life but it sounds like a very satisfactory one: high-paying job, devoted husband, healthy, clever daughter. What if . . . ?'

Willow broke off, putting Sarah Allfarthing in the position of one of the characters in her books. After a moment she looked up and smiled.

'Perhaps she had been told she had a terminal illness and she couldn't face it. Per –'

'If she couldn't face that, she'd hardly have the courage to slit her own throat, would she?'

Willow remembered vividly that one of the reasons Richard had given her for disbelieving in the suicide theory was that Sarah was too courageous for it.

'All right,' she said. 'Then perhaps she had succumbed to one of the suitors and found herself pregnant.'

Stedington looked at her as she had been tempted to look at Tracy. 'Don't be ridiculous. Sarah could have dealt with that easily.'

'What about some professional misdemeanour from early in her career? Isn't that possible? What if someone were blackmailing her – threatening to have her blacklisted by the Bank of England? She sounds far too good a woman to kill a blackmailer. Perhaps she could not face the disgrace.'

'That's the only one so far that has the remotest flicker

of plausibility,' said Stedington, 'but I still don't believe it.'

'Why not?'

'Far too unlikely,' said Stedington instantly before taking a moment to sort out his ideas. 'She wasn't the kind to go in for misdemeanours: too honest. Occasionally more honest than the letter of the law actually demands, which could be tiresome. Besides,' he added more slowly, 'she was always making jokes about blackmail. She'd never have done that if she was a victim herself.'

'What sort of jokes?' Hearing the sharpness in her own voice made Willow say: 'Sorry to sound like an interrogator, but you surprised me. Can you give me an example?'

Stedington shrugged, his powerful shoulders making themselves visible through the tailor's buckram and padding in his suit.

'The kind of thing we all say all day, you know: "Come on, Bill, if you help Ben call over these listing particulars I won't tell about you and the woman at Bognor." Meaningless teasing. Stuff that oils the wheels and stops people getting irritable when one has to make them do tedious and repetitive work.'

Willow considered her own office career and decided that merchant banks must be very different indeed from the civil service. She also wondered how one or two of her Treasury colleagues had managed to adjust when they swapped their government safety and mingy salaries for the excitement and dizzying rewards of the private sector.

'Sarah was jolly good at it. You know.'

'Not really, but I can guess. Look, I oughtn't to keep you now. You must be pining to get home.'

Jeremy Stedington looked at Willow carefully before giving her a meaningless smile and standing up. He seemed oddly tense.

'Will you be here tomorrow?' he asked.

'Definitely in the morning. I may have to pursue my

investigations elsewhere in the afternoon. Good night, and Jeremy . . .'

'Yes?'

'Thank you – for myself and for what you're doing for Richard.'

His dark, good-looking face softened slightly.

'We're all relying on you, you know,' he said as he held open the doors for her.

Chapter 6

WILLOW took the Circle Line back from Monument to Sloane Square and spent the twenty-minute journey jammed between sweating, angry bodies. The hard edges of her briefcase dug into her calves and the handle of someone else's umbrella caught her just above the kidneys. She twisted her head to get a breath of relatively free air and looked at the faces all around her. Most of them expressed dogged endurance, but one or two were suffused with a hate she could well understand. The pressure on her body relaxed at Victoria when the commuters debouched in a hot rush.

All she could think of as she waited for the next stop was ripping off her sticky clothes and getting into a deep cool bath scented with Chanel No. 19 oil. She walked as quickly as possible through the stuffy, dusty streets back to her flat and eagerly climbed the steep stairs.

The moment she walked through the door she knew that she would have to postpone the bath.

Emma Gnatche's pink-and-blue basket lay on its side on the polished parquet of the hall floor. Willow stood quite still, looking at it for a moment and trying not to resent the girl's intrusion. One of her greatest pleasures had always been solitude at the end of the day. Whether she had been writing or battling with her civil-service colleagues, she needed an hour or so of pottering about on her own before she could happily be with other people, even Tom whom she missed so badly.

'Hello, Emma?' Willow tried to make her voice sound welcoming.

The drawing-room door opened and Emma stood there, her pink-and-white face as nearly angry as Willow had ever seen it. She dumped her briefcase beside the basket, thinking: Well, that makes two of us.

'I hope Mrs Rusham gave you some tea or a drink or something,' she said, smiling as she tried to defuse some of the double anger.

'I didn't want anything.' Emma's voice sounded even more patrician than usual and much older.

Willow sighed. The prospect of a restorative bath seemed to recede even further.

'What's the matter?' she said. 'Come and sit down. I need something to drink even if you don't.'

Willow walked straight to the drinks tray and poured herself out a long glass of Vichy water, adding two ice cubes from an insulated bucket that Mrs Rusham had filled earlier. Kicking off her shoes, Willow padded back to her favourite sofa and lay along it, sighing once again as her aching legs rested on the softness of the down-filled cushions.

'Come on, Emma. You look as though I've done something dreadful, and I'm really not aware of anything.'

'I just think you might have told me that you were going to get rid of James Montholme,' said the girl, sounding more like herself and less like the chairwoman of a country Conservative association. 'He was my only source of information about what might have happened that evening and now I can't even –'

'But Emma,' Willow protested, swinging her feet to the

floor so that she could sit up properly, 'you yourself warned me about him. I'd never have thought of asking them to get rid of him if you hadn't pointed out that he could recognize me. It was marvellous that you thought of it. I was really grateful.'

'But now there's nothing I can do for Richard. It's too bad of you, hogging it all to yourself. I know that you're older and cleverer than me, but I'm not a complete fool, whatever you think. You just went ahead and cut the ground from under my feet. I gave up my job to help and now . . . It isn't fair.'

'There's plenty you can do,' Willow said, and set herself to pacify Emma as patiently as possible. Recognizing that she had a genuine complaint helped Willow to keep herself from snapping, but it was still an effort.

Nearly an hour later she had succeeded well enough to say: 'I'm so hot and so revolting that I really must have a bath.'

'I'm sorry, Cressida. You were tired and I lost my temper,' said Emma, standing up at once. She looked younger than she had in the throes of her rage, but calmer too. 'It's just that I'm so worried about Richard. But it wasn't fair of me. I'll get out of your way.'

'Why?' said Willow, suffering from a bad conscience herself. 'Mrs Rusham's bound to have left enough supper for both of us.'

'No, thank you. Really, I must go. I am sorry,' said Emma. 'Will you promise to ring me up when you've something for me to do?'

'Yes, I will.' Willow was so grateful at the prospect of being left alone that she would have promised a lot more than that. 'Goodbye, Emma.'

As soon as she had achieved the solitude she craved, Willow went off for her long-delayed bath. She ran it very deep and hotter than she had originally planned, allowing the scented oil to fill the pretty yellow-and-white room with thick, fragrant steam. Stripping off her clothes and letting them lie where they fell, she got into the bath and reached out one hand for the book that Mrs Rusham had put ready on the table beside her. Also on the table were a small plain glass vase of yellow roses, a *blanc de chine* plate of Cox's orange pippins and an antique tea caddy filled with small, savoury biscuits.

An hour, two apples and three anchovy biscuits later, Willow felt clean and relaxed enough to contemplate the investigation again. Wrapping herself in a huge, soft, yellow bath towel, she walked into her bedroom and chose a loose, cool linen dress the colour of young lettuces. Unable to bear the thought of tights or even stockings, she stuffed her narrow feet into a pair of cream leather espadrilles and went back to her briefcase to collect the list that Jeremy Stedington had given her.

Taking it with her to the kitchen, Willow opened the fridge to see what Mrs Rusham had left for her dinner. It turned out to be a fish terrine with layers of steamed halibut interleaved with salmon mousse accompanied by a sharp, cool sauce that seemed to be made of pulverized water-cress, cucumber and fromage frais. There was a salad of various sorts of lettuce and a plate of radishes, all neatly covered with clingfilm. Willow took a half-bottle of non-vintage champagne from the fridge door and carried everything to the dining room.

As she ate, she read down the list to discover that Robert Biggleigh-Clart himself had been one of the last to leave the bank on the evening of Sarah Allfarthing's death, and the only one on his own. Willow remembered hearing from someone that the chief executive's suite included a bathroom.

'So that he could have washed any blood off himself and changed his clothes,' she said aloud as she cut herself a second slice of the fish terrine.

She looked back at the list and saw that the chief executive had left at five to eight, only just after a group made up of Jeremy Stedington, William Beeking, James

Certes from the solicitors Blenkort & Wilson, and an unnamed client.

Wishing that she had known about the solicitor before she met him outside the lift, Willow pushed aside her plate and poured out the last glassful of champagne. She took it with her to the drawing room, where she remembered to listen to the messages on her answering machine.

There were two from her agent, the first merely asking her to call, the second less temperate.

'Cressida, I know you hate beginning a new book, and that each one is getting more difficult, but they're screaming for something on both sides of the Atlantic. The sooner you start, the sooner you'll get over the horrible bit.'

There was a short pause and then the smoky, acerbic voice added: 'Don't forget, you have signed contracts with them and the delivery date is only four months away. Ninety thousand words minimum in four months. That's quite a lot, Cressida. Get going!'

Willow made a face at the machine and put her finger on the 'stop' button. Eve Greville was right as usual, both about the delivery date for the next book and about Willow's reluctance to get it started. Her first few books had unrolled from her mind with ease, slipping from her fingers to the keys of her word processor as easily as cooked spaghetti falling through the holes in a colander. But recently, since the books had started to command really huge advances – and earn them, too – they seemed far more difficult to write. Willow told herself that as soon as Richard was out of prison she would have to dedicate her time fully to the new novel.

Her insides lurched suddenly as she thought of his freedom and she stood with her finger on the answering machine, staring at the pretty chintz curtains. She remained confident of her ability to analyse all the evidence and make correct deductions from it, but she could not quite hold on to her certainty of Richard's innocence. The thought that her investigation might do no more than turn up corroboration of the police case made her feel seasick. For a moment she was tempted to drop the entire investigation and trust to the barristers that Martin Roylandson would brief for Richard's trial.

Exercising all her tremendous self-discipline, Willow forced the doubts out of her mind, wrote a note on the pad beside the telephone with her right hand and pressed the 'start' button of the answering machine with her left.

'Miss Woodruffe? Martin Roylandson here. I have those photographs we mentioned. Would you like to collect them or shall I have them sent round to you? I shall be here in my office until seven o'clock this evening and from about half past eight tomorrow morning.'

'Damn!' said Willow, thinking of the unproductive time she had spent drinking wine with Jeremy Stedington, the infuriating journey home and her pacification of Emma, all of which could have been spent doing some useful work on the case.

There were no more new messages and Willow rewound the tape on her machine for the following day, carried her dirty plates to the kitchen for Mrs Rusham to wash up, and took her book to bed. Lying back on the soft pillows, she felt the doubts begin to fight back and reached for the telephone to ring Tom Worth. She hoped that his unfailing common sense might help to clear her mind and she knew that his affection would comfort her.

For once she heard the number ring at the first attempt but no one answered. She hung on for nearly ten minutes in case he was still sitting in the garden, but in the end she had to give up. It had been three and a half days since they had talked and she was horrified to find how much she minded being cut off from him.

Sleep eluded her for a long time after she had replaced the telephone, and she woke early. Lying and thinking round and round the apparently insoluble problem of how someone could have got into the Corporate Finance Department, killed Sarah and got out again while Richard was washing his hands seemed unbearable. Since Willow could think of nothing else, it seemed better to get up.

Dressed in the second of her new suits, a discreet navy-and-white spongebag check with plain navy braided edges, she breakfasted quickly on nothing but toast and coffee, and left the flat for Martin Roylandson's office. She got there at twenty past eight and had to wait for quarter of an hour until he arrived.

'Thank goodness!' she said, looking at her watch. 'I've a meeting in the City at quarter past nine, but I couldn't wait for the photographs.'

'Good morning, Miss Woodruffe,' he said pedantically. 'If you will come to the office I shall fetch them for you.'

Willow felt half ashamed of her own bad manners and half irritated by the solicitor's prissiness, but when he handed her a thick manila envelope she smiled.

'Thank you. I must run, but I'll be in touch.'

'I shall await that with interest,' said Roylandson, picking his gold half-hunter out of his waistcoat pocket. 'You should have plenty of time to reach the City. May I compliment you on your new coiffure?'

'What? Oh, I see. Thank you. Goodbye.'

'By the way, our autopsy will be carried out on Monday.'

'"Our"?' Willow stopped with one long leg on each side of the threshhold to Roylandson's office.

'For the defence. It's often done once someone has been charged with murder, even though the pathologist selected by the police is there to serve the prosecution and the defence equally. We have an excellent pathologist coming from Surrey.'

'Good,' said Willow, prompted by his self-congratulatory tone. 'Will you send me a copy of the report?'

'Very well, but you may not enjoy it.'

'Enjoyment is hardly the point, is it? Goodbye.'

Willow left the building and hailed a passing taxi, which got her to the doors of the bank with four minutes to spare. Flashing her visitor's pass at the security men, she said:

'Which one of you is Bert?'

'He is,' said the man at the door, jerking his thumb towards a colleague who was helping a postman load two enormous mail bags on to a trolley. 'They ought to know this isn't the entrance for the post, but he's a new boy. Bert!'

'Yeah?'

'The lady wants a word.'

'Yes?' said Bert, leaving the postman to manhandle his own mistake.

Willow moved further away from the security post so that Bert had to follow her out of earshot of his colleague.

'Mr Stedington gave me this list,' she said, waving it at him, 'and I see that the chief executive left only just after the others last Friday. I wondered, could he have seen them? Was he that close?'

'No,' said Bert definitely, exhibiting no surprise at the question. 'They'd have been gone a good two or three minutes before he appeared. And even if they'd been standing in his way, he'd never have noticed them.'

'Oh, really? Why's that?' Willow risked being late for 'Mr Big' in the interests of encouraging a cooperative witness.

'Well, he was in a rage, wasn't he? I've never seen him look so angry. Livid. And in a hurry.'

'Do you know why?'

'I'm sure I couldn't say, ma'am,' he said, making Willow think that he must have been watching too many cop shows on television. She had never been called 'ma'am' in her life.

'I see. Thank you very much, Bert.'

She left him standing by the door and hurried over to the uniformed receptionists, who asked her to wait while they telephoned the chief executive's secretary. She must have given the all-clear, because Willow was invited to take the lift up to the eleventh floor.

Biggleigh-Clart met Willow at the lift door, which she took to be a mark of signal distinction. He looked quite as smooth as he had done when they had first met, although there were dark shadows under his eyes and faint lines running from his nose to his lips.

That morning he was wearing highly polished black brogues in place of the previous day's loafers, and as she was shaking his right hand, Willow saw that he was wearing a heavy gold signet ring on his left, which she had not noticed before.

'Good morning, Miss King. How are you getting on?'

'Slowly,' said Willow. She followed him into his office, declined both tea and coffee, and went on: 'It's always so difficult at the beginning, rather like setting out on a book. One collects an immense amount of information, but none of it means very much until the story itself becomes clear. Then the details one hardly noticed at the beginning all slot into place.'

'Presumably if there were anything obviously connecting the crime to someone other than poor Richard, the police would have found it,' he said as he walked towards the chamois-coloured sofa by the astral globe.

Willow hoped that she had not flinched visibly as he reminded her of the doubts that had deprived her of sleep.

'Why don't we sit here? It'll be more comfortable.'

'I imagine they would have,' said Willow carefully as she followed him. 'But there must be something we can find to clear him. There must be.' Hearing her voice rising, she stopped talking, took a deep breath and then tried again. 'Can you tell me why you believe him to be innocent, Mr Biggleigh-Clart?'

'He had no need to kill her.' The banker looked frankly at Willow. 'What could he possibly have gained?'

Willow's darkened eyebrows flattened as she frowned. 'That sounds as though you think he might be capable of murder.'

'I'm not sure,' said Biggleigh-Clart, crossing his legs carefully so that he did not disarrange the creases. 'I think it's extraordinarily unlikely, although he can, of course, be ruthless. He'd never have succeeded here if he couldn't.

But I don't know that I could categorically say of anyone that he was incapable of murder. Could you?'

Willow sat and thought.

'Don't you think that almost everyone would be capable of killing under the right form of provocation?' he asked when she showed no sign of answering.

She remembered a play she had once seen in which a group of pacifists had been verbally tormented into showing potential for extreme violence. It had been horribly convincing, but it had been fiction.

'You may be right,' she said, looking directly at the banker, 'but I cannot imagine the provocation that would make Richard kill except in defence of someone else. That at least can't have applied in this case.'

'No. And besides, irrespective of his capability of violence, which is not something I am qualified to assess, I'd have thought that Richard is too sensible to have killed Sarah Allfarthing. It would be such a stupid thing to do. Are you quite sure you won't have coffee? Annabel will be making it anyway.'

The change of subject was so sudden that Willow took a moment to answer the question.

'Oh, well, if you're having some, I'd love a cup.'

Biggleigh-Clart strolled over to the door and leaned out to pass on the instruction. Willow could not believe that he was as unworried as he appeared and wondered why he should take such trouble to hide what would have been wholly understandable anxiety. What had she said that had made him need to interrupt their conversation so abruptly?

'Now, how else can I help you?' he asked when he came back.

Willow sorted out her questions and decided to lead up to the more difficult ones.

'What did you think of Sarah Allfarthing?' she asked, her fountain pen poised above a leather-backed notepad she had taken from her handbag.

'She was wonderful,' he said with a smile that seemed

entirely genuine and only slightly sad. 'I fought hard to get her into Corporate Finance and she justified all my hopes and fulfilled none of the fears.'

When Willow did not speak he added: 'She was everything a woman in banking ought to be.'

'Despite the effect she had on the emotions of her male colleagues?'

Biggleigh-Clart laughed. 'She was no flirt and I don't think it did them any harm to have a glorious-looking, intelligent, well-dressed woman like that about the place. One or two of them might have let their emotions go a bit, but not to any dangerous lengths.'

'I see. I understand that someone sent her roses twice a week. Who could that have been?'

Willow was interested to see a faint hint of colour stealing along the chief executive's perfect cheekbones.

'I sent her a bunch just before she died,' he said with a casualness that might have deceived an uninterested spectator. 'She'd had rather a rough time over the American deal with Richard. I'm sure you've heard all about it. I simply wanted to express the bank's confidence in her.'

'I expect she was grateful.' Willow looked down at her empty notebook and then squared her shoulders. 'This may sound irrelevant,' she went on, 'but I have to ask. I gather that you left the building only a little time before Richard arrived from Tokyo. Were you not risking being late for the dance?'

The handsome face seemed to harden slightly. 'Indeed I was. I was furious.'

'So I understand,' said Willow, allowing herself a glinting smile. It seemed to evoke an answering gleam in the banker's brown eyes. 'Why?'

'I had been waiting for my wife for some time. The plan was that my driver would collect her from Eaton Square, come here, ring up on the car telephone and I would go down. There was some problem with the phones that night and I had been unable to get through to the car to find out what was holding them up. Eventually the chauffeur got a clear line. When he rang me he was still at Eaton Square and he told me that my wife was suffering from a migraine and would not be able to come. Apparently she'd been trying to get through, too.'

'I am sorry. Migraines can be dreadfully painful, can't they?'

'Yes,' he said, recrossing his legs. He looked at Willow carefully and then smiled, not happily. 'But I suspect that this one may have been diplomatic. Neither my wife nor I enjoy the enforced jollity of such occasions, and she does not always understand their importance.' His eyebrows twitched. 'Be that as it may, her decision – or migraine – made me late and the traffic held up my car so badly that in the end I had to take a taxi. Do you wonder that I was angry?'

'Not at all. How was your wife when you got home?'

For a moment Willow thought that he was not going to answer, but with noticeable if not successful efforts towards self-control he said:

'I have no idea. We do not pig it together in the same bed, and I was disinclined to force my way into her room. Either she had had a migraine and needed all the sleep she could get or she had been faking and I might not have been sure of my temper.'

Willow was tempted to write down his exact words, because they seemed so illuminating, but she thought that might make him wary.

'When did you realize that something had happened here?' she asked.

Before he could answer, his secretary brought in a tray with two flowered porcelain cups of coffee and a plate of chocolate biscuits. Willow accepted coffee without milk and declined the biscuits. Mr Biggleigh-Clart added milk to his cup and even stirred in a spoonful of sugar, before taking a biscuit. Willow looked at his broad shoulders and impressively taut figure in surprise.

When Annabel, a slender, well-dressed woman who looked about twenty-four, had left, he answered Willow's last question.

'I began to wonder about Sarah – Mrs Allfarthing – when I saw her husband sitting beside an empty chair. Sarah was unfailing in her attendance at all the bank's functions – except when she was on one of her holidays – and I knew that she had already left her desk by eight o'clock.'

'How did you know that?' Willow asked quickly, thinking that at last she had stumbled on some useful information. She drank some of the excellent, strong coffee and waited.

'Because I rang down to her office,' he answered frankly. 'It occurred to me that she might have been held up too and that it would be friendly to share the taxi with her. But there was no answer.'

'And yet she must have been there.'

'Perhaps she was in the ladies' room.'

Or perhaps, thought Willow, she was already dead. Then she remembered what Richard had told her and sighed. If Sarah had still been bleeding when he found her body, it really did sound as though she had died only minutes earlier. Remembering the denouement of one of Dorothy Sayers's detective stories, Willow wished that women suffered from haemophilia. If Sarah had been a 'bleeder', there might really have been some hope of persuading the police that she had died well before Richard's arrival and that her blood had simply failed to clot.

'Yes?' said Biggleigh-Clart.

Ignoring the time of the murder for the moment, Willow put down her empty cup. 'That was delicious. Thank you. There is one last question that I have to ask,' she said.

'Go ahead. There's no need to look so troubled. Nothing could be worse than having one of our employees dead in such a manner on the premises.'

'It has been rumoured that you and Sarah Allfarthing were more than . . . well, friends,' said Willow, knowing how furious she would be if anyone were to ask her a similar question about her private affairs. He only laughed charmingly.

'Gossip keeps the junior executives and secretaries amused.'

'I see.' Willow's expression was doubtful enough to make him try again.

'I had a profound admiration and liking for Sarah, and her death has left me extremely sad, but, as I have said, she was no flirt and I am not the kind of man to exercise *droit de seigneur* over the female members of staff. I suspect the origin of the tittle-tattle may have been that we belonged to the same health club.'

'Really?' No wonder his figure was so good, thought Willow.

'It opened quite close to the bank last year and we both joined. We occasionally met there and must have been spotted as we sweated side by side in the gym.'

'I'm anxious to find out all I can about her life in the last week or so; do you suppose I could get a temporary membership of the club?'

'No need.' The chief executive got gracefully up off the sofa. 'They give us guest tickets every so often and I've plenty to spare.'

He walked over to his desk, opened the top drawer and took out two pieces of stiff card, which he brought to Willow.

'Thank you,' she said, taking them. 'You've been very frank, and very helpful.'

'It would have been a pleasure talking to you if the subject had been less painful,' he said, his manners as impeccable as his appearance. 'And if I have helped to further your investigation, I am delighted. Please don't hesitate to telephone if you need to know anything else.' He went to open the door for Willow.

As she left the anteroom, she felt uncomfortable and turned to see Annabel glaring at her with something like hatred in her dark eyes. Willow raised her eyebrows, but the girl's gaze did not waver. Eventually it was Willow who turned away, her mind racing towards melodramatic outlines of *crimes passionels* and violent resentments.

The first thing she did when she was let into the Corporate Finance Department by Maggie was to say:

'Did you happen to notice when the chief executive's secretary reached the dance last Friday?'

Maggie looked thoroughly surprised, which reminded Willow that she was supposed to be a training analyst, but she answered easily:

'We went together and got there at about a quarter to eight. We all met up at her flat with our boyfriends and went on from there.'

'I see. Thank you, Maggie.'

Willow walked round to Sarah Allfarthing's desk, regretfully dropping the idea that Annabel might have murdered her out of a jealous passion for her boss. Laying her briefcase on the desk, Willow flipped on the computer in case anyone had sent her electronic messages, but no one had. She temporarily ignored the police photographs in her briefcase and dialled the number of Jeremy Stedington's extension.

'Hello, Jeremy?' she said when he answered. 'Could I possibly have a word?'

'Miss King. Yes, now?'

'Please,' said Willow and took her briefcase with her into his office.

'What's new?' he asked with a friendly grin.

'I picked up the police photographs on my way in this morning and if I look at them out there anyone who peeks over my shoulder will know that I'm not here to look into your training needs. May I borrow a little space?'

'Be my guest.'

Willow thanked him and opened the manila envelope she had collected from Martin Roylandson. Even though she had listened carefully to Richard's description of the body, she could not suppress a gasp as she looked at it.

In neither of her previous investigations had she ever seen a body and she was not properly prepared for the horror of it. Although the photographs at the top of the heap were only black and white, there were coloured ones, too, in which the freshly shed blood was unmistakable, trampled into the carpet, gleaming on the squashed roses, and splattered against the elegant pale-yellow strapless evening dress that hung from the top of the partition.

Perhaps the most horrifying aspect of the photograph she was holding in her clammy hands was the sight of Sarah's gaping throat. Willow could easily imagine what it must have looked like when Sarah's body was suspended from the chair with her head hanging down, flapping like a slaughtered deer's. Whatever beauty she had had in life had been entirely obliterated by the terrifying ugliness of the cut in her neck.

Willow had once tried to disembowel a pheasant someone had given her and the memory rose sickeningly into her mind. She found herself imagining the smell of Sarah's blood. Mingled with the disgust and the terror, Willow felt a profound sympathy for Richard and a sudden resurgence of faith in him. Anyone might have been reluctant to describe a scene like the one in the photographs.

'I say, are you all right?'

Willow forced herself to look away from the photographs and peered at Jeremy Stedington's dark face as though through a fog.

'What?' she asked vaguely and then tried to pull herself together. 'Oh, I'm fine. These are just rather shocking.' She made herself smile and felt the usual relaxation of her muscles. 'I hadn't quite grasped how ghastly it must have been for Richard finding her like that. No wonder he didn't think about things like fingerprints and not disturbing the scene.'

'May I?' Stedington held out a hand for the photographs.

A little reluctantly Willow handed them over and watched the shock driving the blood out of his face. For the first time he looked vulnerable.

'Yes, I see,' he said, obviously determined to keep his voice steady. He handed the glossy prints back to Willow.

'By the way,' said Willow, not averse to catching him while he was off balance, 'I see from the list you gave me yesterday that you were one of the last to leave the building on Friday.'

'That's right. Me and Beeking, James Certes and the client,' he said.

'What about the other side?'

'There was no other side.' Jeremy Stedington sounded rather impatient. 'There's no deal yet; we were planning a possible takeover, which will probably be contested.'

'Oh, I see,' said Willow. 'And you all left together, according to the list.'

'That's right. If you're looking for alibis, everyone at the meeting has one.'

'Right. Thanks. I'd better get back to my cubbyhole and do a little work on your training needs. One or two people are looking at me slightly askance.'

'Suspicious lot, we bankers.'

They both laughed, as though they were trying to banish the memory of Sarah Allfarthing's butchered body.

'Oh, by the way,' said Willow, stopping at the door of his office.

'Yes?'

'I need to talk to the British client who was at the meeting when Richard behaved so badly. I've got his name somewhere; was it Hopecastle?'

'Why?' Stedington's voice and face were both guarded.

'Because I need to know everything about her last weeks. The client may have some memory or insight that I'd get nowhere else. I promise I won't ask any questions about mergers or takeovers.'

'Oh, all right,' said Stedington, flipping through the

cards on his Rolodex. When he had found the one he wanted, he copied the name and address down on a piece of paper and held it out.

'Thanks,' said Willow, coming back from the door to collect it.

Chapter 7

THE following morning Willow was once more woken by the sound of a telephone bell. Still half-asleep, full of a remembered fear, she reached out to pick up the receiver.

'Hello,' she said as she tucked the cold plastic between her chin and her warm shoulder.

'It's only me, Will; don't sound so worried.'

'Tom!' she said, recognizing his voice with a sensation of immense relief welling all through her. 'Thank goodness! Where are you?'

Willow stretched her legs out under the linen-covered duvet and smiled at the telephone as though Tom could see down the wires.

'Back in the flat. I found that I couldn't hang about in the villa without you. I got back yesterday and tried to ring.'

'But you didn't leave a message.' Willow was shocked to hear herself sounding sulky and almost possessive. She quickly added: 'Not that it matters.'

'I wasn't sure who you might have in the flat,' he said, 'and I didn't want to broadcast my feelings through that machine.'

Willow let out a short, snuffling laugh as she turned her

head on the pillow towards the space where Tom's might have been. They had once sat together in her drawing room listening to an absurdly pompous man from her publishers dictating a message on to the machine.

'It's good to have you back,' she said, both more awake and more in control of herself. 'I've missed you. How was the drive?'

'Fine. Dullish, but I had some stunning meals through France. Did you really miss me?'

'Yes,' she said and quickly added: 'I'm glad the meals were good.'

'Will?'

'Yes,' she said, noticing that he was earnest enough to sound a warning.

'Rather against my better judgement, I let myself run into Jane Moreby yesterday.'

'Oh, yes?' There was more hostility than anxiety in her voice, and her muscles stiffened slightly as she waited.

'I have to tell you: her case really does sound convincing.'

Willow removed the telephone receiver from her shoulder and held it away from her while she fought for calm. She pushed herself up against the bedhead and brought the receiver back.

'I know it does. Superficially it looks watertight. But I also know Richard. It is impossible that he should have done it.'

'You said yourself that he'd been under terrific strain before we went away. Perhaps he just flipped.'

'I do not believe it.' Willow put unusual emphasis on the negative and hoped that she sounded convincing to Tom at least.

'I don't –' Tom broke off, trying to protect her from disillusion but not wanting to sound patronizing. 'When can I see you?'

Willow shifted the receiver to her other shoulder and rubbed the red mark it had made on her skin. She had wanted him badly, but she knew it would be difficult not to let him see her doubts if they met and his obvious confidence in Jane Moreby shook her.

'I'm a bit busy today, but do drop in tomorrow if you've time,' she said coolly and then immediately wished she had been more welcoming. Despite his doubts of Richard she missed him.

There was a noticeable pause before he said: 'Fine. I'll do that. Be careful of yourself, Will.'

'I always am,' she said with the smile back in her voice. 'Thanks for ringing.'

She carefully replaced the telephone and got out of bed, deliberately not letting herself think about the things that Tom did to her emotions. Instead she concentrated on what she could do to collect more facts and ideas from which to construct an alternative explanation of Sarah Allfarthing's death.

Pulling on a yellow-and-white kimono that made her hair look richer and darker than usual and her face even whiter, Willow walked through to her writing room to compile a list of people outside the bank whom she might interview. The most important was Sarah Allfarthing's husband and since he was also likely to be the most difficult, Willow decided to tackle him first. Mr Hopecastle, the British client, and the other even more peripheral figures like Robert Biggleigh-Clart's wife could wait until later.

When she heard the sound of Mrs Rusham's key in the front door, Willow called out: 'Good morning.'

'Good morning, Miss Woodruffe,' said the housekeeper, appearing in the doorway. She looked surprised to see Willow working at that hour. 'Shall I prepare your breakfast straight away?'

Surprised herself, Willow glanced at her watch and saw that it was only half past seven.

'It will be ready in ten minutes,' Mrs Rusham promised.

Willow finished her list and, deciding to breakfast in her dressing gown, went straight to the dining room, where Mrs Rusham had already laid out the newspapers. Only a few minutes later, she brought in coffee and a plate of grilled bacon, field mushrooms and tomatoes.

Willow started to eat with pleasure, but halfway through her plateful she remembered the photographs of Sarah Allfarthing's body and swallowing became almost impossibly difficult. Determined not to be beaten by such weakness, Willow forced herself to finish the food. She reminded herself that the oozing saltiness of bacon mixed with the yielding slither of the mushrooms constituted one of her favourite breakfasts and that tomatoes looked no more like blood than Mrs Rusham's red shoes. By dint of describing to herself the tastes and sensations of swallowing to herself as though she were writing about them, Willow managed to eat the lot. The effort was exhausting.

Mrs Rusham brought her a second cup of cappuccino, which Willow drank with relief, enjoying the bitterness that underlay the richness of the frothed milk. When it was finished, she went to bath and dress. For once she did not linger over her bath and was back in her writing room fifteen minutes later. There, after some thought about the best way to approach him, she telephoned Mr Allfarthing and explained simply that she was a friend of Richard's who was working to help his lawyers sort out their defence.

'I see,' he said unhelpfully. Willow waited, but when he stayed silent she went on:

'You see, we do not believe that he could have killed your wife,' she began and then paused, waiting for an explosion of rage or invective.

'No,' said Mr Allfarthing. 'I don't suppose that you do.'

'And I should . . . I know what a dreadful time this must be for you, but I was wondering whether I could come and talk to you, if it would not upset you too much.'

'When do you want to come?'

'As soon as possible, really.'

'All right. Come now,' said Allfarthing.

'You mean at once?' Willow could not believe that breaching his defences was going to be that easy.

'Well, do you want to talk to me or don't you?' he asked with the first hint of impatience.

'Very much. I'll come straight away. It's good of you to be so . . . so very cooperative,' said Willow.

There was a pause and then the sound of a cough before Allfarthing said drily: 'As it happens, I share your belief that Crescent did not kill my wife. Unfortunately the police won't listen to me.'

Willow took a moment to order her thoughts into coherent words.

'Mr Allfarthing,' she said when she could speak rationally, 'that helps me enormously. Thank you. Richard will be as grateful for your faith in him as I am. Shall I come to your office?'

'No. I'm not working at the moment. I find . . . I find it hard to concentrate, and so I'm at home. Do you mind coming here?'

'Not at all. It'll take me a while I suspect.'

'Come by tube. It's quicker than any car. Get off at Epping and take a taxi.'

'Thank you. I'll be there as soon as I can.'

During the long, dull journey out to Essex, Willow discovered that there had been benefits to the unspeakable, hot rush-hour trip she had made the day before. At least with her body squashed between those of all the other travellers, she had not been afraid. It was a different matter, she discovered as the train left central London, to sit alone in a long, scruffy carriage and wait at each stop dreading the arrival of more passengers.

An unwashed drunk shared the seat with her for three stops, before lurching away. Apart from an unhappy girl crying silently in one corner, Willow was alone for the next four stops and then three young men got in wearing multi-coloured, shiny track suits and accompanied by a large rottweiler. They could have been entirely virtuous, but their raucous laughter and their knowing yet unintelligent faces seemed as threatening as their unleashed dog. The tearful girl got out, still sniffing.

Willow pushed her open newspaper higher so that she could neither see nor be seen and counted off the stations until Epping. It seemed paradoxical that the very things that had given her security had taken away various kinds of confidence that she had never noticed while she had them. In the old days she would not have thought twice about making any kind of tube journey, and would merely have been irritated by the drunk and dismissive of the young men.

'Lack of practice,' she muttered to herself as the train pulled into Woodford Station. Two middle-aged women got on, talking happily to each other, and Willow felt herself relaxing.

Fourteen minutes later they reached Epping and a loud-speaker ordered everyone off the train. Waiting until the youths and their rottweiler had left, Willow made her way out of the station to look for a taxi. She found one without difficulty, gave the driver the Allfarthings' address, and sat back waiting to see what kind of house they owned.

The taxi drove through Epping and out into the country, which surprised Willow, who had assumed with unthinking northern snobbery that the whole of Essex was carpeted with housing estates. Eventually the driver pulled up outside what had once been a row of three grey-stone cottages. Knocked into one and wreathed in roses, they looked like the illustration on a biscuit tin.

Startled, Willow paid the taxi driver the ten pounds he charged her and added another as a tip.

'Will I be able to get hold of you later?' she asked.

He felt in the glove compartment and handed her a small cream-coloured card. 'Just ring that number. Or I can arrange to come back and pick you up if you know when you'll be ready.'

'I'm afraid I have no idea how long I'll be. I'll telephone if I need you.'

She got out, pushed open a rustic gate, walked up a short flagged path between well-kept multicoloured borders and knocked on the front door. It was opened almost at once by a man who looked a great deal older than Willow had expected. Sarah Allfarthing had died three weeks short of her fortieth birthday, but her husband looked as though he must be well into his fifties.

He was a tall, slender man with brown eyes, a well-shaped nose and full, almost sensual, lips. The first thing that struck Willow was the obvious fact that he had been weeping. His eyelids were swollen and the whites were streaked with pink.

'Miss Woodruffe,' he said in greeting and held out his hand.

Willow smiled as she shook it and noticed that there were already a few brown spots on the back of it and that the skin had the loose look of approaching age. He might be nearer sixty than she had at first thought.

'It is good of you to let me come,' she said, sounding absurdly like Eliza Doolittle.

He shook his head and ushered her in through the front door. There was no hall: they walked straight into the drawing room. The whole width of the cottage, the room had windows on both sides and was full of wonderfully kept but, to Willow's eyes, ugly furniture. There was a thick, fitted carpet in a careful grey-green colour; the walls were pale grey; and the spindly benchlike Edwardian sofa and matching chairs, which looked out of place under the cottage's low ceiling, were upholstered in dull turquoise velour. Occasional tables from the same period stood about the room, holding silver boxes, photograph frames and lamps made from converted silver candlesticks with turquoise shades.

There was a florid marquetry desk to one side of the wide stone fireplace, which held an incongruous gas-log fire in a brass grate. Balancing the desk on the other side of the fireplace was an enormous television trolley with a video recorder on the lower shelf. An Indian rug with a shriekingly turquoise background lay in front of the fireplace and on the walls hung a series of unremarkable flower prints expensively framed in *faux-marbre*.

Everything that could be polished gleamed and the glossy white paintwork of the doors and skirting boards glistened with recent washing. The expensive magazines that lay on one of the tables were neatly aligned and the cushions arranged in little groups that looked as though no one ever leaned against them.

There were no flowers and no books, there was no dust; and nothing out of place. Willow had seldom felt so uncomfortable in any room she had ever known. Her intermittent feeling of identification with the dead woman dwindled into nothing and she mocked herself for the overactive imagination that had led to it.

'Would you like a cup of coffee?'

Willow turned to her unhappy host, feeling guilty at disliking his house so much, and nodded. 'Thank you. If it's no trouble. May I help?'

'Don't bother. I had to get used to the kitchen once Sarah started at the bank and the last five years have taught me how to cope with it,' he said with would-be lightness. 'Sit down and make yourself comfortable.'

Quite unable to do that, Willow looked instead at the innumerable photographs in their chased silver frames and saw that they were all of Sarah Allfarthing. As she looked through them, Willow decided that she might have been too critical of her own imagination. There was at least one thing that she shared with the dead woman. Sarah Allfarthing, too, had set out on adult life looking gauche and badly dressed; she, too, had changed as she had grown older and learned to achieve an elegant sophistication.

There were photographs of her in her gleaming satin wedding dress, with her dark hair elaborately bunched up to support a crown of white flowers and a long tulle veil. She had looked only mildly pretty then, and both plump and uncertain as she stood with her shoulders drooping and her chin stuck forward in ungainly eagerness.

Other photographs had obviously been taken in hospital as she lay proudly holding a shawled bundle in her arms. Her face had already slimmed a bit and her hair had been cut short, looking roughly unkempt after the ordeal of her daughter's birth. She was on her feet again a short while later, standing outside a small country church with a slightly larger and lacier bundle in her arms.

Her progress through married life was spread out before Willow's eyes, and she saw pictures of Sarah in evening dress, in a long-skirted suit and unbecoming hat, in tennis dress, looking unhappy on skis, collecting a prize at what looked like a village fête, and eventually in one of her banker's suits. In the last photograph she looked as Richard must have known her: slender, long-haired again, and wonderfully confident in her elegance. Her eyes, as dark as her hair, were beautifully shaped and once they could be seen without the distracting plumpness and unbecoming make-up they looked calm and intelligent.

Willow picked up the photograph and stared through the glass, as though the very effort would elicit some useful information from the coloured card. In her mind she could hear Richard saying again: 'You'd have liked her, you know. I've sometimes thought the two of you were rather alike.'

'They don't usually live down here.' Allfarthing's voice so startled Willow that she almost dropped the framed photograph as she turned to look over her shoulder.

'I'm sorry. I . . . I never met her,' said Willow, realizing too late that there was no graceful way of tackling the subject.

'They used to stand on a chest of drawers in our bedroom, but I wanted them about. It bothers my daughter Jeanine, I think, but she's too concerned about me to object. Milk?'

Willow put down the photograph frame and turned to face her host. He was carrying a chequered plastic tray.

'Ah. No, thank you, I'd prefer it black,' she said.

He took the tray to an empty table, poured out the coffee and brought one cup to Willow. When he had fetched his own, he asked her once again to sit down and, as she did so, lowered himself into one corner of the hard sofa and sat waiting for her to start.

'You said that you did not believe that Richard could have killed your wife,' she began, not wanting to weary him with condolences that could mean very little from a stranger.

'That's right.'

'May I ask why? It might help me to convince his lawyer.'

'Sarah liked him,' he said simply, 'and she had excellent judgement. She once told me that if she were ever in difficulties at the bank, she would go to Richard Crescent because, of all of them, he was the only one she could trust not to use her own weakness against her.'

Willow was moved by that posthumous tribute, but she had too much to do to let herself be distracted by her own emotions.

'Your wife was very popular at the bank,' she said in a cool voice. 'I find it hard to believe that anyone would have taken advantage of her.'

Allfarthing gave a short, dry laugh. 'They were all after her, if that's what you mean.'

'I'm sorry. I didn't exactly mean that. I was thinking more of one of the secretaries who was clearly devoted to her. But, since you've brought up the subject of her male colleagues, can you explain why they were all so . . .' Willow hesitated, but he gave her no help. '. . . interested in her?'

Allfarthing's expressive lips thinned and made his whole face look disgusted. He shrugged.

'All sorts of reasons: they could have been afraid of her and wanted to seduce her so that they could prove they were more powerful than she. Or perhaps they saw her as a challenge, like Mount Everest. Some of them probably genuinely fancied her. Richard Crescent was different. She looked on him as a friend.'

'Didn't you mind? Not about Richard, but about all the others?'

Allfarthing shrugged. He picked at a piece of loose skin that hung from the corner of his lower lip, and Willow winced as she saw how painful it must be when he tugged it and how unhappy he must be not to feel that pain.

'To be frank, I hated it,' he said at last. A tiny smile twitched at the edges of his mouth. 'Although I was pretty sure they'd get no change out of Sarah. Sex did not appeal to her as a game, and she'd never have told me about their antics if she had had any serious interest in them.'

'No,' said Willow slowly. 'I don't suppose she would.' She was finding it remarkably difficult to ask questions that might upset him and yet those were the only ones that could be useful. 'What was she like?'

The brown eyes narrowed and the wide mouth relaxed as Allfarthing let some of his memories out into speech.

'Wonderful. She was gentle and funny; kind . . . so kind; lovely to look at; no trouble.'

Willow's eyebrows twitched. There might be similarities between Sarah Allfarthing and herself, but no one would ever describe her as gentle or kind.

'I don't quite understand what you mean by "no trouble",' she said, trying not to sound critical.

Allfarthing's face changed from nostalgia to very slight amusement. 'I've friends down here who have a lot of difficulties with their wives,' he said. 'Some of them drink; others nag; some of them chase young men; and lots of them live their whole lives on a switchback of emotions. One of my clients can leave his wife perfectly serene and content in the morning and when he gets home for dinner she'll be either a nervous wreck or hysterically angry with him for no known reason. Sarah wasn't like that. She was always the same.'

'That's a little hard to believe,' said Willow slowly. She looked around the immaculately controlled living room and suppressed a shudder. 'Did she really have no moods?'

'Of course she had moods.' He sounded thoroughly impatient. 'Every human being does. But there was usually a reason for them and she tried to explain them before I could worry.'

'She sounds very sensible.'

Allfarthing's eyes narrowed as he nodded and his full lips quivered slightly.

'Can you tell me anything about her last few days?' asked Willow, as much to distract him from the emotions she had aroused as for the information her question might produce.

He turned to look out of the window or to hide his expression from Willow. Looking carefully out at the neatly mown garden with its miniature weeping willow, symmetrically positioned sundial and bright bedding plants, he said:

'There wasn't anything different. I've thought about it often since then. She got home relatively early with the usual briefcase full of work. We ate dinner in the kitchen and talked. She started to work in her study (it used to be the nursery) at about half past nine. I went up to bed a couple of hours later and listened to the radio for a bit. She joined me soon after twelve. There wasn't anything unusual. It was all routine. The same ready-prepared meals went from the freezer into the microwave. We talked as usual.'

'Did she seem anxious at all – or afraid?'

The dry, unhappy laugh sounded again and he looked back into the room. His eyes seemed damp and Willow disliked herself.

'She was often anxious. When there was a big deal she was worried that something might go wrong and when she wasn't working on big deals she was bothered that her reputation would sink and she'd be a candidate for redundancy. It's no fun earning money like that – or being a lone woman among so many ambitious men.'

'You didn't envy her the glamour of the City?' Willow was pretty sure she knew the answer to that, but she wanted to give him a chance to get his eyes under control again.

'Certainly not. I couldn't have stood it, but she liked most aspects of it: the buzz and the terror of deals, and all the people. Peacefully auditing local businesses and running my own little firm suits me, but when Sarah left the Revenue to join me, we both realized that it bored her to d– it bored her.'

'I hadn't realized that she had ever worked with you,' said Willow, suddenly discovering something she could ask without risking his bursting into tears. 'Did she ever tell you a story she'd heard at the Revenue about a family who kidnapped their own aunt so that they could vote her shares and sell the family business?'

Mr Allfarthing smiled and looked suddenly much younger. He reached forward for the coffee pot and refilled their cups.

'She and many others,' he said. 'It's one of those stories that accountants and tax consultants tell to amuse each other. I've no idea if it has any basis in fact. I rather suspect that it was made up by a bored accountant one wet afternoon before the budget deluged him with work.'

Willow noticed with interest that his typical accountant was male and wondered what he had really thought about his wife's success.

'How is this helping you?' he asked suddenly. His eyes looked coldly at her.

Disconcerted, Willow drank some more of her coffee and put down the cup.

'I'm not sure yet,' she said. 'I'm still feeling my way through a fog. The one solid fact is Richard's innocence and I'm simply looking for others – however small – to support it. Did your wife have any enemies?'

Allfarthing shrugged and for the first time Willow noticed that he was dressed like a schoolboy in grey flannel trousers, white shirt and navy blazer. His tie was black.

'We once had a dishonest cleaning lady who behaved very badly to Sarah when she sacked her, and there are one or two wives around here who were jealous of her success, but I can't imagine any of them . . .' His voice died and Willow nodded.

'It seems unlikely that it could have been anyone round here. I really meant to ask about enemies in the City.'

'I wouldn't know,' he said, shrugging once again. 'She occasionally burst out about someone who had annoyed her, but it was rarely the same person. She talked more about her friends.'

'Tell me about them,' said Willow, pushing her hair away from her face. The new cut was proving to be less easy to wear than her customary long curls.

'Richard, principally; and one of the lawyers: chap called Certes, James Certes.'

'I think I've met him. He was at the meeting when Richard forgot himself, wasn't he?'

'That's right. He was very good to her when she started at the bank. They met on one of her first deals, a little one, and got on well. He helped her a lot after that.' One more real smile lit his sad face. 'In point of fact he's given our daughter a temporary job until she goes up to university.'

'Is she enjoying it?'

'As much as anyone that age enjoys filing and photocopying, but it'll look good on her c.v. when she starts to look for articles in three years' time.'

Knowing that most murders are domestic, Willow wanted to ask what the Allfarthings' marriage had been like, but she found she could not. With the evidence of Mr Allfarthing's tears, the things he had said about his wife, and all the photographs of her with which he had surrounded himself, it looked as though he had genuinely loved her. She had told him all about the men who had propositioned her, which suggested that she had loved him, too, or at least trusted in his feelings for her.

'Did your daughter get on well with her mother? She must have been very grateful for the job.'

'As well as most mothers and daughters, I suppose,' he said, looking troubled. 'There were occasional fights during Jeanine's adolescence, when she said some things to her mother that I suspect are tormenting her now, poor child.'

He shot his wrist forward so that he could look at his watch, but he did not say anything.

'I mustn't keep you,' said Willow, 'but there is one more thing I need to ask. You said a moment ago that your wife used to tell you about people who had made her angry and that they were often different. That sounds as though there were some who were constant.'

'Only one. A young man called Beeking. He made her really seriously angry recently, and she told me that she had decided to stop talking to him, but he'd always irritated her. He decided to be in love with her almost as soon as he started work at the bank and thought that that gave him rights over her. He used to hack into her electronic mail, look through her wastepaper basket, look in her diary, and even once went through her handbag, looking for evidence that she was having a love affair.'

'I can see that that must have made her furious,' said Willow with considerable sincerity. It would have driven her mad with rage if anyone had done that to her. Her sympathy for Sarah increased. 'He sounds almost unstable. What did you think of him?'

'Beeking? I've hardly ever met him and so it isn't quite fair to say. In fact, I don't think I'd exchanged more than two words with him until I found myself at the same table as him at the bank's dance. He was perfectly civil then, although he grew more and more restive as we waited for Sarah.'

'Didn't you?'

The brown eyes filled with unmistakable pain. He shook his head.

'She worked so hard,' he said, his voice breaking, 'that I thought she'd got stuck in some meeting. I was used to it: the late-night sessions, the limited holidays she could take. I learned never to question her timetable or ask when she'd be home. It fretted her so badly, because she knew how much I minded not seeing her and yet she had to work those kind of hours. I never asked anything, and she always told me what had been going on when she could: when the deal was over or public. That night I just assumed she'd get there eventually. I didn't know . . .'

He buried his face in his clasped hands. Willow, exquisitely uncomfortable, got out of her chair. 'I . . .' she said. 'Is there anything I can get for you?'

'There's nothing anyone can do. Please go,' he said, his voice still muffled by his hands. 'Please leave me alone.'

There was enough suppressed hysteria in his voice to drive Willow out of his house. Standing with her back against the front door, breathing in the warm, spicy scent of some wallflowers in the borders, she realized just how oppressed she had been feeling. It was not only Thomas Allfarthing's grief, which she could do nothing to assuage, but the house itself and its stultifying cleanliness that had made her feel so uncomfortable.

Willow, who had nothing against cleanliness in itself and positively revelled in the way Mrs Rusham kept the Chesham Place flat, could not understand why she had hated the Allfarthings' so much. Walking down the path, she decided that it was the deadness of the room, rather than its lack of dust, that was so depressing. It was like a waiting room for something expensive but unpleasant: dentistry or something legal.

She wondered how Sarah Allfarthing had felt about it and whether she might have chosen her demanding career as an excuse to be away from it or from the possibly oppressive devotion of her husband. Then Willow reminded herself that just because she found other people's emotions difficult to handle, it did not follow that every woman was like her.

Turning back at the gate for one more look at the unexpected house, she thought of the man inside. It seemed irresponsible to leave him alone and desperate. She considered asking one of his neighbours for help. He must have a doctor, she thought, who could be summoned to give him at least chemical consolation.

Just as she was dithering, the front door opened and Allfarthing called from the front door:

'Miss Woodruffe! Do please forgive me. I can't think what came over me. You're stuck here with no transport. I won't be a moment. Just hold on and I'll get the car out.'

'Oh,' said Willow idiotically. 'I mean, that's extremely good of you, but I could easily telephone for a taxi.'

'No, no. Don't worry,' he said, disappearing only to re-emerge with a bunch of keys in his right hand.

He shut the door behind him, double-locked it and then led the way round to the left of the cottage, where a modern garage was screened by a row of Leyland cyprus trees. Inside was a Jaguar, as impeccably kept as the house.

Allfarthing backed out of the garage with considerable panache, which interested Willow, who had a theory about the way people used their cars. There were some who were afraid of them; others who hated them; many who used cars only for convenience; several for whom they offered vicarious power; and a few who loved them and enjoyed the partnership they offered. It surprised her that Mr Allfarthing should be one of the last class.

'Did your wife drive?' she asked into the silence.

'Only to the station and back. She didn't enjoy it.'

'What did she enjoy?'

Allfarthing turned his head to look at Willow for a moment and she thought that once more she caught a glimpse of a real smile.

'Apart from work, she loved exercise: really loved it.

She played squash well and ran miles on those machines. Occasionally I'd join her in London at her health club and row weedily while she ran. She looked magnificent then, her hair flying and her long, straight body moving perfectly in tune with itself. Neither Jeanine nor I could hope to keep up.'

He must have loved her, Willow thought. No one could talk like that who was concealing boredom or disenchantment.

'What about holidays?' she asked, wondering whether she might like exercise herself. Before her sabbatical, she had only ever had enough time to do things she knew that she enjoyed. When she had time she might try some experiments. Once the case was over one way or the other, perhaps. The thought of the ways in which the case might go as much as the sound of Allfarthing's voice stopped her idle ruminations.

'I'm sorry?' she said.

'I was just saying that Sarah didn't like holidays much unless there was plenty of sport. We used to go to those Club Mediterrané places, where she could take as much exercise and watersports as she liked. It suited us both that way and did her good.'

'Do you ski?'

Allfarthing bit his lower lip hard. 'I do, but that was the one sport she didn't like, and since she could rarely take that much time out of the office, I used to go with Jeanine.'

'What about clothes? Did she take much interest in them?' asked Willow, who had been told by everyone else she had talked to about Sarah's wonderful glamour. It was hard to square with the house they had just left. There was something else too that did not fit with what she had heard at the bank, but irritatingly she could not remember what it was.

'I don't really know,' he said, his eyes firmly directed to the road again. 'She had a great many clothes, of course, and since she started to command a big salary she spent a lot on them too, but she didn't ever . . .' He stopped, as though searching for the right word. 'She never preened, if you know what I mean.'

'I know exactly. From all I've heard she sounds a remarkably well-integrated woman,' said Willow, wanting to pay some kind of tribute. Out of the corner of her eye she saw Allfarthing's shoulders sag.

'She was. I'd never . . .' He took a deep breath and struggled on. 'People used to say when I was young that men grow up as they grew older but women always stay the same, as though they were perennially eighteen, and I believed them. But Sarah was different. She grew noticeably all the time, better and better – and I think happier and happier.' He smiled, a tender, nostalgic smile that surprised Willow.

'The only thing that never changed was her nails,' he said.

'I beg your pardon?'

'She bit them,' he said, his voice very gentle. 'She hated it, but for some reason could not stop. It always touched me to see her fingers . . .'

The car slowed down as the traffic lights ahead turned red. Allfarthing drew in breath so suddenly that it sounded harsh.

'It's so unspeakably unfair,' he burst out. 'There was so much more for her and –'

'I'll do my best to find out who did it,' said Willow gently, her mind ticking over at speed as she thought of the implications of the bitten nails. 'And they'll put him away for life.'

The car moved again and a little later stopped outside the tube station. Allfarthing switched off the engine and turned to face Willow.

'I don't know that I care that much,' he said drearily. 'She's dead. It's all over. Revenge is not . . . not something I want.'

'No. I see that. I am really sorry. Thank you for talking to me so frankly.'

Willow saw that he was holding out his right hand and so, in the confined space of the car, she shook it awkwardly before getting out.

Chapter 8

*A*LL the way back to London Willow thought about
what she had learned, building up her picture of the
murdered woman and trying to see where in her hard-
working, sensible, admired life she could have annoyed
someone so much that he – or she – killed her. There were
one or two things that did not fit in with the picture, but
Willow could not see how they might help her.

There was the evidence of the house, which still troubled
her whenever she tried to tie it up with the elegant, grown-
up, successful woman everyone described. There was also
the unlikeliness of the survival of Sarah's marriage. Willow
knew that as someone who had avoided marriage she
was peculiarly cynical about its advertised advantages,
but everything she had seen and heard about married
couples – both as Willow King and as Cressida Woodruffe –
suggested that there must have been at least some friction
between the Allfarthings.

For a moment she was distracted from her investigation
by a sudden picture of herself and Tom in ten years' time
snapping at each other over trivialities as she had seen
so many couples do. A cold determination entered her

mind. It drove out the voice that suggested that both she and Tom might be sophisticated enough to avoid such self-destructive silliness.

Willow straightened her shoulders, ignored her own emotional life and went back to her analysis of Sarah Allfarthing's death.

It was clear that, as her husband had said, Sarah had changed as she grew up, and she might well have grown out of the life they had built together before she had discovered who and what she really was. Perhaps Thomas had not been able to bear to acknowledge that and killed her.

On the other hand, he would hardly have talked so warmly of her development if he had hated it. Besides, Willow thought in frustration, he had an alibi. Suspicious though she was of tales of lifelong marital felicity, she could not see how he could possibly have killed his wife and been sitting at a table at the bank's dance, dressed in an unbloodied dinner jacket, at the same time.

The only people who had shown strong enough feelings for Sarah to make them suspects had all been at the dance when she had been killed. William Beeking and Thomas Allfarthing had sat at the same table. Tracy Blank and her boyfriend had arrived early. The chief executive had been late, but Willow did not see how he could have committed the murder unless he had bribed the security men to say that he had left before Richard discovered the body. That seemed most unlikely, and would have laid him open to appalling possibilities of blackmail.

At Liverpool Street Willow had to change trains and, as she was walking up the escalator, she considered the next person on her list. As a client, Ronald Hopecastle would not have been invited to the dance and Sarah must have irritated him badly. It was impossible to see how he could have got into the bank, let alone the Corporate Finance Department, without being seen and identified, but Willow was prepared to let that aspect of the investigation wait until after she had discovered what he had to say.

She telephoned him and introduced herself as a friend of Richard Crescent's.

'Good Lord,' said the rich voice at the other end of the telephone. 'Brave of you to say so, my dear.'

A moment's silence helped Willow to suppress the rage she felt at being addressed as any stranger's 'dear'.

'And I am trying to find out anything I can that might help him. I wondered if I might come and see you.'

'There's nothing I can do for him, I'm afraid, but come by all means. Now the business is off my hands I've time and to spare, what? For the moment at least. What did you say your name was?'

'Cressida Woodruffe,' she said, wondering whether he could possibly be a fan.

'Girl who writes the books?'

'That's me,' she said, still suppressing rage.

'Come by all means. I'm only sorry m' wife and daughter won't be here. They spend a fortune on your books, what?'

Willow thanked him and walked out of the station to hail a taxi. The journey across London to the Hopecastles' Knightsbridge house took forty minutes, during which she sifted all the information she had already collected so that she could ask the most useful questions.

The taxi dropped her outside a neat white house that was protected from the street by a row of well-painted black iron railings. Bay trees in stone pots stood at either side of the chaste black door and the knocker that Willow used was of highly polished brass.

The door was opened a few minutes later by the master of the house. When she saw how he was dressed, Willow contemplated pointing out to him that for the price of one of his French silk ties his wife could have bought at least four hard-backed books. Discretion stopped her and instead she smiled at him as though she were one of her own beleaguered heroines. He escorted her into a drawing room filled with antique furniture and fluttery double tablecloths and ruched blinds printed with a pattern of bamboo and birds of paradise.

'Can I offer you a drink?' he asked hospitably, waving towards a tray loaded with bottles and square cut-glass decanters. 'I'm having one.'

Willow looked at the squat tumbler that sat on a side table and saw not only that the whisky and soda in it looked dark with lack of water, but also that there were enough sticky finger marks on the glass to suggest that it was not his first drink of the day. In the interest of encouraging him to talk, she accepted a glass of sherry.

'Rare to find a girl who drinks that nowadays,' he said with a beam of exaggerated approval. Willow tried to think what could be the matter with him. She could not believe that he was in the habit of inviting strangers to drink with him in the early afternoon or that he had taken to drink as a way of coping with the boredom of his new freedom from work. He showed enough signs of intoxication to assure her that he was not accustomed to the quantity he had consumed.

'I love it,' she said truthfully and when she had sipped and tasted the sherry, she added: 'Particularly when it is a Palo Cortado like this. Is this the Wine Society's? I think I recognize it.'

'Not just a pretty face, then,' said Ronald Hopecastle, looking both surprised and pleased. He laughed and half stumbled as he went to pick up his own glass. 'Yes, it is. Come and sit down and tell me all about it.'

Willow followed him to a plump coral-coloured sofa that was filled with small tapestry cushions and sat, drooping in one corner of it. She put her glass down on a little table. Copying one of Emma Gnatche's gestures, she scooped her hair behind her ears with both hands and gazed at her feet.

'Well, it's Richard, you see. I simply have to find some-thing that his lawyers can use in his defence. I can't believe . . .' She raised her eyes to the dark ones in front of her and for once let all her terror for – and of – Richard show.

'I don't know that there's much I can do, my dear,' said Hopecastle, displaying signs of distress. 'You see, I saw him lose his temper with her. Had to tell the police that when they asked, y'know. I really did.'

'So they tell me. It's just so impossible to believe that Richard could do anything like that. I've known him for years and he's never once shown any signs of temper.' The plea in her voice was not entirely assumed.

Ronald Hopecastle spread his plump thighs and leaned back against the cushions. His florid face took on an expression of theatrical sympathy. Willow was not convinced by either the relaxation or the sympathy. He looked far too uncomfortable. She hoped that their combined acts were not going to lead him to pat her hand. If he did, she knew that she would have invited it by her own performance, but that would make it no easier to accept.

'He was provoked,' said Hopecastle shortly. 'I must say I could have throttled her myself. I'm afraid it's what comes of having women doing that sort of job.'

'I don't understand,' said Willow, trying hard to go on sounding fragile.

'No man would have felt the need to fill the gap by chatting as she did. And no man would have been so damned silly as to pick a subject like tax fraud at such a moment.'

'You sound as though you disliked her,' said Willow, feeling uncomfortably certain that had this unhappily jovial man actually killed Sarah he would have joined the chorus of her admirers.

'I did.' He laughed. 'She was a pretty tasty-looking creature, but she was out of place at the bank. I thought she was tiresome and in the way. And I didn't like her sense of humour. Couldn't understand why James Certes had such a lot of time for her. He insisted that she was the best of the assistant directors at the bank: older than a lot of the boys of course, but said to be more conscientious and more effective. Couldn't see it m'self.'

'She certainly had a high reputation,' said Willow, still trying to find the source of his uneasiness.

'Oh they've all been falling over themselves ever since she arrived to announce to the world how brilliant she is – sorry, as you were: was. Show that they're not male chauvinist pigs, what?'

'I see. I'd heard that they were almost the last bank in London to take on women as anything but secretaries.'

'Biggleigh-Clart started it when he appeared as chief executive. I gather he'd known her before and persuaded her out of the research department at one of the other banks to join his corporate boys. Doubt if they'll have any more, what?'

Willow found his false interrogatives not only tiresome but positively confusing.

'Do you really think that Richard killed her?' she asked pathetically.

'I'm sure he did. Must have.' It sounded like an article of faith. 'Can't see who else did it – unless –'

He stopped suddenly, looking even less sure of himself, put his knees together and crossed his arms across his chest. Willow mistrusted body-language experts, but she could not miss the message that his was transmitting.

'What's upsetting you so much?' she asked, deciding that directness was her best weapon. There was a long, uncomfortable silence.

'I'd hate to think she might have topped herself,' Hope-castle admitted after a while and reached for his drink.

'No, it's a horrible thought,' Willow agreed. 'But better that, surely, than that someone else did it.'

'Not really.'

He got up, holding up his whisky tumbler, and went to refill it, banging the edge of the decanter on the glass. Willow thought for a bit.

'You were very angry with her, weren't you?'

There was a grunt of agreement before the hiss of the soda siphon drowned it. Willow sat in silence, groping for a reason for his distress. She thought about everything she had heard about the fateful meeting and then remembered what his business had been.

'Did you give her the knife? As a kind of souvenir of the deal?' she asked quietly.

'Oh, Christ!'

Willow had to strain to hear him.

'Wish I hadn't, actually.' The decanter was banged down on the silver tray. Hopecastle downed his whisky and Willow heard him pour himself out another. He walked ponderously back to the sofa, looking even unhappier than he had earlier.

'You see, m'dear, it's a bit of a tradition to hand out presents at the end of a successful deal. They – the bankers – tend to give us acrylic embedments and we reciprocate.'

'Embedments?' It was such a bizarre word, particularly when spoken by a plummy-voiced businessman with too much whisky inside him, that Willow could not quite suppress a smile.

'Acrylic embedments. Haven't you ever seen one? They embed something, a miniature version of the contract usually, in a square of acrylic as a paperweight. And we usually pay them back with something connected to the business, what? I handed out paperknives.'

'In the plural?'

'Yah, but only hers was sharp. It was a silly thing to do. Schoolboyish, you know. But I was so bloody angry. I thought she'd get the point.' He shuddered and held his left wrist against his eyes, letting the glass in his hand bang against his right ear. 'Oh, God!'

Despite her horror of what had happened to Sarah Allfarthing and her continuing anxiety for Richard, Willow could not help noticing the infelicitous pun.

'Listen,' she said, making her voice as warm as she could.

Hopecastle looked at her as a terrified child might look at his mother.

'No intelligent woman – and everyone agrees that Sarah Allfarthing was that – kills herself because someone sends her a knife. It would have been far more likely to make her angry than suicidal. If she was so desperate that she couldn't bear to live with herself any longer, which I don't believe, she'd have killed herself some other way if you hadn't provided the means.'

'But you do see how I feel responsible,' he said, still desperately seeking absolution. 'Even, actually, if it . . . you know.'

'Oh yes, I do see that. But whisky's not going to help you.'

The florid face flushed even more and Willow found herself feeling sorry for him. Tiresome and limited though he might be, he was in genuine despair. She tried to think of something to distract him.

'Is that your daughter?' she asked, pointing to a charming pencil sketch that hung over the ornate pine chimneypiece.

Hopecastle's unhappy eyes lightened slightly and he nodded.

'What does she do?'

He seemed to gather himself together as though remembering something he had once been told. He put down his glass and concentrated.

'Haven't you heard of her? She's a dressmaker – designer, too. Started in business a couple of years ago. Doing very well. I could introduce you, if you like,' he said, squinting at Willow's clothes. 'Lovely figure like yours: she'd make you something smashing.'

Willow felt increasingly sorry for him as he tried to do his best for his daughter's public relations.

'Who are her clients?'

'All sorts. She started with schoolfriends mainly but in the last year she's been branching out. Robert Biggleigh-Clart sent his wife.' An expression of pride and affection banished the horror from his eyes. 'Mandy said she arrived looking as though she expected the village sewing woman and was surprised by the glamour. She ordered two evening dresses! That's turnover of over fifteen hundred quid.'

'Goodness!' said Willow, amused.

'Yes; she's going for the final fitting on Monday evening. She's dressed by all the best people, you know. We're hoping she'll pass the word on so that it goes all the way; even to Kensington Palace, what?'

'That would be a coup.'

'I know. Look, why don't you drop in? Say I sent you and Mandy'll bust a gut for you. Here, I've got one of her cards somewhere.' He lumbered up and went to scuffle in a muddle of papers on a pretty desk in the corner of the room.

Irritably pushing aside a bundle of irrelevant documents, he knocked a pen tray to the floor. Red and blue ink spilled into the mushroom-coloured carpet, two fountain pens rolled under the sofa and a steel paperknife lay with its point towards Willow.

'Oh, Christ, no!' Hopecastle backed into a chair and sat like an image of despair.

'Don't worry. I'm sure we can get the ink out,' said Willow, getting up. She picked up the paperknife. 'Where do you keep the cleaning materials?'

'Haven't a clue, m'dear. Be careful of that!'

'I will,' she said, testing its edge with her thumb. 'But it's not sharp. It's quite safe.' She laid the knife on the desk and knelt on the floor to collect the two pens.

The sound of a key grating in the front door made Hopecastle throw up his head. An expression of surprising relief crossed his face.

'Darling? I've bogged it again. There's ink all over the carpet.'

'Oh, Ronnie.' A light voice, more sorrowful than angry, heralded the appearance of Mrs Hopecastle.

A gentle-faced woman in her early fifties, she took one

look at the mess on the carpet, flashed a smile at Willow and patted her husband on the head.

'I won't be a minute,' she said.

While she was gone, Hopecastle offered Willow the card he was holding in his hand.

'Here y'are.'

She took it and thanked him. 'I ought to go,' she said. 'I'll only be in the way of the rescue operation, but I'll certainly call on your daughter.'

Mrs Hopecastle returned with a bowl of steaming water, a plastic tube of stain remover and several cloths. Willow murmured more farewells and left them to it.

The visit had not told her much that was likely to be of any use, but it had given her a possible entrée into the life of 'Mr Big's' wife, which might help. Willow walked home through the sunlit evening, planning how best to use it.

By the time she let herself into the flat in Chesham Place, she realized how tired she was. She had planned to use the health-club guest ticket to continue to build up her picture of Sarah Allfarthing, but she felt as though she could not face the prospect even of working a rowing machine, let alone running or pulling weights. Telling herself that as it was Friday most of Sarah's fellow members of the club would probably be on the road to their weekend cottages, Willow decided to salve her conscience by dealing with the messages on her answering machine.

Mrs Rusham had already gone for the day, leaving a casserole in the oven, so Willow made free with her own kitchen. Ignoring the delicate cakes and biscuits laid out on the tea tray, she switched on the kettle to make a pot of tea and assembled a thick smoked-ham and Gruyère sandwich as she had had no lunch. When she had poured herself a cup of tea she went to listen to her messages. Hearing Eve Greville's voice, sounding as nearly angry as it had ever been, Willow dialled Eve's number, hoping that she would be answered by the agency's machine.

'Eve Greville.'

Disappointed, Willow gathered herself together to make certain that she did not sound pathetic or defensive.

'Eve; it's Cressida here. I'm so sorry that I haven't been about when you've rung. It must have looked as though I was ducking your calls.'

'Weren't you?' Eve's deep, smoky voice was sarcastic.

'Certainly not. But a friend of mine has been arrested for murder, and –'

There was a gale of laughter at the other end of the telephone, which roused all Willow's self-defensive coldness.

'In twenty-five years of literary agency I have never heard a more creative excuse. Just for that I'll almost forgive you.' All the sarcasm had been dissolved into laughter.

'I'm afraid it's a reason rather than an excuse, Eve.'

'You don't mean it's true? God, Cressida, I'm sorry. I see: I mean, I can understand why the charms of your synopsis have palled. But I really must have something to tell the Americans soon. Can't you give me anything?'

'I've still got four months until the delivery date, Eve. Don't despair. This murder business is taking all my time at the moment, but as soon as it's sorted, I promise that I'll give everything to the book.'

'Can I just tell them what it's about? Then at least they'll stop nagging me.'

'All right,' said Willow, racking her brains for something to say. 'It's about a girl, not particularly clever but bags of native intelligence, whose father sets her up in a dressmaking business.'

'Bit dull, isn't it?'

'No, wait: she starts off making droopy dresses for schoolfriends, but slowly she gets some proper grown-up customers – through her father's business contacts mainly – and learns how to make clothes that are less droopy: probably takes on a professionally trained partner or something. Then as she's learning her job and developing her business skills, she stumbles on evidence of some massive swindle. A big charity. You know those lunches that cost hundreds of pounds to attend. Something to do with that.'

'Slightly better, but I'll need more.'

Willow forced her mind to work. When she was worried about something her imagination needed no spur to create realistic pictures of disaster for her. When she needed it for her novels, it sometimes played possum.

'And falling in love with one of the people who is genuinely involved in the charity – a brilliant, brave, self-denying doctor,' she said, improvising quickly, 'who's come back from a war or a famine zone – she determines to find out what's really happening.'

'More, Cressida. Come on.'

'I can practically feel the lash across my back, Eve. Give me a break.'

'There's no time.'

'All right. Our heroine sets out to find out who the chief swindler is, is violently warned off and just becomes more determined, all the while falling more and more in love with the blameless hero. Only at the end does she discover that the swindler is an old friend of her father's, or one of his best customers or something, or perhaps the doctor's elder brother. Then she has a terrible choice between good and evil, daddy and the boyfriend, success and failure and so on.'

'It's got possibilities, but I suspect you're thinking it out as you speak. Work out a decent synopsis with plenty of colour and interesting background details and it might just do.'

'I think the plot has possibilities,' said Willow, becoming more enthusiastic as she thought. 'It'll have all the glamour of the idle rich at their lunches, upwardly mobile young businesswoman, true love, mystery, moral choice, the vital hint of reality in the daddy-versus-boyfriend ingredient, glitz and sex.'

'Not too much of the last two. Don't forget these are the caring nineties, and she sounds rather young. Glitz and sex are really for jaded heroines in their late twenties and early thirties.'

Willow pushed off her shoes, laughing. 'You're so cynical, Eve.'

'Nonsense. This is a business and you're making – or supposed to be making – a saleable product. Once you forget that, you'll be in trouble and start wallowing in pretension. I must go, Cressida. Get me the synopsis by the end of next week.'

'I'll do my best,' she said, her voice flattening as she remembered Richard and what she saw as her real job. It was a fantastic relief to be free of the civil service at least. The prospect of resigning properly at the end of her sabbatical began to seem not only attractive but right, too. 'Goodbye.'

'Bye.'

Willow put down the telephone and allowed the tape with the rest of the messages to unroll. There was one from Jeremy Stedington telling her that the chief executive had given permission for 'Miss King' to sit in on a client meeting at eight thirty on Monday. Stedington added that one of the lawyers who was to be there had also attended the meeting when Richard had shaken Sarah Allfarthing. Willow smiled as she listened.

The only message that needed any immediate action was one from Emma Gnatche pleading for something to do. Willow drank her tea and then telephoned Emma to invite her round to the flat the following morning so that they could go through everything Willow had learned so far and plan their campaign.

'Thank you, Cressida,' said Emma. 'You're the only hope poor Richard has.'

Before Willow could say anything, Emma had put down the telephone. Her faith made Willow feel guilty not only of laziness but also of treachery to Richard. Yet try as she might she could not completely banish her doubts.

Suddenly the prospect of exercise seemed more enticing

than relaxation and so, instead of taking a drink into her bathroom for a long, self-indulgent soak, she looked for the guest ticket that the chief executive had given her to his health club. When she had found it, tucked into a pocket of her handbag, she telephoned the club to check whether there was a shop selling clothes and equipment on the premises and took a taxi straight there.

Confused by the array of different kinds of Lycra clothes for the various activities the club promoted, Willow eventually settled for a plain green bathing costume, a pair of white tennis shorts and a black T-shirt. When she explained to the assistant that before her swim she planned to exercise in the gym, she was shown several brands of 'aerobic boots'. Deciding against them, she chose the simplest of the available tennis shoes and a pair of white socks. It did not surprise her that her purchases totted up to well over a hundred pounds, but her long-entrenched frugality made her wince when she thought about the likely use to which the clothes would be put.

She spent ten minutes filling in various forms at the reception desk before she was allowed through to the ladies' changing room, which was luxuriously appointed with thick carpet, pale-wood lockers and benches and well-upholstered chairs in front of a row of expensive hair dryers. There were heaps of vivid green towels and towelling dressing gowns, baskets of individual-sized bottles of shampoo and conditioner, and a kind of annexe full of massage tables and all sorts of machines. A wet area beyond the carpet proved to contain saunas, steam rooms, tanning beds and a whirlpool bath as well as the entrance to the swimming pool.

Changed into her shirt and shorts, with her street clothes and money locked away, Willow went to the gym, where she spent a humiliating and useless half-hour trying to use the gleaming white and silver machines. Eventually a sinewy young instructor took pity on her, adjusted the one on which she was sitting, removed several of the weights and showed her how to use it to develop the muscles in her upper arms and chest. That was followed by others designed to tauten bits of her legs, her glutea maxima, and her stomach.

Eventually, aching and covered in sweat, she gave up the machines in favour of the swimming pool. There, having removed all her smudged make-up, she swam with a stately breaststroke up and down the pool, watching for anyone who might have been able to talk to her about Sarah Allfarthing.

There were two youngish men who appeared to be competing with each other to make the greatest splash as they thundered up and down the pool, using their arms like flails. Several slender, tanned women with gold chains around their necks followed Willow's example, but she could not find an opportunity to break into their conversations.

At last, thinking that she might sink from exhaustion if she swam another yard, Willow emerged from the pool, found a towel and retreated to the whirlpool. There she had better luck. Two women with tired, lined faces and the smooth bodies of pubescent girls followed her.

Embarrassed to be wearing a bathing costume while they were naked, Willow moved a little to give them more room.

'Thanks,' said one with a slight smile. 'Ouf, it's hot tonight.'

'That's what I thought,' said Willow, smiling back, 'but I assumed it was always like this.'

The third woman, whose hair was gathered into a bunch of curls on top of her head, explained that the temperature tended to rise towards the end of the week and start off again cool the following Monday.

'Sarah never told me about that,' said Willow in a clumsy attempt to turn the talk to her advantage. 'Isn't it awful what happened to her?'

'Sarah Allfarthing? Was she a friend of yours?'

'Well, not exactly a friend,' said Willow accurately before she had to lie, 'but we met only a short while before . . .

well, before it happened, and she gave me a guest ticket to come here. I was away and when I came back to London she was dead. My name's Woodruffe, by the way, Cressida Woodruffe.'

'The writer? How do you do. I'm Sally Smith and this is Angela Elliott. She's with BJP and I'm at Lowelton.' Neither the initials nor the name meant anything to Willow, but she smiled as though they did.

'It was ghastly,' said Angela, carefully moving her bottom so that the fierce jets of the whirlpool caught precisely the right muscles. 'I hardly knew Sarah, but she seemed a thoroughly good egg. I can't really bear even to think about what happened to her.' There was a pause before she added in patent honesty: 'It's made us all pretty nervous about working late alone.'

'She was great,' said Sally, turning round to face the jets. 'She and I were the first women who joined here and we used to have a lot of laughs at the beginning.'

'I'd noticed that there didn't seem to be too many women around,' said Willow.

'Well, there aren't all that many of us who are willing or able to pay nine hundred pounds a year and a five-hundred-pound joining fee in this bit of London, and not many of the men have put their wives on the list. But Sarah was really chuffed when it opened. She always said she needed a lot of exercise – those enviably long legs, I suppose.'

'Did she come here every night?'

'Not always and never on a Friday. I think it depended on her work and how her husband was. She was terrifically conscientious, don't you think, Ange?'

'I've no idea. It was perfectly clear that she was successful and that that got up the noses of quite a lot of the boys at the bank, but we never got on to intimacies like the trials of our marriages. People don't confide in me as they do in you, Sal.' Angela laughed and Sally joined her, obviously happy with her reputation.

'Did Sarah confide much?' Willow asked. 'She struck me as being rather reserved.'

'She was.' Sally wrinkled up her nose and swung round again with her back to the jets. 'We used to talk a bit about how to cope with flirtatious partners and that led on to other things. I talked more than she did, actually.'

Angela laughed. 'I can believe that.'

'I gather she had quite a lot of trouble with flirtatious colleagues,' said Willow.

'Well, she would, wouldn't she, Cressida? Looking like her in a place like that bank where they've only ever had women as secretaries and tea ladies. The chaps were gobsmacked by her, and not many of them could resist having a go. Trouble was Sarah wasn't keen.'

'Not at all?' said Willow.

'Not really. I think she gave her poor old husband his conjugal rights from time to time, but no one else was going to get a look-in. Let's face it, sex does get pretty boring after a bit. And we're all so damned tired all the time. God, isn't it awful to talk like this when she's . . . ?'

'It's hardly going to hurt her now,' said Angela robustly.

'No, I suppose not.'

'D'you think they've got the right man?' said Willow as casually as she could.

Angela looked at Sally, who shrugged.

'It sounds like it from all I've heard. I don't see how it could have been anyone else.'

'No,' agreed Willow after an uncomfortable pause.

'I'm getting too hot. I'm off for a shower and then a quick steam. Coming, Ange?'

'Fine. Good to meet you, Cressida. Will you join the club yourself? Perhaps we'll see more of you.'

Willow smiled and shook her head. 'I'm not in the City often enough to make it worth it,' she said. 'But it seemed something that I ought to do once she'd given me a ticket. Silly, really.'

The others smiled at her as they stood, pleased with their

perfect bodies, on the edge of the whirlpool. Their breasts were tiny and pointed, their pubic hair had been waxed away at the edges and their buttocks looked almost non-existent. Their exhausted, intelligent faces looked decades older than their bodies. Watching them retreat, Willow thought about the basis of a society that decrees the acme of feminine beauty to be that achieved naturally at about the age of thirteen.

After the two women had left the showers and proceeded chatting towards the steam room, Willow, too, heaved herself out of the bubbling, chlorinated hot water and cooled off.

Chapter 9

THE next morning Willow woke, aching from the un-accustomed exercise, and saw that the previous day's sun had been followed by thick cloud. She lay for a few moments trying to pin down a peculiar sensation of happiness. Richard was still in prison and she had no evidence to support her shaky faith in his innocence. There was nothing to explain the euphoria except for her growing determination to leave the civil service at the end of her sabbatical and that did not seem to be enough.

She had got out of bed and was lying in the bath, feeling the hot water lapping over her breasts, before she traced the happiness to its source. Then she sat up quickly and washed her face in cold water. It was one thing to acknowledge her growing affection for Tom Worth but quite another to let the prospect of seeing him control her moods.

Getting out of the bath and rubbing herself vigorously with a towel, Willow decided to dress in an old and baggy pair of black corduroy trousers. She made a concession towards elegance by choosing a loose multicoloured cash-mere tunic from the Burlington Arcade to wear with them and put her narrow feet into a pair of black suede Gucci shoes. With her face made up with even more than usual care, she went to tell Mrs Rusham she was ready for breakfast.

'You do look more yourself, Miss Woodruffe,' said the housekeeper as she brought a tray into the rosy dining room a few minutes later. 'Have you had some good news about Mr Lawrence-Crescent's case?'

'Not really,' she said, noticing the signs of strain in the normally imperturbable Mrs Rusham. 'But I have discovered that the dead woman stirred up a lot of emotions in people she worked with, and that suggests that the story may not be as simple as the police believe.'

Mrs Rusham picked up a hot plate and carefully laid it down before Willow, removing the domed white china cover to reveal the eggs Benedict she had cooked.

'They look wonderful. Thank you.'

'I've heard that remand prisoners are permitted to have food sent in to them in prison,' Mrs Rusham began, twisting her hands in her overall in a way Willow had never seen before. 'And I was wondering whether you would mind if I were to . . .'

'Cook for Richard? What a wonderful idea! I wonder if it's true. I'll check with Inspector Worth when he comes and let you know. Well done, Mrs Rusham.'

With an approving smile, the housekeeper nodded her head and then disappeared into the kitchen, leaving her employer to pick up the newspaper. Before she had finished the first article or eaten more than half her eggs, she heard the telephone ring. Deciding to let Mrs Rusham answer it, Willow went on eating.

The door from the kitchen opened and the housekeeper emerged, her face back in its customary expressionless formality.

'Chief Inspector Jane Moreby is on the telephone. I told her that you were at breakfast, but –'

Willow had already dropped her napkin and stood up.

'I'll talk to her,' she said, running to the drawing room. 'Cressida Woodruffe here,' she said into the receiver.

'This is Jane Moreby.' It was a crisp voice with a slight northern accent, which took Willow straight back to her bleak childhood and her demanding but unknowable academic parents.

'Tom Worth gave me your number. There are one or two questions I'd like to ask you. May I come and see you this morning?'

'This morning I'm rather busy,' said Willow, instinctively stalling as she tried to ignore the difficult memories of her past.

'It won't take long. No more than half an hour.'

'Very well. I can make time if you'll be here at half past ten. Did he give you the address as well?'

'I'll be there. Goodbye.' The chief inspector rang off cleanly and Willow walked slowly back to her breakfast.

When she had finished she carried the dishes through to Mrs Rusham and told her what had happened.

'You can't allow that woman in here,' said Mrs Rusham, two bright red patches flaring in her cheeks. She gasped. 'Oh, I do beg your pardon! I don't know what came over me.'

'I feel rather like that, too, but who knows? It might help Richard if I talk to her. If Miss Gnatche arrives while she's here, will you entertain her for me?'

'Certainly.'

Willow considered changing out of her trousers into something that might impress Chief Inspector Moreby, but decided to keep them. It seemed important to remind both of them that she was on her own territory and could behave as she chose.

While she waited, Willow was tempted to ring Tom, but since she had been so sharp with him when he asked to see her, she felt it was only fair to wait until he appeared. Instead she telephoned the number on Amanda Hopecastle's card and made an appointment for late on Monday afternoon, hoping that she could engineer a casual meeting with Mrs Biggleigh-Clart while she was there.

There seemed to be nothing else she could do in the half-hour she had to wait for Chief Inspector Moreby except to clean her teeth again and wash her hands. When she had done that she thought it might be useful to have a record of anything that the chief inspector said, so she went into her writing room to find a dictating machine she had once bought but never managed to use for her books.

Taking it back to the drawing room, she thought that the room provided a background that was quite suitable for a successful novelist but seemed incongruous for a discussion about a man in prison on a charge of murder. The golden furniture and paintings, the thickly cushioned sofas, even the seductive mixture of rich creams and yellows of the walls and curtains with the coppery flowers and cushions all suggested peace and luxury and, Willow had to admit, self-satisfaction. It was the room of someone who knew just what she wanted of life and had found a way to get it. Richard's torment, like the pain and terror Sarah Allfarthing must have felt as she saw her murderer pick up the knife, had no place there. The ugliness and reality of them made the room seem fantastically inappropriate.

Chief Inspector Moreby accorded it no more than a raised eyebrow when Mrs Rusham ushered her in a few minutes later. Willow rose from her chair and held out her hand.

'Good morning, Miss Woodruffe,' said the policewoman in an easy voice.

'Do sit down,' said Willow, gesturing to the sofa nearest the door while she took the opposite one. 'You said you had some questions to ask me?'

'Yes. Thank you.'

Jane Moreby sat down and crossed her legs. They were shapely, if not particularly long, and the simple beige pumps she was wearing suited them. Willow waited, oddly nervous. To distract herself she examined the other woman's plain clothes – a pale-beige linen skirt overchecked in black, a thin black jacket and a white shirt – and noticed the wedding ring on her left hand. With her neat, short, mouse-coloured hair, she looked composed, efficient and at ease with herself. Willow was reluctantly impressed.

'How long have you known Richard Crescent?'

'Six years,' said Willow, 'but I don't see how that can possibly be relevant to your investigation.'

Jane Moreby looked at her very directly. 'This is not altogether an official visit,' she said, adding reluctantly: 'I have a great respect for Tom Worth.'

'I see. Then, as it's not official, would you like a cup of coffee?' asked Willow, determined to regain control of the meeting and to ignore the message implicit in the police-woman's remarks.

When Mrs Moreby shook her head, Willow tried again.

'Tom has told you, I take it, that I do not believe that Richard could have killed that woman?'

'Yes. I oughtn't to be here, but in the circumstances I'm willing to listen to anything you have to say. The papers are with the CPS – that is the Crown Prosecution Service.'

'I'm perfectly aware of that,' said Willow coldly. Jane Moreby smiled slightly.

'He has been committed for trial at the Old Bailey. Nothing you can say will change that, but, as I said, I am willing to listen.'

Willow was disconcerted by the other woman's direct-ness. Her visit seemed astonishing and could only have been made out of a serious respect for Tom's opinions. Willow felt both outrage and fear. It was a nauseating mixture. She got out of her chair, almost enjoying the shriek of her stretched muscles, and tugged the expensive cashmere tunic down over her thighs. Walking to the window, she stared down at the big, glossy cars in the street. She saw a plain red Fiesta that must belong to the woman who was sitting so easily behind her.

'I haven't anything much to tell you except that I know him well and I know that he couldn't have killed her.'

'Very few friends of killers see that side of them, and very few can be easily convinced – even by a confession.'

Willow turned back to face the policewoman.

'But you can't possibly have had a confession in this case. Listen: there is no violence in Richard. None. I slept with him on and off for three years and I know. Sex is after all a fairly violent activity. I provoked him often, too, and he was never more than sulky.'

'Perhaps the provocation you offered was not the sort that triggered his anger. Did you know that he was adopted as a child?'

'What?' Willow felt as though someone had hit her hard in the solar plexus. For three years Richard had been the only person in the world who knew her as both Willow King and Cressida Woodruffe. She had trusted him. The thought that he might have kept to himself something so fundamental astonished her.

When she had assured herself that his secrecy could not convince her that he was a murderer, she said: 'He can't have known that. How did you find out?'

'He told me.'

Willow was distressed to see pity in the other woman's grey eyes. It began to look as though she had come not to listen but to warn. Willow could not help imagining what Tom Worth might have said about her.

'Who were his parents?' Willow asked, hanging on to what she knew of Richard and trying to get rid of the sense of injury – and insult – that the information had produced in her.

'That we don't know. He has never exercised his right to have them identified, and only he can do it.'

'But you are suggesting,' said Willow, taking refuge in chilliness, 'that he might have inherited a tendency to violence?'

Jane Moreby shook her neat head again. 'No. What I'm suggesting is that there may be things about him that you do not know. Such as his hot temper. He had quite a reputation for violence at school and university, although he seemed to have conquered it until just recently.'

Willow sat, leaning heavily on the arm of the sofa as she went down in some pain. She had a sudden vision of herself in old age.

'I don't believe it.'

'It's perfectly true. He was once gated for a term when he was at Oxford for injuring another man. Did you know that?'

'In what circumstances?' Willow was battling hard to keep in her mind the picture of Richard as she had always known him.

'On the rugby pitch,' said Chief Inspector Moreby a little reluctantly. It was her first sign of weakness and it galvanized Willow.

'In that case, I suspect it's wholly understandable. Isn't rugby the game where hordes of muddy men fling themselves on each other and kick and bring their opponents crashing down on the field? Don't the players wear special headbands so that their ears are not torn off?'

Willow knew that she sounded like the pompous judges who ask in court for information about modern celebrities of whom they have never heard, but it was the only way in which she could express her complete refusal to accept the policewoman's thesis.

Chief Inspector Moreby shrugged and laid her hands in her lap. Willow noticed that her neat fingers were slightly stained with nicotine and felt another moment's superiority.

'Perhaps if you really do have some questions you could ask them now,' Willow said.

Jane Moreby frowned, asked her for a few innocuous details about Richard's life during the years she had known him and then stood up. Willow sat still, looking up in what she hoped was disdain.

'It is watertight, you know,' said the policewoman with a certain reluctant pity in her eyes. 'Quite apart from all the forensic evidence, the supporting facts of his character and the way he behaved in the previous week's meeting, there simply was no one else who could have done it. You do realize that he laid violent hands on the victim and shook her only a week before the murder?'

'I've heard all about that, but it's irrelevant. Surely there could have been someone else in Corporate Finance when Richard was in the washroom, someone who hid in the bank until it was possible to leave unsuspected?'

Thinking of the mysterious Mrs Biggleigh-Clart, Willow made a mental note to find out whether the chauffeur had actually seen his boss's wife when he was told about her migraine.

'Did you search the whole building?' Willow went on. 'The bank's staff were all accounted for at the dance, but what about a stranger? It's perfectly possible that someone concealed him- or herself until the place was milling with police, doctors, pathologists, photographers and so on and then walked out with the crowd.'

'We had a man on the only unlocked door in the place. Everyone had to identify themselves as they left the building. It is impossible for a stranger to have got through.'

'Perhaps the person was equipped with food and water and camped for the whole weekend.'

'A million-to-one chance.' Chief Inspector Moreby slung her bag over her shoulder. 'And Mr Crescent was not out of the department for long enough for anyone to have got in, killed the victim and concealed himself. Clearly I shouldn't have come.'

She did not apologize and Willow had no trouble understanding the subtext of what she had said: I have wasted my time coming to you out of my friendship for your lover. I came to warn you and you have rejected me. I don't care: you can take the consequences.

Remembering the things Tom had said about Jane Moreby, Willow managed a small smile.

'I do recognize that you meant to help,' she said, but then her pent-up feelings burst into speech: 'But why on earth do you think a man like Richard would have bothered to kill Mrs Allfarthing, even if you've convinced yourself that he's capable of it? He would never be so stupid. He wouldn't have changed into his dinner jacket if he was about to slaughter her, and if he were the sort of man capable of such a killing, he would have found a way to do it that did not leave him covered with blood and holding a knife. He's not a fool, you know.'

'No. He's not a fool. I don't suppose for one moment that he'd planned to kill her. I believe him when he says he had no idea she would be there when he arrived from Tokyo.'

'Then what?'

'He's told us that he changed into his dinner suit at his desk and then went to wash his hands. I suspect that something she said when he came back from the toilet caught him on the raw. He was tired and anxious. His career had reached a plateau: he's probably unlikely to be made a director of the bank and he sees this woman, the first in the department, becoming increasingly successful. Clients are beginning to ask for her to be assigned to the team for their deal. She's getting a big reputation, not just in the bank but in the City, too. You've recently left him. No one has taken your place. He feels a failure. And he can't take it. All his troubles have been caused by powerful women and he's determined to show that he can beat them.'

'Balderdash!' Willow surprised even herself with the old-fashioned expletive. 'That's complete nonsense: more of a fantasy than anything I've ever written. I can see how you've arrived at it,' she went on more quietly as she remembered the poisoner she had identified for Tom only a few months earlier, 'but it does not fit Richard. You've just seized on the most likely suspect – and they're never the actual criminals.'

'Only in novels,' said Jane Moreby drily. 'In real life the obvious suspect is usually the villain. The only difficulty sometimes is proving what we know to be true. In this case all the forensic evidence anyone could want exists. He did it.'

'I don't believe you. And neither does her husband. Doesn't that give you any doubts?' said Willow.

When the chief inspector said nothing, Willow added crossly: 'Haven't recent appeals taught you anything? You may think that your suspects are guilty; you may even doctor evidence to prove it, but –'

'That's outrageous,' said Chief Inspector Moreby in a voice that ripped through the pleasant atmosphere of Willow's drawing room. After a moment the policewoman recovered her temper and in a voice of such patronage that it set Willow seething, she went on:

'Miss Woodruffe, listen to me. Working on your books, away from the rat race, you may not have come across the real terror that a great many men feel when they are confronted with tough, successful women, particularly men who have been educated at all-male boarding schools and colleges.'

Willow laughed and tossed her hair away from her face. She suddenly felt at much less of a disadvantage.

'Of course I have. My good woman, it is not only in the police force that men feel threatened. I think,' she said, remembering what Tom had said to her at the edge of the Tuscan swimming pool, 'that you are allowing your own prejudices to overrun your judgement.'

Willow wished that she had had a bell system installed in the flat so that she could have rung for Mrs Rusham to escort her visitor to the door.

'I appreciate your motives in coming here,' she said graciously, standing up, 'and I look forward to the day when you have to charge the real killer.'

Jane Moreby shrugged and allowed Willow to lead her to the front door. She stopped on the threshold.

'On the other hand,' she said coldly, 'if he's as clever and sophisticated as you believe, perhaps he gambled on our assuming that no one would have been so stupid as to be found as he was with the body in his arms. Had you thought of that?'

Silenced and in acute if hidden distress, Willow merely shook her head. The policewoman crossed the threshold. As Willow shut the door behind her, both Mrs Rusham and Emma Gnatche looked anxiously out of the kitchen.

'Has she gone?' asked Emma, her large blue eyes looking uncharacteristically malevolent. The contrast between the strength of her dislike and her completely conventional pink-and-white prettiness was surprising.

'Yes. Thank God,' said Willow.

'Does she really believe that Richard did it?' asked Emma.

Willow simply nodded, her face bleak and angry.

'Then she's mad. Mrs Rusham and I have been working out all sorts of reasons for her lunacy.'

Willow looked at her housekeeper and saw in her eyes a shadow of the devotion with which they looked on Richard. Clearly Emma's championship of him had attracted Mrs Rusham even more than her sweetness and her intelligence had always done.

'Come on, Cressida,' said Emma, 'let's get down to it. We can't leave him in there any longer than we have to. Don't worry, Mrs R., he'll be back here eating one of your amazing meals any day now.' Emma laid a small hand on Mrs Rusham's arm.

She flushed unbecomingly and said something inaudible before turning back to the privacy of the kitchen.

'Emma,' said Willow as they watched her go, 'did you know that Richard was adopted as a baby?'

'Yes, of course. Everyone knows. It's no secret. Didn't you?'

Willow shook her head. She felt as though mental rats were gnawing at her remaining trust in Richard.

'P'raps,' said Emma, scooping back her hair with both hands, 'he never said anything about it just because it's never been a secret. He prob'ly thought you knew – or that it was too unimportant to talk about.'

'You could be right.' Willow led the way back to the drawing room and went to open one of the windows, as though to let out of the room all memory of Chief Inspector Moreby's certainty of Richard's guilt.

'I know I am. Come on, what do you want me to do? I must do something.'

'Would you talk to Jeanine Allfarthing for me?'

'The daughter? Cressida, I . . . D'you think it's fair to worry her now?'

'No. But nothing about this investigation can be fair. You'll get much more out of her than I could. You belong to her generation, whereas I'm the age her mother was. I've seen her father and he was very frank. He doesn't think Richard did it, but he won't have the same perspective on his wife as Jeanine will. You could learn an awful lot.'

'How would I go about it?' Emma looked daunted but at the same time determined to do her bit.

'I'll ring him and ask if he minds. There won't be anything covert about it. You can listen in.'

Willow telephoned Thomas Allfarthing, apologized for troubling him again, and asked whether 'a young associate' of hers could interview his daughter. He temporized but after some light pressure went to ask her. Four minutes later a meeting had been arranged at a café in Covent Garden.

'What do I ask her?' said Emma when Willow had said goodbye to Allfarthing.

'Anything that seems useful. We need to find out all we can about Mrs Allfarthing. There are only two possibilities for getting Richard out: finding someone else who could have killed her or proving that she did it herself. Roylandson thinks that's unlikely, but I still believe it's just possible,' said Willow, thinking that the hair torn from Sarah's scalp could have been ripped out by a clumsy comb rather than a murderer's hand. 'Jeanine will probably know more about her mother than almost anyone else.'

'I'll try. Thank you for letting me help.'

'Now, have you got any ideas at all about who else it could have been?' Willow hoped that she did not sound patronizing. In all her years in the civil service she had never had an assistant as young as Emma – or as socially confident – and found it hard to know how to manage her.

'The only likely ones seem to be the men who were in love with her and they were all at the dance,' said Emma, shaking her head.

They talked until Mrs Rusham called them to lunch, by which time they had reached no conclusions. Willow was still left with suicide, which seemed unlikely despite what she had said to Emma; the possibility that Robert Biggleigh-Clart had somehow altered the apparently inescapable constraints of time; or the fantastic possibility that there was a previously unknown strain of haemophilia that affected women. When she laughed at herself, Emma asked what had amused her.

Willow explained as they walked together to the dining room.

'Couldn't there be?'

'No. Haemophilia is the result in a male child of a mutation in the mother, but women themselves never suffer from it.'

'There might be something else. Have you asked a doctor?'

Willow stopped and looked down at Emma's stubborn face. 'No, I haven't,' she said slowly. 'I suppose that arrogantly I assumed that I knew everything about it, which of course I don't.'

'Well, do you know any doctors?'

'Yes. There's one at Dowting's Hospital who's a friend of Caroline Titchmell. I've kept in touch with him. But, Emma, if there were any female equivalent of haemophilia, the police would have thought of it.'

'Why? You know quite well that they're not infallible. And they must have wanted a convincing suspect. Why should they have tried to find out about something that could have proved Richard innocent? It would have to be a rare thing, wouldn't it? Otherwise, you would have known about it.'

The mixture of common sense and blind faith in Willow's abilities forced her to take up Emma's suggestion.

'All right, you go on in and start lunch. I'll join you in a second.'

Willow put through a call to Dowting's Hospital on the South Bank and asked for Dr Andrew Salcott. She had met him at the funeral of a murder victim several months earlier, suspected him for a time and then used his friendship for the dead man in her search for his killer. She would probably have lost touch with the doctor if she had not come round after a car crash in which her legs had been broken and found herself in his hospital. As a patient, she had discovered that behind his rollicking, insensitive façade was a man of warmth and experience, and some charm.

'I'm sorry, Dr Salcott won't be here again until Monday.'

'I see. Thank you,' said Willow and then punched in his home telephone number. She had forgotten that it was already the weekend. There was no answer and reluctantly she followed Emma to the sunny dining room, promising to ring him up again.

They settled down to a particularly lavish lunch of artichoke bottoms stuffed with lobster, covered with smoked salmon and glazed with golden aspic, followed by champagne sorbet served in spun-sugar baskets. Emma ate as hungrily as though she had not seen food for several days, but Willow picked. She knew that the unnecessary elaboration of the food was a symptom of Mrs Rusham's distress and could not forget it herself.

Before they had finished, Tom Worth appeared and was shown into the dining room by a tight-lipped Mrs Rusham. Emma had never met him before and looked him up and down with such transparent curiosity that both he and Willow laughed. Their amusement did much to break her constraint and she cheerfully told Tom of Mrs Rusham's wish to send good food into Richard's prison cell.

'Good idea,' he said, grinning. 'Remand prisoners are allowed their own food – and drink. I can't quite remember the quantity of alcohol that's permitted, but I can easily find out.'

'Thank you, sir,' said Mrs Rusham, smiling at him with real approval for once. She suggested to Willow that she should bring another plate so that the chief inspector could join the others for cheese.

'What a good idea,' said Willow at once. 'Tom?'

'Thank you very much,' he said, pulling out a chair opposite Willow's. He nodded kindly to Mrs Rusham when she brought him a plate and a glass and unhurriedly helped himself to claret, a good wedge of Saint Agur cheese and a small pile of digestive biscuits.

Emma watched him while she quickly finished her own plate of cheese. Then she stood up, saying that she had to go home to Kensington before meeting Jeanine Allfarthing and promising to return later to report on her discoveries.

'Don't worry about coming here,' said Willow quickly. 'Just telephone and if I'm not in leave a message. We can talk later.'

Emma looked from Willow to Tom and then smiled self-consciously before going into the kitchen to thank Mrs Rusham for lunch.

'I think,' said Tom when she had gone, 'that she expects me to behave like a caveman and whisk you off for a spot of Stone Age nooky. Pity your housekeeper works on Saturday afternoons.'

Willow frowned at him. Then, remembering how much she had missed him and the hot, slow days and nights they had spent together in Tuscany, she relaxed and held out a hand in wordless apology. Tom gripped it for a moment and then let it go.

'We'll be all right,' he said lightly.

Chapter 10

*F*or the first time since they had met, Willow could not concentrate on making love with Tom. When it became clear that her recalcitrant body was not going to obey her increasingly frenzied instructions to it, she disengaged from his embrace and pushed herself up against the bedhead.

'I'm sorry,' she said, meaning it.

'It happens, Will.' Tom took a long look at her face. 'Don't be so upset. It's not important. It may just be that we've always been in your bed before and you feel strange in my flat – or that you're too preoccupied with the case.'

Willow shook her head and brushed the hair out of her eyes. 'Short hair is far more trouble than long,' she said irritably.

Tom held both her hands. 'It suits you. What's the trouble? Really?'

Knowing that she owed him the truth, she tried to work out what it might be.

'I suppose,' she said at last, 'that I feel as though I'm betraying both you and Richard.'

Tom's broad, attractive face contracted as though in a spasm of pain. Willow remembered her vision of them growing into snappishness and mutual dislike and closed her eyes. In that moment she felt as though she hated herself and Tom and Richard, and most of all Sarah All-farthing's murderer, whoever he was.

'I'm sorry,' she said again.

Tom stroked her white face. 'No need. The difficulty is probably as much mine as yours. I wanted to . . . distract you, and that in itself may have made it impossible. Shall we get up and go for a walk?'

'Would you mind?' Willow opened her eyes and he was both touched and saddened to see the eagerness in them. He shook his head and got unhurriedly out of bed.

'You're going to be awfully hot in that sweater,' he said as she picked up the cashmere tunic. 'Now the sun's out it'll be boiling out there. Would you like to borrow a shirt?'

Willow pulled one of the curtains aside and tried to assess the likely heat.

'I'd love to,' she said, turning back into the room. Tom looked through a pile of shirts and offered her a choice between a plain yellow short-sleeved polo shirt and a long-sleeved office shirt made of thin white cotton woven with narrow blue stripes. She chose the striped one and wore it tucked into her old black trousers, with the sleeves rolled up to her elbows and the neck wide open.

Tom stood looking at her with such obvious approval in his face that she could not help laughing.

'I know,' she said, 'you like this better than all those expensive suits and dresses. But I enjoy wearing them.'

'That's what matters,' he said easily. 'Come on. I'll drive you to Kew and we'll walk along the towpath. There's hardly ever anyone there.'

When he had parked the car and they had walked down the steps at Kew Bridge, he asked her whether she thought she would enjoy the next six months without the Clapham part of her life.

'Definitely.' Willow both felt and sounded tougher now that they had left the dangerous subjects of sex and love behind. The path narrowed and they had to walk in single file. 'Not least being able to spend all my time in Chesham Place. I've discovered that I had come to loathe, really loathe, the Clapham flat, which is presumably why I haven't got round to having the roof mended or the rooms redecorated.'

'Could you really be happy in just one place after all these years?' asked Tom from behind her. 'The mixture seemed to suit you so well, even if you didn't actually like Clapham while you were there.'

Remembering Richard's increasingly petulant criticisms of her fantastic deception and divided life, Willow felt grateful for Tom's calm acceptance.

'I think it may have served its purpose,' she said slowly, 'although I do know what you mean.' She laughed. 'I still have plenty of other fantasies I could put into practice if I find that full-time Cressidery is too much.'

'Such as?' There was amusement in Tom's deep voice and pleasure too. Willow heard it and turned back for a moment to put a hand on his.

'Oh, a little dark cottage somewhere, filled with primitively beautiful old oak furniture and seventeenth-century textiles. An old four-poster bed and big fires and lots of rain outside, and . . .'

'And coming in through the old, old roof,' he said caustically, but still laughing.

'Exactly. Damp and dark and quite different from Chesham Place. But warm too. No, perhaps not damp. Or perhaps I could rescue it from the damp and decay; and make a garden.'

More than willing to encourage her to distract herself from her doomed investigation, Tom asked what she would grow. The path widened again and they strolled on side by side.

'A muddle of apple trees and roses and daffodils in the grass in spring. Nothing obviously designed. Plenty of mossy stone and paths of old brick in a herringbone pattern. Red brick that's gone pale with age. Vegetables perhaps.'

'It all sounds quite sensible – and well within your grasp.' Tom was amused by both the modesty and the domesticity of her new dreams. 'Why not look for a place?'

'Perhaps I will when this is over.'

Willow looked sideways at Tom, surprising an unguarded expression on his face.

'I'm sorry,' she said, trying to be as gentle as he had been, 'but I can't forget R– the case.'

'It's not that,' he said, thinking how badly he wanted to suggest that they should buy the cottage together. 'I just don't like to think of what you may have to face, when . . . if things go wrong.'

Willow's face grew bleak as they stared at each other.

'Even if I fail to stop the trial and even if his counsel fails and he is convicted,' she said at last, 'there's always hope. Thank God for Sydney Silverman.'

Tom's mind was so occupied with Richard Crescent that for a moment he looked puzzled.

'Who campaigned in the House of Commons for an end to hanging, you ignoramus,' said Willow.

Tom grinned. 'Come on, Will,' he said, 'let's speed up. You need to walk off all that anxiety.'

Recognizing her ambivalent reaction to Tom's orders, Willow strode out beside him. They walked for about two miles past the Botanic Gardens and the Old Deer Park before her feet began to hurt and she suggested returning. Tom pointed to an old bench, half-hidden in the frothing white and green bank.

'How about a little sit?'

'Good idea,' said Willow. She looked at the long grasses, already curving under the weight of their ripening seeds, at the cow parsley and the angelica, the dandelions and the nettles and wondered whether to change the decoration of her dining room.

'That silvery pink is rather stuffy in hot weather,' she said vaguely.

Tom looked at her with eyes that were both amused and quizzical. 'What are you thinking about, Will?'

'What? Oh, just my dining room. This green and white is so . . . restful: I was thinking about redoing the dining room.'

Tom thought of several questions he wanted to ask Willow about the way she protected herself from the things she could not bear to think about, but he did not want to make her angry – or to hurt her.

'Why was it, do you think, that the civil service suited you so well?' he asked at last.

Willow turned at once with a wide smile. There had been absolutely no comment in his question, let alone criticism.

'I've been thinking about that,' she said honestly. 'Originally I assumed that I needed to have a job I wanted to escape from in order to have the necessary impetus to write escapist fiction. Then I wondered whether it was all part of my horror of completely committing myself to any one thing.'

'And now?' he said, suppressing a smile.

'Now?' she said, drawing out the vowel. 'Now I think it may have more to do with not wanting to stop playing.' She looked straight ahead through the green-and-white lace that concealed the river.

'I'm not sure that I understand.'

Willow frowned, not in anger but in an effort to find accurate words to use to explain something that she herself had not fully understood. The uncertainty was a new experience for her and she was both interested and disturbed by it.

'While Cressida Woodruffe was a game,' she said slowly, 'it did not matter terribly what the books were like or what anyone thought of them.'

She stopped talking and concentrated on the glittering patches of water that were revealed by tiny gaps in the tangle of wild flowers.

'DOAP was still the real world. It was hard work, dull, frustrating and completely safe. If I get rid of that safety net then what was entirely frivolous becomes reality and starts to matter. I'm rather afraid that I simply won't be able to write escapist tosh any longer.' She turned to face him again. 'D'you see now?'

'Would it matter so much?'

'Of course,' she said. Catching sight of the expression in his brown eyes, she added a warning: 'Don't tell me I ought to write something serious.'

Tom got up and held out a hand. Willow took it after a moment's hesitation and allowed him to pull her up from the bench. They set off in silence back along the towpath.

'Why not?' Tom asked about ten minutes later when they were once again walking in single file.

'Because,' said Willow, who was ahead of him, 'people need escapist tosh; I'm good at providing it; there's nothing wrong with it; and I loathe it when people make me feel defensive about it.'

'Okay,' he said in a friendly voice. Willow was left feeling that she had been unreasonable, but she was too tired – and too reluctant – to try to explain herself any further.

When they reached the car, Tom wanted to take her out for tea, but Willow shook her head.

'I'd be horrible company,' she said, 'and I want to get back.'

'May I come with you? Will, I'd never ask if things were normal, but they're not. I'd like to be about just in case you need anything. I'll read the papers and sit quietly. Please?'

Torn between wanting to be alone with her anxieties and her feeling that she had never matched his generosity or tolerance, Willow at last agreed.

True to his promise, Tom settled himself on one of her sofas with the day's newspapers while she retreated to her writing room and telephoned Andrew Salcott once again. That time he answered.

'Hello, Andrew. It's Cressida Woodruffe here.'

'Well, hello! How are you? Still scribbling away?'

'That's right.'

'Well and truly recovered now, I hope. How are your legs?'

'Not bad at all. I'm fine, really, despite trying to force myself on with the new book, which is giving me a few research problems.'

'Do I detect a sly request for professional advice here?'

Making herself smile, Willow said: 'Actually, yes. You're obviously a brilliant diagnostician. What I'm after is some information on blood clotting, and –'

'Can't help, I'm afraid. I'm no haematologist.' He laughed. 'I used to think that phagocytes were places where gender-benders met.'

'It's not particularly specialized information,' said Willow repressively. Much as she enjoyed word games, she had more urgent things to think about. Besides, she was not sure what phagocytes were and did not want to display any greater ignorance than was necessary. 'I was just wondering whether there's anything like haemophilia that affects women.'

There was a short pause and then the sound of a cigarette lighter and a deep inhalation.

'Well, yes; as far as I can remember there are several known causes of hypoprothrombinemia. Von Willebrand's disease affects both sexes, for example. Not enough work has been done on blood coagulation, though; they keep discovering more and more odd conditions that cause pro-thrombin deficiency. And there's always the effect of the anticoagulants.'

'What?' It all sounded hopeful to Willow, especially the bit about more and more odd conditions, and she cursed herself for having wasted so much time before talking to him.

Her ignorance seemed inexcusable. After all, she had considered haemophilia during her meeting with Biggleigh-Clart and yet had dismissed it. If she had had Emma's humility she might have asked the necessary questions days ago. Willow disliked admitting her own inadequacies and in a sudden access of self-consciousness remembered how doubtful the two bankers had been about her sleuthing ability.

'What are the anticoagulants?' she asked.

'Warfarin, heparin, phenindione – all given to patients at risk of thromboses.'

'Warfarin? Isn't that rat poison?' Willow could not ignore a memory of Richard's disgusted face one evening when he told her that mice had been found in the building next to his flat and threatened to invade it.

'It is used as a rodenticide, but in therapeutic doses it prevents clots in humans. In bigger doses, it deals with human clots, too. Hah! Hah!'

Willow took a moment to laugh dutifully and then asked her next question.

'Would it prevent clotting altogether or simply delay it, and if so, for how long?'

'It's impossible to say without more data.' Salcott's voice still held overtones of his rollicking laugh, but he was sobering as he talked. 'They all have different timings. If I remember right, warfarin, for example, when taken by mouth rather than intravenously or intramuscularly, is most effective thirty-six hours after it has been taken and passes off after about forty-eight hours.'

'Oh. But it would be true to say that there are conditions, naturally occurring or medically induced, that would slow down the normal clotting of blood in women?'

'Definitely.'

'And would they show up in a postmortem?'

'Crime novels now, eh? That's a new departure.'

Willow said nothing and Salcott, his voice still sounding his amusement, proceeded to answer.

'Warfarin and the rest would be very easy to detect. I take it that you want something undetectable by ordinary work?'

'Yes.'

'Why?'

'Well, say you have a body with its throat cut and the blood still dripping: I need some explanation for the blood still being liquid about half an hour after the killing. Is there anything?'

Salcott laughed. 'An inordinate number of things. What is the position of your body?'

'Half suspended on a chair with its head down and the blood dripping out.'

'Then it would go on dripping for hours.'

'Really? But I thought blood clotted almost as soon as it met air,' said Willow with a vivid memory of the haemophiliac victim in one of Dorothy Sayers's novels.

''Fraid not. All sorts of things could affect it.'

'Tell me a few that I might be able to use,' said Willow, wondering why everyone concerned had apparently accepted that the time of death was limited by the freshness of the blood.

'Apart from the ones I've already given you, I'd suggest a Vitamin K deficiency that would affect the formation of prothrombin and stop the platelets adhering normally. There are plenty of other things, too, but I haven't even thought about any of this since I was a student. You'd do better looking it up in a decent medical encyclopedia or talking to a competent pathologist.'

'Except that I probably wouldn't understand an encyclopedia,' said Willow with deliberate and not wholly artificial pathos. 'You've been very helpful. Thank you, Andrew.'

'Glad to hear it. You sound more cheerful. Dinner one of these days?'

'Lovely. May I ring you?'

'Be sure you do. Last time you said that, the next I saw of you was with both your legs in plaster.'

'That was hardly my fault.'

'No. I'm glad you're keeping in touch. See you soon. And take care.'

Willow thanked him and went into the drawing room.

Tom looked up, let the *Independent* drop to the floor and got up.

'You look wonderful,' he said. 'What's happened?'

'Something encouraging. I came to ask whether you'd like tea. Mrs Rusham will have left us something. I know it's rather late, but what about it?'

'I'd like it a lot.'

They went together to the kitchen and found the usual selection of savoury sandwiches, keeping fresh under a clean, damp teatowel, and a plate of small cakes. Tom filled the kettle while Willow reached into one of the immaculate cupboards for a teapot. She took the first one her fingers met, which proved to be of Herend porcelain, dumped it on the worktop beside the kettle and removed the teatowel from the sandwiches.

'Hm, crab and watercress. Good,' she said, putting two tiny brown-bread triangles together and taking a bite of both.

'You look hungry,' said Tom with a wide smile.

'I've just realized that I am,' she said. 'I've been finding eating difficult, but things are looking up.'

'Don't –' Tom began and then stopped. The kettle switched itself off and he warmed the pot, added three spoons of Earl Grey tea and then turned back to face Willow, who was still eating. There was an expression of triumph and conscious greediness in her face.

'Don't what?' she said through her mouthful of bread and crabmeat.

'Don't build too much on whatever it is.' Watching the increasingly stubborn look in her pale-green eyes, he hastily added: 'I'm not asking you to tell me what it is, merely to guard against disappointment.'

He carried the teapot to the table and put it on a cork mat. Willow swallowed and collected two matching cups and saucers and sat down at the table.

'If I tell you,' she said, 'would you feel obliged to pass it on to Moreby?'

'Not necessarily. If you were about to make us all look like fools or worse, I might have to warn her, but not if you've just had a wizard wheeze.'

Willow managed to laugh.

'Nothing like that. It's just that the main reason for them to suspect Richard was the condition of the victim's blood. It was still completely liquid when they were found; there was no jellifying, no clotting, no separation into the clot and the serum. Everyone seems to have taken that to mean that the blood was shed only a few moments before the computer man found Richard with the body.'

'Not entirely,' said Tom cautiously. 'There's also the short-circuiting of the keyboard. That alerted him and it must have happened as soon as the blood got into the machine.'

Willow poured out the tea and added milk from a carton out of the immense fridge while she thought. After a while her face cleared.

'Listen, Tom; there's a perfectly good explanation. The body was hanging head downwards when Richard tried to lift it, which is partly why it would still have been dripping blood. We know that he stumbled and generally made a terrific mess. He probably kicked the keyboard nearer the dripping blood, which would mean that the time when the computers went down was immaterial after all.'

'That's possible, but –' Before Tom could finish, Willow had rushed on.

'Or perhaps it was Richard who tipped over the flowers so that it was their water that caused the trouble and not the blood at all. He did say that the flowers were all over the floor when he first saw the body, but he could have been muddled.'

Tom looked sceptical.

'Even if either of those were true, I don't see that they really help. He is the only person in the place who could have killed her.'

'Nonsense,' said Willow more robustly than she would

have believed possible before her talk to Salcott. 'If she died even half an hour earlier, then she could not have been killed by Richard.'

'Then who did kill her? There was no one else there.'

'You're not thinking, Tom, or else Moreby hasn't briefed you properly. There was the chief executive, for one. He was alone in his office from the time that his secretary left; he has his own bathroom, in which he could have washed off any bloodstains before he changed; and he was late for the dance.'

'What would he have done with his bloody clothes?' asked Tom, watching her in pity.

'Anything. Locked them in his private safe that evening and smuggled them out in a briefcase later. Opened up his antique astral globe and dumped them there. Your colleagues,' she added drily, 'clearly never thought of searching the place.'

'With Crescent covered in blood and his fingerprints all over the murder weapon, it's hardly surprising.'

Very coldly indeed, Willow said: 'They ought to have listened to his story and checked it.'

Tom reached out for one of her hands. Willow put them both in her lap.

'Come on, Will. Be reasonable. It's a ludicrous story. You must see that.'

'But that's exactly why they should have checked it,' she said, feeling deeply critical of her own doubts again. 'Surely no one of Richard's wit and brains would invent a story quite as stupidly unconvincing as his.'

'Perhaps not, but why on earth would the chief executive have wanted to kill Mrs Allfarthing? And even if he had, why do it at the bank?'

'God knows. The secretaries undoubtedly believe that he was in love with Sarah, as do most of the other employees, although he denies it. He cleverly told me that he had tried to ring Sarah up about eight, when he discovered that his wife was not going to the dance after all, and he told me that he thought Sarah must have gone because she didn't answer. As it turns out, she could really have been dead by then.'

'It sounds pretty unlikely,' said Tom. 'You must see that.'

'Oh, I do, but at least there's a possibility now that we could shake Moreby's case. Admit that.'

'All right, I'll admit it. But I don't think you'd get very far in court.'

'Nor would she, trying to pin down the time of death like that. From what my medical source has told me, any decent pathologist could throw doubt on it.'

'All right. Then what about the smell?' asked Tom.

As though disregarding his own question, Tom picked up a sandwich and began to eat. Willow, who remembered her own vivid imaginings when she studied the police photographs, knew just what he meant.

'Richard was very preoccupied when he got back from New York,' she said slowly, 'and he dashed into the office in an enormous hurry. He might easily not have noticed the smell of blood. There's a very efficient air-circulation system. There are people in that department who smoke and yet I've never been conscious of the smell of their cigarettes.'

She, too, chose another sandwich and refilled her tea-cup.

Tom watched her and recognized in her uncharacteristic excitement the relief of serious anxiety. Although he longed to protect her from the discovery of Richard's guilt, which he knew would almost break her, there was nothing he could do. He changed the subject abruptly by asking her what she thought of the book reviews in the day's newspapers.

Willow allowed herself to be diverted and their day together began to improve as they talked. When Tom hugged her just as he was about to leave, Willow let herself relax against him and even began to feel the sensations her body had denied them both earlier. Feeling it himself, he let his hands move to her breasts. The crispness of the cotton could not disguise their sudden response. Willow gasped.

He pulled back a little way so that he could gesture to the closed door of her bedroom. There was an amusingly enquiring smile in his eyes. After a moment Willow nodded and led the way.

Later the next day, when he had gone, happy and in love, Willow settled down to telephone Emma Gnatche.

'I'd have rung you myself but I didn't want to disturb you.' Emma's voice was breathless with terror or excitement.

'I know. But I'm longing to hear how it all went.'

'Are you alone?' As Emma asked her question, Willow realized that the breathlessness might have been caused by embarrassment and felt herself blushing slightly.

'Yes. Come on, what did you discover?'

'Well! Quite a lot, actually. At first Jeanine was weepy and full of her mother's praises, but after a bit we got talking and I . . . I . . .'

'What's the matter, Emma?'

'Well, I said some pretty awful things about my own mother, and I wish I hadn't.'

'Don't worry, Em, she'll never know and saying them probably helped Jeanine.'

'It certainly got her talking.' The dry, half-amused tone reminded Willow that although Emma was young and in many ways astonishingly naive, she had never been stupid.

'And?'

'Disentangling the useful facts from the guilt, resentment and self-justification, I think the most important thing she told me was that her mother used people and manipulated them into doing things for her.'

'A lot of successful people do that, either with cajolery or the threat of anger or withdrawal of patronage.' Willow hoped that she was not sounding contemptuous or superior.

'This sounded a bit different. Jeanine said that her mother flirted until the men she needed succumbed to her charms and then went cold on them and forced them to compete for her favour. She also said that her mother was terribly selfish and made Mr Allfarthing live a miserable life without her while she swanned about completing her machinations.'

Willow thought of all she had read and written about daughters and their fathers. She herself had never had the opportunity of intervening between her parents and was rather glad of it, but she had met and read of several couples who were being driven apart by their daughters. In almost every case the gravamen of the daughter's charge was that her mother was making her father unhappy. The possibility that the reverse might be true never seemed to occur to those crusading girls; nor did the thought that their interventions might make matters worse.

'Nothing Mr Allfarthing said or did suggested that his wife made him unhappy while she lived,' said Willow, feeling both sorry for Sarah and relieved that she herself had no daughters. 'By the way, did Jeanine say anything about her mother's health?'

'Yes,' said Emma. 'I asked whether there had been any problems.'

'Well done!'

'Thanks. It seemed quite an obvious question to ask.' Emma sounded surprised.

Willow smiled in appreciation and pushed herself more comfortably back into her long sofa.

'And she told me that her mother had had no more than the usual colds and flu and a few gynaecological problems.'

Willow was silent, trying to make use of that information.

'I did ask,' said Emma, sounding embarrassed again, 'whether she thought that any of those might have been, well . . . the result of any of her flirtations.'

Willow could not help smiling at Emma's mixture of practicality and tentativeness.

'Did she give you any kind of answer?'

'Oh, yes. She was quite open about it and said that her mother was too cold to let any of her adorers sleep with her.'

'She does sound a nice, affectionate girl.'

'Don't be like that, Cressida. She's awfully unhappy. And it does sound as though her mother was pretty beastly to her.'

'In what way?' Willow was surprised to find herself identifying with Sarah Allfarthing and tried to moderate her partisanship.

'Oh, making all kinds of rules that she herself would never have dreamed of keeping; sneering at Jeanine's spots; trying to make her dress as though she were forty, too; forcing her to work for one of the adorers. Um . . .'

There was a sound of paper rustling. Willow waited.

'A man called James Certes. He's the partner at Blenkort & Wilson who Jeanine does most of her work for. Apparently he'd do anything for Mrs Allfarthing: recommend clients, help her out of scrapes, anything.'

'Did Jeanine say what he was like?'

'Only that he's incredibly demanding and makes her do all sorts of unoffice chores for him. And he insists that she and the other temps and clerks hang about in case something comes up even when there's no urgent work. She had to wait for him on the night it happened so that he could dictate a whole lot of notes about his meeting at the bank when he came back. Whenever she protested he told her it was good for her to discover what real life is like. She thinks her mother told him to force her to work hard and she can't wait to go.'

'Is she leaving?'

'Not before the agreed time. She said she'll stick it out until the end of the summer and then never go near a firm of lawyers again.'

Willow sat up straighter. 'What's she going to do? Her father told me she was planning to be a solicitor.'

'Well, actually, she wants to be a chef and so I've promised to introduce her to Sarah Tothill, who can give her some good advice. But you must promise not to tell her father anything about it. He's too loyal to his wife to take the news properly quite yet.'

'Emma, you've done really well. Thank you.'

'There's lots more and I've been trying to type it up, but my machine's gone on the blink. I did wonder.'

She left Willow to interpret the elliptical sentence.

'Whether you could use my word processor? Certainly. Come tomorrow, if you like. I've got to go out early to sit in at a bank meeting, but Mrs Rusham will let you in. Use the telephone, the photocopier, whatever you want. She'll feed you.'

'Gosh, super! Thanks, Cressida.'

Chapter 11

*B*EFORE she left for the bank at seven thirty on Monday morning, Willow typed and faxed a letter to Martin Roylandson asking him to get his pathologist to check whether the condition of Sarah Allfarthing's blood provided any real evidence of the time of her death and whether she suffered from a lack of Vitamin K or any other deficiency that would affect the clotting time. Willow then scribbled a note for Emma and left the flat.

Reaching the bank with ten minutes to spare before the meeting, Willow took the time to stand just inside the doors of the Corporate Finance Department, trying to imagine Richard rushing in and turning to his right without noticing that there was anything wrong. It was perfectly true that no one at the door would be able to see past the big baffle behind the secretaries' desks. But could anyone have failed to smell all that blood? Could anyone have avoided noticing the splashes that must have extended beyond the line of the screen?

Willow wished that she had brought the photographs with her. She was fairly sure that there had been blood at least two foot away from Sarah's desk.

'The carpet's dark grey,' she told herself angrily. 'It might have been impossible to see blood against it. And he was in a hurry.'

'You all right, Miss King?'

Willow started and looked to her right. Jeremy Stedington stood there, his arms full of files and papers. She had neither heard nor seen him until he appeared round the screen.

'Fine,' she said sternly. 'Am I late?'

'No, but you do look faint and –'

'I'll be perfectly all right. Is it time to go down? I'll dump my briefcase. Just a moment.' Willow walked round to Sarah's carrel and laid down her black case, leaning heavily on the edge of the desk as she waited for her head to clear.

She swallowed down the hot saliva that had filled her mouth, took a comb out of her handbag to tidy her hair, and turned her back on the place where Sarah had died.

'You still look pretty white.'

'Don't worry about me, Jeremy. Just occasionally I feel horribly sick when I think of what that poor woman went through. Sometimes I even feel as though it might have happened to me.' She laughed to drive out the fantasy, but she neither was nor sounded amused.

'Perhaps I shouldn't have given you her desk,' he said, 'but, as I told you, I knew it would help the department's jitters if they saw someone coming and going there normally. I watched Maggie walk quite close to the chair on Friday without turning a hair. The strategy is working, but it's rough on you.'

'Good. Poor things,' she said absently. 'Jeremy, why are the desks arranged in that bizarre fashion? Wouldn't it make more sense to have a passage down the middle and let at least half the staff look out at the daylight?'

'We tried that,' he said, holding open one of the double doors for her. 'But it didn't work well. The partitions between the desks were lower, too, and the boys complained that they could never concentrate on their documents. This way, they get more of an illusion that they're on their own while not sacrificing the proximity necessary to keep everyone abreast of what they need to know. And they can always turn round and see the daylight.'

'Those on the right, anyway. How is that fixed? Who are the ones who get daylight behind them?

Jeremy Stedington shrugged, but he looked slightly self-conscious, too. 'A variety of reasons. Pecking order, mostly.'

'So Richard was higher in that than Sarah?'

The lift doors swished open and Willow preceded her escort into the lift.

'Good Lord, yes!'

'That sounds very emphatic,' she said, gritting her teeth as she remembered Chief Inspector Moreby's contempt for Richard. 'Why?'

'Well, he was a lot more experienced; done some bloody good deals, Richard; and he was –'

'One of the boys?' Despite her partisanship, Willow could not help sounding a little sarcastic. Stedington's face flushed.

'I was going to say "one of us", which is not the same but which you might have misunderstood even so. Here we are. Come on; mustn't be late.'

Willow hurried after him and at the doors of the meeting room she grasped his left sleeve.

'Jeremy, stop. This is really important. What did you mean? Why wasn't Sarah Allfarthing one of you?'

'Cressida,' he said, throwing discretion to the winds. 'This is my job. I must concentrate on the meeting. We can talk afterwards if you like. But, please, don't distract me now.'

'Sorry.'

They walked in to the room, where a plump, smiling woman in her fifties was sitting talking happily to a slight man in a dark suit.

'Mrs Zelland,' said Stedington in the voice of a child

presented with a new bicycle at Christmas, 'how good to see you.'

'Jeremy. I do hope you're feeling better.'

'Very much, thank you. May I introduce you to Miss King? She's not one of us,' he said and stopped for a second. 'But she's observing the way we do things here with a view to advising us on our training needs. Miss King, this is Hughina Zelland.'

Willow was already extending her hand towards the client when Jeremy pronounced her name and the shock of it made her pull it back.

'I know; isn't it ridiculous?' said Mrs Zelland, holding out her hand.

Willow managed a short laugh and shook the hand, which felt soft but quite dry. 'Not at all,' she said, recovering her composure, 'merely surprising.'

'It was my father. He wanted a son and by the time I was born – I was the sixth, you see – he knew he'd have to make do with me.'

'Yes, I see. And what is it that your company does, makes?'

Mrs Zelland smiled and Jeremy Stedington hastened to explain.

'Mrs Zelland owns Powers and Jenkinsons.'

'Good Lord,' said Willow involuntarily. She knew perfectly well that Powers, which had once been a small but effective textile concern in the north of England, had expanded under its present management until it not only supplied many of the major chains with clothes, and owned its own shops and factories under a variety of names and in several countries, but also extended into other industries.

'You've kept yourself well out of the public eye, Mrs Zelland,' said Willow, thinking of the lunches, the interviews and all the other efforts designed to publicize the achievements of women in business.

'And it's to stay that way,' she said, still smiling comfortably, but with a flash of determination in her eyes.

'Naturally,' said Willow coolly. To emphasize her independence, she turned to the young man who had been sitting quietly at the conference table and recognized him.

'Oh, yes, and this is James Certes,' Stedington said as the doors opened and a group of people were ushered in by one of the uniformed receptionists.

'We've met,' said Willow, examining him far more closely than she had at their first encounter.

'So we have,' the lawyer agreed, as he stood up to shake hands.

Willow thought that he was a surprising figure. From the descriptions of him as one of Sarah's admirers, Willow would have expected him to be at least the same age as the dead woman, but he looked as though he were in his middle thirties at the most. He was dressed in an oddly unconventional suit: baggy and too long in the leg. It was the kind of suit that men in television or possibly publishing and journalism might have worn and as different as possible from the pinstriped convention. Willow thought that he looked just the kind of man likely to appeal to a tetchy adolescent like Jeanine and wondered whether Sarah might really have asked him to give her daughter a hard time.

Watching him as he said something suitably polite to her, Willow thought of one reason why he might have chosen to dress so oddly. He was not only slight but short as well; his smooth hair was angelically fair and his face beautifully modelled. The catchphrase 'small but perfectly formed' might have been invented for him, and Willow could well imagine the diffidence he might feel among the huge, powerfully built men she had met in the Corporate Finance Department. At first sight Certes's trendy clothes were more noticeable than his shortness and made him look different rather than insignificant.

Having shaken his hand, Willow turned back to Jeremy Stedington, who introduced her to the new arrivals: two bankers from a much bigger and better-known merchant bank, their client, who owned some dreary, cheap clothes retailers, and his lawyer.

'There don't seem to be many of you today,' said one of the bankers, a young man called Andrew Crants, with a disparaging smile. He was accustomed to big deals and disliked the sensation that his less important rivals had the better client.

'We're two short at the moment,' answered Stedington, sounding harsh.

Mr Crants winced and flushed slightly as he remembered what had happened to Sarah Allfarthing.

'There'll be plenty of backup when we need it,' said Jeremy dismissively. 'Let's not waste time. Our client is not prepared to offer work to all the staff or to take over certain outstanding liabilities. I will summarize . . .'

Willow's mind slipped. She had no interest in whether Mrs Zelland was going to extend her empire or at what price. What did interest her was the way the meeting was conducted and how tempers might be raised. As she sat half listening and watching avidly, she tried to picture that other meeting when Richard's latent violence had been aroused.

Once she caught James Certes looking at her with interest and she quickly made a meaningless note on the lined pad she held in her lap. A little later she caught Jeremy's eye and was surprised when he winked. After that she studiously avoided eye contact with anyone.

Halfway through the morning the temperature of the meeting had begun to rise and Mrs Zelland to show considerable restlessness. People began to make excuses to leave the room for a moment, as though they needed a chance to regain their self-control, and Willow began to listen more closely.

'It's perfectly clear what she's trying to do,' said the other side's client in an unpleasantly nasal London accent. 'She wants the sites. She's no interest in the workrooms or the staff or the good will we've built up in south London over a hundred and fifty years. She's going to asset strip, and –'

'You have no assets,' said Mrs Zelland coldly. All traces of motherliness had gone and she looked every inch a top profitmaker. 'Your shops are dismal and need gutting and complete refitting. Your workroom machinery is out of date. Your staff is ill-trained and has the lowest morale in the business.'

She sat back. The man opposite her reddened and seemed to swell, as though someone were pumping him up with compressed air. Willow was interested to see young James Certes lay a hand on his client's wrist and gently squeeze it.

'If you think it's all so frightful, why the hell have you been buying up the shares and putting me through all this?' demanded her opponent.

Mrs Zelland smiled. 'Because I hate to see anything so badly managed,' she said. 'And south London needs something better than you've given them. They're not charladies any more, you know.'

Four people started to talk in tones of outrage.

'If I might interrupt.' James Certes spoke quietly but there was something about his confidence that stopped the others.

Willow listened as he calmed them all down and proceeded to suggest a solution to the various difficulties. Jeremy Stedington followed his lead and the meeting slowly sank towards a consensus. There were still a few legal niceties to be discussed when Mrs Zelland announced that she had spent enough time on a small matter and needed her lunch.

'What a good idea, Hughina,' said James Certes with a charming smile. 'Why don't you let Jeremy take you away? I'll fiddle through all the tedious details with Andrew, Tom and Jonathan.'

'Excellent.' Mrs Zelland turned to Willow, who was sitting writing more meaningless notes. 'Miss King? I'm sure you don't need to watch the lawyers pick nits all afternoon. Why not come and witness some client management?'

Laughing, Willow looked towards Jeremy Stedington, who nodded slightly.

'Thank you, Mrs Zelland. I'd like that immensely.'

While the client was in the lavatory, Willow turned to Stedington.

'Sarah was the dog on this deal, wasn't she?' she asked, having picked up the bank's pejorative term for the junior members of the Corporate Finance teams.

'Not really the dog, you know. That was Beeking; we just didn't need him today. Sarah was an assistant director, after all.'

'Sorry. I hadn't appreciated quite the degrees of doggedness. But she was working for you on the deal?'

'Yes. I thought you might get something useful from watching the residue she's left. I'll have an urgent telephone call to make at some stage during lunch and you can cross-examine the client about her.'

'You're a brick, Jeremy. Now tell me quickly before she comes back: why wasn't Sarah one of you?'

'She didn't muck in,' he said. 'We're all out for ourselves –'

'Naturally.'

He smiled slightly. 'But she was ferocious in defence of her own territory – and . . . and she lived by different rules; wouldn't work the same hours, didn't drink with the boys, that sort of thing.'

'In fact she was a woman,' said Willow, thinking rather bitterly of the different attitudes obtaining in the bank and the world outside it. To Sarah's husband the hours she had worked seemed very long, and yet to her fellow bankers she had been a slacker.

Stedington only shrugged, but his face looked angry. Before Willow could say any more, Mrs Zelland re-emerged and they all went out to lunch.

Willow learned very little about Sarah Allfarthing from

the encounter, but she did discover during Jeremy's diplomatic absence that he was in the process of a particularly messy and unhappy divorce.

'I hadn't realized,' Willow said quickly. 'No wonder he's taken some of my frivolously feminist remarks so badly.'

'He's been deeply unhappy. From his point of view poor Sarah's tragedy has not been altogether bad.'

Willow was still finding it difficult to relate Mrs Zelland's soft plumpness, her pearls and her old-fashioned perm to her ruthless mind, and she remembered Martin Roylandson's having accused her of judging by appearances. Gathering her wits, she asked in what way the murder had helped Jeremy.

'Sarah had been carrying him through the last few deals they did together. I'm not sure how much he understood it, but her absence has certainly forced him to concentrate again.' Mrs Zelland's eyes looked uncomfortably shrewd.

'Did she have anything to do with the divorce?'

'I shouldn't have thought so. I'm the last person to deny that powerful feelings do grow between people who work together.' Mrs Zelland looked down at a magnificent sapphire on her left hand with a bitter expression. 'But those two showed no signs of it.'

'What are the signs?' Willow was interested, both as novelist and investigator.

Mrs Zelland's eyes twinkled, the bitterness receded and she looked once more like someone rehearsing for the part of a sweet old lady.

'The odd catching of eyes, avoidance of physical contact, picking up each other's half-spoken sentences, knowing too much about each other's past and interests: that sort of thing. It's hard to categorize but unmistakable when you see it.'

'You sound pretty convincing,' said Willow and then, remembering that she was supposed to be interested in training, asked: 'Does it affect efficiency?'

'I'd have said: inevitably. At the beginning it heightens

everything wonderfully. Both parties will work harder and better, partly because the sexual spurt gives them added interest in their jobs and partly to preen before the beloved; but later both tendencies slacken. I think it's always a mistake in the end. And when it is the end, of course they tend to be wiped out for a time, completely useless and desperately unhappy. People should be warned to look out for it in themselves and in their subordinates and stamp it out at once.'

'I suspect you're right,' said Willow. 'It's an aspect of management training that we don't normally address.'

'No,' said Mrs Zelland drily. 'I don't suppose you do. But it's becoming more important now that women are establishing themselves in less and less subservient jobs.'

'Do you think it had some part to play in the tragedy here?' Willow asked.

'I suspect it may have.'

'Do you believe in the police's suspect?'

'I never met him. James always insisted that we have Sarah as the assistant director on our deals.'

'What a pity,' said Willow with obvious sincerity. Mrs Zelland looked at her once again and Willow longed to be able to tell her the truth and ask for advice. There were brains behind that placid exterior that even Willow could admire, and a detachment that she envied.

'I wonder what's happened to Jeremy,' she said.

'Keeping out of our way for a bit,' said Mrs Zelland. 'He doesn't much like women at the moment, poor boy. I suspect he'll skip the rest of lunch and drag you back to the office when he comes back.'

'Before he does, will you tell me one thing?'

'If I can.'

'Was there something going on between James Certes and poor Sarah? It seems curious otherwise that he should have particularly asked for her on his deals.'

'He was a lot younger than she – not that that means much,' said Mrs Zelland. 'I'd often wondered, and when I saw how badly her death affected him I did think he might have cared for her. You won't have noticed, because he's adept at keeping his face, but he's been quite, quite desperate recently. And yet I think it might have been something other than an emotional attachment.'

'Such as? I'm sure you've some idea.' Willow's smile was a great deal more twinkly than she suspected, and Mrs Zelland responded to it.

'Yes, I have. I came to the conclusion that it might have been simply because he felt easier with her than with the men. He's quite small, as you saw, and by and large merchant bankers are big.'

'Yes, I've noticed that,' said Willow with a laugh. 'Big and loud-voiced.'

'And then I suspect he felt he had more influence with her. He's a very creative boy, you know. When everyone else is thrashing about trying to impose their will on the rest, James is quietly working out how to get round the obstacles instead of trying to beat them down by main force. I think Sarah might have been more receptive to ideas from a lawyer than the bankers usually are. She had less machismo to protect.'

'Do bankers despise their lawyers?'

'Both sides despise each other, dear. And when you've got accountants, too, it's hardly bearable. They've all got to score points off each other and the client is left paying the bill for their vanity. That's why I don't let them all get together on any of my meetings.'

'I'd wondered about that today,' said Willow simply for something to say.

'Oh, pooh! Today's was a deal so small as to be almost irrelevant. But I've done some quite big ones with Jeremy Stedington.'

'And always with James Certes?'

'Since he became a partner at Blenkort & Wilson, yes. There's Jeremy. Wait and see if he's prepared to have pudding.'

Willow laughed and then laughed again as she watched the gentle but inexorable pressure that made him agree to eat a raspberry sorbet before going back to the office. Mrs Zelland left them outside the restaurant and they walked back together.

'Impressive woman,' said Willow when they were out of her hearing.

'You're telling me – but nice with it.'

'You sound surprised. Haven't you ever met that combination before?'

Stedington looked down at her. Despite her height, he was a good six inches taller. There seemed to be contempt in his face.

'Are you trying to trap me into saying that I hated Sarah and killed her because I can't take professional women?'

'No.' Something in Willow's short monosyllable seemed to carry conviction, for his face relaxed and he started walking again.

'Niceness and impressive ability do seem quite rare in combination, but as you've no doubt been told I am feeling pretty jaundiced about women at the moment.'

'All anyone has told me – and that was Hughina herself – is that you've been going through a messy divorce. No details.'

'Messy!' It was extraordinary how angry he sounded. 'Messy is a serious understatement. You're obviously a feminist. Listen and tell me if I'm mad and chauvinist to think what she's done is outrageous.'

Stedington walked over to a bench covered in pigeon droppings and sat down. Willow, glad that she was not wearing any of Cressida's expensive clothes, followed reluctantly.

'I thought we were getting on fine; we'd got past all the stages people warn you about: the end of the first flush of excitement; the strains of moving house; her giving up work and having nothing to do all day; the first baby and all those broken nights; less thrilling sex; and so on.'

He stopped and when Willow looked sideways at him she saw that his face was set and hard.

'And?' she asked gently.

'And she came to me one morning and told me that she'd been having an affair with my best friend for four years, that our youngest child might even have been his, and that she was leaving me for him.'

'Some friend!' Willow was fairly sure that expressions of sympathy would be unwelcome.

'I know. But even so I wanted to push to get things right again. It wouldn't have been the same, but I was damned if I was going to give up that easily.'

'Didn't you hate her for it?' Willow watched a pigeon with a club foot hobbling and flapping its way among the sandwich crumbs on the pavement.

'No. I hated what had happened, but . . . she was my wife.' Stedington looked more puzzled than unhappy, as though he were still trying to understand what had happened to him. 'I'd loved her for so long it couldn't all just be put away because of what she'd told me.'

Thinking that he sounded unrealistically saintly, Willow waited for the rest.

'We got divorced and because we've four children under ten she got half the value of the house, which really meant keeping it, and a huge proportion of everything I earn. Is that fair?' He pushed both hands through his hair in a way that reminded her sharply of Richard. 'Particularly when I didn't want a divorce at all and she'd been unfaithful all that time.'

Accustomed to the stories of betrayed and deserted wives, Willow was silenced. If the story were as he had told it, it sounded so unjust that it made her feel as angry as all accounts of cruelty were beginning to do.

'It sounds horrible,' she said frankly. 'Obviously the court didn't want to penalize the children by driving them into poverty, and doing a job like yours you're hardly in a position to look after them yourself. But I agree, it sounds bitterly unfair.'

'Bitterly. That's right. I'm bloody bitter.' He turned his head away. 'But it didn't make me slit Sarah Allfarthing's throat.'

'I'm sure it didn't,' said Willow after an uncomfortable pause.

In her embarrassment she half remembered something he had said to her about the way Sarah worked, which seemed important. Before she could pin down the memory, Stedington turned on the bench beside her and gripped her arms above the elbows.

'How can you possibly say that? You don't know me at all.'

'You've an alibi,' said Willow coolly, ignoring his unpleasantly tight grip. 'You were in a meeting that you left in company with several others.'

He laughed then, with a short cracking sound, and released her.

'You're all right, Miss King,' he said. 'Richard always did have good taste in birds. I'd better get back. Are we going to see you this afternoon?'

'For a bit, but I'll have to go at about four. I'd better ask some training questions to establish my own alibi. Tell me one thing. Does Mrs Biggleigh-Clart involve herself in charities or is it just her husband?'

'Yes, she does,' he said, pushing his long body off the grubby bench and waiting for Willow to join him. 'But not in such a practical way as Bob. She runs something called FACA – Fight Against Child Abuse – and she's involved with most of the other children's charities, even if it's only at the level of buying a place at lunches and concerts.'

'Always children?'

'Always.'

'Do they have their own?'

'No. I believe there's some kind of problem. That's bloody unfair too, because they're some of the best people I know. They've kept me going during all this hell.'

'Poor things,' said Willow, thinking of the unhappiness

that most people lived with every day of their adult lives. Her own long isolation seemed petty and stupid, as did her double life and all its secrets. Surely, she thought, she could have got over her loveless childhood and learned to live with other people without putting herself through such extraordinary hoops. She smiled up at Jeremy and turned the conversation to the people who had been at the morning's meeting.

He echoed Mrs Zelland's encomia of James Certes's talents, but in a voice that made Willow wonder how well the two men actually liked each other. She asked Jeremy directly.

'Quite frankly, I think he's a little shit – personally. But that doesn't mean that I don't like the fact that he pushes his clients towards us, or that he's not good at his job. I suppose it's because he's slippery, and angry in a rather neurotic way.'

'Really?'

'Yes. He showed no signs of it today, but he can come out with some pretty spiteful remarks – always calculated, I think, to cause maximum embarrassment to the opposition, which is useful to us. But I don't like it. Occasionally he can be morose, too, which is tricky. He's –'

'Not one of us?' suggested Willow, laughing.

Jeremy joined in and agreed, adding: 'I could never fathom Sarah's passion for him.'

'Passion sounds an odd word. One of my informants said that she was cold.'

'Oh, not sexual passion. Your informant is right: she wasn't the type to go in for leg-over situations. But she was always on the telephone to him, teasing him, asking for advice, getting him to do little chores for her. I rather suppose that's why the idiotic Tracy is going to work at Blenkort & Wilson. She could hardly have got the job on merit.'

They reached the elegantly designed doors of the bank and Jeremy checked his watch.

'I must dash; there's an important meeting. Thanks for listening – and not beating me about the head with feminist claptrap.'

Willow watched him run up the shallow steps, his powerful thighs pumping inside the well-cut trousers of his suit. She followed more slowly, thinking of Tracy, and was glad to see her at her desk, looking as bored as usual, when Maggie opened the locked doors.

'Thanks, Maggie. Busy?'

'Fairly. But if you need something I could squeeze a few minutes.'

She looked so desperate that Willow shook her head. As she passed the workstation she said pleasantly to Tracy:

'I've just met your new boss. He seems a nice fellow.'

'James Certes? Was he here today? He usually calls me up when he's coming. He must have been very busy today.' Tracy looked rather put out.

'When do you join him?'

'End of the week,' said Tracy, her expression changing to one of almost seraphic delight. Cynically, Willow wondered how long that pleasure would last. She also wondered why someone as reputedly clever, slippery and creative as the lawyer would want to employ a secretary like Tracy.

'I must go and do some work,' said Willow before she disappeared round the screen to sit once more in Sarah Allfarthing's place. For two hours she worked on her tentative training suggestions, typing carefully on the replacement keyboard and ignoring the thought of Sarah's blood spurting out of her severed neck.

At four o'clock Willow filed her work, turned off the screen and collected her belongings.

She waved goodbye to the two secretaries and took the lift downstairs. By the front door she found herself standing next to James Certes, who was standing with a light mackintosh hanging over his arm talking to one of the lawyers representing Mrs Zelland's opponent.

'Your meeting went on a long time,' Willow said by way

of greeting. The two lawyers turned, irritation showing on both their faces until they recognized her. Then they both smiled politely.

'A lot of dull details to sort out,' said Certes. 'Was the meeting instructive from your point of view?'

'Not enormously,' said Willow, grabbing the opportunity he offered. 'I'd hoped to get some clue to why there was such a disgraceful scene the other day and so help to construct a stress-management course that might help prevent another. But you were all so calm and well-behaved.'

'I've heard about that scene,' said the opposition's lawyer. 'I gather it had a disastrous sequel, too.' He shook himself violently. 'I'd better be on my way. Get those papers over to us tomorrow, James, and I'll do my best to get a signature.'

'Great. Thanks, Tom.' The lawyer turned to Willow. 'I'm afraid I must go, too, Miss King, but it's been a pleasure meeting you.' He held out his hand. When Willow took it she expected a limp grip and was pleased by its firmness.

'You probably have some pretty strong views about the way the bank's employees carry on their business,' she said, still holding his hand. 'Perhaps we could talk some time.'

'Give me a call. I'll buy you a drink,' he said, 'and share my frustrations with you.'

Not certain whether he was trying to make a joke, Willow smiled and instead suggested taking him out to lunch. He agreed, looking a trifle surprised, and they made a firm appointment.

'I can't think why the bank didn't ask us our views direct,' he said as they emerged on to the front steps. He squinted up at the sky. 'It looks pretty clear still, but there's thunder in the air. Any of us could tell them what their employees need in the way of training.'

'I'll look forward to hearing your views,' said Willow, holding out her hand once again. Certes shook it and set off back to his office.

Willow saw the encouraging yellow light on the front of a

cruising taxi and ran down the steps to grab it before the rain came. She gave the driver the address of Amanda Hopecastle's Fulham house and tried to think that she was getting closer to something that would prove Richard's innocence.

Everything she had heard seemed to taunt her subconscious into doubting him again, although most of the time she could manage to make her rational mind reject the doubts. If Jeremy Stedington could live with his much-loved wife and not know that she was unfaithful, perhaps it was possible for Willow to have made love with Richard and not known him to be violent after all. If Mrs Zelland could look sweet and behave gently and yet run a ruthlessly successful multimillion-pound operation that extended from eastern Europe to the United States, then Richard might be capable of killing. And if Richard were so different from the man she thought she had known, then Tom, too, might be a stranger.

Chapter 12

THE main part of Amanda Hopecastle's house gave no indication of what Willow discovered when she was escorted up the carpeted stairs to the converted attic. The hall and staircase were decorated with sprigged prints, scrubbed pine and ruched Austrian blinds, but the loft was white, airy and almost harshly lit.

There was a long cutting table, marked out in metric squares, an industrial sewing machine and an overlocker. A worktop under the windows supported a professional steam press and a variety of irons, while a group of adjustable sewing forms stood nearby. A large cork board was covered with sketches, swatches and photographs of finished clothes, all neatly attached with matching red or white round-headed pins. Under it ran a shelf, from which hung brown-paper blocks of all kinds. To either side of the board were large racks holding polythene-covered rolls of fabric. It was the room of an amateur, but an efficient and hard-working one.

Amanda Hopecastle herself looked rather as Willow had expected. She had her father's height, but not his bulk, and a lot of dark hair which she kept away from her face with a piece of twisted brocade. The gilded lavishness of the material contrasted agreeably with the fraying ends that peeked above the knot on the crown of her head. Her skirt was quite straight and very short, showing off her long legs clad in matt black tights.

She led Willow to a pair of chairs to the left of the cutting table.

'Now, what can we do for you?'

'Well, I need a long dress,' said Willow, lying, 'for a charity ball I've got to go to.' She grimaced as though she dreaded the occasion.

'They are dull, aren't they?' said Amanda sympathetically. 'Some of my clients actually seem to enjoy them and they're a great source of income for the likes of me, but what a waste of time!'

'I think we're going to get on,' said Willow, agreeably surprised by the dressmaker's down-to-earth manner. 'Can you show me some of the things you've done?'

Amanda waved towards the cork board. 'It's all there.'

'I'm not very good at judging two-dimensional stuff. Have you anything nearly ready here?'

There were no obvious signs of reluctance as Amanda got out of her chair and threw open the double doors of a cupboard that ran the whole width of the house. In it were several garments in different stages of construction. After some thought she abstracted two, took them out of their linen bags and slung them over the dummies.

'There,' she said as she finished hooking up the second dress.

Willow looked carefully from a distance and was genuinely impressed. The first dress was a mass of ivory silk ruffles with large baroque pearls hanging here and there, and the other a slim column of very dark violet-coloured velvet that hung from the dress form in sophisticated simplicity.

'I like the contrast,' she said, with her eyebrows raised. She walked closer to the dresses and Amanda obligingly picked up the hem of the frilled one and showed Willow the inner structure.

'The hem is finished with horsehair braid. None of the more modern equivalents seems to give such effective stiffness without weight,' said Amanda. 'And we always bind the seams with a Hong Kong finish.'

'How did you learn it all?' asked Willow.

It occurred to her that if she really were going to write a synopsis for Eve Greville, she ought to take the opportunity of sucking as much information out of Amanda Hopecastle as possible. It also occurred to her that she might be able to put the cost of the dress she was going to have to order against her expenses for tax purposes. Determined to ask her accountant's advice, she watched Amanda and was amused to see her looking self-conscious.

'I've found a wonderful tailor,' she said, 'who was trained years ago in Vienna and then worked in New York. She's taught me and the girls who sew for me. She also found us a marvellous cutter. I'm told she's very old-fashioned, but the difference she's made to my stuff is incredible. I can't afford either her or the girls for more than mornings yet, though.'

'She's done you well. I must say that the velvet seems more me than the frills, but I'd be interested to know what you suggest. I don't really want quite such nakedness over the shoulders.'

'No, I see,' said Amanda leading the way back to the two chairs. 'Might you need to wear the dress at a formal dinner?'

'I might well,' said Willow, with a brief ludicrous fantasy of winning the Nobel Prize for Literature. She laughed at herself and Amanda smiled sympathetically.

'We could always make you a sleeveless dress with a little jacket.'

'I'm not really happy in sleeveless things. Is that a terrible bore?'

'No. Just a challenge. Look, I think the best thing would

be for me to take your measurements and make a few notes about the colours you wear and think about it all. Then, when I've a few sketches, I can ring you up and we'll see how it goes. Does that suit you?'

'It sounds excellent,' said Willow, wondering how she was going to be able to spin out the taking of measurements until the arrival of Mrs Biggleigh-Clart.

Just as Willow was putting on her clothes again after the measuring, which she had interrupted with as many questions as she could invent, there was a discreet buzz on the intercom. Amanda answered it. Willow put her head round the edge of the screen and called out:

'I'll be a minute or two, Amanda; don't wait.'

With almost audible surprise, Amanda clumped down the stairs. Willow tidied herself up, combed her hair again and was re-blackening her eyelashes when Amanda returned with her next client.

She was just as tidy as her husband, although in her the finish was less immediately obvious than her smallness. She could not have been much more than five foot tall and her bones looked birdlike. Her fine dark hair was brushed plainly back over her impeccably shaped head and tucked into a ruched black velvet bow at the nape of her neck. Her face was lightly made up above the smoothness of her simple wrap dress of black linen and there was a string of fat pearls just covering her collarbone.

'This is Cressida Woodruffe, you know, the writer,' said Amanda, looking slightly put out.

'How do you do?' Mrs Biggleigh-Clart approached Willow with her hand held out. 'I do so love your books.'

So effective was the woman's social technique that Willow had no idea whether she had even heard of Cressida Woodruffe until that moment. The two of them shook hands and Willow managed a flashing smile.

'It's Clara Biggleigh-Clart, isn't it? Didn't we meet at that big Save the Children lunch last year?'

A moment's doubt flickered in the dark eyes, but the

smile never wavered. 'That must have been it. I knew that we'd met somewhere. Have you had much made by Amanda?'

'Nothing yet, but I've been so impressed by the evening clothes I've seen that I'm about to commission a long dress.' Willow moved a little way from the elegantly dressed dummies and Clara gave a tiny scream.

'Amanda, darling! They've come out so well. I love the pearls, don't you, Cressida?'

'I think they're stunning,' said Willow frankly. 'I hadn't realized these dresses were yours. I must say I'd love to see them on.'

There was a short pause, but Willow was confident that anyone as professionally charming as Clara would find it difficult to be direct enough to snub her.

'Why not? Unless Amanda minds?'

'Well, no; not if –'

'Splendid!' said Willow. 'Even a dummy doesn't really show how these things move, does it?'

She settled herself back in one of the two chairs while Clara and Amanda disappeared round the back of the painted screen. They kept up a flow of charming banter, complimenting each other and chatting as Clara's dress was delicately laid over the top of the screen. Willow hoped that it had been well dusted. Then Amanda appeared to remove the frilly dress from its dummy.

A few minutes later Clara emerged, looking rich, beautiful and surprisingly young, her shoulders rising out of the pearly foam. An immense, ripping crash echoed and boomed across the sky and made Amanda jump. When it was followed by the sound of deluging rain, Willow smiled in satisfaction.

Attempting to join in the cosy talk about the dress's merits, she thought of ways to ensure that Clara realized she had come to the dressmaker's house on foot.

As the other two watched their reflection in the three long mirrors, Willow began to feel uncomfortable with their unconfined and narcissistic femininity. Eventually both client and dressmaker pronounced themselves satisfied with the dresses. Amanda proceeded to lay each one on the cutting table and fold it around layers and layers of tissue paper until it would fit into the firm dress box that had her name stamped diagonally across it in flowing scarlet lettering.

'Shall I send you the account?' she asked.

'Yes, darling. Do please do that.' Clara peered out at the rain that cascaded down the windows in silklike festoons.

'Do you have a car, Cressida?'

Willow, who had been ignoring all Amanda's hints and glances for the past hour, got to her feet.

'No, I haven't. But never mind. I'm sure I can pick up a taxi.'

'Don't be ridiculous.' The reprimand was offered in the full cosiness of Clara's easy charm. 'My driver is waiting downstairs. We can easily drop you. Where do you live?'

'Chesham Place, actually,' said Willow, successfully imitating Emma Gnatche once more.

'But that's so easy! It's only round the corner from us. Come along.'

After what she hoped was a gracefully insincere refusal, Willow allowed herself to be persuaded. When the two of them had left Amanda Hopecastle and were sitting in the back of the midnight-blue Daimler, protected alike from the rain and from the chauffeur's hearing, Willow decided to abandon finesse.

'I particularly wanted to meet you,' she said, 'and I'm afraid I have forced myself on you.'

The smile that Clara bestowed on her passenger was different from the earlier version, sharper, more intelligent and much more critical.

'I did wonder what it was that you thought I could do for you,' she said, sounding crisper too.

'I'm an old friend of Richard Crescent,' said Willow, 'and I'm trying to find something – anything – to help him. It has been suggested to me that Sarah Allfarthing might have committed suicide and I just wondered whether you had any views. I'm trying to talk to everyone who might have known her.'

'I see. What makes you think that I might have any views at all?'

Willow looked out through the translucent grey sheets of rain to the blurred buildings of the King's Road.

'Because I know that Jeremy Stedington has an immensely high opinion of you; because I've been told that you are extremely intelligent; and because I cannot believe that you never heard any of the gossip about Mrs Allfarthing and your husband.'

'That's frank.'

'It seems to me that just now frankness is my only re-source,' said Willow, letting her voice wobble slightly. 'To wrap it all up would take for ever, besides being patronizing.'

The big car slowed for some red traffic lights and a bus drew up beside it, blocking Willow's view of the shops. She turned to look at Clara, whose face was just as beautiful without its conscious gaiety.

'You're probably right. If frankness is to be the order of the day, I should tell you that I disliked her intensely.'

Willow hoped that she did not look as surprised as she felt.

'My husband was obliged to find her an asset since he had fought so hard for her appointment, and I resented the way in which she traded on that.'

'Resented it on his behalf?'

'On his behalf?' There was an edge to Clara's voice that intrigued Willow. It suggested that she was a stronger character than she allowed herself to seem. 'Perhaps partly. But more on behalf of all the women who don't push as she did, and who would probably have done a better job. She was extremely pushy, you know.'

'How did you meet her?' asked Willow, watching the

traffic lights turn green. The car purred smoothly across the intersection. Clara moved her lips slightly in a minute but eloquent gesture of distaste.

'Once she persuaded Robert to invite her and her husband to dinner. It was the only time they ever came and luckily I'd refused to have anyone else with them. He – Allfarthing, I mean – was both embarrassed by her and determined not to show it. I thought he was a decent man if a little suburban. She spent the evening trying to show me that her influence over my husband was greater than my own. At least that's what her antics seemed to be about.'

'How curious! Didn't your husband mind?'

There was a delicate laugh from the woman at Willow's side.

'He said that he had not noticed anything and that I was imagining it.' She leaned forward to look out of her window at the rain. 'But as I told you, his pride would not let him admit that he had made a mistake over her.'

'Was that why you decided not to go to the bank's summer dance?' Willow spoke as quietly as she could and with as little urgency.

'Partly. I never wanted to go at all and then when . . .'

'When?' Willow asked when Clara said no more.

After a long pause she turned and put one tiny hand on Willow's wrist. In the poor light Willow thought that she looked sympathetic.

'She telephoned me, you see, and I don't think that suicide could have been further from her mind. I'm sorry.'

'When did she telephone?' Willow let the urgency out in her voice.

'At about half past six, I suppose.'

'May I ask why?'

The car swung round into Sloane Square and Willow, who had been paying no attention to the route, over-balanced and had to cling to the strap above the window to prevent herself from falling on the fragile figure beside her.

'She wanted, or so she said,' said Clara with contempt, 'to ask me what I would be wearing that evening.'

'But how extraordinary!'

'Wasn't it? I think her exact words were: "It suddenly occurred to me that we might have chosen the same designer and I wanted to make sure that you wouldn't object to my wearing yellow." I think she must have got the idea from that television advertisement.'

Willow was puzzled and said so. Clara laughed once more.

'I suspect that the message she was really trying to pass was that she knew she was more beautiful than I am and that she would do her best not to upstage me.'

'She sounds thoroughly unattractive,' said Willow, wondering what to believe. Nothing – even Emma's report of Jeanine's adolescent outpouring – she had heard from anyone else suggested that the dead woman would have stooped to such childish gamesmanship.

'Oh, she was attractive all right.' There was bitterness in the cool voice. 'Nearly everyone except me thought – or pretended to think – that she was just wonderful.' She stopped and looked away from Willow.

'Did you decide straight away that you wouldn't go to the dance?'

'What? Oh, no. I went to have a bath and change, planning to wear something she could never have afforded and to get all my diamonds out of the safe, but then I thought that was rather petty. To dignify her by joining in with her games was not something I wanted to do.'

'And so you told your chauffeur about the migraine.'

'That's right. I didn't tell him myself, of course. I simply asked the housekeeper to let him know and then I went out to a small restaurant with a friend and home to bed at half past ten.'

Willow was silent, wishing that Tom Worth were in charge of the police investigation. If he had been, she could have told him what she had learned and persuaded him to question Mrs Biggleigh-Clart and find witnesses to her alibi. But Chief Inspector Moreby would never do it. Willow looked down at Clara's hands. Could they have driven a knife far enough into Sarah Allfarthing's throat to cut the blood vessels and so kill her?

'I didn't do it, you know.' The soft voice broke into Willow's thoughts. She managed to laugh.

'I don't see how you could have done,' she said. 'She was a lot bigger than you and could have fought back.'

'Perhaps not.' The car turned into left into Lyall Street. 'If I had stood behind her and suddenly grabbed that long hair she always flaunted, twisted it and dragged her head back. With my other hand I could have picked up the knife very quickly and cut her throat. It would have been easy if the knife had been sharp enough.'

'But your fingerprints would have been on the knife and there would have been blood all over you. And you would have found it hard to get out of the building.'

'Perhaps I hid until the next day and bathed in Robert's bathroom.'

'But he met you at breakfast the next morning.'

'Ah yes, so he did.' There was a slight chuckle in the dark beside Willow. 'I'm sorry: it's not fair to make fun of you when you're trying so hard to help poor Richard Crescent.'

The car stopped in Chesham Place. Willow decided that she did not like Clara Biggleigh-Clart at all.

'You've a fine imagination,' said Willow with an unfair sneer. 'Can you use it to tell me who might have wanted her dead?'

'Almost anyone,' said Clara with a readiness that suggested she did not care what Willow thought of her. 'Her poor embarrassed husband; my poor husband whose pride would not let him sack her; Jeremy, whose life she probably made into a misery with her teasing. Any of them might have wanted her dead, but even my imagination cannot make me believe that any of them killed her.'

'Even Richard?'

'I would never have thought him capable of it, but life is full of surprises. I rather wish I'd known him better. You see, I'm afraid that he must have done it and when I had the chance to know him I never realized what depths he had. Good night, Miss Woodruffe.'

Willow made herself smile into Clara's sparkling black eyes and thank her for the lift, although her heart was banging away inside her ribcage and her hands were sweating badly.

As she walked up the stairs to her flat, she wondered whom she could ask for a realistic assessment of Clara's character, which might help to remove the sting of what she had said. Jeremy Stedington had sounded too partisan to be useful and it seemed hardly fair to badger Mr Allfarthing. It was not until her key was turning in one of the locks of her front door that she thought of the perfect source. Without calling out to Mrs Rusham or even waiting to see whether Emma Gnatche was still using the word processor, Willow went into the drawing room and picked up the telephone receiver.

She punched in the number of the *Daily Mercury* and asked to speak to Jane Cleverholme.

'I don't know if she's still there, but I'll try for you,' said the switchboard operator. Willow waited impatiently, thinking that gossip columnists really ought to work longer hours.

'Diary.'

'Jane? Is that you? It's Cressida Woodruffe here.'

'Cressida! How good to hear from you. How are you?' The cheerful voice banished Willow's impatience but as she forced herself to chat it was quickly followed by a slightly colder version.

'Ah, I see,' Jane said after a few minutes, 'you want some more information from me.'

'Yes, I'm afraid so, Jane. Your job just makes you the perfect source of the kind of gossip I need now.'

'Well, since you did let me into a lot of dirt about that

multiple murderer, I suppose I'll have to admit that I owe you.'

'Terrific,' said Willow, deliberately ignoring the coldness. 'Tell me about a woman called Biggleigh-Clart.'

'The charity queen? Wife of Mr Beautiful the Banker?'

'The very same,' said Willow, her face relaxing. 'I don't need to know that she's glamorous and spends a fortune on her clothes and is a wonderful fund-raiser. I've already heard all that.'

'You want the dirt, in other words. There isn't a lot. We did a piece about her recently and dug away like anything without much result. She really does do good work for her charities. She's said to be faithful to Mr B. the Banker. The only slightly unkind thing we could get anyone to say is that she does love a drama. The charities aren't quite enough to keep her amused during her gorgeous husband's long hours of work and it's been suggested that she tends to stir up lovely emotional crises in people so that she can soothe them down and enjoy herself.'

'Doesn't she have any emotional crises of her own?'

'Apparently not.'

'How dull for you!'

'That was caustic.'

'I know,' said Willow, smiling at the absent Jane. 'You're just so very good at what you do that it's hard not to take the mickey a bit.'

'I'm going to take that at face value instead of looking for the sneer. And now I must run. There's a big do on tonight and I'm on call.'

'Just like a doctor. Thanks, Jane. You've been helpful even if you didn't produce the answer I wanted.'

'Good luck!'

Jane put the telephone down before Willow could ask her what she meant. Hearing the empty buzz in her ear, Willow put down her own receiver and went to find out whether she had the flat to herself.

To her delight she found that Mrs Rusham had already

gone, leaving her a chilled *millefeuille* of seafood with a jug of avocado sauce in the fridge. Willow left the kitchen, calling Emma's name, and was answered only by silence. Putting her head round the door of her writing room, she saw that the only evidence of Emma's visit was a neat pile of typescript in the middle of the desk.

Willow started to unbutton the jacket of her suit as she went to run herself a bath. To be alone again seemed the height of luxury. As she undressed and soaked herself in the warm, scented bathwater, she thought about the cottage of her recent fantasies and began to consider the practicality of them. Selling the Clapham flat would probably raise about half the price of a comfortable, weatherproof cottage with enough land for her orchard-garden. She started to plan, trying to decide whether to have the flat decorated before she put it on the market or whether that would be merely a waste of money. In its present condition it might depress any potential buyer and yet Willow hated it so much that she just wanted to be rid of it.

The skin of her toes and fingers had begun to pucker and blanch before Willow reluctantly dragged herself out of both bath and fantasy. She felt guilty of wasting time and mental capacity on her own daydreams when there was Richard's horrible reality to consider. By way of compensation, she took Emma's notes into the kitchen with her when she went to eat the *millefeuille*, and sat reading them.

After a few mouthfuls she decided to let herself concentrate on eating until she had finished the *millefeuille*. The combination of crisply flaky pastry and the firm, sweet flesh of lobster, scallop and prawn demanded her full attention, and the cool, herb-scented sauce tended to drip over her lap and the notes if she tried to eat and read at the same time.

Later, when she had brushed the crumbs from her lips, eaten a lusciously ripe peach and piled her plates in the sink for Mrs Rusham, Willow poured herself a glass of a wonderful Trockenbeerenauslese wine she had bought in half-bottles as an experiment. She took it through to the drawing room and began to work in earnest.

Two hours and another glass of wine later, she knew that she needed to talk once more to Richard. The thought of facing him before she was certain of his innocence was horrible, but she would have to do it. If Martin Royland-son's pathologist could prove that Sarah could have died before Richard reached the bank, Willow knew that she would be able to relax. If the pathologist could not help, she would have to find a convincing alternative theory and to do that she had to talk to Richard.

When she was lying in bed, feeling slightly more confident and happy, Willow reached for the telephone and called Tom Worth. They talked for a few minutes before he said:

'How are you getting on?'

'A few ideas are beginning to crystallize out of the mush of information I've been collecting, but I'm nowhere near a solution.'

'You sound happier. I've noticed you don't mix metaphors when you're upset.'

Willow laughed, for once actually enjoying a piece of criticism.

'I do like you, Tom,' she said. 'And it's true, I am feeling more chirpy. For a time I even began to doubt Richard's innocence, but I've found that there are things about Sarah Allfarthing that just don't add up. She wasn't perfect and there are gaps in her life story that I can't fill. Somewhere, somebody knows what she was really like – and really up to. And there are plenty of other people who have motives just as strong – or weak – as Richard's for wanting her out of the way. I'm going after them.'

There was a pause before Tom, with uncharacteristic tentativeness, said: 'Please be careful. Remember what you promised after you were half strangled by Ben Jonson.'

'That sounds as though you think it might not be Richard either.'

'I have a great respect for Jane Moreby,' said Tom slowly.

Willow waited, not certain whether he had anything more to say.

'But perhaps not quite as much respect as I have for you,' he finished.

'Thank you for that, Tom,' said Willow, surprised and touched. 'I'll do my best to keep the promise I made you then. I won't act as a tethered goat unless I absolutely have to.'

As she spoke, Willow had a sudden vision of the police photographs of Sarah's body and felt the first disgusting symptoms of fear for her own safety. In spite of her earlier experiences of murder, she had not thought of the savagery of Sarah's death in connection with herself until that moment. Willow quickly said good night to Tom, ignored his protests and got out of bed to check the locks on all her windows before bolting the front door.

She went back to bed and lay cursing the vivid imagination that was the source of all her comforts as she tried to banish the pictures of knives and blood and severed heads that blocked the sleep she badly wanted.

It came at last, but soon her mind was tormenting itself with a dream in which she was trying to reach the back of a butcher's shop where a woman's naked body was hanging from a bloody hook. The body swung, as though in a fierce draught, and Willow could see the long dark hair blowing away from a face that seemed to have no features. Every time she took a step towards the woman, Willow was forcibly held back by hard hands belonging to some man she could not see. The long hair seemed to change colour from Sarah's dark brown to a more familiar dark red as Willow struggled to move forwards.

Half aware that she was dreaming, Willow tried to wake herself out of the nightmare, but it was not until a bell shrilled through her silent flat that she was released.

Shaking from remembered terror, grateful for the summons, she slid out from under her linen-covered duvet and reached for her dressing gown. The bell rang again and she went to the intercom beside the front door.

'Yes?' she said into it, wondering why Tom should need her so late.

'Thank God you're awake. Let me in, there's a darling,' asked a deep masculine voice that sounded thickened by drink or injury. It did not sound at all like Tom's. Willow said nothing as her suddenly sweaty hand slid on the hard plastic of the receiver.

'What're you playing at? Let me in.' The voice was louder in her ear and her knees began to shake.

'Who are you?' Willow asked, trying not to sound either pathetic or frightened. She felt both to a shocking degree.

'If you don't bloody let me in, I'll break the door down. You know perfectly well who I am, and we've lots to talk about,' said the voice, sharpening with every word. 'Stop playing games and let me in. I'm fed up with all this pussy-footing you've been doing. I want you to face me and tell me what it is you think I've done. There isn't any proof, you know.'

The sound of two fists pounding on the street door came unmistakably through the intercom. Anger came to Willow's rescue at last, bringing with it both warmth and a certain confidence.

'If you do not stop making that noise I'll send for the police,' she said, banging down the receiver.

Ignoring the bell that continued to shrill as her unwanted visitor put his finger on the button and kept it there, Willow walked to her drawing room to look down into the street. Her tormentor was invisible, hidden from her by the roof of the stucco porch. The cars that were parked along the gutter seemed familiar, but she could not have sworn that there was not a strange one among them. Still looking down, she reached for the telephone and tapped in 999.

'Emergency,' said an efficient voice. 'Which service do you require?'

'Police,' said Willow and then gave her name, address

and telephone number. When the police answered, she explained what had happened. A soothing man at the other end of the telephone took down the details.

'Is he still banging, miss?' he asked at the end of her account.

'Yes. And he's still pressing the bell. It's making an awful noise. It'll wake all the neighbours.'

'That's probably no bad thing. Don't worry. We'll send someone as soon as we can.'

'Thanks,' said Willow. 'I'd be grateful.' She replaced the telephone receiver and went into the kitchen to make herself a hot drink. It was a long time since she had wanted cocoa, but it seemed an appropriate comforter in the circumstances.

After a very long, very noisy eight minutes, the sound of banging and bell-ringing stopped abruptly. Willow waited, with her hands wrapped around the warm mug, for the police to ring her bell and tell her what had happened, but no one did.

Taking her mug to the drawing room she went back to her chair by the window and watched the apparently empty street, wondering what had happened. She was about to go back to bed when a small police car drove slowly along the road, parked opposite her front door and waited. After a while a uniformed officer got out and eventually disappeared under the porch, only to emerge a moment later, simultaneously shaking her head and talking into her radio.

Willow went back to bed at last, half reassured, wholly embarrassed and wondering whether the police would ignore any further calls from her flat after the false alarm. Still unable to sleep, at half past two she took a pill.

Chapter 13

WAKING with a heavy head and hallucinatory memories of yet more nightmares, Willow made herself get out of bed soon after seven so that she could unbolt the front door before Mrs Rusham tried to get in. Feeling too sick to want coffee and too shaken even to try to talk to Tom, Willow made herself some China tea, which she took into the bathroom.

After several cups of tea and three-quarters of an hour soaking in hot water, she felt less ill and considerably less pathetic. Her head still ached but her eyes no longer smarted and the nausea had subsided. She put on a simple but comfortable linen skirt and a loose shirt and went to see what Mrs Rusham had produced for her breakfast.

Relieved to see a mixture of soft fruit around a small mound of *fromage frais* instead of the cooked fish or bacon she had feared, she told her housekeeper what had happened during the night and settled down to eat. Coffee began to seem less daunting once she had finished the fruit and after drinking two cups of fragrant cappuccino she felt much more herself. Her confidence had returned and with it her fierce determination to prove Richard innocent of the murder of Sarah Allfarthing.

A handwritten letter had emerged from the fax machine in Willow's writing room as she breakfasted and she tore off the paper as soon as she reached her desk.

'Dear Miss W [she read]
There is nothing in the postmortem report to confirm or deny your theory that the victim could have suffered from a Vitamin K deficiency. Blood tests for it can be carried out only during life. But the pathologist agrees that clotting time can't be specified as closely as the police have suggested. From the physical signs in the body it is true that death could have occurred some time before my client's return to the office. I can let you have a copy of the entire report if you would like it.

Useful though the uncertainty may be in helping defence counsel throw doubt on the prosecution case, it does not alter the fact that my client was the only person alone with the victim that evening, the only person whose fingerprints were on the weapon and the only person who showed signs of bloodstains.

Equally the uncertainty in the time of death has no effect on the time that the blood short-circuited the computer.
Yours,
Martin R.

Willow sat down at her desk with the fax in her hands. A mixture of anger and fear shook her as she reread it. At that moment her fear was no longer that Richard might have done the killing, but that she might never be able to prove otherwise. His counsel might get him off by weakening the prosecution's case, but that would not be enough.

To calm herself, Willow leaned back in her chair, looking around the small book-lined room and remembering the satisfying days in which she had sat there writing the novels that had made her financially independent. They had been her passport to freedom not only from the civil service but also from the shibboleths of her upbringing. She knew perfectly well that she would never entirely rid herself of the legacy her well-meaning but destructive parents had left her, but, surrounded by a luxury they would have despised, she did not blame them for it.

Her admiring inspection of her own possessions did not provide the usual sedative and she turned instead to her alternative specific against emotion: work. Pulling the telephone towards her, Willow rang up Martin Roylandson, asked for a copy of the full report and arranged to visit Richard at half past two that afternoon.

The solicitor was his usual prissy self and she kept their conversation to a minimum, breaking it off on the excuse that someone had come to the door of the flat. That was true – Willow had heard the bell ringing as she dialled the solicitor's office – but Mrs Rusham had already said that she was quite prepared to deal with any visitor, even the possibly violent man who had disturbed her employer's sleep.

Hearing the sound of voices stop and the front door close, Willow emerged from her writing room to find out what had been going on. Mrs Rusham turned with an enormous, cellophane-wrapped bouquet in her arms. She stopped at the sound of Willow's step and held out the flowers.

'Aren't they magnificent? Here's the card.'

Reluctantly admiring the big fan-shaped bunch of apricot and cream-coloured roses, pinks and freesias, Willow took the small white rectangle and read:

My husband asked me to send you these in abject apology for his idiocy last night. He is very sorry to have disturbed you when he mistook your house for ours and

to have behaved so badly. We both hope that you will be able to forgive him.
Susan Callanture.

Willow closed her eyes and breathed deeply in both relief and sympathy for the unknown Mrs Callanture.

'Poor woman,' she said. 'Yes, Mrs Rusham, they are lovely, aren't they? Can you deal with them for me? You're so good at flowers.'

'Why, thank you,' said the housekeeper, but she did not retreat. 'I've been wondering: have you heard anything from Mr Crescent?'

Willow shook her head. 'Not yet, but I'm going to see him today.'

'Oh, I'm so glad. Miss Gnatche rang me at home yesterday to ask if I'd heard anything, because she hasn't managed to speak to you for a while. May I telephone her to say there will be news later? She is most terribly anxious, you know.'

'Yes, of course. Telephone whoever you like,' said Willow, disliking the sharpness that had crept into her voice but unable to prevent it. Mrs Rusham's adoration for Richard had always amused her, as had Emma's hero-worship of him, but if they were to build some kind of alliance in which Willow figured as a harsh, unsympathetic witch who kept them both from their beloved, life in the flat would become intolerable.

Feeling unfriendly and at odds with herself, Willow went back to her office to wait for the pathologist's report that Martin Roylandson had promised to send her through the fax machine. When the report came she read it slowly, checking the precise meaning of various technical terms in a medical dictionary. Apart from the encouraging comment that there was absolutely no evidence that could confine the time of death to the period between Richard's arrival in the department and his call to the police, there seemed to be nothing in the report that could help her case.

Depressed, she changed into her noncommittal dark-blue suit, ate Mrs Rusham's perfectly prepared watercress soup and a salad of artichoke bottoms, tiny broad beans and shreds of chicken, and left Belgravia for the prison.

She drove there in the new Metro she had recently bought in exchange for a ridiculously large Mercedes she had hardly ever used, parked just outside the plant nursery that sat with incongruous cheerfulness at the foot of the forbidding fortress, and, having exchanged her contact lenses for spectacles, went to present her credentials at the gate.

The uniformed warder looked her up and down, consulted a list pinned to his clipboard and eventually let her through. He escorted her down a long corridor smelling of drains and disinfectant to the green-painted interview room.

Willow put her briefcase on the floor beside her hard plastic chair and waited for Richard. When he was brought in by another warder, she was relieved to see that some of his desperation seemed to have gone. He still looked tired and unhappy, but there was no longer a hunted expression in his eyes; he had straightened his back and shoulders and was walking with much of his old arrogance. His hair was much cleaner than it had been the last time they had met, and his nails had been neatly cut.

The warder left them alone and Willow reached out to touch one of Richard's hands.

'You look better,' she said, pleased.

'I suppose one becomes accustomed to almost anything, and Mrs Rusham's pies and pâtés are making a big difference, not to speak of those wonderful half-bottles of fizz. Thank you for them, Willow,' said Richard, adding with a hint of a smile: 'They're doing almost as much for my morale as my infinite faith in you. How are you getting on?'

'I'm not sure yet,' she said, wondering whether to tell him about the uncertainty over the time of death or not. In some ways it seemed cruel to keep it from him, but Willow decided that a continuing anxiety was likely to be less damaging than the sort of violent swings between hope and despair that she had been feeling. If he was innocent, as she was determined to believe, then she wanted to save him from those.

'I have collected an enormous amount of information,' she went on, 'and I've reached the stage where I need to talk to someone I can trust about various people at the bank before I start to interview them.'

A curious smile twisted Richard's lips. It seemed to mock Willow and yet demand something from her. She had never seen Richard smile like that before and it disturbed her.

'You still trust me then?' he said. 'After everything you've learned? I'd say that was quite remarkable for a woman with all your experience.'

Willow felt as though she had trodden on a live electric wire, jolted, breathless and tingling with fear.

'Shouldn't I trust you?'

The mocking smile left Richard's face and a hardness appeared in his blue-grey eyes.

'Only you can decide that,' he said in a voice of such cold anger that Willow began to sweat. Annoyed with herself, determined to believe in all she had known of him and felt about him, she put the sensation down to her disturbed night and said as coolly as she could:

'Richard, what are you doing? Are you trying to make me doubt you?'

He shrugged and then brushed his hands over his face and through his hair again. Willow waited as he sat staring at her. He opened his mouth as though to speak and then shut it again. At last his face relaxed into its more familiar self-deprecating smile.

'I suppose that the very idea of a friend who has un-questioning faith in me is such a lifeline in this nightmare world that I'm trying to push you and push you so that when you don't crack I can be sure of you,' he said, sounding more like himself.

Willow still did not speak. She wanted to reassure him, but he had shaken her badly and she needed time to assess what had happened.

'Christ!' he burst out into the silence. 'You of all people ought to know that I'm not capable of slitting someone's throat. You know more about me than anyone. We were lovers for three years, Willow.'

He spread his hands palm upwards on the table. They both looked at his hands and remembered the nights they had spent during those years. Willow shivered and then tried to force herself back into rationality.

'Yes, I do know you're not capable of murder,' she said when she could speak again, 'despite what various people have told me.'

'Well, thank God for that. You were beginning to worry me.'

'That makes two of us then,' said Willow more lightly. 'By the way, why did you never tell me that you were adopted?'

Richard put his hands in his lap again as he stared across the plastic-covered table at her, obviously puzzled by her question.

'Didn't I? It wasn't particularly secret. If I didn't, I suppose I thought you wouldn't be interested.' He looked carefully at her as though trying to understand her. After a while he murmured: 'I see. You think that because I never told you that the parents who brought me up had not actually bred me I might have lied to you about other things, and that I might be not only a liar but also a murderer?'

'No; no, of course not. Put like that it sounds absurd,' said Willow. She took off her spectacles and rubbed the space between her eyes.

'You've had your hair cut,' he said suddenly.

Willow laughed and felt better. 'Yes. I'm sorry to have

sounded wobbly. I suppose the strain of it all must have been been getting to me. I didn't sleep much last night and I've lost a lot of my various sorts of armour recently.'

'I had noticed that,' said Richard more gently.

'And that policewoman came to see me and tried to show me how little I know you.'

'What? That's outrageous! Have you told Roylandson?'

Willow shook her head. 'She came out of the best motives, I think, and at some risk to herself. Look, Richard, we ought both to calm down and start work. All this emotion is misleading and –'

'Dangerous?' There was a light back in Richard's eyes and a tenderness she had not seen for some time. 'You always did hate messy feelings. All right: what do you want to ask me?'

Gripping the handle of her briefcase as though it were a piece of that discarded armour, Willow hauled the case up in front of her and got out her notes and the small dictating machine.

'D'you mind this?'

Richard shook his head. She switched on the machine.

'Right. Now on the basis that we know you did not kill Sarah Allfarthing and assuming that it is mad to suggest a wandering vagrant did it, the most likely possibilities are limited to the security men, Robert Biggleigh-Clart, Bill Beeking and James Stedington. There are also Mrs Biggleigh-Clart; the client who was at the meeting that night, whose name I don't know; and the lawyer, who was James Certes of Blenkort & Wilson.'

'Quite a long list,' said Richard with audible self-control.

'I know, and I've no basis for including any of the people from the meeting, because I don't see how any of them – even if he left the meeting room for long enough to kill Mrs Allfarthing – could have cleaned himself of all her blood.'

Richard shuddered and Willow leaned across the hard table to touch his hand.

'Sorry,' she said. 'But we've got to hang on to every possibility, however absurd.'

'All right. What can I do?'

'Tell me things. What is the relationship between the Biggleigh-Clarts like?'

Richard pushed his chair back and crossed his legs, laying one ankle across the other knee.

'I suspect it's like most City marriages that have survived a quarter of a century. He has always worked bloody hard and she's had to build her own life around that. They don't see an enormous amount of each other, but from all I've heard when they do meet they're perfectly civilized.'

'It sounds rather bleak. D'you think that there is any foundation to the rumours of Biggles's infatuation with Sarah Allfarthing?'

Richard put his hands in his pockets and pushed his chair on to its back legs.

'You'll break your coccyx if you tip the chair right over,' said Willow, sounding like a nanny.

Richard grinned briefly. For once he looked as though he might be thinking of Sarah without seeing her mutilated body.

'He thought she was gorgeous and interesting – and funny, too. And so she was.' There was nostalgic sadness in Richard's eyes and in his voice. 'She was utterly different from Clara, and interested in the things that interest Biggles. Yes, I suspect he did think she was marvellous. Whether they had actually had an affair, I don't know. I think it's unlikely that she'd have wanted it even if he did, but . . .'

'Did they have any opportunities for making love?' asked Willow when it became clear that Richard was not going to finish his sentence.

'I'd have thought they had plenty. He sometimes whisked her off for expensive lunches from which they did not re-emerge until late afternoon. And occasionally they would be visiting the same clients in Europe or America at the same time. Hotel rooms and all that. But, you know, the more I think about it, the less I can see Sarah sneaking off for an illicit bonk with anyone, let alone Biggles.'

'Some people are rather less complimentary about her than you,' said Willow slowly.

'Does that make you suspicious of me or her?'

Willow shook her head and shrugged. After what they had just been through she was determined to keep any remaining doubts to herself.

'I liked her,' said Richard, sounding helpless. 'But it's true that there were people who didn't find her spell as compelling as I did. Stedington was one. He thought she was pushy and he found her jokes tiresome. Or perhaps Clara persuaded him into saying so. She has a lot of influence over him.'

'What sort of jokes? Practical? Smutty?'

'Don't be idiotic.'

Willow was glad to see that Richard was fast regaining his normal confidence and the automatic rejection of her suggestion, which would once have infuriated her, made her smile.

'Neither of those. She just added a spice of fun to the most ordinary transactions. If she wanted to twist someone's arm for a favour she'd pretend she knew something discreditable, and –'

'That doesn't sound particularly charming,' said Willow, remembering that Jeremy Stedington had said much the same.

'Don't be sour, Willow. You're deliberately misunderstanding. It was a joke.'

'Sophisticated stuff!' said Willow in derision.

'You wouldn't understand unless you'd been there. It was the kind of banter that makes people grin and stops the working day seem too long and boring. Most successful people have their own technique: that was hers.'

'I see. Richard?'

'Yes,' he said, letting his chair settle back on all four legs.

The sound of them hitting the hard floor echoed round the room and reminded Willow of her fading headache.

'The police are of the opinion that you were jealous of Sarah's success and afraid that she would soon overtake you.'

Richard laughed. 'Come on, Willow. You know better than that. She was a good two years older than I am. She had only recently got her first foot on the ladder and I've been an assistant director for years. I have faithful clients in all sorts of worlds; she was always terrified of being marginalized and relied pretty heavily on James Certes's recommendations.'

'Well, that's something, then. Good. I'll tell Roylandson.'

While she made a note, Richard asked her what else she wanted to know.

'Who do you think might have done it?' she asked for the second time and watched Richard's face whiten.

'That's an impossible question.'

'Difficult but not impossible. You know all these people. You must have thought about which of them could have done it.'

'I suppose . . .' His voice faltered. 'No, it's unlikely to have been the client, whoever he was. I suppose . . .'

'Come on, Richard. Loyalty and finer feelings are all very well, but if we're to get you out of here, I need to know everything you can tell me.'

'I suppose,' said Richard with reluctance, as though the words were being dragged out of him, 'that the most likely, or rather the least unlikely, is Beeking. You're right. I have been thinking about it, over and over again. He's the only one who's ever seemed at all weird, and there's no doubt that his feelings for Sarah were intense – and exceedingly possessive.'

His skin took on a grey tinge.

'It's a detestable thought and you mustn't . . . don't go accusing him.'

'I'm not that foolish. But I must talk to him and find out if he could have left the meeting for any reason and if he kept a change of clothes in the office.'

Richard nodded and his hands went to his collar as though to straighten his tie, but he wasn't wearing one. Willow remembered all the newspaper accounts she had read of men hanging themselves in prison.

'You must keep yourself together while we search out what really happened that night,' she said urgently. 'Emma and Roylandson and I are all working on it. We will get there, but it's taking time.'

'How is little Emma?' he asked, his eyes and his voice softening.

'Desperately anxious for you. She'd send her love if she dared.'

'Will you send mine to her?'

'Yes. But will you answer me one more question?'

Richard straightened his shoulders and controlled his mouth. 'Fire away.'

'I've been thinking about what everyone's told me about Sarah and there seems to be a discrepancy. Her husband suggested that she worked the same sort of appalling hours that you've always worked, and yet Jeremy said that one of the reasons why Sarah wasn't one of the boys was because she refused to work so hard. Could she have had a lover outside the bank, d'you suppose?'

Richard's expression sharpened. He looked interested, alert and suddenly hopeful.

'I suppose it's possible and it's certainly true that she used to knock off pretty early some evenings. If it is true it could widen the field a bit, couldn't it?'

'Yes, I think it could.'

'She could have asked him to meet her at the bank, knowing that everyone else would be at the dance,' said Richard. 'I suppose if she were really besotted, she might even have given him the number of the doors. Willow, you're brilliant.'

'Don't get too excited, Richard. It's only a guess, but I'll look into it. Now, just one more thing: when you first saw Sarah's body, where were the roses?'

'Roses? God knows. Why?'

'I know that you were concentrating on her body,' said Willow, ignoring his question, 'but it is important.'

Richard's eyelids closed and after a while he shook his head.

'I can't be absolutely certain. I can see them in my mind's eye all mashed and bloody all over the floor, but whether that was then or while the police were milling about accusing me of things, I don't know.'

Willow smiled. 'So it is just possible that they might have been knocked over while you were wrestling with her body?'

'I suppose it's possible,' he said, 'but I can't be sure.' His eyes suddenly sharpened. 'You mean that if I knocked them over then it could have been their water that got into the keyboard and not the blood at all.'

'Exactly. Obviously some blood got in – everyone could see it – but the damage could have been done by the water.' There was both triumph and relief in Willow's smile. 'And it is only the damage to the computer that gave the police their supposedly accurate time of death.'

'But the difficulty is,' said Richard sadly, 'that I can't swear to spilling the bloody roses.'

'Pity. But if you do remember, will you tell Roylandson?'

Richard promised and they both stood up. He gripped her hands when she kissed him goodbye and she felt almost like the mother of an eight-year-old prep-school boy leaving him alone at the beginning of his first term.

'Richard, I . . .' she began and then stopped.

'I know,' he said. 'You want to take me out of here. But I know that you're doing all anyone could and, believe me, I'm grateful.'

'Good. You will –'

'I'll keep myself together,' he said, 'and now you'd better

whizz off while my upper lip is still reasonably stiff. Be careful, won't you? I mean, be careful of Beeking.'

Willow nodded and went to knock on the heavy door. The warder let her out and, mindful of the upper lip, she left without looking back at Richard again.

She felt too worn out to tackle Beeking then, so she took a taxi straight back to her flat and salved her conscience by fetching the sheaf of horrible photographs of Sarah's corpse. Taking a powerful magnifying glass, Willow studied each one in an attempt to find something that would help. The minuteness of her search took some of her attention away from the horror, but more than enough remained to make her feel as though her mind and her stomach were being forced through some disgusting churning process.

Eventually, when she could not bear it any longer, she went to the kitchen to report to Mrs Rusham that Richard was delighted with the hampers she was sending to the prison.

To her astonishment, there were tears in the housekeeper's fierce eyes. Willow decided to forgive her for her alliance with Emma Gnatche.

'How is he?' asked the housekeeper.

'Not too bad considering his anxieties and the fact that he's in prison. He's stopped panicking and he looks quite healthy again.'

'Thank you,' Mrs Rusham murmured and then added with remarkable viciousness: 'I'd like to flog whoever's done this to him.'

'What about some tea?' asked Willow, unable to cope with the power of her housekeeper's emotions.

Mrs Rusham recovered herself and promised to bring a tray to the drawing room. 'I've put your post in there already.'

Willow went to slip out of her shoes and lie full-length along one of the sofas with the pile of letters beside her. There was one from Eve Greville saying that Cressida's various publishers had all expressed modified rapture about the dressmaker's romance, though the Americans had pleaded for the heroic young doctor to be doing some kind of relief work in Central or South America. The letter ended:

It is really important that you deliver on time: not simply for contractual reasons but so that the book does not miss the Christmas market next year. You've built up your success steadily and part of the reason has been your steadfast production of a book a year. If your publishers don't think they are going to get next year's book in time they'll be reluctant to give you the full treatment this autumn. Their plans for *Simon's Simples* are lavish and there are only six weeks until publication. Don't risk it!

Willow shrugged and tossed the letter on to the floor as the first in the heap for filing. She knew that Eve was right, and she would be furious if her publishers did not market her new book properly, but until Richard was free she could not concentrate on anything else. The next letter she picked up was from her accountant and it brought her off the sofa at once.

Cursing herself for forgetting to pursue the few facts she had of Sarah Allfarthing's last few weeks, Willow was about to telephone her accountant to ask him about the fraud story Sarah had told Richard's American clients with such disastrous consequences when Mrs Rusham brought in the tea tray. Postponing her enquiries for a while, Willow returned to her sofa for tea and crustless tomato-and-basil sandwiches. As she ate and drank, she opened the rest of her post.

None of it was particularly interesting – a mixture of bills, requests for details of her life and work for various international directories of writers, and a few fan letters – but the sandwiches were wonderful. At the bottom of the pile of letters was a plastic-wrapped catalogue of ingenious machines and bits and pieces. She had once ordered a tiny vacuum cleaner for the keyboard of her word processor from one such catalogue and ever since had been bombarded with them.

They had lost their early charm for her but even so she flicked through the pages while she drank her second cup of tea, wondering whether she could possibly need sixty paintbrushes or even a karaoke set. Deciding that she did not, she turned the page and came upon the description of a mackintosh made of thin plastic that could be wrapped up into a packet six inches by four. Staring down at it, she thought to herself: so that is how a shortish man or woman could prevent the spurting blood from Sarah's cut throat from marking his or her clothes. If one of the men from Stedington's meeting had had such a mackintosh then he might have been able to leave the meeting, kill her and return with no sign of blood about him.

Remembering her promise to give Emma Gnatche something useful to do, Willow finished her tea and went to sit at the mahogany Pembroke table in the window. She telephoned her accountant first and after some persuasion made him agree to investigate Sarah Allfarthing's fraud story and discover whether it had any factual basis at all. When he had made her agree in turn to check her annual accounts and return them quickly, Willow rang off and tapped in the number of Emma Gnatche's small Kensington house.

Emma sounded delighted to be asked to do anything and at once agreed to get hold of one of the foldable mackintoshes so that they could experiment with it.

'I'll bring it round as soon as I've got it,' she said. 'How was Richard when you saw him? Mrs R. said you'd be going this afternoon.'

'He was much better,' said Willow, adding: 'And he asked me to send you his love. I'll tell you all the news when we meet. Goodbye.'

'Bye, Cressida. Thank you.'

Willow replaced the receiver and got up, but the thought

of Tom kept her standing with one hand on the telephone. She did not like interrupting him at work unless she had no choice, but at last the memory of the agonized night she had spent alone in the flat sapped her willpower and she tapped in the number of his office. She soon discovered that he was not at his desk and when she tried to ring his flat she heard only his recorded voice.

'Well,' said Willow, staring at the unresponsive telephone, 'I suppose he's left me with my pride intact.'

It was cold comfort.

Chapter 14

WILLOW had a better night's sleep, disturbed by nothing worse than anxiety dreams, and woke soon after six o'clock to mull over her long talk with Richard. It was clear that she ought to tackle William Beeking as soon as possible. Knowing from Tracy that he usually ate his breakfast in the bank's canteen, Willow decided to join him there. She did not want to be alone with him in case Richard's reluctant suspicions were correct, but the canteen seemed likely to be safe.

She left a note for Mrs Rusham, left the flat at five past seven and made her way to the bank. Even at that early hour the underground was full and as stuffy as an unventilated basement laundry. Eventually the train stopped at Monument and she got out with hordes of others.

Bert greeted her at the door of the bank with a cheery wave that made her feel almost at home there. She took the lift up to the canteen on the fourteenth floor and was agreeably surprised to find a civilized dining room with the same spectacular views down to the river that she had seen from the chief executive's office. The word 'canteen' had always conjured up a picture of rickety card tables set up in a village hall, but the bank's was different.

White-clothed tables for four were ranged around the three glass walls, while bigger round tables stood in the middle of the room. There was a tactful amount of space between each of the tables and plenty of evergreen plants to break up the room and provide a sensation of privacy. A long serving counter filled the fourth wall, and waitresses bustled among the tables removing debris and replacing the tablecloths and napkins.

Willow collected a tray and chose a modest breakfast of fruit, coffee and rolls from the wide selection, paid and turned with the tray in her hands to see if there were any sign of Mr Beeking. She found him quite quickly, reading his *Financial Times* and tucking into bacon, eggs, sausages, tomatoes and kidneys. She walked slowly over to his table and said:

'Would you mind awfully if I joined you? I hate eating alone or with complete strangers.'

'Not at all,' he said, politely folding up his newspaper.

Willow set down her tray and murmured: 'Do please go on with the paper. I never meant to disturb you.'

Beeking smiled. He had a pleasantly tanned face with a rounded chin and grey-green eyes. His blond hair was thick and lay in fat waves over his head. She had accepted the general view that Sarah had disliked his attentions, but it occurred to Willow as she watched him rearranging his crockery to accommodate hers that he did have charm. It was even possible that Sarah might have enjoyed his company: unlikely but possible.

'Actually,' said Beeking, 'I'm rather glad of the opportunity of having a discreet word with you out of the department.'

'Really?'

'I don't know how much weight your report is going to carry, but I do think that one of the most crucial areas of training is that of the support staff.'

'Oh, I quite agree,' said Willow, smiling encouragingly at him as she began to spoon up her grapefruit. His voice did not quite fit the boyishness of his looks. There was a slightly resentful edge to it that grated on Willow's ear.

'Our secretaries – even the relatively efficient ones like Maggie Blake – are poor at managing their time and distinguishing between the relative urgency of the tasks in front of them.'

'I see,' said Willow a little coldly. 'I thought you meant training them so that they could take on more of an executive role.'

'What? Heavens above! That sort of thing doesn't happen in banking. They wouldn't want it in any case. They're Essex girls, after all.' He plunged his fork into a plump kidney at the edge of his plate and the blood from its pink interior spurted up through the holes he had made and out on to the glistening yolk of his fried egg. Suddenly queasy, Willow looked away.

'I gather that Tracy is leaving,' she said in order to keep the conversation open.

'Ah, yes. But that's because . . . that was engineered.'

'I don't understand.'

'She used to do most of her work for a colleague . . . er, Sarah Allfarthing.' He looked across the table to Willow with a questioning expression.

She thought of looking surprised but realized in time that ignorance would not be at all convincing. Beeking must have known that his colleagues would have been passing on gossip about the dead woman and, besides, there had been reports of Sarah's death in all the newspapers.

'Yes, I have heard what happened to her,' said Willow. 'I understand that you and she were particularly close friends. I'm so sorry.'

His blond head drooped over his breakfast for a moment but then he looked up with what seemed to be a consciously brave smile.

'I tried to shield her a bit; that's all. Whatever you may have heard.'

'Shield her?' Willow put down her spoon and pushed aside the empty grapefruit skin. It was interesting that all the men who were reputed to have loved Sarah Allfarthing were trying to play down their feelings. 'Shield her from what?'

'I don't know how much you've heard about the way she was treated here,' Beeking began. Willow wished that she had a portable and concealable lie detector so that she could distinguish between the contradictory stories to which she had to listen each day.

'I've heard that she was much liked – and successful.'

'But at a terrible cost to herself,' said Beeking. He pushed his fork into the yolk of the egg and it collapsed to mingle with the spilled blood from the kidney. As Willow watched him, she saw the corners of his mouth turn down. He swallowed, looked away and signalled to one of the waitresses.

'Could you take this away?' he asked when she arrived.

'Yes, of course. Aren't you well, Mr Beeking?' she asked in a soft Southern Irish accent. 'Or was there something wrong with your breakfast?'

'I'm fine, Maeve,' he said with another brave smile. 'Just not very hungry today.'

When she had gone he turned back to Willow.

'She's very sweet but a little oppressive in her concern. She monitors my eating habits and tells me when I look tired. Touching though it is, it can become wearing.'

'She seems to know you well.'

He shrugged. 'I come in here for breakfast most days.'

'You were telling me about Mrs Allfarthing,' said Willow as she noticed that he had been distracted by the kindly waitress. He stopped staring after her and turned back to Willow. 'You said that her success was achieved only with difficulty.'

'Well, she was a woman in a man's world. She had to

suppress all her natural inclinations towards gentleness and quietness – and she hated it.'

There were few things that made Willow angrier than the assumption that women were born patient and gentle and self-denying. She wanted to give Beeking a short lecture on gender and sexism, but since it was important to keep him on her side she confined herself to a simple question.

'How do you know that?'

'You could see it,' he said with a pitying smile. 'Watching her in meetings and around the office, I could always see when she was trying to screw herself up to be tough. She found all direct confrontation difficult and would much rather use her wits to avoid it. I used to see her sometimes literally shaking after she'd had to talk to difficult clients on the telephone. The others never noticed. They were completely taken in by her patina of confidence.'

'You clearly knew her well.' Willow poured herself a cup of coffee and buttered one of her rolls.

'Yes,' said Beeking quietly. 'I think I knew her better than anyone else here.'

'That sounds almost as though you must know who killed her,' said Willow without thinking.

Beeking looked at her as though she were demented. 'Everyone knows. The man has been arrested.'

Willow shrugged and managed to look disinterested. 'Oh,' she said. 'I'd heard that one or two people don't believe he could have done it.'

'You shouldn't listen to uninformed gossip. I'm perfectly certain that he did. If only . . .'

'What?'

'If only I'd waited for her that night,' he said. For the first time since they had been talking he looked genuinely distressed. 'I'd asked her if I couldn't take her to the dance as soon as I could get out of a meeting I had to attend, but she said she had something important to ask Richard and would wait for him.'

Shocked, Willow just stared at Beeking. He seemed puzzled, but after a moment his eyes cleared.

'Richard Crescent, the bugger who did it.'

'Oh, I see,' said Willow. It was a feeble comment, but it was enough to satisfy Beeking. 'I don't understand, though, did you go straight to the dance from your meeting?'

'Yes. Why?'

'It's silly, I know,' said Willow shaking her head, 'but I just remember Tracy's telling me that the party was black tie. Surely you weren't wearing a dinner jacket in your meeting?'

'Heavens, no,' said Beeking with a laugh. 'No. Stedington and I decided since we were so late that we simply hadn't time to go home and change. We went as we were.'

'Oh, I see. You hadn't brought evening clothes to the office?'

He shook his head. 'Only people like Sarah who lived out in the sticks did that.'

There were a lot more questions that Willow wanted to ask, but she did not want to risk arousing any suspicions of her motives and so she turned the conversation back to the training of secretaries and heard yet more stories of Tracy's incompetence.

Beeking eventually swallowed the last of his toast and drained his coffee cup.

'I must go, but this has been a useful meeting. I'd like to see a copy of your report; perhaps it would help if I went through the draft with you.'

Willow raised her eyebrows.

'That's a charming offer,' she said with patent insincerity, 'but our practice is to show the reports only to those who commission them. I'm sure a copy will reach you in due course. Thank you for your suggestions.'

He strode out of the room and there was a tightness about his shoulders and his legs that suggested he was angry. Willow watched him stop for a moment by the door and say something to Maeve that made her smile and blush.

Willow slowly ate the rest of her rolls, bought herself a second pot of coffee and drank it as she stared out of the window towards the river. Beeking was one of the few people she had met – apart from the police – who appeared to be convinced of Richard's guilt. He was also the only person apart from Clara Biggleigh-Clart whom she would willingly have suspected, and he seemed the likelier murderer of the two.

Taking the lift back to the Corporate Finance floor, Willow considered Beeking. It was possible that all his unattractive habits might have had their origin in his lowly position within the department. His patronage of the waitress, his contempt for the secretaries, his constituting himself as Sarah's possibly unwanted champion, and even his ready acceptance of Richard's guilt might all have been tools to shore up his subsiding self-esteem.

On the other hand, Willow thought as she walked out of the lift and rang the bell at the doors of the Corporate Finance Department, many of his characteristics fitted the basic profile of a certain type of murderer. It was only a few months since she had read most of the latest works on serial killers. The fear that had kept her from sleeping properly returned with full force.

The doors began to move in front of her and Beeking stood there with his charming smile in place.

'Thank you,' said Willow, unclamping her teeth. 'I'm sorry to have disturbed you again.'

'We're all alone,' he said, still smiling. 'The others rarely get here as early as this.' He was standing with one hand on the right half of the double doors, blocking her way.

'What a good opportunity to get some work done in peace,' she said, forcing herself forwards. He moved just enough for her to pass without touching him. 'How you all manage to concentrate with telephones ringing and people talking all round you, I can't think.'

She set off towards her own desk and felt him following her.

'Are you sure I can't help with your report?' he said, leaning over the back of her chair.

'No, no. Really. Thank you. I must get on.' He did not move away from the chair and Willow could not force herself to sit in it while he had his hands on the back of it. The thought of Sarah's death filled her mind. Beeking's hands were very white and a little pudgy. Had one of them twisted in Sarah's long, dark hair and forced back her head while the other drew a knife across her throat?

'Are you all right? You look awfully pale.'

At the sound of his voice, Willow brushed a hand across her forehead and wiped away the sweat. She swallowed, feeling her Adam's apple swelling and blocking her wind-pipe.

The electronically locked doors parted with their usual squeak and Willow heard the sound of two pairs of heavy shoes thudding over the carpet. Her throat unblocked itself and she began to breathe again.

'I think I must have swallowed a crumb at breakfast,' she said. 'My throat doesn't feel right at all.'

'Poor you,' said Beeking, relaxing his hands on the chair back. 'I'll fetch you a glass of water. Sit down and rest.'

Vowing that she would never drink anything he produced, Willow swallowed again and nodded. He disappeared and she sat down, her head balanced on her right hand, wondering whether she ought to pass her suspicions of Beeking on to Jane Moreby. The young banker who had the carrel next to Willow's gave her a cheerful greeting as he whisked his chair out with one foot and slung his briefcase on his desk.

A moment later his jacket was adorning the back of his chair, he had switched on his screen and was settling down to work. Willow waited for Beeking and his glass of water. When it came she thanked him with as much politeness as she could summon up and waited until he had disappeared before pouring the water into the nearest huge, fan-leaved castor-oil plant.

It was some time before she could make herself start her own work, but eventually the possibility that she had made Beeking suspicious forced her to switch on her computer and type in her password in case anyone had sent her confidential messages. There was one from the chief executive himself.

I warned you [Willow read] that I would stop you at once if I felt you were exceeding your brief. I have to say that I think your interrogation of my wife was outrageous and underhand. If you wanted to talk to her it would have been more honest – not to speak of more polite – if you had asked me to arrange it.

I have considered terminating our agreement, but am prepared to extend it provided that I have your assurance that there will be no more similar escapades. If you wish to speak to anyone not in the bank's employment, you must consult me or Stedington first.

Please give me your assurance by return.

Willow read the message twice before she was prepared to concede that Biggles might have a point. It would have been much simpler – as well as more economical – to have asked him to fix a meeting for her. Wondering whether she was addicted to secrecy for its own sake, Willow typed in a message of apology and sent it off. That done, she called up on to the screen the notes she had made about the bank's training needs.

Telling herself that she was in no danger at all unless she was stupid enough to allow herself to be alone with any of her suspects again, Willow worked for the rest of the morning. She read through those of the completed questionnaires that had been returned to her to design a series of lectures, workshops, role-playing exercises and study papers for the various levels of staff in the Corporate Finance Department.

In between tapping her suggestions into the keyboard

she kept thinking of Sarah Allfarthing and the possibility that she might have a lover outside the bank.

About to write down all that she had been told so that she could work out where to go in search of proof, Willow caught a glimpse of the man on her right swinging his legs up on his desk and turning to grin at her. She smiled back and pushed her chair back so that she could ask about his views of the bank's training needs as a prelude to getting his views on the dead woman's character.

He had been on one negotiating course already, he told her, and had plenty to say about its failings, but he was less articulate about the kind of training he thought might be useful. After some tactful probing Willow realized that he found it hard to admit to any lack in himself or his competence, so she asked him to tell her about the difficulties that the most junior staff had when they first joined the department. That seemed to be easier and he gave her some quite useful information.

When she asked him about Sarah Allfarthing, she was surprised to see a wide smile spreading across his face.

'She was lovely,' he said just as the telephone on Willow's desk began to ring. 'It was the vilest thing . . . quite incomprehensible. I say, hadn't you better answer that? It might be Biggles.'

Willow picked up the receiver and heard one of the receptionists telling her that James Certes was awaiting her in the lobby.

'I must go,' she said to the young banker, 'but it's been very useful talking to you. Perhaps we could continue later?'

'Delighted – unless a deal gets in the way.'

'That reminds me,' said Willow as she got up and picked up her linen jacket. 'How are deals allocated? It seems to me that some of you get far more than your fair share of the work.'

'Chance, really, I suppose. And how we've performed before. And whether the client has asked for us. Or,' he added with a humorous grimace, 'whether the client has particularly asked not to have us.'

'Do you think that the system could be improved?'

'I'm sure it could be.'

'Then do you think you could give me a rundown of the criteria that are used now and the ones that you think would be more useful? That would be a great help.'

'Sure,' he said, looking a bit surprised. Willow reminded herself that she was a training, not a management, consultant and left him. As she waited for the lift, she tried to remember what it was that she had wanted to ask James Certes, but the effect of her encounters with William Beeking seemed to have removed her capacity to think sensibly about anything except the safe anodyne of her cover job. At least, she told herself bracingly, that might help to convince Certes.

He got out of the dark-red bucket chair as she eventually emerged from a lift full of chattering people and stood, hand outstretched. Willow walked forwards, thinking again how unlike a City solicitor he looked with his delicate face and his fashionable suit. As they met, she shook his hand, and pushed the memory of William Beeking's very different hands out of her mind.

'Where would you like to eat?' Willow asked. 'I haven't booked anywhere, but as it's quite early we ought not to have difficulty getting a table.'

'There's a champagne bar round the corner where I sometimes used to go with poor Sarah Allfarthing,' he said. 'It's pleasant and quick.'

'Fine. Lead on.'

They walked abreast, falling into single file when builders' scaffolding or other pedestrians demanded it, making stilted conversation when they could, and it was not until they were sitting side by side in the cool dimness of the bar watching a waiter open a remarkably expensive bottle of champagne that Certes asked Willow how he could help her.

The cork eased itself out of the dark-green neck of the

bottle, hardly assisted at all by the waiter's deft fingers, and the wine hissed as it rose.

'Yes, that's fine,' said Certes as he tasted it.

Willow thought that since it was she who was paying for the lunch and she who had selected the champagne, it ought to be she who tasted it.

'Not bad,' she said when she eventually had the chance. She was tempted to go through the whole performance of looking, smelling and rinsing her teeth with the wine, but she resisted.

'I was hoping,' she went on with a sweet smile, 'that you could tell me something about the performance of the bank's corporate financiers from the point of view of your clients. I have interviewed almost everyone within the department and have a fairly clear idea of what needs to be done; your views would be very helpful.'

Certes laughed and held his glass up to the light, watching the bubbles rise and bounce as they hit the surface.

'From the clients' point of view they should be quicker, cheaper, less prone to error, vanity and other human defects.'

'Naturally,' said Willow, managing to laugh with him. 'I suspect that the same could be said of anyone in any field of expertise – even the law, perhaps. Have you never made a mistake? Not even a teeny-weeny one?'

'That sounds unnecessarily frivolous,' said Certes as repressively as though he had suddenly lost his sense of humour.

'Sorry.' Willow was surprised but determined to be polite. 'They all carry on at the bank as though life was a tremendous joke and I seem to have caught the habit.'

'Well, they oughtn't to. A most remarkable woman was killed there and they should bloody well show a bit more respect.'

'I think they're using frivolity as a way to deal with the horror of what happened to her. They all speak of her with tremendous respect – and affection.'

Certes drank a large mouthful of champagne. When it had gone down his throat he apologized.

'I suppose it's because I hold them all responsible,' he said with a paradoxically sweet smile, 'that I get so worked up.'

'Responsible? How?'

Certes shrugged and Willow saw the end of his real shoulders at least three inches inside the line of the shoulderpads in his jacket.

'They gave her a very hard time when she first went there and because of it made her into something they couldn't handle. Richard Crescent may have killed her, but it could have been almost any of them.'

'I find that almost impossible to believe,' said Willow, staring down at the rising bubbles in her glass. 'There are women in merchant banks all over London and none of them has been killed. Why should Sarah Allfarthing have been any different?'

She looked up and saw the beautiful eyes narrow into almond shapes.

'They hated Biggleigh-Clart for forcing her on them and then hated themselves for falling under her spell; and so they took it out on her. If she hadn't been the only woman or if she'd been less alluring and unattainable, things might have been different.' He drank some more champagne and drew one of the two menus towards him. 'Why are you so interested?'

'Who wouldn't be?' said Willow, reaching for the other menu. 'It's not prurience – at least I hope not – but I've been sitting there at her desk day after day, surrounded by people who talk about her, and I haven't been able to ignore it. I don't think anyone would be able to dismiss it. I've been feeling . . . well, a lot of sympathy for her.'

'I think you'd have liked her,' said Certes, looking at Willow over the top of his menu. She was surprised and showed it.

'You've something of the same mixture of glamour and

toughness,' he said, adding slowly: 'however hard you try to hide it.'

Willow tried to concentrate on the menu and ignore the suggestion implicit in what he had just said. Eventually she chose another mixed smoked-fish salad and hoped that it would be better than the one she had had in the cocktail bar.

'By the way,' she said when the waiter had taken their order, 'before we get down to business, will you tell me one more thing about the dead woman?'

There was a pause.

'Why not?'

'It's just that I've been wondering how she managed to persuade you to offer a job to that tiresome secretary in her department.' Willow had the impression that she had given Certes a shock, but he smiled encouragingly and so she went on: 'Mrs Allfarthing must have told you about the things the girl does: the confidential letters sent out in the wrong envelopes, the mislaid telephone messages, and all the rest.'

Certes's smile became impish and he suddenly looked very pleased with himself.

'Oh, she did. Poor Sarah: that girl was one of the many crosses she had to bear at the bank; and it was almost the only one I could do anything about. It was my idea.'

'Your idea?'

'Yes. Oh, good, here's the food.'

The waiter laid down two plates of well-arranged salad, each with generous slices of smoked salmon, eel and halibut. Willow was relieved that her judgement had not deserted her. When the waiter offered them horseradish sauce, she saw that it was the authentic version of whipped cream into which fresh horseradish root had been grated.

'You were going to tell me about your idea,' Willow said as soon as the waiter had gone. Certes laughed. It was a pleasant sound and Willow could not help smiling at him.

'You've Sarah's tenacity, too. The two of you would have got on well. It was a day rather like this. We were lunching and I could see that she was almost beside herself with rage. I asked why and eventually she told me about something Tracy had done that was catastrophically crass even for her.

'I exploded. It was obvious that she should be sacked. Sarah said bitterly that she had tried to get her out but that Tracy had been there too long for it to be possible without going through all the performance of giving her three written warnings and monitoring her performance and explaining exactly where she fell short. No one Sarah talked to was prepared to bite the bullet and go through with it and she could not do it on her own.'

'And so you offered her a job? Knowing –'

'Wake up, Miss King,' he said, taking a huge bite of smoked eel. Willow had to wait while he chewed and swallowed. 'At Blenkort & Wilson she'd be on probation; we could throw her out at no notice the moment she did anything wrong at all. And it was quite safe; from all Sarah had said over the years I knew that Tracy would do something wrong within a few days. All it would cost us would be her salary for a few weeks. Cheap, really, as part of practice development.'

'I beg your pardon?'

'Practice development. If we made Sarah properly grateful, she'd recommend us to clients of hers who needed lawyers. Simple.'

Battling with her distaste for the story and a rather large bone that had got left in the smoked eel, Willow asked whether Sarah Allfarthing had accepted the plan at once.

'Oh, no,' said Certes, picking the champagne bottle, dripping, out of the ice bucket at his side and refilling both their glasses. He grinned. 'She was far too straight. But I brought her round in the end. I owed it to her.'

'Really? Why was that?'

'She'd done a lot for me one way and another,' said Certes, drinking some more champagne. When he had put his glass down again, he looked at Willow with what appeared to be insincere and rather unpleasant self-deprecation. 'There was one particular occasion when she and I were both at the same dinner: rather an important one at the Biggleigh-Clarts'. I'd been mad enough to take a girlfriend who was . . . well, not as discreet as she might have been. She drank too much and started making the most appalling remarks. It was thoroughly difficult and the more I tried to intervene, the worse it got.'

He fell silent, staring down into his glass. Willow waited, wondering why she should feel such complete lack of sympathy for him.

'And then Sarah took a hand,' he said at last. 'How she did it I still don't know, but she managed to save the whole evening. She took the creature in hand, talked to her, took her away to the loo and calmed her down. She was like that, you see: efficient and kind. I owed her a lot.'

'Was that why you helped to find her clients?' asked Willow.

Certes sat quite still, a puzzled frown on his face.

'They all say how much you helped her career at the bank,' Willow went on, trying to think what could be so worrying about her question.

'Do they? Ah, well. Yes, it was partly that.'

Something in the acute way he was looking at her suggested to Willow that it was time to turn the conversation back to her cover job and she asked Certes what the bankers lacked in the way of skills and management techniques. As she listened to his answer and went on to ask more questions, Willow found herself impressed with his intelligence and perceptiveness but still repelled by him. Mrs Zelland had said that he was enormously creative, but Willow preferred Jeremy Stedington's description of him as brilliant but slippery – and a shit.

The story of Tracy's new job seemed typical of him: very clever and quite ruthless. It also seemed fundamentally cruel and Willow could not believe that the Sarah Allfarthing for whom Richard had such affection, could have agreed to it. As she acknowledged the discrepancy, Willow felt a clenching in her guts. Richard's affection might well have blinded him to the side of Sarah that Clara and Jeremy Stedington disliked, but it was just possible that his apparent affection was merely a cloak for some quite different emotion.

Losing interest in James Certes, Willow finished her lunch. She walked back to the bank with her mind in a muddle of fear and renewed suspicion. All the vivid impressions her imagination offered seemed to quarrel with the few facts she had, each of which seemed to become shadowy whenever she tried to use it.

She wished that she had been able to talk about it all to Tom, but he had not yet returned her last telephone call. She told herself that he was probably very busy, but she knew that he might also be awkwardly torn between his loyalties to her and to his colleagues.

There had been plenty of times when Willow had been reluctant to see Tom, but, unreasonably, she hated the thought that he might be loath to see her.

Chapter 15

WHEN Willow returned to her desk in the Corporate Finance Department, the carrel to the right of hers was empty, but the young banker had left her a note:

Dear Miss King,
I have been thinking about your suggestion for allocating deals more sensibly and I can't after all produce any useful advice. Until all of us are equally successful and effective, the directors and team leaders will always want the best. The best will always be the busiest and will only turn down a deal if they absolutely have to. Thus the natural order means that the best will always be working slightly below par because they have too much to do and the less good will get less experience because they're less in demand. I can't see any way round it. Sorry.
Yours (off to Milan on a big one),
C.P.

Without planning to, Willow looked along the row of dark-red screens to Bill Beeking's desk and saw the back of his curly fair head bent conscientiously over his work. 'Less in demand indeed,' she muttered to herself as she packed her papers away in her briefcase and switched off her computer.

She left the department by way of Jeremy Stedington's office. He did not look particularly pleased to see her and snapped:

'Is this necessary? I'm extremely busy.'

'Yes,' she said, undeterred. Having checked to see that there was no one in the corridor behind her, she asked her question: 'I know you don't want to tell me, but I need to know who the client was at your meeting on the night of the murder.'

'For Christ's sake! What difference can it possibly make now?'

Willow said nothing.

'I suppose you'll stand there, clogging up my office, until I tell you,' said Stedington bitterly. 'It was Ronald Hopecastle. Don't pass that on.'

'Why not?' asked Willow, diverted.

'None of your business. Now leave me alone.'

'Please may I ask just one more question?'

'Bloody hell! Oh, all right, but be quick.'

'Can you tell me whether anyone left your meeting on the night Sarah died?'

'Definitely. Probably each of us left at one time or another. Why?'

'I just need to know if anyone had a chance to telephone out of the bank,' said Willow, hastily thinking up an innocuous excuse.

'Several,' he said again, looking irritated. 'I left to shout at that idiot Tracy for sending down the wrong papers. Beeking nipped out at least three times to fetch things or photostat or telephone after the secretaries had gone. Yes, he definitely made at least one call for me and could have rung someone else. The client went to wash at least once - and so did Certes.'

There was a slight sound of amusement that banished the impatience from his rich voice.

'What was funny about Certes's absence?' asked Willow.

'Poor bugger'd eaten an iffy take-away the night before after a meeting with some of our rivals, and he had to run to the bog several times.'

'I see,' said Willow, wishing that he had told her that only one of them had left. 'Thank you, Jeremy. There's just one more thing . . .'

'Not now,' he said, really angry. 'I'm expecting a conference call at any minute. They're bloody difficult to concentrate on even when they're entirely within this country and there's no damn fool woman asking idiotic questions. This one is between me, a Frenchman in Tokyo, an American in Atlanta and a Japanese in San Francisco. I need –' His telephone rang. 'Get out!' he said to Willow and she obeyed.

She carefully walked down the window side of the department on her way out so that she did not have to go anywhere near Bill Beeking. As she passed Richard's empty desk, she saw Tracy arguing with the man who sat on his right. Hurrying to the secretarial workstation, she said quietly:

'Maggie?'

The girl looked up. Her eyes were clearer than they had been at the beginning of the week and her smile seemed a little less unhappy.

'Yes? Can I help?'

'You were fond of Mrs Allfarthing, weren't you?' said Willow, still quietly.

'Very,' said Maggie, closing her eyes for a moment.

'She worked hard, didn't she?'

The dark-brown eyes opened and focused on Willow's face.

'Yes, she did, but not like some of them.' Maggie gestured towards the double row of desks. 'She never worked all night unless it was really necessary and she always took all her holidays. She said it was silly to ruin your health for a job. She was so sensible.'

Maggie looked away from Willow. With her head bent

over her keyboard, she started flinging her fingers across it in a maniacal dance. Willow took the hint and left, having got the information she needed.

The tube was a lot less disgusting in the middle of the afternoon than during the rush hours, and she arrived at Chesham Place cooler and more herself than she had expected. She went straight to the kitchen to warn Mrs Rusham that Emma Gnatche would be there for tea and found the big room empty except for an extraordinary mess of what looked like tomato ketchup and olive oil all over the floor. Willow stood in the doorway for a moment, trying to work out what Mrs Rusham could possibly have been doing. For one dreadful moment Willow wondered whether her housekeeper could have given in to the strain of Richard's ordeal and gone mad.

Distracted by a sound from her writing room, Willow went quickly to investigate. When she got there she could not suppress a laugh of extreme relief. Emma Gnatche was sitting in Willow's swivel chair, while Mrs Rusham stood behind her dressed in a plastic mackintosh that reached three inches above her ankles. A brilliantly polished Sabatier steel knife lay on the desk. At the sound of the laughter Mrs Rusham turned, blushing furiously.

Emma swung the chair round.

'Hello, Cressida. I just don't think this would work. Look,' she went on, pulling Mrs Rusham's hand round to the front of her own neck, 'the blood would have spurted forwards and down – which you can see in the photographs – so that it's the hand and cuff that would need protecting most, not the body of the killer. It's gauntlets he'd need, not a mackintosh.'

'I think you're right, Emma. Besides, if anybody came into my office dressed like that on a summer's evening I would ring 999 at once – even if it was someone I knew. Blast!'

'And then there's the difficulty of folding it up again if it was all covered in blood. We did all kinds of experiments in the kitchen, and –'

252

'So I saw,' said Willow drily and then smiled reassuringly as Mrs Rusham, who had been standing in silence, flushed with humiliation or anger.

'I shall fetch your tea, Miss Woodruffe.' She unbuttoned the coat and handed it to Emma, who thanked her enthusiastically.

'It was a relief to be able to do something,' said Mrs Rusham, 'even if it was useless.'

'She's awfully sweet when you get to know her, isn't she?' said Emma when she and Willow were alone again.

Willow patted her shoulder. 'Sweet isn't exactly the word I'd have used of Mrs Rusham, but she's extremely fond of Richard. I always thought she'd never approve of anyone except him, but you seem to have got through all her defences. Well done,' said Willow, trying not to smile at the incongruity of the pair of them flinging tomato paste all over the kitchen. 'I'm sorry about the mac,' she went on. 'It was a poor idea. I ought to have thought of the way the blood would spurt. I hope you didn't have to trail all over London for it.'

'No. It was easy to get hold of it.'

'Good,' said Willow vaguely. Something was teasing the edge of her mind, some idea that kept just out of reach. After a few moments, she added: 'I suppose we ought to go and have that tea. It's not really fair to keep Mrs Rusham waiting. Come on, Emma.'

Willow led the way to the drawing room, cursing her inability to focus on the half-formed idea. There was something she had heard, or seen, that held the key to Sarah's life and Willow could not remember what it was. The sensation was tiresomely familiar: it was like waiting for an orgasm or a sneeze. She could feel it gathering in her brain, she longed for it, and yet she could not bring it to fruition.

Emma became motherly over tea, pouring it out for Willow, urging her to eat more sandwiches and to put her feet up on the sofa. Willow let her do it and then tried to pin down her ideas by putting them into words.

'You see, Emma, there are things they've all said about Sarah Allfarthing that don't ring true. Everyone agrees that she was fun, clever, successful and glamorous. Some of them were in love with her and some of them weren't. Richard says she was never cruel and that her loyalty meant she would do almost anything to avoid hurting someone who cared about her. Beeking says that she hated conflict. Her husband, whom she married when she was eighteen, says she'd changed enormously over the years.'

Willow took a bite of her sandwich and put the rest down on the plate beside her.

'What is it?' asked Emma, watching in fascination.

'It's somewhere in all that. Married at eighteen to a man older than she; now enormously changed. She was, too. When they met she was a trainee with the Inland Revenue; pretty but plump and naive. When she died she was beautiful and sophisticated.'

'Yes?' The fascination in Emma's round blue eyes was dwindling into perplexity.

'She was married for over twenty years to the man who appealed to her when she was young and unaware of what she was really like. Their tastes are now completely different. He told me that. She exercised ferociously . . .'

'Presumably,' said Emma, picking up a sandwich that oozed with mayonnaise, 'to keep herself from getting plump again.'

'Yes,' said Willow, laughing. 'But she bit her nails, too. Doesn't that suggest to you someone trying to distract herself from things she did not want to acknowledge in her own character?'

'You mean that she was tired of him but too kind to tell him so?'

'I think she might have been. Too loyal to want to destroy their marriage and yet too different to feel at home in it any more. He says that she worked terribly hard, took hardly any time for holidays and often had to work overnight in the office.'

'Bankers do have to,' said Emma, licking her fingers. 'Richard and James Montholme often have.'

'And yet one of the secretaries who worked for her says that Sarah Allfarthing always took her full holiday entitlement – which is six weeks – and rarely allowed anyone to make her work all night.'

'You mean she was having an affair after all?' Emma's eyes dilated. 'With Richard?'

Willow shook her head. 'Not with Richard; I'm certain of that at least.'

The mental sneeze was coming closer to the surface. She considered the distance she herself had come from the plain, hard-working northern twenty-one-year-old who had joined the civil service as a trainee and of the things she had craved as she changed.

'No, I don't think it was a lover at all.' Willow sneezed. 'Everyone seems to agree that she wasn't interested in sex. Her husband said so in almost as many words and no one at the bank believes she slept with any of the adorers. I think it was space and solitude she wanted, not more emotional complications.'

'I don't understand,' said Emma.

'I don't think it was another man she went to when her husband thought she was working. I think it was a house. Somewhere away from both London and Essex; a place she could go to be just herself and have a bit of blessed loneliness.'

'Why would she want that?' The astonishment in Emma's voice made Willow laugh. She pushed herself off the squashy clotted-cream-coloured sofa and padded towards the telephone in her bare feet. She looked over her shoulder.

'Various reasons,' she said, not wanting to explain why she believed that she understood the dead woman's needs so well. She rang Martin Roylandson's office and when she had been connected to his extension, she told him her theory.

'Could you find out if it's true? Even if she used a false

name in the place where the house is, presumably somewhere there must be a record of its true ownership.'

'I'm sure there is, but it could take weeks to find it. And if Mrs Allfarthing really wanted to keep it secret, wouldn't she have simply rented it for a while? Then there need be no record of a purchase.'

'What about asking the police to help?' asked Willow, thinking that Roylandson was a lot brighter than she admitted.

'I don't think that would be sensible at this stage,' he said, giving Willow the distinct impression that he would rather not look foolish in their eyes. 'If there were such a house we'd need to know rather more about it before making them a present of whatever evidence it might contain. I'll do my best to find out.'

'Let me know if you do get anything, and I'll see what I can do. There is one person who may be able to help,' said Willow, thinking of Mr Biggleigh-Clart.

'I'm delighted to hear it.' The solicitor's sarcasm hardly touched Willow. 'By the way, there were no scratches on Mr Crescent because Mrs Allfarthing had bitten nails.'

'Yes, I know,' said Willow, not quite able to suppress her satisfaction at having got there first. 'Goodbye.'

'He does think Richard's guilty,' she said as she walked back towards the sofa and Emma. 'That's why he's being so useless. Tom told me that Roylandson is one of the best when it comes to defending the innocent but not so good at getting the guilty off a charge. Damnation!'

'We'll just have to persuade him of the truth,' said Emma. She sounded confident, but her big blue eyes were pleading.

'We will. Emma, I've a private call to make. Do you mind if I disappear for a moment?'

'Of course not. Or I could go and talk to Mrs R.'

Willow shook her head and went into her bedroom. She had absolute faith in Emma's honesty and knew that she would never listen in on the drawing room extension.

Lying back on the Irish lace coverlet, she dialled the bank's number and asked to speak to the chief executive. A few moment's after she had given her name to Annabel he came on the line.

'I'm rather busy this afternoon. Is this important?'

'Very,' said Willow. 'I've an idea that Sarah Allfarthing trusted you.'

'I like to think so,' said Biggles, sounding fractionally warmer.

Willow stared at the French oil painting on the opposite wall and mentally substituted the elegant figure of Sarah Allfarthing for the frothily dressed enchantress on her ribboned swing. They both seemed to have had the same effect on the besotted men around them.

'And I suspect that she told you about her house,' said Willow, striving for a casual voice.

There was silence at the other end of the telephone and she wondered whether she was making an idiot of herself.

'I can't believe that she would have gone away without letting anyone at the bank know where she'd be, and you seem the most likely candidate for that confidence.'

'How did you get on to it?' Biggleigh-Clart sounded both perturbed and rather annoyed.

'A mixture of intuition and deduction,' said Willow. 'It wasn't very difficult when I started to match up the things everyone had said to me about her. There was time missing. She had to have spent it somewhere and you all told me that she wasn't the kind to take a lover.'

'So do you want congratulations?' The last of the warmth had gone.

'No.' The denizens of DOAP would have recognized the crispness in Willow's voice and she heard it herself with gratitude. 'I want the address. Presumably, since you've apparently told neither her husband nor the police, you promised not to pass it on to anyone, but she's dead now.'

Biggleigh-Clart said nothing. Willow tried again.

'If her murderer is to be brought to justice, I need to know the address of her house,' she said.

'How will it help you?'

'I'm not sure, but I need to see the place. It'll help me to know her if nothing else and that in itself will be useful.' There was another reason, but Willow was not prepared to articulate it to anyone on whom the slightest suspicion had fallen. After a little more persuasion, he reluctantly disgorged the information:

'Mill Cottage, Blewton, Berkshire,' he said. 'It's about an hour's drive down the M4. Between Pangbourne and Goring.'

'Thanks,' said Willow. 'Is there a telephone number?'

'No. Sarah always took one of the bank's portable phones when she went there. It saved trouble – and identification of her whereabouts.'

Willow was already off the bed while he was talking and as soon as he stopped she said:

'And the key? It wasn't on her key ring, because her husband identified them all for the police. He told me so.'

'I believe that she collected it when she went to Blewton. I don't know where, though,' said Biggleigh-Clart, 'And I have a feeling one other person had a key, but she never said who.'

Willow thought she heard some satisfaction in his voice and frowned. Shrugging, she said: 'Before you go, there is one other thing I need from you.'

'Time is getting short. Can you tell me quickly?'

'Yes. I know that places like the bank often make a taped record of all the telephone calls in and out.' Willow paused so that the chief executive could either confirm or deny what she had said. But he did neither, simply waiting for her to continue.

'And I need to listen to the calls that Sarah made and answered on the afternoon before she died. Can you get the tape for me?'

'If there were such a tape in existence, it would be highly

confidential and I would not be able to release it to anyone except the police on production of a warrant,' he said formally. 'If that's all, I must say goodbye now. No doubt I shall see you at the bank soon.'

'Goodbye,' said Willow, frustrated.

She had assumed that there might be a tape and his response suggested that there was. Willow tried to picture herself suborning the guardian of the tapes like a Second World War heroine or breaking into the bank and stealing them like a fictional American private eye. But neither fantasy was remotely convincing and she was left with the knowledge that the only way she could get hold of the tapes would be to persuade Chief Inspector Moreby to demand them. Willow dropped the receiver on to its cradle, deciding to concentrate first on the evidence that Sarah's cottage might produce.

On her way back to Emma, Willow felt the second mental sneeze begin to form. It was almost as though her mind had been galvanized by the success of discovering Sarah Allfarthing's cottage and was working properly for the first time since the murder. Willow went to fetch the pictures of Sarah's body once again. She looked at the top one and smiled before riffling through the rest to make certain she was right. The sneeze was achieved and the satisfaction considerable.

'Cressida?' Emma's voice, sounding doubtful, brought Willow's head round. 'Are you all right?'

'Yes, I am. Emma, come here. Look at this: what strikes you about the evening dress?'

Emma obediently bent her neat blond head over the horrible coloured photograph.

'It's smart,' she said doubtfully, 'sleeveless, silk, pale yellow, covered in blood . . . What do you want me to tell you?'

'It's covered in blood,' said Willow with quiet satisfaction. 'Emma, what woman brings an evening dress – a pale-yellow silk one – into the office and has it hanging on her partition all day without any kind of protection?'

Emma straightened up and turned to Willow, her eyes bright as diamonds.

'The cleaner's bag! You think that that's what he used. That sort of plastic is even finer than the mackintosh. But what could he have done with it when he'd killed her?'

'Exactly. It's not in any of the photographs. The police must have gone through all the rubbish that night. In fact I know they did because that's why they were so sure there was no suicide note. They must have searched and so the cleaner's bag can't have been there.'

Emma was scooping back her hair over both ears, which Willow knew was a sign of embarrassment or distress.

'What is it?'

'Don't be cross,' said Emma, sounding like a frightened child.

Ashamed of having been the cause of such fear, Willow shook her head.

'I just thought that if there wasn't any blood on it, they might not have mentioned it. D'you see what I mean?' Emma still sounded afraid and Willow made herself relax the muscles of her face. 'Suppose Sarah had decided to dress because Richard was so late and taken the plastic off and put it in a wastepaper basket, and . . .'

'That's sensible,' said Willow carefully and was relieved to see the fear dying out Emma's eyes. 'But I don't think so. She had expensive clothes and took care of them. Wouldn't she have kept the plastic to put her suit in?

'I suppose she might have,' said Emma, looking happier. 'But if he did use it, how did he get rid of it?'

'That's the question. I suspect he bundled it up, carefully keeping the blood to the inside – perhaps even sellotaping it so that it would stay folded up safely – and then he must have put it somewhere about himself and kept it until he could get rid of it.'

Willow was silent, thinking of the river, of the innumerable skips around London where any piece of bloody plastic could be buried beneath rotten timbers, obsolete kitchen cupboards and ancient bricks, of the municipal dumps, and of the literally thousands of accessible dustbins throughout the residential areas of the city.

'But where about himself? It would never have fitted in his pocket without an obvious bulge.'

'No,' said Willow slowly, 'but what about under the arm? Or perhaps in his groin.'

'Ugh! And then where would he have got rid of it? It could be anywhere.'

'I know. It's hopeless.' Willow thought of something that she could usefully do, checked that her guest had finished tea and then said: 'Emma, I've got to go out now.'

'Can I come with you?'

'I don't think so,' said Willow instinctively. As she watched Emma's disappointed face she almost changed her mind, but a powerful need to be alone when she discovered Sarah's secrets kept her silent. 'I'll ring you up when I get back.'

'I think you ought to have someone with you,' said Emma in a small voice, 'if it's to do with the case. If you've been asking questions at the bank and of all Sarah's friends and relations, you may have frightened . . . I think you ought to have protection.'

Willow smiled as she looked at Emma's slender figure, neatly dressed in a pair of well-pressed jeans and a pink-and-white-striped shirt with a frilled collar.

'I'll be fine,' Willow said. 'No one is going to do anything to me that would betray the fact that Sarah's killer is not already in prison.'

'When will you be back?'

'I'm not sure: three hours perhaps.'

'Please, may I wait here? I won't be a nuisance. Please. Then I'll know that you're all right.'

Willow looked at her in silence for a long time. Emma's affection was warming, but it was constraining too. Remembering that she was trying to find a way between the deliberate loneliness in which she had lived in Clapham and the falsely based friendships of Cressida's life, Willow found a way to smile. Emma's face relaxed.

'It's sweet of you to mind about me, Emma. Yes, do stay here if you'd like. Make Mrs Rusham give you some dinner and help yourself to anything you want to drink.'

Emma folded her lips together and looked like a child's drawing of stubbornness. Willow laughed.

'You won't make me any safer by starving yourself,' she said, adding with a smile: 'But what you could do is ring Martin Roylandson and tell him I've found the house. He'll know what that means.'

Emma wrinkled her nose into a mischievous grin.

'All right, but please take care. Will you tell me where you're going?'

Willow promised, dictated the address of Sarah's house, and went to change out of her suit. She was tempted to ring Tom and ask her to go to the house with her, but that seemed both pathetic and unfair so she stamped on the impulse. A few minutes later, dressed in the serviceable black corduroy trousers and a dark blue shirt, with a sweater slung around her shoulders, she collected the camera she used to take visual notes for her novels and tried to think what else she might need. She knew that she had a stout torch in her car, along with a toolbox that she had never opened but that was said to contain everything that anyone could need to service a car. If she could not find the key to Sarah's hideaway, at least she ought to be able to break in.

Chapter 16

*I*T TOOK Willow fifty-five minutes to reach Blewton in her inconspicuous Metro and another fifteen to discover that there was no Mill Cottage in the village. There was a small grey church with an elegant house beside it; there were two telephone boxes, a post office, a row of cottages, a pretty humped stone bridge with a pub at its foot; but no mill.

Clouds blocked out the sun and a few big drops of rain banged down on the windscreen as Willow searched. She drove past the pub several times and noticed with pleasure that it was called the Goat and Compasses. Her late rebellion against her cool, rationalist upbringing was beginning to give her a sentimental attraction towards the religion her parents had rejected in their pursuit of provable scientific truth, and the prospect that 'God Encompasseth Us' pleased her. She also liked the joke.

It occurred to her to stop at the pub and ask for directions, but she wanted no witnesses if she had to break her way into Sarah's house.

Slowly it dawned on her that the mill in question was likely to be a watermill and that if it had once served the people of Blewton it would probably have been upstream of the village. Parking her car at the edge of the simple stone bridge, she turned off the engine, wound down her window and listened to the chuckling rush of the river. Then, switching on the ignition again, she drove carefully over the bridge and turned right.

The road she had chosen began to seem unlikely as it wound away from the river, narrowed, turned to hard ruts under her wheels and threatened to end only in a farm. She had almost decided to go back when the unsurfaced track turned once more to her right. The half-hearted rain stopped and the clouds parted enough to let the last of the evening's sun sparkle for a moment on a distant prospect of water. Willow drove on, round a final bend, and found her way barred by an ancient gate.

She got out, discovered that the gate was chained and padlocked, and climbed over it. It was clear almost at once that the house before her had once been part of a working mill and that for the moment at least it was unoccupied. Returning to her car, she backed it down the horrible, rutted track for about half a mile until she reached a patch of trees she had noticed on the way. There she drove her little car carefully up the shallow incline and in between the sparse trees until it was partly concealed from the road. Anyone searching would find the Metro easily, but a casual passer-by might not see it.

Sliding a heavy spanner from the toolbox into the back pocket of her trousers, she slung the small camera around her neck and collected the torch. Equipped for every eventuality she could imagine, Willow then locked the car and made her way back to the empty house.

It looked splendid in the dying sun of that summer's evening, the rosy orange of the roof tiles glowing and the brick walls mellow. Nothing had been done to prettify it. There were fat pincushions of moss all over the roof, looking rather like dark-green sea urchins, and the paintwork was old and flaking in some places. The garden consisted simply of apple trees growing in rough grass.

But with all its dilapidation, the house looked honest and welcoming – and empty.

Willow could easily imagine Sarah leaving behind all the anxieties and importunate figures of her London life for this benevolent peace, where, presumably, she could be herself and ignore their expectations of her.

Walking round the front door, Willow noticed that there were no dustbins to be seen, and was not sure whether to be relieved or disappointed that she would not have to pick over the accumulated rubbish for clues. When she reached the door, she felt along the top of the lintel and under the doormat and underneath various adjacent stones, but could find no key.

She was reluctant to break a window and circled the entire house, skirting the flat millpond and inhaling the scent of the waterweed and the gently rotting wood of the great millwheel, in case there was another door or hiding place for a key. Halfway round she passed the entrance to the mill itself and tried the door. To her surprise it was not locked and she made her way in, walking gingerly and recoiling in horror as her steps alerted some creatures that started scrabbling in the gloom.

Willow switched on her torch. At the sight of a group of what must have been rats, she retreated quickly to the door, gripping the architrave as she tried to control her towny disgust. It was there that she found a big iron key, hanging on a rusty hook screwed into the wood.

She tried it first in the door of the mill itself and was so encouraged when it did not fit that she ran to the house, tripping on a stone buried in the rough grass and banging her knee painfully as she crashed down.

After several false starts the key turned and it was only as Willow was actually stepping across Sarah's threshold that she realized there might be a burglar alarm. When Willow heard neither warning beep nor the shrilling of an alarm bell, she relaxed, pulled the door shut behind her and locked it, pocketing the key. She took a few moments to calm herself before she started to look round.

For a while she wondered whether she had made a disastrous mistake and forced her way into a mill belonging to some quite different village. There could have been no greater difference between the house outside Epping and the interior of the mill. Its walls were simply whitewashed and the floor covered with the flat, plaited rush matting that comes from Suffolk. The big chairs and sofa looked a lot more comfortable than the original millers would have had but they were simple and rather shabby. There was an old oak refectory table, faded by sunlight, pushed under one of the windows. It held a muddle of papers, two tarnished brass candlesticks, a pewter mug of dried grasses and berries, and a cracked but beautiful old china dish. The curtains at the small windows were unlined rep of a clear, bright red.

It was not until she found her way across the room to the table and saw a pile of letters addressed to Miss Sarah Allfarthing that Willow knew for certain she was in the right place. She read them all, but there was nothing in them to help her or to embarrass their owner. All of them were concerned with village matters or the house. Willow put them neatly back in their envelopes and went through the rest of the papers. There were several newspaper cuttings, but none of them referred to anything to do with the City. Some were recipes for food or potpourri, others were articles about moral dilemmas of one sort or another: recent decisions by appeal court judges, abortion, euthanasia, the allocation of scarce financial resources, the line to be drawn between political interference in distasteful regimes and the protection of the innocent suffering under those regimes.

Skimming through them, Willow wished once more that she had known Sarah Allfarthing. Burying her sharp regret, she tidied the papers on the table and set about looking for something that might help to find Sarah's murderer.

The house was small and contained nothing in the way of

secrets. The wardrobe in the bigger of the two bedrooms held one pleasant-looking grey-green dress, trousers, flat shoes, shirts, jerseys and underclothes. All the clothes were well worn and shabby, although there were signs that each small tear or lost button had been carefully repaired and replaced. The room itself was as simple as the ground floor. Once again the walls were white, and the high soft-mattressed bed with its blackened brass bedstead was covered in a beautiful but tattered red-and-white patchwork quilt that hung to the ground. There were small unmatched oak tables at either side of the bed. One was empty; the other held a lamp, a cheap quartz alarm clock and a copy of Paul Fussell's *The Great War and Modern Memory*, which interested Willow, but did not seem particularly significant.

It must, she thought, have been part of Sarah's flight from the successful life that had threatened to imprison her. Perhaps it had helped her to read of the ways in which the doomed young men in the trenches had been immortalized; or perhaps she had simply wanted to soak herself in an experience as unlike her own as she could.

Willow, remembering how moved she had been when she had read the book, picked it up and flicked through its pages, reminding herself of it. As she laid it carefully back in the dustless space it had left on the table, she thought with a rueful smile that it ought to have held in its pages a letter or even a photograph that would have given her the necessary clue for which she was searching.

She looked carefully around at the rest of the room, gently pulling aside the plain red curtains and lifting the rush matting. But there was nothing to be found.

The second bedroom was bare, the bed unmade and covered only with a dustsheet, the cupboard and drawers empty. It seemed very clear that no one had ever shared the house with Sarah. For a moment Willow felt as though she had betrayed something important by invading its solitude, and began to understand why Robert Biggleigh-Clart had kept it secret even after Sarah's death.

Only when Willow remembered Thomas Allfarthing's description of Sarah's affection for Richard did she think that the dead woman would have thought the invasion justified if it ultimately proved his innocence. Willow's discomfort dwindled and she went back downstairs to the small white kitchen and switched on the light.

The largest thing in it was a chest freezer. It had a lock, but when Willow tried the lid, it lifted easily. There, too, she found neither shocks nor evidence. Instead there were neat piles of boxes and heaps of bags, each one containing a single helping of meat, fish, vegetables or fruit. There were small loaves of bread and a few rigid containers labelled 'chicken stock' and 'mushroom soup'.

Willow carefully closed the lid, making sure that it clicked into place, and then turned to the sink. It was scoured clean. She opened the double doors underneath and saw various cleaning materials, rubber gloves, a bundle of cloths and a lidded bucket.

When she undid that, she found a mixture of dry rubbish, which she painstakingly examined. There were carefully washed-out milk cartons, old envelopes, a newspaper and a plastic dry-cleaner's bag. Willow took it out and carried it to the kitchen table, where she examined it minutely. There was nothing on it at all, except some dried tea leaves. Disappointed, but not very surprised, she bundled it back into the bucket, switched off the light and left the kitchen.

Although Willow had found nothing useful in the cottage, she was determined to make some record of her visit and took careful flash photographs of each room, opening the cupboards and making visual notes of their contents. Then, impelled by something she did not trouble to understand, she went back to Sarah's bedroom and lay down on the bed. Not bothering to switch on a light, Willow put her arms behind her head and lay in the gloom, thinking about the woman who had owned the house.

Gradually, as Willow went through everything she had

ever been told about Sarah Allfarthing and the little that the house revealed, she lost her conviction that the murder must have been sparked off by the emotions that Sarah had stirred up in her colleagues.

Various things she had heard or noticed returned to Willow as she ruminated: Bill Beeking's saying that Sarah had stayed behind in the office because she wanted to talk to Richard; Thomas Allfarthing's conviction that Sarah trusted Richard and would have gone to him if she were in any kind of trouble; and the stories her colleagues had told about her sense of humour.

Sarah had joked about blackmail in her efforts to persuade people to do things for her. Perhaps someone who had a genuinely shameful secret had misunderstood her jokes or perhaps, faced at last with something serious, Sarah had no longer been able to joke and had decided to take some kind of action.

Willow's heart started to bang against her ribs and her breath to shorten before her mind even acknowledged the unspeakable thought that hit her then. Could it have been Richard who had once done something reprehensible that Sarah had discovered? Had she, trusting him, confronted him with it and driven him to try to silence her?

Much as she detested the idea, Willow could not prevent her novelist's imagination from presenting her with a version of Sarah's death in Technicolor brutality. Richard's hands, which Willow knew so well – the hands that had so often stroked her, comforted and excited her – twisting in Sarah's hair, seizing the knife and slicing through the clear, pale skin of Sarah's neck, through the thin layer of yellow fat that lay below it, through the veins and arteries that spouted blood.

With an effort that made her clench her muscles and drive her tongue forwards between her painful teeth, Willow forced herself to remember the pictures that that same, treacherous imagination had given her of William Beeking's soft white hands only a few hours earlier.

She told herself that her ability to see in her mind Richard killing Sarah did not make it true. With a groan like a bull sealion in the grip of sexual passion, Willow turned over on to her front. The patchwork bedcover was rumpled beneath her and her face lay on Sarah's pillow. The scent, sharp and clean, that rose from it must have been of her shampoo. Sick, ashamed of herself, and unhappier than she had been for a long time, Willow got up off the bed, plumped up the pillows, straightened the duvet and pulled the patchwork cover taut again. Suddenly she smiled. If Richard had killed Sarah, he would never have been so muddled about the vase of roses. He had immediately understood the significance of her question about them and yet had still let her see that he did not know whether they were on the desk or the floor when he first saw the body.

The sound of a car's engine made her stop tidying the bed, with both hands flat on the pillow. She half turned her head and saw that the last of the day's light was going. The car came nearer and stopped. Not wanting to risk showing herself at the window, Willow flattened herself against the wall and listened. She could hear the unmistakable sound of someone trying the chain at the gate, dropping it against the wood and climbing over. Footsteps crunched on the bits of gravel between the rough grass of the orchard-garden. A key was driven confidently into the lock on the front door.

Willow pushed her fingers into the back pocket of her jeans to touch the key she had found in the mill. Her fingers felt the cold metal of the heavy spanner and she drew it out to grip it uncomfortably in her clammy hand.

Filled with a mixture of terror and social embarrassment, she looked around the small room for a hiding place. She thought of the wardrobe and rejected it. Steps began to sound below her as the intruder walked about the house. As soon as she heard them on the uncarpeted wooden stairs, Willow lowered herself quietly to the floor and slid under the bed. The huge patchwork hung down on either side and she blessed the fact that there was matting on the floor. If it had been simply wood, there would have been tell-tale marks in the dust where she had dragged her body across the floor.

Lying still among the curls of mattress dust and unswept long hair, terrified of the prospect of sneezing, Willow heard the bedroom door open.

The steps were slightly squeaky as their maker walked from the door to the bed. As Willow lay, rigid and breathing silently, shallowly, through her nose, she heard the noise of metal clinking on to wood. A duller sound followed, perhaps of a book. Just by her head the patchwork counterpane moved.

Willow's head turned towards the half-seen movement instinctively. Her hair seemed to make an astonishingly loud swishing noise as it dragged against the matting. Hot and cold pulses followed each other down her arms and legs, leaving her sweating and aching. Her hand clenched on the hard metal of the spanner as her eyes focused on the blunt ends of a pair of sports shoes. They were so close that despite the lack of light she could see a layer of distressed pale-grey rubber, a band of dirty cream, and then slightly grimy white leather, stitched and punched to let out sweat and smells.

She tried to make her mind concentrate on what she could smell so that she might identify the intruder, but there was only acrid sweat that could have belonged to anyone, petrol and a warmer, pleasanter scent that might have been coffee or chocolate. She could not decide.

The shoes were of a kind that could have been worn by either a man or a woman. Foreshortened as they looked to Willow, they gave no clue to the size of their wearer's feet. Into the sickness of her disappointment and her fear came one consoling piece of knowledge.

They were not Richard's feet. Richard was in the custody of a famous, uncomfortable, overcrowded prison. Richard was guarded and protected. If they were the murderer's feet, then the past was safe again and Richard innocent.

If Richard were truly innocent, then the worst of Willow's fears could be ignored and she could once more believe wholeheartedly in Tom Worth. In her relief, she understood properly how much her doubts about Richard had affected her feelings for Tom, shrivelling them as a sharp frost burns the new shoots of early spring.

One of the shoes moved out of Willow's sight, breaking her train of thought and making her hands clench as they lay on the matting parallel with her thighs. She could feel the heavy key pressing painfully against her buttock, but she could not move it. The fine canvas that covered the bottom of the bed hung three inches above her until it was suddenly pressed down.

It was almost impossible not to put up a hand to protect her face, but the other fear was greater and she lay waiting. The second shoe disappeared and the bedsprings crunched. The canvas brushed Willow's nose and her teeth clenched over the tip of her tongue.

The two of them lay there, one above the other, for a few minutes as though they were both waiting for something. There was a scrabbling sound just above and behind Willow's head and she instantly thought of the rats in the mill. Something hard and cool hit her forehead. One hand flew up from her side and a finger stuffed itself between her teeth. Looking up she could see the outline of a gloved hand withdrawing from the gap between the bedspread and the wall.

The bedsprings creaked again as the hand disappeared; once more the canvas descended. Willow's wrist felt something hard above the canvas. The shoes reappeared as the canvas lifted away from her face, this time with their heels towards Willow. They squeaked across the room. There was the sound of a door opening and then more complicated noises of metal rubbing metal and something softer. The door closed and the squeaking feet moved on, out of the bedroom, paused and then unmistakably went into the other rooms before going down the stairs.

Willow took her finger out of her mouth and in the dusty gloom of her hiding place saw her teethmarks, dark red and deeply embedded on either side of a hard white ridge of her flesh. She waited.

The sound of an engine hit her ears as comfortingly as the siren of a police car would have done. She rolled out from under the bed and ran to the window, determined to see the number of the car. Trying to keep herself from showing at the window, she peered out, saw a cloud of exhaust and the shape of the pale numberplate in the dusk, but she could not even identify the make of car, let alone distinguish the figures on the numberplate. Frustration seized her and she slammed her fists against the whitewashed wall.

It felt like half an hour, but was probably no more than a few minutes, before she had controlled herself enough to return to the bed and find out what had been dropped on her face. It turned out to be a single cufflink. Holding it in her left hand, she switched on the bedside light. The link was of gold enamelled in dark blue and she knew it at once. She had bought it herself, one of a pair that she had given Richard for Christmas about two years earlier.

Picking the curls of mattress dust out of her hair, Willow began to search the room for a second time. She found several of Richard's possessions that had not been there when she had arrived. There were clothes of his in the wardrobe, old and easily identifiable by anyone who knew him. There was a wallet with his initials on the bedside table, together with a crossword torn from a newspaper and half-completed in his writing. Inside the wallet were some innocuous and uninteresting letters addressed in various hands to 'Dear Richard', some money and, perhaps most damning of all, a plastic card, like a credit card, proclaiming his membership of a tennis club. There were also several wrapped condoms.

Remembering that there had been no sign of used contraceptives in the only rubbish container in the cottage, Willow was grimly amused to think of the lengths to which the intruder might have gone in his efforts to establish Richard's presence in the mill. She checked the date of the crossword. It had been printed the weekend before Sarah's death.

Underneath the wallet lay a copy of one of Cressida Woodruffe's novels. Outraged, Willow opened it and read the mocking dedication she had written in it two years earlier:

'Richard, this frivolous (but profitable) trifle is for you: not to read, because I know you won't, but to keep certain in the knowledge that you are the only one who knows its origin. W.'

The knowledge of her incompetence suddenly hit her. If she had been properly qualified for the job she had taken on, she would not have cowered in the dust under the bed but grabbed the ankles of the intruder who had stood beside the bed, kicked her way out of her hiding place, disabled him – or her – and solved the mystery. At least she should have got up more quickly so that she could have been in time to read the numberplate of the car. And she would never have deposited her fingerprints on the false evidence that had been planted all around her.

All she was equipped to do was look and think and write notes and take photographs. As she thought of that, Willow despaired. What police officer was ever going to believe that the photographs she had taken were genuine? No one, least of all Jane Moreby, would credit that the evidence had not been tidied away for the shoot and then replaced.

Willow found that smiling at herself helped to bring her back to earth and decide what to do. She searched the rest of the cottage, this time without touching anything, and found shaving equipment and more wrapped condoms in the small bathroom, and another book with Richard's name on it downstairs.

She decided that the most urgent thing was to get to a telephone and speak to Martin Roylandson, Jane Moreby and Tom Worth. Of them all it was Tom she wanted most, but he who had least reason to be informed of what she had, at last, discovered.

Taking one more look around the cradle of Sarah's solitude, Willow left the mill house and, carefully keeping out of the moonlight in case the intruder had silently returned, she retreated to her car. She tripped often and once buried her left foot in some unspeakable country substance that clung and stank. When she reached the car she found some large leaves and cleaned as much as she could away from her shoe and ankle, wiped her hands on the thin, prickly grass, gasping as they ran into a bramble branch, and drove back towards the potential comfort of the Goat and Compasses.

When she reached it, she parked the car among all the others on the asphalted space at the back of the building, checked the state of her left foot in the light of its open windows and walked in to order herself half a pint of dry cider. As she carried the overflowing glass to a vacant seat by the telephone, she looked carefully at her fellow drinkers. There was no one whom she recognized, although several people stared with unembarrassed interest at her. Taking a book out of her shoulder bag, she settled down and before she had finished half her cider the other drinkers had resumed their own arguments, courtships and discussions.

Disguising her hurry, Willow put down both drink and book, found some coins in her bag and took out her address book. The only answer she got from Martin Roylandson's office was a machine and when she dialled the number of his home she did not get even that.

Reluctant to talk to Jane Moreby without any kind of legal advice or protection, Willow pressed the follow-on button and dialled the number of Tom Worth's flat. Once again she was answered only by the machine.

'Damn,' she said on to the inviting tape, pressed the follow-on button and dialled the number of Jane Moreby's office. She was answered by a member of the chief inspector's staff, who could not say when she would return and declined to give Willow any other numbers that might be more successful. Leaving a message to say only that she had rung, Willow cut the connection, put the rest of her change into the telephone and rang the number of her own flat, hoping that Emma Gnatche would not be too carefully mannered and discreet to answer it.

'Hello, this is Cressida Woodruffe's telephone.' Emma's gentle voice shook slightly.

'Emma, it's me,' said Willow. 'Is . . . ?'

'Thank God! We've both been most desperately worried. You said you'd be back by eight.'

Willow watched the liquid-crystal display that told her how much of her money was being used up and quickly said: 'My money's about to run out. Will you ring me back? Have you got a pen?'

'Yes, here,' said Emma.

Willow dictated the number of the pub's telephone, and put down the receiver just as the last number of the display started to flash.

While she waited for the telephone to ring, Willow looked down at her watch and saw in surprise that it was only nine o'clock. She felt as though she had lived through about twelve hours since she had left Belgravia.

'Emma,' she said as soon as they were reconnected, 'you said "both". Is Mrs Rusham still there?'

There was a pause and then Tom Worth's voice, solid, deep and controlled, said: 'It's me. Are you all right?'

'I'm fine. I rang your flat. Tom, I need your advice.'

'What's happened?'

'Something rather alarming that absolutely exonerates Richard,' she said, trying to keep her voice low and dull enough not to interest anyone else in the pub. 'But I can't see its convincing Jane Moreby, even if I had managed to get hold of her.'

'Why are you talking so quietly? Is there someone there?'

For answer, Willow held the receiver away from her face for a few moments.

'Oh, I see. It's a pub or something?'

'That's right. The Goat and Compasses in Blewton. I suppose you couldn't get here?' said Willow casually. 'I don't quite see how to explain it all on the telephone and I need a witness.'

'Will, of course I'll come. Is it conclusive evidence?' There was enough urgency in his voice to make Willow say:

'I think so. I can't get hold of Martin Roylandson and I don't know how best to put it to Moreby so that she'll believe it.'

'I see. You know, Will, I won't be able to disguise anything or bend it. I shall have to pass everything on to Jane.'

'I know you will,' said Willow and went on in as quiet a voice as possible: 'I've discovered that our late friend had a bolthole here and while I was searching it someone else appeared and, not realizing I was there, added some bits and pieces of Richard's. D'you see what I mean?'

'All right,' said Tom when he had asked how she was. 'I'll get hold of Jane and persuade her to come with me. If I can find her, we should get to you in a bit less than an hour. Emma and I've been looking at the map for the last forty minutes. See you.'

Willow put down the receiver and then, leaving her book and drink on the table, walked back to the bar to ask whether there was any food to be had. The publican, a cadaverous man with a straggly moustache, offered her shepherd's pie, fisherman's pie or ham sandwiches. Attracted by the simplicity of the sandwiches, Willow instead ordered shepherd's pie with vegetables on the grounds that it would take longer to produce and eat and therefore give her an excuse to wait until Tom appeared.

He came at last, when she had finished the pie, which turned out to be rather good, some commercial ice cream and a cup of stewed filter coffee. He stood in the doorway looking reliable, tough, intelligent and almost unbearably welcome. Willow despised herself for having sent for him, but she still could not think what other action she could sensibly have taken. She got slowly up off the hard chair that seemed to have cramped all the muscles on either side of her spine and went to greet him.

His hand lightly brushed her cheek but he did not smile.

'You look all right,' he said. 'A bit pale and harried, but all right.'

'I am. Now.' Willow flushed and looked down at her watch. It seemed absurd to find his very presence comforting. 'D'you want something to drink?'

'No. We both gorged on your food and drink before you rang. Let's get on with it. Presumably you don't want to talk here.'

Willow collected her bag and book and accompanied him outside to the big, dark Saab he always drove when he was off duty. She saw the slight, fair-haired figure of Emma Gnatche sitting in the front seat and stopped.

'Where's Jane Moreby?'

'Out on a case. I got through to her, but she can't come.' He looked slightly embarrassed. 'She asked me to have a look at what you'd found and said – promised – to listen in the morning.'

'That doesn't sound very hopeful. And why on earth did you bring Emma?'

'Because she was sensibly worried for you and because I could see no good reason to refuse what she desperately urged,' said Tom in his normal voice. 'Come on. Where is this house?'

'You're turning this whole thing into a family picnic,' said Willow crossly, 'a farce.'

'It may have its farcical aspects,' said Tom in a hard voice, 'but that's just too bad. Now stop worrying about your dignity or letting Emma too far into your life and tell me what's really happened.'

Willow winced slightly as she heard his accurate analysis of her objection to Emma's presence. She told him in minute and exact detail everything that had happened since she had arrived in Blewton.

'D'you want to follow me or shall I come in your car?' she finished.

'Let's go in mine. The less disturbance of the ground the better if it really is the victim's house.'

Willow opened the door to the back seat of the Saab, got in and answered Emma's touching but intrusive questions about her wellbeing. She gave Tom directions to the mill and at his request stopped him just before the wood where she had hidden the Metro. He drove up on the verge and said:

'You two had better wait here while I go and investigate, but before I go I want you to tell me again exactly what you did, where you went and what you saw. First of all: how did you get in?'

'I found the key hanging on a hook inside the mill itself.'

'All right. What did you do when you got in?'

'I searched the house for any signs of anyone else having been there. There weren't any. She obviously used it to get away from people.'

'Sounds familiar.' There was enough expression on his face to tell Willow that Tom was momentarily diverted from the investigation. She saw Emma looking from one to the other of them in surprise. Ignoring her, Willow said directly to Tom:

'Yes. That's exactly what it felt like.' Willow shook her head as though she had been swimming under water and needed to clear her eyes and ears. 'But there were no clues to anyone else's presence at all. Everything I saw pointed to Sarah's having been alone.'

Willow tried not to feel – or sound – defensive.

'Then, after I'd taken the photographs, I heard a car. I'd parked mine well away from the house and locked the door behind me and whoever it was must have thought the house was empty.'

'Go on.'

'I . . . It's . . . Oh, damnation. I was too much of a coward to do anything but hide,' said Willow, staring out at the dark windscreen between their two faces, which were turned uncomfortably towards her. 'Until whoever it was had got back into the car and started to drive off.'

'Thank God for that,' said Tom once more, frowning through the windscreen. Willow looked at the back of his head and her lips twitched into an involuntary smile of acknowledgement. He turned back and nodded at her to continue.

'When I had failed to get the number of the car, or even see what kind it was,' she said, 'I went through the house again and saw what he or she had done. It's foully inconvenient that I have no witnesses to the fact that the stuff wasn't there before, but at least it proves to us that Richard really is innocent.'

Emma's face hardened into an accusing mask as she spoke for the first time since they had reached the mill.

'Do you mean that you thought for one minute that he might not be?'

Willow thought of the horrors through which her imagination had put her, of the disgust she had felt of her own suspicions, and the terror that had lain over her life.

'Yes,' she said simply. 'I'm sorry, Em.'

Chapter 17

'ALL right,' said Tom when he came back to the car. 'I believe you, although there's not enough evidence to convince a picky court. It doesn't get us far. I'm damned glad that you didn't try to tackle him, but it's a pity that you didn't get a look at his face.'

'"Bloody amateurs",' suggested Willow, trying to make a joke to make herself feel better.

'That's right,' said Tom with a sidelong smile. 'Why, as a matter of interest, didn't you tell Jane Moreby about the house as soon as you'd worked out that it existed, instead of coming down here on your own?'

Willow's sense of failure dissolved into comforting anger.

'Because she doesn't listen to anything that suggests she might be wrong.' Her voice was tight and very cold. 'She is convinced that Richard is guilty. I doubt if I'd have managed to persuade her to go and look at the house, and if she had it would probably have been too late. The killer would have been there first and all Moreby would have found would be corroboration of her fantasies.'

'Steady on, Will,' said Tom, forgetting the silent presence of Emma Gnatche beside him.

'I know you like her,' said Willow more moderately, 'but I also know that only incontrovertible proof is going to shake her conviction of Richard's guilt and I don't want to go back to her with anything less.'

Tom looked in his driving mirror at Willow's face. In the thin light of the half-obscured moon, it looked livid and ill. Her pale-green eyes had almost disappeared into the pallid mask.

'You must. I can't possibly conceal the existence of the house from her now that you've seen fit to tell me, or the existence of someone planting clues.'

'Tom.' Emma Gnatche put a hand on his arm. 'You mustn't –'

'He's got to, Em,' said Willow. 'He's a policeman. But while he's trying to persuade her that I'm not lying, you and I will just have to get the rest of the evidence.'

Emma looked slightly comforted until Willow laughed bitterly.

'You'll have a tough job persuading her, Tom. Your Jane doesn't like me at all.'

'No,' he agreed, looking in his wing mirror as he swung the heavy car round in a tight turn and drove back to the pub. 'I know she doesn't.'

When he had lined the car up beside Willow's Metro in the car park of the Goat and Compasses, Emma got out, murmuring something about 'finding the loo'. When she had gone, Tom turned back to Willow.

'Are you all right?'

'Not really. But I'll survive.'

'You were badly frightened, weren't you?'

Willow looked at him in the weird glow of the multi-coloured lights that hung along the eaves of the old pub and longed to throw herself on his chest and howl out all the terrors that had tormented her and make him tell her that she had not done badly, that her mistakes could be corrected, and that by her cowardice she had not condemned Richard to life imprisonment. Fortunately for her self-esteem, the interior of the car did not allow any such exhibition. She contented herself with leaning forward until her forehead touched the rough wool of his sweater. One of his hands stroked her short red hair. She drew back from the comfort that she wanted so badly that she mistrusted it.

'I was a little anxious,' she admitted. 'But what's eating me is mainly rage that I was stupid enough to go on lying under that bed when I could have got the evidence that we need.'

There was a pause before Tom said quietly: 'If it was the killer, I doubt if he'd have let you live, knowing that you had identified him.'

'I had a spanner,' said Willow, breathless at the brutality of Tom's observation. After a moment she changed the subject: 'I don't suppose your wretched colleague will believe any of this. She'll probably assume that I made it all up and planted Richard's possessions in the cottage myself.'

A short laugh from Tom dispelled some of the painful tension in the car.

'What, as a diversion? You wouldn't be stupid enough to do that, Will, would you?'

There was silence in the car. Willow drew even further back from Tom. She remembered her own doubts about Richard and her conviction that one of the worst fears is the one that suggests the people closest to you are strangers who might do anything.

'No,' she said. 'But there's nothing I can do to make you believe that. Just because . . . because we're friends doesn't mean that you can actually be certain of the truth of anything I say.'

Tom turned in his seat so that he could face her fully. There was humour in his eyes and immense affection.

'Don't agonize, Will,' he said. 'There were fresh tyre marks at the cottage, quite different from the ones the Metro made in the wood.'

'Bloody amateurs is right,' said Willow after a moment of

mixed resentment and relief. 'I didn't even think of the tyres.'

A man staggered out of the back door of the pub and stood, with one hand against the wall, peering about in the gloom. After a moment he shrugged slightly, took his hand from the wall, unzipped his trousers and proceeded to relieve himself in the open. Something in his arrogant stance as he planted his legs apart and arched his back made Willow say:

'And Freud believed we envy that. How I sympathize with Queen Elizabeth I!'

'As I once said to you, you and Jane Moreby have a lot in common,' said Tom with a friendly smile. 'She'll need to talk to you about this. Don't let your antagonism show. It's going to be hard for her to climb down; try not to make it more difficult than it needs to be.'

Thinking to herself that she wanted to make everything as hard as possible for Jane Moreby, Willow nevertheless knew that Tom was right.

'That sounds as though you do believe that this exonerates Richard,' she said, sounding completely reasonable and uncritical. Tom grinned at her in approval.

'Yes, I do. But as you told me on the telephone, it isn't enough; it's also not my case so what I believe is irrelevant. Here's Emma. Do you want her to drive you back to London?'

'Certainly not,' said Willow, opening her door. 'I may have scared myself witless, but I am perfectly capable of driving. You can take her back.'

'There are things I must do here, Will. It would be better if she went back with you – and if you stayed at her place tonight.'

'What have you got to do?' Willow demanded, stung by the suggestion that she needed to be protected by eighteen-year-old Emma.

'I must get the local men to seal the mill and keep an eye on it until Jane can get here.'

'Oh, I see. All right. I'll see you, then.'

Tom gripped her wrist as she was leaving the car. Emma was still a few yards away from them.

'You've done well and bravely. You'll get him out, Will. And . . .' He looked up at her. 'You know that I love you, don't you?'

Fighting all sorts of emotions and sensations, Willow nodded and turned away. She had joined Emma by the time she decided to turn back.

'You're right,' she said, leaning down to speak through Tom's open window. 'I am tired and I will get her to drive me.'

Tom looked at her in silence and then smiled in acknowledgement of all the unspoken messages she had offered him. Willow joined Emma once again and gave her the keys to the Metro.

They said little on the journey back down the motorway except to agree that Emma would drive to her house and Willow take the car on from there. She was determined to ignore Tom's suggestion that she should stay with Emma.

Having seen that Emma was safely inside her small pink-and-white house south of Kensington High Street, Willow got into the driving seat of her car and went back to Belgravia. She paid careful attention to the speed limit, although the roads were not at all full and thirty miles an hour felt like walking pace after the motorway. As she drove through the first section of Eaton Square, she saw lights on in the Biggleigh-Clarts' second-floor flat. The thought of their sterile, civilized unhappiness together made her shudder in the illusory safety of her little car.

She could not stop herself from thinking of Tom and the awful feelings of dependence that he aroused in her. The events of the day had left her jumpy, exhausted and lonely; and yet the prospect of another person within that loneliness was still daunting.

Having parked the car, Willow got out and walked up the steps to her front door, wondering if she had been foolish to refuse the sanctuary of Emma's house. With her hand on the key to the street door Willow remembered what Tom had said earlier about what could have happened if the murderer had seen her at the mill. Her hand shook as she wondered whether she had betrayed herself with all the questions she had been asking.

The killer had left one of Cressida Woodruffe's novels on Sarah's bedside table. Could it have been a sadistic hint that he or she knew who 'Cressida' was and what she was trying to do? Would there be someone waiting at the top of the stairs for her?

Remembering the spanner she had left at the mill house, Willow went back to her car and took the biggest of the remaining tools from the box in the boot. With its comforting heaviness in her hand, she forced herself up the stairs to the door of her flat. She stood outside it for several minutes, listening.

When she was certain that there was no sound at all, she slid the Chubb key as quietly as possible into the lock and tried to turn it. There was some immovable barrier and the key would not turn.

At that moment Willow almost turned tail and retreated to the flat in Clapham that she had been determined to sell, but she remembered the disaster of her cowardice at the mill and tried the key again, turning a little to the right in case that would loosen the barrier. The key turned right with ease and the lock clicked into place.

Standing outside her own front door, shaking and breathless, it took Willow some time to remember that the last people to leave her flat had been Tom and Emma and that neither of them had a set of keys. They could neither have double locked the door nor switched on the burglar alarm. For all the time they had been away her flat had been secured only with a Yale. Willow wondered whether it was true that such locks could be picked with any plastic credit card.

When she eventually summoned up the courage to open

the door and step across the threshold, she found the entire flat in darkness, which was unusual. On the nights when she was expected home, Mrs Rusham had always left on the lights to welcome her.

With the door open and darkness ahead of her, Willow leaned back so that she could put her finger on the bell. It trilled through the empty silence.

'Hello!' she called uselessly. 'Is there anyone here?'

As her voice echoed in her head, she knew that no one lying in wait would answer. It occurred to her to fetch one of the downstairs tenants, but then she remembered the night she had summoned the police when she was in no danger and decided she could not bear to look such a fool again.

At last she switched on the hall lights and proceeded to the kitchen. With the spanner in her right hand, she felt for the light switch with her left.

The light showed her the room, as tidy as Mrs Rusham could make it, and as empty. The big Aga gleamed and the long worktops were clear. The cupboards looked untouched and the luxurious bunch of mixed green herbs stood comfortably in its Italian pottery jug of water by the sink.

Leaving the light on and the door open, Willow tried each room in the flat, flinging open cupboard doors and bending down to look under the sofas and the bed like some demented spinster half afraid of intruders, half longing for company.

'Which I suppose I am,' she said to herself when she was certain that she was alone. Then, when she knew she would not have to run from anyone, she bolted and locked the front door.

The only signs that there had been people in the flat after Mrs Rusham's departure were the plates and glasses that Emma and Tom must had left in the drawing room. Feeling stupid but still tingling from her self-induced fear, Willow put down her spanner and poured herself an inch of Laphroaig whisky, into which she splashed some water.

The first peaty, familiar taste of it steadied her and she lay along the sofa. By the time she had finished the drink, her muscles were beginning to relax and the cold sweat to dry all over her body. She lay for a few minutes more, enjoying the flame-coloured flowers that Mrs Rusham had arranged in the glass cylinders that were temporary substitutes for a matching pair of black Ming vases she had once owned. Calmed and feeling more tired than anything else, Willow went to run a bath.

While the hot water was pounding the scented oil into foam, she remembered that she had seen some paper protruding from the fax machine while she was searching her writing room for an intruder and went to fetch the message. She refilled her whisky glass and took it with the fax into the bathroom. While the scented steam curled the edges of the thin, shiny paper of the fax, Willow read what her accountant had to tell her.

Re your tax-fraud story, my information is that it is based on fact. An extended family called Bicklington-Heath (if you can believe it!) owned a business. The family members who actually ran the company wanted to sell it, making themselves a great deal of ready money. Some of their older relations who had plenty of cash wanted to keep the business for sentimental reasons. Eventually they were all persuaded to agree to sell their shares – except for one elderly single aunt of the chairman.

Without her agreement nothing could be done and the chairman would have been in a very nasty situation without his share of the cash (he had some vast personal tax bills he'd deferred for five years that had become inescapable). He persuaded a married cousin to invite the aunt to move from her lonely 'retirement' flat to the big, jolly family house. The cousin and her husband promised to take care of the old girl. It's said that she was happier than she'd been for years with all that friendly company and family food.

'And sold the shares in gratitude?' said Willow aloud, picking up the clean flannel that Mrs Rusham had left on the table by the bath. Willow reached forward to rinse it under the cold tap, wiped her face with it, took a long swig of whisky and went back to her letter.

The chairman reported her dead, got probate and took over her shares in the company. He and the cousins kept her well supplied with money and she was happy. They voted her shares, sold the company and pocketed their rewards. It turned out that they'd anticipated nature by only four years; she died of a massive coronary.

The fraud was discovered by an idiotic mischance, which I suspect you will sympathize with.

Willow raised her own eyebrows at that and read on with an added spur of interest.

Unknown to the family that was caring for her, the aunt wrote one day to her old tax office to say that she had not had a tax return for the past two years and was getting worried about her undeclared income.

Reaching for her glass, Willow smiled. Her accountant had often suffered from her demands that her tax returns be filed within the statutory thirty days, despite the fact that the Revenue did not actually want them so soon and applied no sanctions and charged no fines unless the returns were not filed by the end of six months. She looked back at his letter.

The man who had perpetrated the fraud – the chairman – hanged himself, leaving a typed note confessing to everything and exonerating the rest of the family, who, he wrote, had believed he wanted them to house his old aunt in gratitude for her agreeing to let him vote her shares. I hope that this is of some use.
Yours,
Peter.

Willow shuffled the three sheets back into place and put them on the table. She lay back against the curved enamel of the bath, sipping her drink and trying to decide whether any family could be so innocent of such a fraud. She fell to wondering, too, about the pronunciation of Bicklington-Heath and whether it could be contracted in some way, as Cockburn, Featherstonehaugh and Cholmondeley are contracted to Coburn, Fanshaw and Chumley.

There were a great many questions that needed answers, but in the aftermath of terror and relaxation, Willow felt far too sleepy to do any more that night. Her doors and windows were all securely locked; her body was warmly comfortable for the first time in hours; and there was at least a quarter of a pint of whisky seeping into her bloodstream.

She tried to calculate how much pure alcohol that signified and as she was dividing five fluid ounces by 43 per cent, she fell asleep in the bath.

When she woke in bed the following morning she could hardly remember having got herself out of the bath, dry and into bed. Various of her muscles ached badly and she had a headache, but she felt better than she had any right to expect. Checking her clock she saw that Mrs Rusham was due to arrive in about ten minutes and decided to get up.

When they met half an hour later, Willow was dressed in the dark-blue linen suit with a cream-and-emerald striped shirt. Her face was discreetly made up and she had put a pair of modest emerald studs in her ears in place of the plain gold knots she had previously worn to the bank. She felt reasonably well in control.

Willow thought that Mrs Rusham looked ill, but she said that she was perfectly all right and quickly presented her employer with an impeccably cooked omelette flavoured with chives, parsley, tarragon and chervil from the jug by the sink.

'I must apologize for the mess we made yesterday,' she said as she brought Willow a second cup of cappuccino.

Willow smiled and shook her head. 'Please don't,' she

said. 'You were helping. We all want Richard safe and anything is justified if it gets us any nearer.'

Mrs Rusham nodded. It occurred to Willow that her housekeeper hated looking a fool almost as much as she herself did.

'I disposed of that mackintosh; I hope that's all right?'

'Fine. Don't you worry. I think we're nearly there, Mrs Rusham.'

The frown on the housekeeper's heavily modelled face lessened but she did not smile. She thanked Willow and retreated to the drawing room to relieve her feelings by restoring it to its customary pristine order.

Willow drank the coffee slowly and tried to concentrate on *The Times* until it was late enough to begin making telephone calls.

The first was to her accountant, whom she thanked for all the work involved in his fax.

'I'm sorry to ask for even more,' she went on, 'but do you know the name of the chairman's cousin? The married one who looked after the old lady?'

'Cressida, what is all this about?'

'That doesn't matter. Do you know? Or shall I try someone else?'

The accountant sighed, obviously reminded himself that he was talking to a good client who always paid his fees on time, and said:

'I don't know, but I can probably find out. I'll ring or fax you when I know.'

'Thank you, Peter. Goodbye.'

She was about to ring Martin Roylandson when she heard the sound of her own front-door bell. Mrs Rusham went to answer it and Willow waited in her writing room, listening.

'If you will come into the drawing room, I shall see if Miss Woodruffe can see you,' she said, giving no clue to the visitor's identity.

A few moments later, she came into the writing room,

shut the door behind her and said: 'It's that policewoman again.'

'Chief Inspector Moreby?' said Willow.

Mrs Rusham nodded.

'Thank you. Would you tell her that I'm on the telephone and will come as soon as I can? Perhaps you could offer her some of your coffee, too?'

The expression on Mrs Rusham's face suggested that she would rather provide prussic acid. Willow grinned in private sympathy and waited until she was alone again to telephone the solicitor.

'Mr Roylandson? Cressida Woodruffe here. You're going to disapprove of what I've done.'

'Good morning, Miss Woodruffe. What is it that you have done?'

Wishing that he would occasionally use some everyday slang or a few sloppy elisions, Willow told him how she had proved the existence of Sarah Allfarthing's cottage and what had happened there.

'I do not know that I particularly disapprove of that – although I might wish that you had seen fit to include a witness to your outing.'

'There's more,' said Willow.

'I see.' Mr Roylandson sounded grim and Willow made herself smile so that she did not sound accusatory.

'When I failed to get hold of you last night I told Chief Inspector Worth what I had discovered and he has passed the information on to Chief Inspector Moreby.'

'Ah, I see,' said Roylandson coldly after a short pause. 'You were correct, Miss Woodruffe; I am angry. You really ought to have confided in me before telling all to the police. I might remind you that they are on the opposite side to you in this case, whatever your private relations with them.'

'My private affairs are nothing –' Willow began, but Roylandson carried on as though he were a steamroller and she a newly tarred stretch of road.

'Even if you have no evidence, your suppositions could

292

have been helpful in court. What you have done is to give the police plenty of time to collect the evidence that disproves them.'

'You haven't much faith in my discovery,' said Willow drily. 'I rang you this morning to tell you that Chief Inspector Moreby is sitting in my drawing room now, waiting to question me about it.'

'What a fortunate circumstance it is that I have no urgent meetings first thing this morning! I should be with you in fifteen minutes. Can you confine your confiding impulses until then?'

'I expect so. Goodbye.'

Willow thought that she heard Roylandson laugh just before he put down his telephone. She walked quickly and quietly into her bedroom to comb her hair and check her make-up. When both were flawless she went to face Jane Moreby, who was sitting in one corner of the big sofa reading the *Independent*.

At the sound of Willow's step, the policewoman looked up and put her newspaper on the table at her side. She stood up and formally shook hands with Willow.

'Tom Worth wanted to come with me this morning, but I thought that you and I would do better alone,' she said abruptly.

'You may be right,' said Willow, 'although that does sound as though you think we should be facing each other with drawn swords on some blasted heath at dawn.'

Jane Moreby frowned.

'This isn't a game, you know,' she said after a pause. 'I can understand your impulse to dramatize everyday life into the sort of thing you put into your novels, but –'

'It may be the stuff of everyday life to you,' Willow answered with deliberate coolness, 'but it is entirely strange for me to have one of my best friends unjustly in prison, and I have not the slightest intention of dramatizing anything. By the way, I have asked his solicitor to come here.'

She looked down at the gold Cartier watch.

'He should be with us in about ten minutes,' she said, and thought she saw contempt in Jane Moreby's eyes.

'Tom says you took photographs of the mill house before the alleged planting of evidence,' she said. 'May I see them?'

'I haven't had time to have them developed,' said Willow, 'and I think I'd better ask Mr Roylandson's advice before I hand over the film to you.'

'May I sit down?'

'Oh yes, please do,' said Willow, speaking more naturally. 'I'm sorry; I didn't mean to keep you standing like a candidate for a domestic job. Is Mrs Rusham making you coffee?'

Jane Moreby suddenly smiled and revealed herself as a younger, more appealing woman than she had seemed in all her severity.

'I declined, which was . . . silly. If it's not too much trouble I should love a cup.'

'Good,' said Willow, also relaxing. 'I won't be long.'

She waited in the kitchen while Mrs Rusham made a pot of strong coffee and heated a jugful of milk. By the time it was ready and she had laid a tray with crockery and a plate of biscuits, Martin Roylandson had rung the doorbell.

Willow let him in herself and took him to the drawing room, where Mrs Rusham had carried the tray of coffee.

Chapter 18

WILLOW poured out three cups of coffee and offered one to the police officer and another to the solicitor. They helped themselves to milk and sugar and both avoided the biscuits.

'Chief Inspector?' said Willow, sitting back and waiting.

'You do understand that this is all quite irregular, don't you?'

'Certainly,' said Martin Roylandson, straightening his tie, which had been so tightly knotted that it protruded from his shirtfront in a stiff arc.

'Chief Inspector Worth has persuaded me that although there is no admissible evidence of what Miss Woodruffe has told him about her investigation of Mrs Allfarthing's cottage, he believes her account is truthful. I have been down there this morning and seen what little evidence there is.'

'Which is?'

Willow was about to answer the solicitor herself, but Jane Moreby was quicker.

'A collection of items that are readily identifiable as belonging to Richard Crescent. I have a list here which I can copy for you later. According to Miss Woodruffe's story none of them were in the cottage when she first arrived. There was undoubted evidence that a car different from hers had recently driven up to the locked gate in front of the mill. The tyres are standard and used on a variety of middle-sized cars.'

'Hm,' muttered the solicitor, 'nothing much there. It could have been anyone's.'

'Precisely. But it is enough to make me reconsider my earlier certainty about your client's guilt. I am not convinced, but I am willing to listen to what Miss Woodruffe has to say.'

Willow could not prevent a triumphant smile from stealing on to her lips, but Martin Roylandson looked at her repressively. He took a deep breath through his flexed nostrils and put his coffee cup precisely in the middle of the table nearest him.

'I am naturally relieved to hear you say that, but I need assurances from you about the consequences to my client.'

'Obviously I can't give you assurances of any kind, except that I will listen,' said Jane, looking at Willow for a moment as an ally against the solicitor.

Willow nodded briefly and then turned to him. 'There are things we need to know that only the police can find out. Are you willing to let me tell Chief Inspector Moreby what I know and what I suspect?'

'I should prefer to hear it in confidence first, but that is hardly practical at this juncture. You had better start on the assumption that I shall stop you if I believe it to be necessary in the interest of protecting my client.'

'Very well. I believe that I now know why Sarah was killed and how it was done; later today I hope to have some evidence to prove who did it, but I am unlikely to get enough to stand up in court. I need you,' said Willow turning to Jane Moreby, 'to search Richard's flat for evidence of the burglary that must have provided the evidence I found at the mill. And I also need you to force the chief executive of the bank to release the tapes of all the telephone calls made to and by Sarah Allfarthing on the last day of her life. He has refused to let me have them.'

'I can try persuasion,' said the policewoman. 'I doubt if I could get a search warrant on the basis of your suppositions. Why do you think she was killed?'

'There are two more things that I need,' said Willow, ignoring the question.

'Yes?'

'One is a re-examination of the computer keyboard. Everyone has assumed that it was the blood that leaked into it that short-circuited it, but I think it could have been water from the roses.'

'I don't see what relevance that could have, but it's easy to check,' said Jane Moreby.

'You've calculated the time of death on the basis that as soon as her throat was cut the blood leaked into the keyboard and shut down the computer.'

'That's right.'

'But I think that while Richard Crescent was trying to pick up the body he must have tipped the vase of flowers over. I suppose that traces of vegetable matter left in the water by the roses might even show up on his dinner jacket. You could get your scientists to check that, too. I am sure that a vaseful of water would have been much more likely to have damaged the electrics than more viscous blood.'

'That's debatable,' said Jane Moreby with a slight smile. 'But I can look into it. What else do you want?'

'The report of your fingerprint expert.'

'The only prints on the weapon were those of the victim and Richard Crescent,' said Jane Moreby.

'I can believe that, but there must be others on some of the things that were sitting on the desk. Your people took away everything that was there. What did they find?'

'A variety of unidentified prints. But they're hardly relevant. Why do you think Mrs Allfarthing was killed?'

Willow considered for a moment and then absent-mindedly took a biscuit from the tray.

'This may be rather longwinded,' she said when she had swallowed a mouthful of chocolate and ginger biscuit. 'But I want you to see the steps that have led me to my conclusions. All right?'

Jane Moreby nodded, but Martin Roylandson abstracted the gold half-hunter from his waistcoat pocket, swung it round on its chain so that he could study the face and then said:

'I have a meeting in fifty-seven minutes.'

'I'll be as quick as I can,' said Willow. 'Do help yourselves to more coffee or biscuits. Now, it has become obvious that unless Sarah was killed in some *crime passionel*, which I consider to be unlikely, the reason she died must lie in the meeting at which she told her story of the tax fraud and Richard shook her.'

'Why?' As she spoke, Jane Moreby crossed one slim leg over the other. Her face which had begun to show signs of friendliness had returned to its earlier detached obstructiveness.

'Because the meeting is the only thing that could have caused any change in Sarah's life. You were sure that she was killed because of the tensions she aroused at the bank, but everyone there has had five years to get used to those tensions. I cannot believe that they smouldered for so long and then burst into such violent flame for no reason.'

'Go on.' Although the words were encouraging, the tone was not.

'The story of Richard's shaking her must have fled round the bank. Everyone there has heard of it, talked about it and decided on his guilt or innocence of the murder on the strength of it. But there were other people involved in that meeting. Apart from the Americans who had all gone home before the murder, there was the British client, whose deal was almost ruined and who actually gave Sarah the knife, which had been honed to an unprecedented sharpness; there were Richard's colleagues; and there were the lawyers.'

Watching Jane Moreby's impatience and sensing Martin Roylandson's, Willow decided to edit much of her summary of the events that must have led up to Sarah's death.

'I do not believe for one moment that she was killed because of the deal. It went through at a relatively small extra cost. I think that she was killed because of the story she told.'

'Are you suggesting,' said Martin Roylandson, leaning foward to pick up a biscuit and a plate from the tray, 'that someone at that meeting had been implicated in the tax fraud that Mrs Allfarthing described?'

'Yes.'

'It seems rather unlikely,' said Roylandson fussily collecting the crumbs he had scattered around his plate.

'Perhaps at first glance, but if you look more closely you might see more likelihood. Most of the people I have talked to at the bank have said that Sarah frequently made jokes about blackmailing people into doing things for her. They all say that it was her way of being one of the boys and oiling the wheels of everyday work.'

'It sounds peculiarly unpleasant and not in character with what I have heard of the victim,' said Jane Moreby, still obstructive and refusing to meet Willow's eyes.

Mr Roylandson put down his plate and with an irritable shake of his shoulders recrossed his legs. Willow paid no attention.

'I think that someone who heard about her tax story believed that the blackmail was ceasing to be a frivolous joke and becoming serious,' she said.

'I suppose that there is a dim kind of pattern there,' said Jane Moreby, looking and sounding unfriendly.

Willow picked up the three sheets of her accountant's fax and handed them to Mrs Moreby.

'This is an account of the story she told from another source. I believe that the person who killed Sarah Allfarthing is also a member of the Bicklington-Heath family, probably a child of the married cousin.'

'Why?' Jane Moreby took the shiny curl of paper.

'Because,' said Willow with slightly raised eyebrows, 'there is no one at the bank or in any way connected with it called Bicklington-Heath. It's possible that he changed his name, or pronounces it differently, but I don't think so.'

'And you believe this character killed Mrs Allfarthing because he thought she might have shown him to have been involved in an ancient scandal? It seems remarkably far-fetched.' Jane Moreby sounded almost disappointed, which slightly encouraged Willow. 'Not least because no action was ever taken. At this length of time, no one is going to reopen a dead fraud case.'

'No,' said Willow definitely. Martin Roylandson's head lifted suddenly as though someone had called his name.

'Then what?' he demanded.

'The case was not pursued at the time because the chairman of the company hanged himself, having typed a letter admitting the fraud. I think that whoever killed Sarah might also have murdered the chairman. Something Sarah said – either at the meeting or later – led that person to believe that she knew it and was going to betray him.'

Roylandson looked interested and as though he were about to speak but Jane Moreby started first, without raising her eyes from the fax she was reading.

'It is remarkably difficult to engineer a hanging,' she said, 'without leaving evidence.'

'Evidence might have been ignored,' said Roylandson judicially. He drew his lips into a little red bunch and then turned it in so that he looked like a toothless crone. 'With a suicide note,' he went on, 'a strong motive, and a hanged body, it is entirely probable that the local police did not even look for evidence of murder.'

'I suppose so,' admitted Jane Moreby, looking up at last.

'And there are ways,' said Willow, who had been exercising her imagination. 'If I were doing it, I think I would suffocate my victim first with – say – a polythene bag. Not enough to kill him, but just enough to render him unconscious. I doubt if that would leave much evidence.'

'Possibly.' Jane Moreby sounded unconvinced. 'But it's all irrelevant. At this distance – what? Twelve years – no one is going to be able to prove it.'

'I know. But we have a limited number of suspects. It must surely be possible to find out whether any of them . . .' She broke off as the telephone bell provided a welcome interruption. 'Excuse me.' She picked it up before Mrs Rusham could answer it and gave her name.

'Will, it's Tom. Are you all right?'

'Fine. I'm with your colleague now.'

'Ah. I'll ring you back later then.'

'All right. Thank you, Tom. Goodbye, my love.'

'Whether any of them has relations called Bicklington-Heath,' Willow continued, turning back to the other two.

'You must see that it's far-fetched,' said Jane.

'Frankly, I think it's hardly as far-fetched as that a harassed and gentle man like Richard Crescent would for no good reason that anyone can produce take a knife and slit the throat of a woman of whom he was sincerely fond and who undoubtedly trusted him.'

'I doubt that we shall ever agree about the depths of your ex-lover's character,' said the policewoman rather spitefully. Willow wondered whether it was the uncharacteristic endearment she had used on the telephone that had annoyed her antagonist.

'There are a great many problems you simply haven't addressed,' the policewoman went on more moderately. 'I have already sent officers to Richard Crescent's flat to investigate any possible burglary, but I need something more solid before I can divert any more manpower.'

'What worries you, Chief Inspector?'

'Where was the blood? None of the people at the bank that night had any blood on them except for Richard Crescent.'

Willow smiled, the triumph seeping back to her mind and her lips. She got up and went to fetch the police photographs from the drawer of the mahogany pembroke table. She carried them to Jane Moreby's chair.

'Look.'

Jane Moreby looked down at the garishly coloured portrait of Sarah's body. Willow pointed to the long dress that hung with bloodstains like horizontal exclamation marks across its skirt.

'Where is the plastic cleaner's bag?' she asked.

Jane Moreby sat very still indeed. Martin Roylandson straightened his back and asked to see the photographs. Jane handed them over.

'Perhaps there wasn't one,' he said, looking through the pile.

Jane Moreby, who had been staring at her neat black-calf pumps, raised her eyes. She looked at Willow and nodded.

'There must have been. It was yellow silk. She'd not have left that hanging without protection all day.'

'Are you sure the bag wasn't already in a wastepaper basket?' asked Roylandson, happily playing devil's advocate. 'Perhaps she had started to change.'

'There wasn't,' said Jane, sounding tired. 'I can check the reports again, but every wastepaper basket on that floor was sifted in case she'd left a letter.' She looked across the floor towards Willow. There was a small smile on her lips at last.

'It seemed that the most obvious defence would be suicide, and I wanted to be certain there was no possibility of our overlooking any evidence. I'm sure there was no mention of a plastic cleaner's bag in any of the searchers' reports.'

'Perhaps the dress hadn't been hanging there all day. Perhaps . . .'

'I can check that too.' Jane Moreby opened her big handbag and took out a small, black-covered notebook in which she wrote herself an order. She looked up at Willow with a new respect. 'What did he do with it?'

'I suspect he wrapped it round his knife hand and arm and then when he had killed her scrumpled it up, blood inwards, and put it down his trousers or perhaps in the armpit of his shirt,' said Willow. 'I don't think it would have fitted in his pocket. Then he'd have retrieved it from his boxer shorts or wherever he'd hidden it and chucked it away once he was well away from the bank. I don't imagine you've a hope of finding it.'

'It could be anywhere,' agreed Jane Moreby in a gloomy voice.

'I know, but there is still one chance of identifying him. It is just possible that he might have sellotaped the bundle together so that none of the blood could escape and seep through his clothes. If that's so, he might have left a print on the sellotape. You see, if it's like the substitute they gave me when I used Sarah's desk it's in a flimsy holder; to get any tape out you need to put a finger on the roll.'

The policewoman wrote herself another note.

'All right,' she said. 'Who is he?'

Willow turned to look at the solicitor, who nodded his dessicated head.

'I think he's either William Beeking or James Certes, the solicitor from Blenkort & Wilson.'

'Why?'

'Beeking seems suspicious because he's angry, unhappy and manipulative. He monitored everything Sarah did and everyone she saw. It is just possible that he did so because he knew she'd worked for the Revenue at the office where the fraud was first suspected and wanted to know whether she remembered it and could identify him. It's also possible that "Beeking" is a contraction of Bicklington-Heath, isn't it?'

'Hm. And Certes? Why do you suspect him?' Jane Moreby sounded quite unconvinced.

'He was close to Sarah and not only often did chores for her but also recommended his clients to ask for her whenever they used the bank. Given what we know of her blackmailing jokes, I suspect she may have used them on him to engineer such favourable treatment.'

'Supposition,' said Jane Moreby crisply. 'And not very useful.'

'True. But listen: everyone tells me that he's remarkably creative and can see ways round difficulties quicker than anyone else, just the kind of mind to plan the deception of the Bicklington-Heath aunt. One of the bankers told me that just occasionally Certes's ideas are so creative that they create all kinds of trouble for his clients. So far he's always got them out of it. And he's the only of them all who wears suits loose enough easily to conceal the bulge made by a thin plastic dry-cleaner's bag.'

'Even if I accept that,' said Jane, 'there are two insurmountable problems. Like Beeking, Certes was in a meeting with Mr Hopecastle, the client.'

Willow stood up, smiling.

'Everyone at those meetings leaves at some stage. Beeking was sent to the Corporate Finance Department several times by Jeremy Stedington and Certes left the meeting room often on the excuse that he had diarrhoea and once returned, ostensibly from the lavatory, looking quite sick. He could easily have killed Sarah then.'

'And the doors?' asked Martin Roylandson, looking positively happy. 'What about the code number of the Corporate Finance Department doors? Beeking knows them, of course, but Certes can't.'

'I think he could.' Willow smiled at herself. 'But I don't want to make a fool of myself explaining how. I need to ask a few questions at the bank today.' She turned to the policewoman. 'Will you try to get the tapes, Chief Inspector?'

There was a pause before she nodded.

'Well done, Miss Woodruffe.' Martin Roylandson checked his watch and stood up, straightening his cuffs. 'Chief Inspector, you and I need to talk about my client's position. I must not stay any longer or I shall miss my meeting. Perhaps we could meet later in the day?'

Willow listened while they made an appointment for half past four. When she escorted Mr Roylandson to the door, he surprised her by shaking her hand in a firm grip and congratulating her.

'I do think we've a chance now. I'd never have advised what you've just done, but it may work out all right. Good day.'

Willow shut the door behind him and went back to see Jane Moreby re-reading the fax.

'I can photostat that for you if you like,' Willow said.

'Have you got a machine here? Good. Thank you. Will you be at Roylandson's office this afternoon? It would help.'

'Very well.'

Jane Moreby got up and after some hesitation offered Willow her hand.

'I'm not ungrateful, you know,' she said stiffly. 'If Crescent is innocent, then . . . then I shall owe you several apologies.'

Willow waited a moment and then said:

'It would be better to offer them to Richard. I'll see you later.'

When Jane Moreby had gone, Willow went into the kitchen to keep Mrs Rusham up to date and to ask her to have the photographs of Sarah Allfarthing's cottage developed.

'We are getting there, Mrs Rusham. It should not be too long now,' said Willow as she left the flat.

When she reached the bank she went straight to Tracy's desk. When she looked up from her work, Willow said quietly:

'Did you ever tell James Certes about Mrs Allfarthing's inability to remember numbers?'

'I might of,' said Tracy, looking astonished. 'So what?'

Willow smiled. 'So nothing, Tracy. But tell me: when you were describing her stupidity to him, did you give him any examples of the sorts of numbers she couldn't remember?'

There was a moment's pause before Tracy said: 'Yes. He didn't believe me, you see.'

'I do indeed. After all, you told me the number of her briefcase locks, didn't you? Might you have told him the code for the doors to this department?'

For the first time since Willow had known her, Tracy looked afraid.

'No,' she said positively, and then added: 'No, I don't think I would have done that.'

Her wedge-shaped face was red. Willow knew that she would get nothing more definite, but she thought that Jane Moreby might. It seemed astonishing that anyone could be stupid enough to pass on such information and then fail to connect her indiscretion with the murder, but from all the accounts of Tracy's errors and omissions, Willow was prepared to entertain the possibility.

Wanting a relatively private telephone so that she could ring Jane Moreby, Willow went to Jeremy Stedington's office. Finding the door open, she looked in.

'Jeremy? Is this a bad time, too?'

He looked up at once with the old smile on his face and pushed his left hand through his hair.

'No. It's a good time for me to apologize,' he said, pushing his chair back and stretching out his long legs. 'I really am sorry I was so sharp with you yesterday afternoon. It was just that I had rather a hairy deal on the go and I couldn't cope with distraction.'

'I know. All I wanted to ask you is whether you would write me a statement about everyone who left your meeting on the night that Sarah died, giving the order in which they left if you can possibly remember it.'

'I'll try,' he said doubtfully. 'Is the order so important?'

'Only for my files. I want to produce a full account of every single thing that happened in the bank that evening. It'll help get my mind clear,' said Willow and then added, trying to sound quite casual: 'By the way, was Bill Beeking involved in your conference call yesterday?'

'Yes. You saw him coming into my office.'

'I thought I had. Did he stay? I mean, what time did he leave the bank?'

'Look here, what is all this? Do you want to talk to him? If so he's out there at his desk now.'

'No. I just want to know what time he left yesterday.'

Stedington shrugged and pulled his chair back to his desk.

'I suppose he went at about seven fifteen. I stuck around a bit longer.'

'Thank you,' said Willow. It was quite possible that Beeking could have got to the Blewton mill if he had left then and been lucky with the traffic. 'What sort of car does he have?'

'Pocket rocket – Peugeot 205 – like everyone else at his level.'

'Thanks,' said Willow, leaving the office before Jeremy could ask her any more questions. She would have to wait to ring Jane Moreby until Jeremy had left his office. Back at the carrel that had once been Sarah's, Willow dialled the chief executive's secretary to ask for an appointment with the great man.

'I am afraid that he has had to go out to an urgent meeting, Miss King,' said Annabel, sounding pleased with herself. 'He is unlikely to be back until early this afternoon.'

'Oh dear. Have I only just missed him?'

'By about half an hour.'

Wishing she could ask whether the police had had time to demand the taped records of Sarah's telephone conversations, Willow arranged to see him at three o'clock and put down the telephone. She heard someone walking behind her and whirled round in her swivel chair, almost overbalancing.

'Maggie! You startled me.'

'I am sorry, Miss King,' said the girl. 'It's just that I'm likely to have a bit of free time this afternoon, round about four o'clock. I'll have finished all the reports by then and the boys will take some time to finish the next drafts.'

There was a charming, rueful smile on her face, which made Willow sympathize with the frustrations of her secretarial life.

'Do you suppose there's a free meeting room? It would help if we could talk in private.'

'Yes. Number four will be free then. It's a tiny one with no natural light,' said Maggie, looking a bit surprised. 'Shall I book it?'

'Would you? That would be wonderful,' said Willow, waiting until Maggie had gone to turn on her computer and put in a little time reading the last few completed questionnaires that the bankers had been returning to her over the previous few days.

A hand descended on her shoulder close to her neck and tightened. Still holding a questionnaire in her left hand, Willow turned and saw Beeking grinning at her. She shivered.

'You startled me,' she said, hating both her breathlessness and his obvious pleasure in it.

'I know. I wonder why? Should I apologize?'

'It doesn't matter. What can I do for you?' Willow wondered whether he could possibly have overheard her being indiscreet.

'I was just going to ask whether you were planning to lunch in the canteen,' he said with a charming smile and an inclination of his blond head.

Willow smiled as kindly as she could. He could hardly do her any injury in the bank's canteen and she still had questions to ask him.

'Actually, I was just thinking of getting some lunch. There's no reason why we shouldn't go together. Come on.'

Chapter 19

*I*T WAS not until they were settled in their dark-red chairs with their chosen lunch in front of them that Willow said casually, as though it did not matter at all:

'What was it you did that made Sarah Allfarthing stop talking to you, William?'

He looked up from his cheese salad as blood rose unbecomingly in his tanned cheeks. He shrugged and his lower lip pushed up the top one into a pout. For once Willow saw him not as sinister but as unhappy, even perplexed.

'I'd worked out how she'd managed to get her career here off the ground and I tried to do it too,' he said at last. Then he shrugged. 'I thought she might be amused and help me, but she . . .'

He dug his fork into a piece of cheese and lifted it. The cheese crumbled and fell back to the plate. He dropped the fork and put his hands in his lap.

Willow glanced round to see whether anyone else was watching them, but the rest of the lunchers appeared to be absorbed in their own affairs.

'Blackmail, you mean,' she suggested.

He looked up and Willow saw a sickening mixture of resentment and misery in his hazel eyes.

'She told me I was a stupid mischief-maker,' he said sullenly. 'And when I pointed out that it was exactly what she did, she laughed at me and said if I couldn't tell the difference between a joke and a piece of despicable manipulation then I needed to see a psychiatrist.'

'That was cruel,' said Willow lightly, wondering whether she was wrong in her certainty that the Bicklington-Heath fraud was at the root of Sarah's death. Had the humiliation she had inflicted on Beeking tipped him over into violence? Willow made her voice as kind and firm as she could.

'I never knew that she could be unkind. People keep telling me how wonderful she was.'

'She could be a bit sharp sometimes.' Beeking tried to eat his piece of cheese again and was successful.

Willow watched him carefully. She did not want to propel him into making a scene. Deciding that he seemed well in control of himself, she risked another question.

'What did you use to blackmail her? I know that you watched her. What was it that you had seen?'

A satisfied smile banished some of the resentment and most of the unhappiness from his face.

'I told her that if she didn't include me in all the deals she got through Certes then I'd tell Mrs Biggleigh-Clart about the time Sarah and Biggles made love.'

Willow sat up straight and stared at him as though she were trying to see through his fleshy face to his brain.

'But they didn't,' she said, her green eyes narrowing. 'Mrs Allfarthing was sexually cold and refused all advances from everyone.'

'Oh, but they did: just the once. That's why Biggles was so keen for her to go to America.'

'I don't understand.' Willow, who had given up all interest in her heap of cottage cheese and tinned pineapple, put down her fork. 'America?'

'She wished that she'd never done it and told him that it was all over. He was so desperate for more that he told her that if they couldn't be lovers, she'd have to go to the States to work in our office there.'

'How on earth do you know all this?' Willow was so surprised by what he had said that she had no idea whether he was telling the truth, lying to persuade her of his innocence of murder, or merely fantasizing.

Beeking looked stubborn, and pleased to be stubborn, as he ate some more of his salad.

'I'm afraid that I don't believe you,' said Willow with a superior smile before she fell to pretending interest in her own lunch.

Beeking's eyes lightened and his lips curled into the old smile of boyish charm. He reached into the inner pocket of his jacket and pulled out his wallet.

Just like Little Jack Horner, Willow thought.

He abstracted a handwritten letter on thick white paper. He read it, looking happier than ever, while Willow sat like Tantalus under the fruit trees of Hades. At last he offered it to her. Remembering Tantalus, Willow was reluctant to reach out for it.

'Go on. Read it.'

She took the letter, noticing that it had once been crumpled into a tight ball and that the handwriting looked very like that which she had seen at Biggleigh-Clart's desk.

Sarah, life is becoming intolerable. I know that none of what has happened is your fault and it's therefore unjust that I am asking you to go away, but in this case justice has to take second place to expediency. I cannot go to New York. You could – and it might help you too. It's the only way I can see us ever being able to get back to normal. It won't hurt your career here. Just give me six months to get myself in order and you can come back with all your promotion prospects intact, even enhanced. I am not trying to blackmail you into parting with sexual favours. But I am asking you to help me help myself get over you.

You have told me often that you trust me. Trust me in this: I would not ask you to go if there were any other way.

This was supposed to be a love letter, but it's a poor effort – and that in itself is a measure of how badly I need to be free of you for a time. It's not a long time: only six months. Please, Sarah, think again. I am fighting for my sanity.

RB-C.

So that was why she wanted to talk to Richard, Willow thought. She looked up to see Beeking watching her.

'Why didn't she shred it?' she asked.

'She probably would have,' said Beeking, showing no signs of the bad conscience Willow thought he should have. 'But I saw her crumple it in her fist as she read it. I suppose she was angry with him. And then Jeremy yelled for her and she had to rush away.'

'And you picked it up, didn't you? And she knew it had to have been you. And that's why she wouldn't speak to you again when you refused to admit that you had it. You're a proper masterpiece, aren't you, William? And what about that other one?'

'What other what?' Beeking seemed puzzled.

'There was another handwritten note in your wallet. What's that?'

'Nothing very interesting,' said Beeking, shrugging.

'William,' said Willow, making her voice as authoritative as it had ever been in her civil-service days, 'let me see it.'

And so he handed it over and Willow started to read. When she had discovered that it was no more than a shopping list, she looked up to see Beeking laughing at her.

'You're all the same, you managerial women,' he said.

'You think that you own the world and can make the rest of us do anything you want. But you're wrong; just as she was wrong. People won't stand for it.' He held out his hand.

'Why do you keep an old shopping list?' asked Willow, having checked that among the notes about tomato ketchup, pasta, anchovies, olives, detergent, shampoo and tampons was nothing useful.

'It's all I've got in her handwriting,' he said, still smiling. Something in his face infuriated Willow and she felt all the anger that must have flooded through Sarah as she discovered what had happened to Robert Biggleigh-Clart's letter.

'Did it please you that she died like that?' she asked slowly. 'With her throat slit and her blood pouring out over the floor?'

The white-clothed table was suddenly thrust into Willow's stomach. Her glass of water tipped and poured its contents down the front of her jacket.

'You're disgusting!' Beeking hissed into her ear.

Willow recoiled and saw him stalking out of the restaurant. The pretty young waitress ran after him, only to return disconsolate a few moments later.

Willow pushed the table back, mopped her front with a dry part of the tablecloth and got up, feeling shaken and full of sympathy for Sarah. Between Beeking's uncontrollable snooping and Biggles's passion, she must have had a hellish time. Knowing that she would have to talk to him about that passion, Willow began to dread her meeting with the chief executive.

When it was time to go up to his office she did what she could to tidy her damp suit, brushed her hair and presented herself at Annabel's desk. The secretary got up at once and ushered Willow into the main office.

The chief executive rose as Willow walked into the room. He looked as impeccable as ever, but the skin around his eyes was tightly stretched and there were shadows in them that she had not seen before.

'Miss King,' he said without smiling. 'What can I do for you this time?'

Willow smiled at him deliberately and took the chair opposite his desk. He sat down. Annabel closed the door behind her.

'I asked for this meeting because I wanted to know various things about Sarah's cottage,' Willow said, starting with the easiest question.

He shrugged. Once again Willow noticed the breadth of his shoulders and the tautness of his figure, a tautness that could only have been the product of well-conditioned muscles.

'There's not a great deal I can tell you. I've never been there, and as far as I know no one else has either. Sarah rented it so that she could be entirely alone. That's all she told me, except for giving me the address.'

'And you've never told anyone else?'

'No.' Biggles's well-shaped head drooped slightly. He sighed. 'No doubt it's sentimental, but I had promised her that I'd keep her secret and her death did not seem to be a good enough reason to renege.'

'Not even by telling the police?'

'You sound appalled,' he said with a faint smile. 'What good would it have done them? She was killed here, not there. If I'd told Inspector Moreby about the cottage, she would have passed it on to Allfarthing. Since Sarah always went to such lengths to keep him in contented ignorance of her own unhappiness, I thought that I had better do the same.'

'Was she so unhappy?' asked Willow, passing over his extraordinary assumption that Sarah's secret cottage would be irrelevant to the investigation of her death and his ruthless decision to edit the truth he told the police.

'Yes.'

'And was that why you fell so badly in love with her?'

At the sound of her deliberately quiet voice, he looked furious.

314

'Come on, Mr Biggleigh-Clart. I have come to understand a great many things during the last few days, including that. Don't bother to deny it – or to accuse me of impertinence. It is a material fact.'

'Why?'

'Don't be obtuse. You know it is, which is why you didn't want me here: not because of the sensitive information about your clients' affairs but because you dreaded anyone finding out about you and Sarah. You knew that if the police found your last letter to her they'd have thought you had a pretty strong motive.'

The chief executive's façade remained impeccable, but his eyes looked tormented.

'So she didn't destroy the letter,' he said, his voice sounding quite detached.

'No. She would have, but something got in the way and it was retrieved.'

'I see. You're partly right about her unhappiness, I suppose,' he said, swivelling his chair so that he could look out over London.

Willow watched the back of his silver head.

'I've never talked to anyone about this before.'

'I've been listening to a great many people talking,' said Willow drily, 'and few of them have been wholly truthful. Nevertheless I make a good listener.'

'I'd always liked her and thought her attractive,' he went on, ignoring Willow's interruption. 'And I respected the work she did, but it wasn't until we talked in here late one evening that I really began to know her. All we did then was talk, but we found that we were more alike than I could have believed possible.'

He swung his chair round to face Willow again. 'Can you understand that?'

'Oh, yes.'

'But she had more guts than I. I suppose I've abdicated from the struggle at home and just ignore it. She tried – really tried with that dull stick of a husband of hers.'

He fell silent and turned back to stare out over the office towers and the few delicate spires of the post-Plague churches.

'And then?' asked Willow just as the telephone buzzed, breaking into his confessional mood.

'Yes, Annabel?' he said into the receiver. 'I'll tell her.'

He looked up at Willow.

'Apparently your solicitor has something he needs to discuss urgently before some meeting or other. The message wasn't very clear, but he's in his car in the car park downstairs.'

Willow looked down at her watch. It was half past three. She could not think what Roylandson might have discovered that was so urgent. Biggleigh-Clart's face had closed up again and it was clear that all his defences were back in place. There were still a lot of questions that had to be asked.

'I suppose I'd better go down. It can't take long. Will you be here if I come back?'

He looked at her, a faint smile tweaking his lips and an almost frightening intelligence showing in his brown eyes.

'All right. I will be here,' he said. 'You can take the lift straight down.'

Willow did as he said and emerged into a low-ceilinged concrete world in which the dim, fluorescent lighting, the weird acoustics and the overpowering smell of dust and engines contrasted strangely with the expensive luxury of the gleaming cars that waited in multicoloured rows. She looked round and, seeing no one, called out:

'Martin? Are you there?'

She started at the sound of a horn and called again.

'Over here,' said a voice from her left.

She walked forwards just as the door of a low red sports car opened and James Certes got out.

'Whom were you expecting?' he asked with a charming smile as he stood with one foot on the ground and one balanced in the doorway of his car.

'My solicitor, Martin Roylandson,' said Willow, stopping under one of the few ceiling lights.

'I never said I was your solicitor,' he said, stressing the pronoun. 'Some of those telephone girls are aburdly casual about the messages they take. Come and sit in the car. I need to talk to you.'

It sounded perfectly reasonable, but Willow, who was already cursing herself for her stupidity in going to the car park alone and defenceless, was not prepared to go any closer.

'You can talk to me here,' she said.

Certes removed his foot from the car and shut the door. The noise sounded remarkably loud as it echoed from one concrete wall to the next. He strolled towards her, looking trendy in his baggy suit and quite unthreatening. Willow stood her ground.

'What do you want?' she asked. 'I was in the middle of a meeting with Robert Biggleigh-Clart and he's expecting me back any moment.'

'Don't worry. I can easily explain your absence when I go up to talk to him. He won't be surprised that you've fled when he hears just exactly who you are.'

Willow raised her eyebrows.

'But I think he will be surprised to know that your training consultancy doesn't exist and that you have consistently lied to him. He might have no difficulty believing that you are the mistress of Richard Crescent, but it may shock him to discover that the only reason you are here in the bank is to uncover old scandals.'

'What makes you think that?' asked Willow.

'Though how you think any scandal, however dramatic, could help to disguise your lover's guilt, I can't imagine,' said Certes, ignoring her interpolation. 'I suppose it comes from your ridiculous novels.'

'And what do you know about my novels?' she asked, wishing that she had a tape recorder up her sleeve.

'Plenty, Miss Cressida Woodruffe. You will never be able

to get your lover off, you know. Since I quite like him, even though you make me laugh, I thought it would be only fair to give you a chance to get out before I unmask you.'

The contempt in his voice acted on Willow's mind as contempt always did. All doubts about herself were banished in her determination to force him to swallow his insults.

'You're losing it,' she said calmly and when he merely looked puzzled, she added: 'I wasn't at all sure that it was you at Mill Cottage, but now you've given me all the confirmation I need.'

His fair, beautiful face looked quite blank.

'You saw the photographs of me at Richard's flat, didn't you, and took his copy of *Mandragora for Amanda* then. You know, you're beginning to panic and it's having a catastrophic effect on your judgement. I am as little interested in the bank's scandals as Sarah was in the Bicklington-Heath fraud.'

Certes said nothing and Willow was not even certain that his expression had changed, but there was a new alertness in his stance that suggested she had shocked him.

'You've been dropping hints about what you did all over the place. I suspect a psychiatrist would even say that you wanted to be caught. You even invented the story of the Biggleigh-Clarts' dinner as a reason for all your favours to Sarah. I know that you never dined there at the same time as she did.'

'Just what are you talking about?' asked Certes, slipping his right hand into the pocket of his suit.

'Sarah telephoned you that day, didn't she? Did you forget that the bank tapes everyone's calls?'

When Certes said nothing, merely looking at Willow as though she were talking in a code to which he had no key, she went on:

'She wanted to ask your advice about a letter she had had . . . she probably called it "worrying" or "upsetting". In your panic, you assumed that the letter was about your part in the fraud.'

'You really are a romancer, aren't you?' Certes's voice was as light and easy as usual, but between his parted lips Willow could see his teeth clenched. Sweat glistened on his upper lip, catching the light like sequins on a dress.

He moved forward again, with his right hand still in his jacket pocket. Willow moved back until her way was blocked by the concrete wall. Its hardness make her whole body jerk as she hit it.

'You've been wary of her, haven't you, ever since you discovered that she had worked in your great-aunt's tax office at the time of the fraud?' she said, determined to regain control of their dialogue. 'I wonder when you actually began to get frightened by Sarah's jokes about making you do things for her because of what she knew about you. They must have started to niggle and then bothered you more and more until you were convinced she knew who you were. And then came the day when she told the story of the fraud in front of you.'

Willow smiled and slowly shook her head.

'I'm not surprised you flipped. You must have thought that she was about to start putting the screws on seriously.'

'You're talking total crap, fit only for a woman who writes sentimental rubbish,' said Certes, standing about three feet away from her. 'I don't suppose you even understand the words you use.'

'Did she summon you to her office that night?' said Willow and, when there was no answer, supplied her own: 'No. She was too conscientious ever to give you the number of the doors, even though Tracy wasn't.'

Something in his face told Willow that her supposition about Tracy's indiscretions had been correct.

'Sarah must have asked to see you urgently because of her letter and you assumed that it had to do with the fraud. My God! You must have been in hell all these years, thinking she knew and wondering how long she'd tease you with it and make you work for her before she reported you to the Law Society. How you must have hated her!'

Certes's face did change then. Shocked that its delicacy could express such viciousness, Willow tried to back, pushing herself painfully into the concrete.

'I must go,' she said. 'The chief executive is expecting me.'

'I don't think you ought to go anywhere until you have told me what all this nonsense is about.' Certes took another step towards her and gripped her left arm with his right hand.

'Let go of me,' said Willow icily.

'Tell me what you mean,' he said.

Willow twisted her arm and pulled, but she discovered with an unpleasant shock that for all his smallness he was much stronger than she and she could not free herself. Relaxing her muscles, she felt a corresponding lessening of his grip, although he did not let go. She told herself that there was no need to be afraid of him. The car-park attendant's kiosk was not far away, even if it was out of sight, and Certes would hardly risk killing her with a witness so close.

'All right, I'll spell it out,' she said, trying to breathe normally. It seemed important not to give him the satisfaction of knowing that she was afraid. 'I think that it was you, as a law student, who found the answer to the Bicklington-Heath problem; you who knew that no death certificate is required to obtain probate. Your uncle – or whoever the unfortunate man was – took all the blame when the scam went wrong. Did he kill himself, or did you help him along?'

As she said that, Willow realized that she had gone too far. The grip on her wrist was released but before she could move or call out, Certes's knee was between her legs, his right hand jammed against her mouth, forcing her head against the wall. His body pressed against hers in a terrifying parody of the act of love. Choking, trying to get enough of a grip on the flesh of his hand to bite it, Willow brought both hands up behind his head, wound them in his short hair and pulled with all her strength.

'Bitch,' he said as he leaned away from her far enough to crash his hand against her cheek in a backhand blow that was heavy enough to smash her face into the wall. The side of her head caught on a rusty bolt and she felt blood pouring out of her scalp and down her face.

'The police know all about you,' she said, coughing and tasting salt blood as it oozed between her painful lips. 'And Biggleigh-Clart knows I'm here. You'll never get away with this. The panic will get worse and you'll betray yourself over and over again. Let me go.'

He slammed his left hand against her mouth again as he fumbled in his pocket with his right, keeping her pinned against the wall with the weight of his body. When he looked up she saw that he was way beyond the reach of reason. His mouth was cruelly twisted and his eyes were wild.

It isn't a knife, she said to herself, trying to keep looking at both his face and his hand. It can't be a knife. Fight, damn you. She pushed her shoulders back against the concrete in an effort to thrust him away with her pelvis and her legs. But she could not force him to move. Her mind would not work properly; she could not think what else to do. At last it told her to shout. She moved her head just enough to get a grip on his fingers with her teeth. As as he flinched and let his hand slip to her neck, she yelled:

'Help!'

It was not loud enough. Swallowing a mouthful of blood and gagging against the taste, she tried again. 'Help!'

No one came.

Out of the corner of her eye she saw Certes bring a thin polythene bag up out of his pocket and knew what he was going to do. She forced her bloody face down against the hard bar of his arm, bending her head this way and that so that he could not get the bag over it with only one hand and pushing as hard as she could against him. She felt the imprisoning arm move and his upper body arch back so that he could use both hands.

Without thinking what she was doing, Willow lifted her right hand in a horizontal V-sign and drove her nails hard into his eyeballs. The pressure against her collapsed as Certes doubled up, screaming, his hands covering his face.

Willow yelled for help again, running between the Porsches and the MR2s, the Jaguars and the Daimlers towards the far end where an illuminated arrow offered hope. As she rounded the corner at the bottom of the ramp up the street, she saw a uniformed man sitting in the glass cubicle. From yards away she could see the earphones over his head. She ran and banged on the glass door.

'What's the trouble?' he asked before he looked at her properly. Then he grabbed her arms. 'What have you done to yourself? What's happened?'

Willow simply pointed behind her and together they ran to where Certes was crouching against the wall with his hands half covering his face.

'Christ!' said the attendant when he caught sight of the man's eyes. 'D'you do that, miss?'

'Hang on to him,' said Willow. 'I'm going to get help.'

'There's an emergency phone on the wall there. Get an ambulance quick.' He looked back at the huddled, roaring man on the floor. 'And the police.'

'I will,' she said and reached for the telephone, which she had never even noticed.

After that she hardly remembered anything until she was sitting on a hard chair in the casualty department of the nearest hospital waiting to have her face dressed. The police had talked to her, she knew, although she could not remember what she had said to them or they to her. One of them was sitting beside her, though whether for protection or restraint she could not remember.

The pain in her cheek, where her own teeth had slammed into the soft flesh and torn it, seemed to be increasing and she kept shaking. Suddenly, she remembered that the chief executive had been expecting her to go back to his office. She stood up, looking around for a telephone.

The young constable beside her got up and put a hand nervously on her shoulder, trying to persuade her to sit down again. Willow told him that she had to call the bank. He insisted on going with her to the telephone boxes.

She spoke to Biggleigh-Clart and explained something of what had happened.

'I know all about it,' he said with a short, humourless laugh. 'That sort of thing can't happen here without my being told. How are you? They said you weren't too badly hurt.'

'I'll be all right,' she said, feeling as though her tongue was twice its normal size and her whole head hurt. 'Have you given the police the telephone tapes?'

It was not what she had planned to say and she could not understand why she so badly wanted to know.

'Yes, I have.'

'Thank God.' Willow suddenly felt desperately tired as she realized why it was so important.

There was still no actual evidence of Certes's guilt. The police would obviously believe that he had assaulted her when the saw the state of her face, but she had done far worse damage to him. She felt sick and afraid of herself. Certes might never be charged with Sarah Allfarthing's murder. He might not even be guilty. Biggleigh-Clart was talking but she could not hear him.

Willow felt a tap on her shoulder and turned to see the young constable gesturing at Jane Moreby, who was walking down the passage towards them.

'I must go,' she said into the telephone. 'I'll report later.' She put the telephone down as he made another inaudible protest.

Willow turned to face Jane Moreby, who looked angrier and colder than ever.

'Are you all right?' she said.

Despite the expression on her face her voice was almost

gentle and Willow, who had been expecting criticism at the least, nodded, suddenly unable to speak. Her legs began to shake again and all the terror she had not allowed herself to feel in the car park overcame her and with it the horror of what she had done to Certes's eyes. She couldn't see properly and she couldn't stand up. The voices all around her were buzzing in her ears so that she could not distinguish any words.

'I'm sorry,' she gasped, as she leaned against the wall, her forehead feeling the coolness of the cream-painted wall. 'Just give me a minute.'

The constable put a shoulder under her right arm and helped her back to the chair where she had been waiting. Jane Moreby sat down beside her.

'A doctor's coming. Don't worry.'

'Was it Certes? I must know.' Willow said urgently. 'Was it him?'

'Yes,' said Jane definitely. 'I'll tell you exactly what we've found when your face has been dealt with and you've had a chance to recover. But you were right about enough to make it all pretty clear: his mother was a Bicklington-Heath before she married; Sarah Allfarthing did ring him up that day; and it looks as though one of the fingerprints on the sellotape is his. We don't know how he got into the Corporate Finance Department, but we're working on it. Don't think about it any longer. We can make a good case. Richard Crescent will be released as soon as the formalities can be dealt with. Martin Roylandson is very efficient. Ah, here's the doctor. Can you give her something?'

'Tracy told him the code for the doors,' said Willow as the doctor led her away. 'I'm sure of it. Don't go away.' Jane Moreby said nothing.

When a nurse had cleaned the dried blood from Willow's scalp and face, and washed out the inside of her right cheek with something that stung and burned, the doctor examined her. He asked her all kinds of questions, tested her eyes, probed the pain in her face for serious damage and ultimately decided that nothing had been broken. He put two stitches in her scalp, gave her some powerful painkillers, and told her to go home and rest.

Willow emerged, shaky but just about in control of her legs, to find Tom Worth waiting for her. He stood up as he saw her and came to take her arm. He seemed to promise infinite safety and Willow reached out for him.

'Jane had to go, but I'll take you home,' he said and Willow almost wept in relief.

'I'm sorry, Tom,' she said when he had helped her into his car. 'But it's not a broken promise. I didn't set out to trap him or provoke him. It was stupidity, not –'

'Hush, Will,' he said, taking her to the door. 'You don't have to apologize. I just wish . . .' He stopped, took a deep breath and went on: 'I just wish that I had been there. But you're all right. That's what matters.'

He drove her back to the flat, where Mrs Rusham was waiting.

'It's nearly over,' said Willow when she had soothed her housekeeper's concern for her injuries. 'Richard will be home soon.'

'I know. Chief Inspector Worth told me. I'm so sorry about what's happened to you, Miss Woodruffe. I've made up your bed and there's some consommé ready for when you've had your bath.'

Willow managed a smile, although the widening of her lips hurt ferociously.

'Thank you. But you shouldn't have waited. It's far past your time.'

'I wanted to wait. The soup is in a pan. It just needs heating.'

'I can cope with that, Mrs Rusham,' said Tom cheerfully. 'You go on home. I'll look after her.'

Willow said good night to her housekeeper and went to wash the grime and sweat off her body. When she was dry she put on a new silk nightdress and went back to her bedroom. There were fresh linen sheets on the bed and new flowers in the vases. And Mrs Rusham had lit a fire in the swept hearth, despite the heat of the August evening.

With a painful smile at the incongruity of it all, Willow slid into bed and lay against the pillows. Tom brought her a tray with a flat bowl of soup and a plate of thin brown bread with the crusts cut off. She lay drinking it and watching him fetch himself a glass of whisky and sit down in a low chair at her side.

The curtains had been drawn and the only light in the room came from the fire and the pink-shaded lamps on either side of the bed. They cast an easy glow over the pretty room that seemed worlds away from the violence in which she had indulged that afternoon. Willow put down her spoon, feeling sick.

'Have I blinded him?' she said suddenly.

Tom looked up. The low flickering firelight accentuated the bump in his broken nose. He shook his head.

'No. You hurt him badly, but not as badly as that.'

Willow let her head fall back against the pillows and closed her eyes.

'Thank God.'

'You don't know enough yet to damage anyone badly. It was a good effort, Will, and I'm proud of you. But when you're over this I want you to let me teach you how to look after yourself, and to know exactly how much damage you're doing. Will you?'

She nodded.

'I'd be grateful. I realized at Mill Cottage that I needed to know,' she said. 'By the way, where did Jane go?'

'Back to work. He's under arrest, but still in hospital. She thought you might like to hear the telephone call Sarah made to him and so she's made a duplicate of the relevant bit of the bank's tape. D'you want to hear it now?'

'Yes, please. There's a cassette player in my writing room.'

Tom went to fetch it and a few minutes later Willow was listening to Sarah Allfarthing's voice for the first time.

It was deep and very pleasant with a slightly husky edge to it.

'Could I speak to James Certes, please?'

'I'll put you through.'

'James? It's Sarah here. Something rather frightful has happened that I must talk to you about.'

'What? What have you heard?' The sharpness in Certes's voice told Willow a lot about his state of mind. He must have been living in almost constant fear of discovery.

'It's a letter I've got here. I think we really ought to talk about it. I shan't take any action until we've met, but I shall need to do something quickly. It's horribly important and rather a shock.'

'What?'

'I can't possibly say over the phone.'

'I'm coming to Jeremy's planning session this evening. We could meet after that.'

'I can't. I've got to go to this wretched dance tonight. We're all supposed to be on duty in our glad rags by seven forty-five. Are you busy tomorrow at lunchtime?'

'Yes, but if it's really that important I could cancel.'

'It really is.'

'You intrigue me.' Certes's voice was light, almost teasing.

'Oh, don't,' said Sarah. 'It's horrible.'

'All right. I'll meet you at the champagne bar at twelve forty-five.'

'Thanks. Don't talk to any of them about this tonight, will you?'

'Certainly not. I'll see you tomorrow.'

Tom clicked off the tape.

'It is hideously ironic, isn't it?' said Willow. 'Certes was one of the two people whom she considered to be her friends. If she hadn't trusted him, she'd never have summoned him like that to talk about her difficulties with Biggleigh-Clart and Certes would never have got himself in a position where he needed to kill her.'

'But why do you suppose he went up to her office? I'm probably being thick,' said Tom with the smile Willow loved, 'but what did he hope to achieve?'

'I suspect,' Willow answered slowly, staring into the fire, 'that he believed everyone would be at the dance and he seized the chance to get hold of the letter. If it had been as inflammatory as he thought, she'd hardly have left it in the bank, but . . .'

'But she'd hardly have put it in her evening bag either,' said Tom.

'No. And in the message, she did say she had the letter "here". I think he remembered Tracy's telling him the number for the doors and decided to go up to find it. We'll never know what happened when he saw Sarah there, what she said, why he still thought she was blackmailing him. What is clear is that he was in such a panic that he killed her. Poor woman.'

'Yes,' said Tom and for a moment they both thought of the clever, elegant woman with the husky voice who had tried to keep her husband, her daughter, her colleagues and her clients happy while still driving herself to succeed in a world in which she would always be mistrusted.

'But what could she have done to him even if she had been blackmailing him?' said Tom at last.

'Told the Law Society and stirred up enough dust to have him struck off the roll, I suspect. Even if she had never managed to persuade the police that he had had a part in his uncle's hanging, that would have been enough to ruin him. As a partner at Blenkort & Wilson, he must have been earning about £150,000 a year, I suppose – and far more in the good years. To a man as vain and self-obsessed as he that could have been an adequate reason to kill her.'

Tom looked at her, understanding her bitterness because it was what he felt whenever he was confronted with someone who believed that his or her own comfort and security were more important than the life of another human being.

'Will you sleep tonight?' he asked at last.

Willow's eyebrows joined over her nose as she frowned.

'If I take a pill,' she said. 'Will you stay?'

'Sure,' Tom answered comfortably as he got up to take away her tray.

Chapter 20

A WEEK later, once her mouth had healed and she had finished the synopsis for her agent, Willow hosted a lunch to celebrate Richard's release from prison. His long-standing affection for Sarah Allfarthing meant that for him at least the celebration was muted, but Willow, Emma and Mrs Rusham were united in triumphant pleasure. Even Tom Worth was pretty cheerful.

Willow had suggested to Mrs Rusham that they should all go out to a restaurant, but the housekeeper had begged, in breathless desperation, to be allowed to cook for Mr Lawrence-Crescent. Just as desperately, she had refused to eat with them.

She had not, of course, stopped at cooking. The silvery-pink dining room was filled with flowers. All the silver had been polished until it gleamed and so had the furniture. The surface of the mahogany table was so shiny that it reflected the sprays of ivy and pale roses that trailed over the edge of the silver quaich in the centre. There were tiny dishes of newly roasted and salted almonds on the table, and handmade chocolate truffles filled the matching Georgian bonbonnieres on the sideboard, while more champagne than the five of them could possibly have drunk in three days lay on its side in the enormous fridge in the kitchen.

While Mrs Rusham brought in course after course of ambrosial and spectacularly presented food, the four of them ate without saying very much. The bisque of langoustines was followed by a boned and stuffed chicken flavoured with white truffles, which in turn was succeeded by an immense platter of eight different vegetables, each one separately sauced.

Tom and Willow spoke to each other occasionally and watched Emma Gnatche adoring Richard. He visibly relaxed under her care, smiling more easily and eventually even making a few jokes about his time in prison. Emma, looking both older and happier than Willow had ever seen her, topped his stories with an account of her experiments with Mrs Rusham, the plastic mackintosh and the tomato ketchup.

Richard leaned back in his chair laughing as Mrs Rusham brought in the pudding and he thanked her even more warmly than when he had first arrived at the flat. She flushed unbecomingly as she put a tower of spun sugar, raspberries, cream and meringue down in front of Willow and then turned to Richard.

'It was a pleasure,' she said formally, 'to do anything we could.'

Richard stood up and put both his hands on her shoulders. 'You've been wonderful,' he said and leaned down to kiss her cheek.

Mrs Rusham's heavy face quivered; she tried to speak, shook her head and moved back.

'This looks superb,' said Willow, understanding how difficult it was for Mrs Rusham to answer Richard's declaration.

She looked at her employer with rare gratitude and turned in silence to the sideboard to pick up the plates, which she distributed before fleeing back to the safety of her kitchen. The other four looked after her with sympathy and no little embarrassment, which Willow eventually tried to dispel by handing round the elaborate pudding. Emma refilled Richard's glass and they began slowly to talk again.

'Tell me one thing,' said Richard, clearing the sweetness of the meringue out of his palate with a draught of champagne.

'What haven't you worked out?' asked Willow, amused.

'Do you think Certes actually meant to kill her?' said Richard, the happiness shrinking out of his face as he remembered what he had found that night.

'I don't think he can have planned it, or it wouldn't have been so messy. He couldn't have known that the plastic cleaner's bag would be there, even if Hopecastle had told him about the knife. I think it was a spur-of-the-moment decision. I cannot imagine that he'd have left a print on her sellotape if he had had time to plan properly. He's far too sharp.'

Tom leaned across the table to refill Willow's glass.

'Perhaps he thought that he was so damned clever it would not matter.'

'I doubt it. I think he was probably very shaken by the killing.'

Emma, looking shaken herself, said: 'But why did he think he could get away with it? He couldn't have known that Richard would be coming back from Tokyo to be the perfect suspect.'

'I don't imagine he thought at all,' said Willow. 'I think he was in the most frightful panic and simply assumed that with no blood on him he would never be suspected.'

'Or,' Tom added drily, 'perhaps he assumed that no one would believe Tracy could ever have been stupid enough to tell him the number of the doors.'

'Perhaps,' said Richard with a rueful grimace, 'but anyone who's ever worked with her could believe it. What I don't understand is how he knew about Sarah's cottage and got hold of a key.'

'Oh that's easy,' said Willow at once. 'She was so determined to keep the place secret from her husband in case its existence hurt him that she would have made all her arrangements through Certes. We know that he did all kinds of chores for her and as a solicitor would be the perfect person to negotiate the rent and perhaps even sign the lease on her behalf. I only hope that there will be some documents in his office to prove it.'

'But none of it really matters any more,' Emma said with a delighted – if proprietory – smile at Richard. 'Not now that you're out of prison.'

As Willow watched Richard smiling back at Emma, she remembered the mystery of his parentage and for one wild moment asked herself whether Mrs Rusham could possibly have been his mother. There was nothing in his long, good-looking face or his very English colouring to suggest it. Her once inky dark hair and her sternness of feature would surely have stamped themselves on the genetic inheritance of any child she bore; and the coincidence would have been ludicrous; but it might have explained her painful devotion.

'. . . don't you think, Willow?'

'Sorry, Richard, my mind was miles away. What did you say?'

He smiled and she could see from the angle of his right arm that his hand must be lying on Emma's knee.

'Emma has just told me how young she felt and I was merely observing that she seemed to have grown up enormously.'

'Enormously,' Willow agreed, watching them with delight. She noticed that Tom was looking quizzically at her and she nodded slightly to show him that she understood what he meant and that she enjoyed the sight of Emma's bond with Richard.

'Then perhaps I'm old enough for one of you to tell me

something,' said Emma, raising the hand that must have been covering Richard's to scoop her hair behind her ear. 'Will you?'

'Probably,' answered Tom cheerfully just as Willow was doing sums in her head and deciding that Mrs Rusham could only have been about fourteen and a half when Richard was born. 'What is it?'

Emma looked from Richard's familiar, beloved features to Tom's craggy, amused face, which she had once found dauntingly masculine and rather dangerous.

'Why do you two keep calling Cressida Will or Willow? It's been puzzling me for some time.'

Her sweet pink-and-white face was framed by its customary pearls and black velvet hairband, but her big blue eyes were shrewd. The two men turned from her to Willow.

'It's your story, Will,' said Tom.

'Well,' said Willow, taking a gulp of champagne for Dutch courage, 'it's a simple story, really, Emma.' Her voice sank to the quiet sing-song of an old-fashioned nanny trying to send her charge to sleep at night and she told Emma a fairytale version of her past.

'Don't look so surprised,' she added when she had come to the end, 'it's only a late twentieth-century variant on "The Ugly Duckling" or "Cinderella".'

'With a few differences,' said Tom. 'I'd have said it must have been more Arthurian than either of those.'

'A quest?' Willow said interested. 'Perhaps.'

'I never thought I'd live to hear you announce it,' said Richard, raising his glass to her. She could not tell whether he was mocking and found herself stiffening at the possibility. 'Are you going public?'

'I doubt it.' She suddenly smiled again. Mocking or not, she liked them all. 'I'm beginning to think that perhaps I've overrated secrecy, but I still haven't got to the stage of wanting to lay my inadequate and dreary past before the shocked eyes of the fans.'

Into the silence that followed came Mrs Rusham with a

tray of coffee. Willow insisted that her housekeeper should sit down and share that with them at least and later, when they had finished the coffee and the truffles, they all went into the kitchen with her to load the washing-up machine.

When Mrs Rusham had eventually got them all out of her kitchen, no one quite knew how to end the celebration until Willow, understanding what both Richard and Emma wanted most, urged her to give him a lift back to his flat.

At the front door Richard turned back to thank Willow yet again, adding:

'If only I'd been clearer about the bloody roses it would have been much easier for you. I'm sorry, Will; I just couldn't remember spilling them when you first asked me.'

'Don't worry, Richard,' Willow answered. 'As Emma said: none of it matters any more. Off you go.'

'Do you mind that?' asked Tom as Willow shut the door behind them. She shook her head.

'What, Richard and Emma wandering off into the sunset hand in hand? No. I think it's excellent. How permanent it'll be, I've no idea, but they'll both enjoy themselves and that's the main thing. Besides, I've been wanting to get rid of them for some time.'

'Really?'

'Yes. Really.' She put her arm around his waist and added: 'I owe you a holiday, Tom. I know you've used up all your leave for the moment, so what about a weekend in Paris?'

'Only,' he said with a consciously wicked smile as he opened the door to her bedroom, 'if you can afford to whisk me off to the Crillon.'

'Done,' she said. 'What a splendid idea! And I can buy you some cufflinks at Cartier while we're there. You need a present and what with all of Richard's drama I haven't been shopping for weeks.'

336

Tom shut the door behind him and stood looking at her with a derisive glint in his eye. For once she enjoyed it.

'Withdrawal symptoms, eh?' he said before he kissed her. 'I think you ought to try a little cold turkey. Why don't we go to a tiny hotel I know in Saint Germain and forget presents? You surely don't need Cressida's extravagance any more.'

Willow laughed. She felt an extraordinary ease with him, as though she had known him for a lifetime that had been quite different from her own.

'You may have just heard me burning boats, my dear friend,' she said with mockery to match his own, 'but I'm damn well keeping all my life rafts.'

IN THE BLOOD

Also available in the series:

The Morse Poetry Prize
Edited by Guy Rotella

CARL PHILLIPS

In the Blood

THE 1992 MORSE
POETRY PRIZE
🖝 SELECTED AND
INTRODUCED BY
RACHEL HADAS

Northeastern University Press
BOSTON

Northeastern University Press

Copyright 1992 by Carl Phillips

Library of Congress Cataloging-in-Publication Data
Phillips, Carl, 1959–
    In the blood : the 1992 Morse poetry prize / Carl Phillips ; selected and introduced by Rachel Hadas.
      p. cm.
    ISBN 1-55553-135-0 (pbk.)
    I. Title
PS3566.H476I5   1992
811'.54—dc20   92-25012

Designed by Ann Twombly

Composed in Weiss by The Composing Room of Michigan, Inc., Grand Rapids, Michigan. Printed and bound by Braun-Brumfield, Ann Arbor, Michigan. The paper is Glatfelter Offset, an acid-free sheet.

MANUFACTURED IN THE UNITED STATES OF AMERICA
97 96 95 94 93 92   5 4 3 2 1

For Joanna

ACKNOWLEDGMENTS

Grateful acknowledgment is made to the editors of the following magazines in which some of the poems herein first appeared or are forthcoming. *Agni*: "The Glade," "Leda, After the Swan." *Boston Literary Review*: "holy, holy." *Calapooya Collage*: "For Chiron," "The man we're looking for," "Passion," "Still Life: Treadmill with Mirror." *Callaloo*: "Blue," "Death of the Sibyl." *Chaminade Literary Review*: "Undressing for Li Po." *Creeping Bent*: "Sappho and the Camera." *Kenyon Review*: "In the Blood, Winnowing," "Memories of the Revival." *Paris Review*: "Fra Lippo Lippi and the Vision of Henley." *Poet Lore*: "Africa Says," "Film Noir." *River Styx*: "Elegy." *Stone Country*: "From the Sun's Tower," "With Love for the Night Patrol." *Visions*: "On Being Asked to Recall the Annunciation." *The Worcester Review*: "Luncheon on the Grass."

"With Love for the Night Patrol" won the 1989 *Stone Country* Poetry Competition.

Lines 25–26 of "Conversion" are from the writings of St. Symeon, as quoted in Joseph Campbell's *The Hero with a Thousand Faces* (Princeton: Princeton University Press, 1973), p. 39.

I would like to thank the Massachusetts Artists Foundation for a fellowship that assisted in the completion of this book.

Thanks also to Alan Dugan and my fellow poets and critics at Castle Hill in Truro; to Doug, for last-minute support; and especially, for more than I can say, to Joanna.

Contents

Introduction

Universal and private, lurid and hidden, transcendent and terrestrial—such are the contradictions on whose scaffolding *In the Blood* stretches itself like a pair of wings (and wings are a favorite image throughout the book). The opening poem, "X," programmatically embraces oppositions, as X = anonymity shifts to X = eros:

> X,
> as in variable,
>
> anyone's body, any set
> of conditions, your
>
> body scaling whatever
> fence of chain-metal Xs
>
> desire throws up. . . .

Another variable of X is the cross. *In the Blood*'s epigraph from Romans offers a schematic chiasmus: "for what I would, that do I not; but what I hate, that do I."

And chiasmus feels appropriate. Reading this book without knowing its author's identity, I came to think of him (him, I believed, not her) as a person composed, like his poems, of pained contradictions—eros tugging against anger, despair, isolation. But I soon felt I could depend on the verbal texture of the poems to be silken smooth, their tone rueful, amused, urbane.

Perhaps X is a student of the classics or art history. Certainly his frame of reference embraces Chiron, Achilles, Sappho, Gabriel, Fra Lippo Lippi, not as occasions for erudition or word-painting but as variations on the essential X of flesh and spirit.

xi

only now, after the mechanical
drown   recover   drown of the oars in
their hands, do I understand wings

and the scaled-down pattern for
suffering that every wing, surely,
is lined with

("Fra Lippo Lippi and the Vision of Henley")

The same wry attention marks the poems—more immediate, perhaps, but always angled, nuanced—of the body:

Recently, I woke up holding your leg, and decided
to give it my full attention. It seemed
thirty-two inches of road winding steadily out
into nowhere, land that wouldn't hold up
in good light.

("Loving the Town Planner")

Internal evidence would seem to indicate that X, whose name I
presently discovered to be Carl Phillips, is a poet of color who is
erotically drawn to other men. The reductiveness of such terms is
one lesson of *In the Blood*, with its language of dreams and wakings,
its chiastic wings, its constant dissolving of one world into another:

Under the night, somewhere
between the white that is nothing so much as
blue, and the black that is, finally, nothing,
I am the man neither of you remembers.
Shielding, in the half-dark,
the blue eyes I sometimes forget
I don't have. Pulling my own stoop-
shouldered kind of blues across paper.
Apparently misinformed about the rumored

stuff of dreams: everywhere I inquired,
I was told look for blue.

                                        ("Blue")

Color, gender, even mortality ("there was this morning now, / in the
shower, when you know / you are dying") are crucial themes, to be
sure, yet they are ancillary to Phillips's essential (*EX*istential?) vision, a
vision whose poetics are slyly set forth in one of the many ostensibly
painterly poems in the collection, "Life Lessons from Art":

> Leave every room its share
> of dark corners. . . ;
> always, the flesh . . .
>
> should be the primary source of light:
>
> if there are windows,
> they are only to show some emblem
> of the world you have chosen
> largely to ignore. . . .
>
>   leave the bulk
> of your work unsigned.

With each successive reading, I find that *In the Blood* gains
steadily in grace and mystery. Part of the controlled power of these
poems results from their reticence—a rare commodity in much poetry these days, but not at all incompatible with passion. I shall look
forward to seeing more work by X (in Wallace Stevens's words, "the
sharp flash, / The vital arrogant, fatal, dominant X") in the future,
and I trust that what he uses the epigraph to excoriate is not his
practice of the art of poetry.

RACHEL HADAS
December 1991

xiii

. . . for what I would, that do I not;
but what I hate, that do I.

Romans, 8:15

I

X

Several hours past that
of knife and fork

laid across one another
to say done, X

is still for the loose
stitch of beginners,

the newlywed
grinding next door

that says no one
but you, the pucker

of lips only, not yet
the wounds those lips

may be drawn to. X,
as in variable,

anyone's body, any set
of conditions, your

body scaling whatever
fence of chain-metal Xs

desire throws up, what
your spreadeagled limbs

suggest, falling, and
now, after. X, not

just for where in my
life you've landed,

but here too, where
your ass begins its

half-shy, half-weary
dividing, where I

sometimes lay my head
like a flower, and

think I mean something
by it. X is all I keep

meaning to cross out.

ৠ Passing

When the Famous Black Poet speaks,
I understand

that his is the same unnervingly slow
rambling method of getting from A to B
that I hated in my father,
my father who always told me
don't shuffle.

The Famous Black Poet is
speaking of the dark river in the mind
that runs thick with the heroes of color,
Jackie R., Bessie, Billie, Mr. Paige, anyone
who knew how to sing or when to run.
I think of my grandmother, said
to have dropped dead from the evil eye,
of my lesbian aunt who saw cancer and
a generally difficult future headed her way
in the still water
of her brother's commode.
I think of voodoo in the bottoms of soup-cans,
and I want to tell the poet that the blues
is *not* my name, that Alabama
is something I cannot use
in my business.

He is so like my father,
I don't ask the Famous Black Poet,
afterwards,
to remove his shoes,
knowing the inexplicable black
and pink I will find there, a cut
gone wrong in five places.
I don't ask him to remove

his pants, since that too
is known, what has never known
a blade, all the spaces between,
where we differ . . .

I have spent years tugging
between my legs,
and proved nothing, really.
I wake to the sheets I kicked aside,
and examine where they've failed to mend
their own creases, resembling some silken
obstruction, something pulled
from my father's chest, a bad heart,
a lung,

the lung of the Famous Black Poet
saying nothing I want to understand.

✒ Life Lessons from Art

—for Evy

Leave every room its share
of dark corners,
its shelves of relics,
or replicas of same,
to cast additional shadow;
always, the flesh—be it

the girl-student's lifted
arm, the bit of neck escaping
from the meister's lace cravat—

should be the primary source of light:

if there are windows,
they are only to show some emblem
of the world you have chosen
largely to ignore, a plow, or a ship
with sails folded, griffins rising where
the eye of the cartographer fails,
skies doubling as the pasty brow of God.

As appropriate, paint yourself
into the grain of a half-eaten slice of orange,
the cameo holding the infant's
baptismal gown together,

include your reflection
in the doorknob, the porcelain
sconce, the tea-service the newly
married couple has already forgotten,

anywhere they'll think to look last.
With these exceptions, leave the bulk
of your work unsigned.

⚓ Mix

Later would come the good school and what I'd learn there,
about the rasp of two hands shaking on a thing
being only one way of fucking in small, public spaces.
In the meantime, or in that meantime part of the room
I was always, all over again, finding back then,
they were of course talking about sex. As of
the new jazz, that anymore would rather meander
through than jump the ear as it used to.
Or anything all but sure, a good deal,
the sweeter than sweet it always
tastes like, just before closure:

a lot of talk, and everybody, each slightly
more than his neighbor, swallowing
air like olives,
then smooth stones,
then something undefined,
but larger. Larger, and less smooth.

✒ Still Life: Treadmill with Mirror

Oh, he was beautiful (even
a man, even here, can say it),

racing toward his own good idea
of what beauty must be when it goes
all steamy and determined
in place.

This is the last long afternoon of Kid Narcissus,
I was thinking,

any moment something different will happen.

Much later, I thought of that poem about the urn—

you know, where everyone's barefoot and pastoral,
robes loose and slightly
raised, like there's really wind
or some kind of headway being made:

beauty, chasing tail forever.

Film Noir

We've just pulled out of
a dream sequence,

in which your ears were throwing stiff
unnatural shadows onto the bed
behind me, the lighting wanted
to give something away . . .

And I'm noticing
that your arches are the only
beautiful things left about you,
though they've fallen away
somewhat, like the letters
to the several names
you've suggested

for what we're doing here.
Accident isn't one of the choices.
You say something like
accidents are things wished for
too late, when wishing has become
another plug to stop the mouth
going round with itself.

At this point
I'm about to look up and see
lives and buildings occurring
behind you; I haven't yet
said my next line,
that the skyline is no longer
your body by the handful;
strictly speaking,
we've only just entered
the neighborhood of the climax,

but this is where it should end,
the music lurching in, like unwanted
police backup, each of us
nervously passing our weapons
between us, the two of us
dissolving, as the door falls down.

✒ On Being Asked to Recall the Annunciation

Clearly, no one was expected; nothing
had been prepared. The lighting had the reel
of medieval struggle to it, of a body trying
to remember having lain beneath love's
crooked drill, routinely jumping its grooves,

when
Gabriel walked into the room cast as a woman,
smoking a cigarette the way a man would,
downward, in pinches, stoppering up
small gaps in the space around him. He wore
nothing at all but his green boots, the toes
sharp and turned outward, away from
the impertinence of so many acres of flesh going
unshared. I'd already begun forgetting

to ask likely questions: where were his wings,
for example, was there anything I could bring him?
It became impossible

not to believe each word as it fell, the way
hands too soon fall away from prayer.

✍ Elegy

Poor Eros: sadly, as in the boning of fowl
or of angels in defeat, someone has snapped
his wings off, and now, fitted out in his

leatherette sash, spitting bad Greek from
either side of a mouth not at all like the
mouth in his pictures, he goes thin and un-

recognized. Who expects the winged horse
and Icarus, one failing, one not, tattooed
on his ass where it rises to the motorcycle's

nudging? Or, instead of the delicately pared
bud of legend, a cock heavy with travel, re-
ceding within its saurian folds in time with

the booted foot's effortless shift from gear
down to gear? At all the old cafés, look, how
even as he passes by, the aging citizens steam

the windows and miss him, remembering his boy's
way of entering a scene just to break it, his
pink legs working whole crowds into longing.

⚜ On the Notion of Tenderness in Wartime

The news
that you are reading the journals of Delacroix
arrived safely,

thank you. For days
the only word here has been water: everywhere,
scratched into the sun-cracked bellies

of every turned-over-and-over-again stone,
I see it, but I am told
this happens—any day now,

the rains.
Last night I remembered our bodies
coming apart that first time,

you saying "now we're alone in the world."
Sometimes, even here,
it can still get that quiet.

ᴥ *With Love for the Night Patrol*

After the echoes unwrap about us,
the world is unchanged: trees broken and prone
like cool stigmatics, bit of bird in the bush,
wagerable sounds. There is rain, and
the same doubt I couple with the breaking
of dangerous habits. It is difficult
to know what to walk away from.

We tramp through loosely stitched, folding miles
of field whose pattern eludes us. A child's gown
clings to the spokes of an abandoned wheel,
maybe there were houses here.
Every shift of light rears and tips
toward instruction, a clue, the way
things do at home, in a faucet's spit
and cock, in the flight
of a knife.
We push our eyes absently at shadow,
and move on, feeling ready for very little.

I've seen the moon bruise a good jaw down
to pearl, as if scrubbed by rough cloth,
or the fine dirt in the air.
I have marked how the body's action loses
its signature in crisis, frames pitched and
wilting in unison, how legs and arms
dumbly flutter like spent occasions
into the wind.
Mostly,
I think of those many-sectioned dreams in which
night is figured with bodiless advice, missed entries,
deaths that are none of the several small ones

you've come to expect, and you resign yourself
to your own dead weight, when ascending is
the only right move and you know it, you know

you're in the part nobody reads.

ꕥ *Africa Says*

Before you arrive, forget
the landscape the novels are filled with,
the dull retro-colonial glamour
of the British Sudan, Tunis's babble,
the Fat Man, Fez, the avenue that is Khartoum.
Forget the three words you know of
this continent: *baraka, baksheesh,*
assassin, words like chipped knives thrust
into an isolation of sand and night.
These will get you only so far.

In the dreams of the first night,
Africa may seem just another body to
sleep with, a place where you can lay
your own broken equipment to rest.
You have leisure to wonder at her being
a woman, at your being disappointed
with this. You come around to asking
what became of her other four fingers,
how she operates on six alone.
You wipe the sweat from
your chest with her withered hand, raised
and two-fingered; observe, as she sleeps,
how that hand casts the perfect
jackal on a wall whose color
is the same as that of the country

itself, a dark, unpalatable thing who
uses a bulbed twig to paint her lids
in three parallel zones that meet and
kiss one another. She smells of henna or
attar, or rises steeped in musk that in other
women does not stray from between the legs.
She says she has no desire to return

with you. Don't be surprised if
she takes nothing you offer, and moves
on bare feet away from you, or if
you wake feeling close to something,
the gauze damp and loose at your face.

And should you choose to leave, know better
than to give the city a farewell sweep of
the eye. To the pith-helmeted mosques, the slim
and purposeless boulevardiers, the running
sores at the breasts of the women who beg
beside stalled trains, you were never here.
For this reason, you may decide to stay put,
thinking you have left nothing finished.
You may have an urge
to make each move count.
You may have learned nothing at all.

৶ৠ Sect. VIII

I.

Not Achilles, no longer listening
to what is said in the officers' mess, or what
the waves, fingering the beached ships,
echo, that the hero is down,
down and angry . . .

             "Not Achilles, but the knife
in his hand, is what matters," says the captain,

"the knife, and then whatever it is drops from it,
parings of dried fruit, beef, the decidedly
unheroic moons of his nails:

each its own epic, like the blade before it,
the fingers and power behind them
before that."

           Similarly, of interrogation, on
the taking of soldiers in hand, "keep the smile,"
he'd say, "but the good thing it means he's
remembering, or has just that moment

thought of—that I would make my own."

II.

A hand moving through hair cut to look more thin than it is
was the captain.
           Or imagine any field of battle, with its
dust, limbs finding themselves abruptly alone, men
who ride a desperate cause like one more
of the enemy's women:

the eye that, from all of this, would pick out
some more particular thing,

              the fine twist, for example,

the body goes into, hard agony coming upon it,
or the blind hole of a man's mouth together
with the air it has come still around,

this too was the captain, pocketing detail for later,
the long hours when detail
was found wanting.

III.

The captain,

cool beneath his tent of bleached canvas, pulling
the legs from insects—whatever flies in,
that he captures—

                    ranging each of them, bent-kneed,
severed, that cannot know how stupid, now,
all reflex is, across the flats
of his still-beautiful hands . . .

this must be one of those hours.

Never mind the sun beating the sand clean of everything
but the question nobody, anymore, is asking,

or the sentries, with their talk of the heat and
madness and dying and, smattered in between,
the small way scandal has of saving
its debut for the end;

let this moment, as much as anything else,
be the captain,

his, briefly, to fill in
as he pleases. "If this is all, in the end,
any man wants,"

he used to say,
"it is easy enough, it is easy."

ᴥ *Sappho and the Camera*

I must say,
O Captain,

yours alone
is the face that, even now,
is filled in with all that
the others lack, cleanly marked
as the apparent and clear
correct answer.
Crowding the photograph
with distractions, stray
shin-guards, blonde
regalia, horns sprouting
from a neighbor's crown, the rest
serve merely to make
more prominent
the wisdom of choosing you
to rest upon. You are the only
line that fits, the one
point to which
the eye swerves buoyant
with direction, you are

most fairly captured.

From the Sun's Tower

Your hands, shining, drawn in
from the rain, rise no cleaner,
notice, for your holding them out.
The body that floats naked
in the hotel window is yours still.
This is your own blue cock; your legs
are the thin ones, though not unheroic.
Just shy of thirty, they
feel it, fall loosely apart,
or collectively strut the dark, simply
because. For similar reasons,
you may paint your eyes in the morning,
shave only one side of your face,
put a pearl in your nose.

When the winds, or the liquor,
or your ass gives entirely out
to promises, faces, you've money enough
to say no to the hair in the bidet,
the bad water. But there are also
the walled miles to any move elsewhere,
as easy as dreaming your own arms
back, the plate you broke mended,
the stranger's head unopened.
There are the assumptions made by night:
you'll learn to pronounce the names for food
and the neighborhoods you wake to; the next body
must be the one you'll have stayed for.
And then, too, where are the waiters
more lovely?

⚡ Going Under

So what, if the nurses on this particular shift
are all eunuchs, their slippers, as they
pad the buckled tiles, thin

from dreaming back the cool marble of a history
they remember hearing tales of somewhere,
just history now? So what?

For you, the doctor has shaved his dark, difficult
face, something other than the shit- and
fly-covered walls for your

eyes to travel. For you, his lips close, just
behind and above your head, around snatches
of the St. Matthew Passion—

how many angels, even those in countries less
babbling than this one, can do that?
Captain, be easy, this is only

what it is at last to be falling: why else don't
the doctor's hands, as any stranger's
before, take you anywhere special

now? How else can you not want to touch it, his
dwindling brow, want the darkness coming
down to be his ears, like wings,

unfolding to shade you all the long way home?

II

Leda, After the Swan

Perhaps,
in the exaggerated grace
of his weight
settling,

the wings
raised, held in
strike-or-embrace
position,

I recognized
something more
than swan, I can't say.

There was just
this barely defined
shoulder, whose feathers
came away in my hands,

and the bit of world
left beyond it, coming down

to the heat-crippled field,

ravens the precise color of
sorrow in good light, neither
black nor blue, like fallen
stitches upon it,

and the hour forever,
it seemed, half-stepping
its way elsewhere—

then
everything, I
remember, began
happening more quickly.

༄ Birdland

For attention upon arrival, arrive naked,
save for a single rhinestoned pair of field-
glasses. Affect a perfectly natural interest
in ornithology, i.e., profess to know
the male when you see him, or that in any cast
of starlings, no two are the same; let the eye,

with no prompting—like any bird's eye—
attend to the ankle, whether banded or naked,
in flight, and fly with it. As for the casting
of the hard trick, drawing birds from the field
to within some more observable range, know
this too is easily mastered: play to the interest

in any sudden appearance of food, stir interest
by not stirring—remember this, their eyes
are most liable to settle on what they know
or believe to be safe clearing: a pool, the naked
body stumbled upon in some field,
not turning for the wind, one bloodless finger cast

as signal flag, softly waving, broadcasting
it's safe to go down, come closer. A cool disinterest
is, above all, essential, in the particular field
you've entered. Fear, too keen a light in the eye,
and you'll have lost all the edge your body's nakedness gave you—any bird worth half a tail-shake will know

what you've pretended all this time not to know,
or really don't, anymore, already having all but cast
to either side what clear vision remains, eyes nakedly
parading the room, in each a dangerous uninterest
in what the other one sees, a failure of the eyes
to telescope, hence a marked inability to field

whatever meets them head-on. In this case, a field
of birds you begin to sense you already know
from somewhere, to do with that space the mind's eye
now slowly pulls forward, a room, windows of overcast
sky, and in the room the only point of real interest,
what the two bodies, sheetless, bone-naked,

closed-eyed, and busy shifting the casterless
bed elsewhere, miss: the sound a naked interest
will make—birds alighting in a field they know.

✍ Goods

Bed-wetter, probably: solver of problems
in parts, only.

　　　　　Dreamer of trees always falling,
and the hard rains after,

　　　　　　　I'm sure.

. . .

"Let's just say," he says, picking up speed,

the sun, from behind, doing a Hollywood thing
with his hair,

　　　　　"I am mostly not a bad man."

Still,

. . .

I can picture him
getting rough with the good china,

how I'll feel about that.

✌ Loving the Town Planner

You bring me to lovely places: today, a beach
where nobody swims; they all stand erect
and braced at the shore's end, waiting for waves
to meet them, wary of riptide. The water
is the same green everyone's wearing this summer,
what the catalogs call "new basil." I like
the onion rings sold at the beach-house, as
delicate, thin, and necessary as your fingers
marking my chest with a dagger of wet sand,
while you speak of direction and travel.
Travel, for you, is a pickup truck and a damp gym bag,
stuffed with maps of your town, underwear that
may be clean, depending on where we're going next.
You drive along streets whose names are all suburbs
of London (though we're very much in America), and
show me three ways to find your house, that way
guaranteeing I can't find it and turn up some night,
drunk and howling your name in the driveway.
You've got an odd set of concerns.

As the sand burns, your words buoy us both up
to cooler places, the abandoned farm
you took me to a month ago, last week's cove,
protected by law, so that people like us
can lie about naked and undisturbed into
the next two centuries.
                              You get around,
don't you? I understand that, out here.
It's only in closed rooms that I don't know
what's what, when the only coast
is a mattress overshooting its box-spring,
the most exotic view the sun through
the hairs your Siamese leaves on broken furniture.

31

Recently, I woke up holding your leg, and decided
to give it my full attention. It seemed
thirty-two inches of road winding steadily out
into nowhere, land that wouldn't hold up
in good light. When I fell back asleep,
I dreamed I was glowing like an old capital
that everyone was slowly leaving for freshly erected
shadows of a newer city. There was a lot of bad dancing.
I was not unhappy. You were an architect who wore clothes.

Now you're taking my picture with an invisible camera.
I blink as it clicks, and wait to feel something
has just this moment changed for us, but I know
that only happens in certain poems. The truer vision
is that absolutely nothing is changing: I will send you
for more food, since you need to be all the time
moving; I'll watch your legs turn outward, framing air
and leaving it in wishbones behind you; you'll take me
to your room, show me the new air-conditioner, and
look at my body as at a small island whose far side
keeps rolling from view into sheets of fog,
just when you think you've got it all
mapped and on paper.

◁ Luncheon on the Grass

They're a curious lot, Manet's 'scandalous
lunch partners. The two men, lost
in cant and full dress, their legs sprawled
subway-style, as men's legs invariably are, seem
remarkably unruffled, all but oblivious to their nude
female companion. Her nudity is puzzling and
correct; clothes for her are surely only needed
to shrug a shoulder out of. She herself appears
baldly there-for-the-ride; her eyes, moving out
toward the viewer, are wide with the most banal,
detached surprise, as if to say, "where's
the *real* party?"

Now, in a comparable state of outdoor
undress, I'm beginning to have a fair idea
of what's going on in that scene. Watching
you, in clothes, remove one boot to work your
finger toward an itch in your athletic sock,
I look for any similarities between art
and our afternoon here on abandoned
property. The bather in the painting's
background, presumably there for a certain
balance of composition, is for us an ungainly,
rusted green dumpster, rising from overgrown
weeds that provide a contrast only remotely
pastoral. We are two to Manet's main group
of three, but the hum of the odd car or truck
on the highway below us offers a transient third.
Like the nude, I don't seem especially hungry,
partly because it's difficult eating naked when
everyone else is clothed, partly because
you didn't remember I hate chicken salad.
The beer you opened for me sits untouched,

going flat in the sun. I stroke the wet bottle
fitfully, to remind myself just how far
we've come or more probably have always been

from the shape of romance. My dear,
this is not art; we're not anywhere close
to Arcadia.

✦ Badlands

I have my own likely pictures,

of you picking up speed toward sunset,
admiring in your hands at the wheel
that charm that comes from whatever, after
long desire, fumbles initially;

you've stopped for cards you won't send,
you write of the land as of a whore unfolding,
of mirage as one more name for the body
and the scars of detail that crowd it,

dead man's babble . . .

Like flesh like rice paper like anything else
whose beauty lies in the tearing,
the days as we have them,

this desire to kiss and finger each edge
as it blooms.

ᶴᶰᵉ The Conditioning Trick: Home Method

As a start
I confine myself to a handful of rooms
and give simple things an attention
you'd laugh at: in the kitchen,
actually roasting the peppers
myself, baking with ingredients I've brought
to room temperature, rinsing
the salad greens until the leaves,
patted dry,
sway pliant as prophecy
into my hands.

In the bedroom
impossible flowers rise
from the curtains you chose for me.
I look past them and invent my own
names for the sky: watered gin,
a child's scarf after rain, the diva's
backside, Vincent the Sometime
Dark and Sometime
Fair.
I add up the seams in the wallpaper, and keep
landing squarely on the same
unwieldy prime number, the number
of birds to hope for in augury,
or of creases to find on the sacrificed animal's
liver.

I've removed both lights
from the bathroom, and the wings of the blinds
are kept folded,
but like all of my difficult thoughts,
you still turn up in the shower.
I talk myself out of the dream

that at this point is all
you can believably be:
"the blue tiles," I say, "are not you,"
though they match the blue lines
at your ankle and breast; "the patterns
soap makes in the drain are not
those you traced on the back of my neck;
and these hands,
that beneath the steady, regimented
water, seem like nothing
so much as tongues, passing over, unfolding me,
these hands that must know me from somewhere, these
too," I say, from a mouth not mine,
"are not you," until

your limbs become
the steam and vision I have bent
three rooms, a small life, around.

✍ *Undressing for Li Po*

Li Po,
the moon through the vertical blinds
is laying its bars down,
I see black, tapered lives, and
the paler ones in between, all the sticks
of my life left to mend.
Fingering the two flat prayers
at my chest, one pierced with a gold ring,
the other rouged with a broken wedge
of mouth-paint,
I'm remembering your fondness
for wine, Li Po, you desiring your own
reflection, or the moon's, the same thing,

and dying from it.
At the mirror, to the man I love
too much, I am trying to say
that I have no need
for his tattooed body, his
hands at my wrists, the cicatrix
of woes tilting down
from beneath the belly—

that I'm tired
of flesh tumbling over the dwindling sword
of itself,
something like joy . . .

Li Po, Li Po,
the moon is picking its way
over used swabs and razors, pots of cream,
my face where I left it, on the dressing-table.
I am thinking
mountains,

good wine,
plash of exile,
letters to nowhere, the poems,
untrimmed affection,
distance, boats coming
more still than the water
in their wandering.

Li Po, last night,
drunk again, I stood naked downstairs,
just dancing, dancing . . .
I watched my feet recover and lose again
their apricot, moving in and out from
the moon's light,
watched my body lose all particulars
save clean grace, what I'd forgotten.
I imagined dancing with a man seven feet tall,
the moon making a small planet of his face,

I thought of you again, Li Po.

⚜ The Glade

Here, complete with half-swallowed cry
of small game rising, stirring
the light, is that ease

with which a legend goes
languorously down on itself,
slow-dying;

this is the air left behind, thick
with the whir of bees flagging, smell
of meadow that's spent all its arrows,

where every dream is
of difficult breathing, of desire
as a finally grounded bird

whose limbs and blue-black wings
dangle from the dreamer's mouth,
refusing to come loose . . .

Here,
where his body lay, gather up all
the broken-stemmed flowers;

photograph the water, that in
the wind repeatedly makes for shore
and misses—

these, for dark Narcissus
who, whatever else and more
he may have been,

was never ours.

III

🍃 Conversion

Unprodded, you stop taking appearance as granted
and effortless, not only the sex lives of friends,
yourself, but more tangible objects, springing
smug as fact from shelves and bins: produce,
canned goods, duplicate wedding gifts. You consider
which tap comes first, hot or cold, domestic tools
passing from one hand to another, the direction
you settle on to stir things.

There will be distractions: a torn trash-liner
crackles from the telephone cables, the wash cycles
alternately stall or howl and thrust across
the air; know that these are not it, continue
looking. Ignore the bad lawnwork, walk like
a raven back and forth between the wet sheets,
tugging their pegs.

Daily life can narrow to a mythology of efficiency.
Waiting for God to come into your house, to drag
one foot like water over the curled dhurrie, you
tell friends you have chosen a contemplative life,
tipping ash onto San Callisto's chipped brow, and
offering up that lack-of-better-to-do patience
that passes for a sensitive wisdom, a quality.
You may find within yourself a tendency to dress
in oracular shades. You don't say that your
dreams are of shouting for God *as fire to iron,*
as the light to glass through a weight
of veils on your mouth; how, in the bath, you trace
the names of minor saints in fingers around
the bend of your hips, and feel an arousal that
no longer seems misplaced.

One morning the rooms all swell, so that cleaning
becomes a hieratic gesture, the dust on your
parting knees the kiss of promised dispensation.
There seems not enough and much still to be
done. The light passes in and out of you, stiff
miracle, merging, leaping, unuttering. These
could be angels, you don't know. You lie on the floor
with your next lover, a traveler who listens
to white gospel and is constantly speaking
of walkers, flyers, divers, the three
orders of jinn, as of something to beware of.
Don't hear this part. Take his waist like
a wheel for direction, your own flesh for
a malleable prayer. Drift lovely and absolute
as vision toward him, beyond him, out several
doors at once.

✺ holy, holy

You're expected to know
that God may be the gnats clouding
the violets across a room, the clatter
of beaded curtains when there's no wind
in the hallway and no one's been at the wine,
a chafed hand smudging violation
between two legs, the missing finger,
any stick in a hole—he's said to be
that mysterious.

But more often, he cameos as that which lacks
surprise,
the mountie,
the seller of chances,
the anatomist with a figure to cut;

approaches the body as if it were something
more pliant, foil, good cotton;

comes equipped with the requisite
roll to the floor for passion, limbs
no more articulate than the stiff
crease in the pants he will always remember
to fold first.

Presumably, there are details
you might wish to refer to, later:
the mouth that goes without saying,
the bloom of hair at the ear,
the make of the car . . .

while, in another part of the house,
flags are burning,

alien tankers are penetrating home ports,
there are chinks in the National Security;

it's all rather quick and unrelenting.

You keep meaning to ask what all the fuss is about.
You return the nightstand to its original position.

✎ Memories of the Revival

On the fifth day,
done with praying
for long life, television
skin, a little more ignorance
on the part of whatever
powers might be,
done with squeezing divine allowance
from the knees' indignities,
you take the grotesque by his
oversized ears, and lead him
into your bed, where over

and over and over, you tell him
that practice is its own
strange perfection,
and direct his eye to what

he can't possibly understand:
how the heat has brought out
the artery and bronze in his arms,
to an arousing degree,

how the ravaged skin of his back
reminds you of schoolchildren, seen
from a height, the same pinched
squashes of color . . .

Or perhaps, leaning at a shutterless window,
you watch his hands, on command, shift
crabwise, stiff with bad habit, against
the small, hairless drama of his body,
producing a sound somewhere between

a rake's bite into unexpected flesh
in the leaves, and a wounded dog dragging
its torn trunk over a wet, pitted road.

Later, you have the same dream
as usual, of your body rising
like steam off virgin soil, while
across a yellowed distance the rains
resaddle, flinging whole capes and skies
of possibility behind them,

clouds listing toward bluff. Occasionally,
you wake to the carelessly pitched
limbs beside you, and you watch
the skyline burning down
on his unlikely drum of a chest,
then fall into the other dream, the one

where you've been standing for hours,
waiting for the trees to renew
their shoving.

ꝰ Fra Lippo Lippi and the Vision of Henley

If, in depicting the angels, I cannot
avoid something, as well, of what
the river that day cast before me,

the musculature of the rowers' arms,
together streaking the air of those
otherwise empty, unremarkable hours;

if only now, after the mechanical
drown   recover   drown of the oars in
their hands, do I understand wings

and the scaled-down pattern for
suffering that every wing, surely,
is lined with, do, Monsignor,

forgive me. By your grace, again,
this is what happened: at first,
only the heat, the cool water . . .

Visitation

When it was over, they told me
that the creak of wings folding
was only the bed, that shutters

do not clap of themselves. Morning
was what it had always been, any woman
marooned in the air,

                              the nicked
blooms of suggestion, in the lamp,
in the lemonwood stool, every seam
or pocket slowly retrieved,

were the usual ones, what
everyone knows. Father spat
into the unswept yard below,
as if it too were an unseemly desire,

and passed through the door.

I am no mystic. I know
nothing rises that doesn't
know how to already.
In my ears, only the clubbed
foot of routine, no voices, no

clatter of dreams: but I saw
what I saw.

Design for the Lost Corsair

For that apocryphal-as-
dream effect, let the deck
surrender to the magnolia's

parchment flowers.
Within the damp hair of
the eunuch loosely chained

to the rail, one-slippered and
dancing still, though he
needn't, camellias,

one blowsy hibiscus
to shade the mad captain's
one eye, staring into the sun,

and across the hero's wasted brow
that not even sleep, now, will
smooth, the rose, laid so.

Everywhere,
dangling like spit or
prayer from scurvy-soft mouths,

in broken fistfuls taken up
and cast onto the water,
the lily, for

rudderless promise, for
sliding over the world's edge,
into whatever comes after.

✌ Death of the Sibyl

The world, when it comes, is not the fist
and palm of a lover's roulette, nothing
to brace for. There are no visions.

The blue stops here, as the walls do,
light spills with the candor of money
or jangled music on the morning's disorder:

the knife, streaked and at rest, spent
fruit, plates round and flat as an old,
unquestioned routine. Outside, the hours

drift and pick at the air, as if coming
and going were grave decisions, as if there
were still an immediacy, somewhere, to

things as they are. You know better.
Your body isn't the restive field it was,
clouds share none of the marbled indifference

of statues, whose absent limbs and dark-socketed
heads once triggered desire. Surely this
is the backside of God, to lie down

in a room of no accidents, touch your own
flesh or not, to nobody's direction, grip
sheets in your mouth and know passion is

little more than a wound to be straddled,
shadow something less than pearls in
retreat. To feel empty as seed to fire,

hear the rush of whole lives passing
elsewhere, without you, and still believe
you have not been entirely abandoned.

IV

~ evangels

Wonderful,
as in

truly replete
with wonder,
is what it is,
how the body finds
in its own
aboriginal coil
all it needs, finally,
of blood and the gospel.

Watching you, bound
at the hands and
being led like some
Peter or Joan or Agnes,
those relentless,
imperturbable wielders
of agony, toys
for any whip or
shackle going,

I know
that the world might be,
for any of us,
reduced to the driver's
hair gone ecstatic
under the wind's passage,
the derisively indifferent
flesh of his mouth,

his fine hand unsnapping
the door to an unmarked car
the press and cameras

spill away from.
No,
I take back
the "might be"—hour
after looped
hour,

that is all
the world is.

 # Miserere

And
after the dream of my brown hands turning
beneath the clear water that runs
forever on command through
the houses I clean,

I woke to find
my hands were still
not as brown
as the water the tap spat
into my glass,

not as brown as the brown
that the light, by the time it had
made its way through the stained
blinds down to your face,
had become, all you have ever
known of how the day comes

to be. And I thought to be thankful
for all the work the world, in torn
skyfuls, brings us, and how
O somebody, somebody, as
they say, must do it. And beneath
your slowed breathing, fuck
that, I heard a voice like mine
keep saying, fuck that, and the black
that I saw was not my hands
or your crumpled lashes or
your mouth still opening and closing
around some last dream of your own.

𝒮𝓌 The Arsonist as Lover

Sigh into it, and smoke will rise
off iced vodka as it will from no other
clear liquid. We tilt our eyes
like dolls and breathe small birds
across the veranda's plum shadow:
as if this were their cue, a small girl's
nameless legs from a tree
skirt the light in stiff trapeze.

Sun limns the half-pediment
of the house that rises at our property's
hem, as steadily as a smooth pregnancy,
round, with no eyes for a hitch.
I wake early
and watch the men settle
like butterflies, freckle with red
and bronze backs the roof, the exposed
beams of morning; they are so tiny, seen
through the sky's clean distance, I cup
and release them one-handed,
and come back to the one dream:

I dream we are, you and I, seeking
an omen between ourselves, and it is
the same one, though neither of us
can know that, waiting for the hour
to fill us, as when the grey doves,
in movies, in unison rise
and crowd the air, pushing the light
before them until the sky is all
breast and pearl momentum. The most
ordinary things become sign for us,
so that when the girl drops softly

onto the lawn, she's the answer
approaching; look, you say, her hair
is a house on fire.

ᴥ For Chiron

Nothing expected hurts
as it otherwise should, so
no, you did not hurt, Professor,

even that first time. I had dreamed
already the green line of subway
before your directions, your shadow
a tall drink in a room of skyline rising
off glass surfaces, everywhere
glass. That much I saw before
seeing, the incidental angle to your
bed, traveling wet with clues among well-suited
men on the train in daylight, showering you into
the loose tiles of the dormitory bathroom. All
as expected: half-note of surprise to every
return, my dim passing away from you,

the clouds I watch now in June, broad
years from you, waiting for your shape to drop
on a life I make for myself.
I like to think of me moving across
that part of your life
where you somewhere
lie remembering (though this is

the one thing I never
expect) what still
bewilders, each time you wake to it,
lifting yourself to different faces.

✍ The man we're looking for

says pee
for piss, and nobody
minds

claims he's never seen
in one room three
attractive women

is often asked what
he's waiting for,
does

and does not
wear more than one ring to
a finger, an ear,

has a fondness
for the letter K, on
T-shirts, good cuff-links,

the first and last pages
of books he provides
his houseguests

bends clinically over
a woman, certain men, as over
a new drink

laughs the laugh
of his most recent victim,
owns it, in this respect

seems
a collector of sorts,
a connoisseur,

e.g., knows
a concealed weapon
when he sees one

has been variously described
as dangerous, small of hand, half-
heroically

gaited, worth giving
pause at, bit of the
masher,

gorgeous. Be alarmed, but steady;
these are simply
the facts as we have them,

ma'am.

 *Passion*

Initial sketches didn't include
that lily on the table
or the nude homunculus in repose
where the signature should be.
In both cases, flesh tilts
toward its own weak reflection, growing
and growing on the eye,

though you are still very much
the focus, striking the four-footed
martyr's pose as if God were
a tireless cowboy, and sacrifice
a matter of cool business.
Your legs, as they bleed
off the canvas, suggest
the embarrassing lack of proportion
a life will allow.

There is something here distinctly
not from the lives of the saints,
perhaps only what the mind, returning
to the portrait as toward a bad but
familiar plan, keeps coming away with:

that not everything deserves illumination;

that your body was never more unforgettable
than now.

⚜ In the Jury Box

The way he told it,
it wasn't an unnatural thing.
He had always looked past those
whose limbs had already twisted
themselves into muscle, who knew
how to go about moving through space
with the ease that comes from much use.
It was the others he'd watch, their
slim, frangible necks notching the air,
or ducking before the push of the wind
across a playground, unfinished knees
flying in sprints through the unsettled
rooms of the body, sometimes stopping to
scratch themselves like men, then boys
again, rumbling, loosely sneakered, past.

He told how he'd follow them, wait
for them to break themselves up,
choose one to approach; he told of
the bees and his thin, irredeemable
shadow blacking the lawns' yellows—
forsythia, dandelion—how he'd listen
to the clatter of the old year's leaves
upon the new grass, remember the toenails
and sand at the bottom of his bed long
summers ago, the body's casting
off of debris, the dry archaeology
of childhood. These were the details,
tenderly delivered, that all but
endeared him to us.

So that even at its most horrible point,
his story touched us with a fear
that is, too, a kind of beauty—we

saw it all, his body rising
in handfuls from his shirt of worn
broadcloth, the gnats drawn to its absence
of color at dusk, the way he flourished
his body like an unbeatable hand or
a fine career, fell as tentative as snow
upon the squall of a strange boy's
body, and bore down upon him
as if he were trying to push something
finally away from himself. And, almost
an afterthought, the confusion, the
killing, later, the distraction of flesh
rendered still and useless, how
to cover it all so well he might never
think to feel this way again.
For a moment, the room came still
as at the presence of something
holy or so unthinkably dark that it
became something holy, each of us, to
a man, to a woman, dreaming his hot and
briefly mad flesh tattooed upon our own.

ꙅ Fast

First the snapping down of clouds
from Michelangelo fingers to abbreviated
snouts, getting on with it,

too many of that squeamish-crowd kind of wild
kind of rose you can't find at the plaza,
none of that composure,

and downshore, at the edge of what my eye
could still see, the usual matter of the flesh,
the lanky symbol of it, scuttling

crabwise, as symbols tend to,
away . . .
then just this air of indifference:

"wind," they said, when it occasionally
settled, settling the way hands
that find no hold at first

eventually do,
or again "wind" when it picked up,
bringing the bone out in their faces.

On Holy Ground

Four days into the country,
you determine
there will be no translation:

there is only the one sky,
whiter than any saint,
than the fire
they say will refine us all,

and your empty hands
that scrape it.

Back in the wreckage
of the good hotel,

the occasional
pulled lament of a body climbing
free of the pool;

the smell of flesh
abrading itself,
in showers, on native linen,
reminds you of home.

◢ Blue

As through marble or the lining of
certain fish split open and scooped
clean, this is the blue vein
that rides, where the flesh is even
whiter than the rest of her, the splayed
thighs mother forgets, busy struggling
for command over bones: her own,
those of the chaise longue, all
equally uncooperative, and there's
the wind, too. This is her hair, gone
from white to blue in the air.

This is the black, shot with blue, of my dark
daddy's knuckles, that do not change, ever.
Which is to say they are no more pale
in anger than at rest, or when, as
I imagine them now, they follow
the same two fingers he has always used
to make the rim of every empty blue
glass in the house sing.
Always, the same
blue-to-black sorrow
no black surface can entirely hide.

Under the night, somewhere
between the white that is nothing so much as
blue, and the black that is, finally, nothing,
I am the man neither of you remembers.
Shielding, in the half-dark,
the blue eyes I sometimes forget
I don't have. Pulling my own stoop-
shouldered kind of blues across paper.
Apparently misinformed about the rumored
stuff of dreams: everywhere I inquired,
I was told look for blue.

V

In the Blood, Winnowing

I.

Before the dumb hoof
through the chest, the fine hair
of wire drawn over the head, snapping
free the neck's blue chords,

before the visionary falling away
from a body left mumbling to itself,
consigned to the damp sling
of tropic circumstance,

there was this morning now,
in the shower, when you know
you are dying,

you are dying and your body—
a lozenge or a prayer, whatever goes
slim and unimportant when the tongue
has grown overly zealous—

contracts under the steam,
under the light that shows up on your skin
as a deep red the shower's curtain
alone can't account for.

II.

What is it but
yours, the one hand
drawing the scrotum (no longer
yours) back upon itself?
When you come
into the other hand, it's like
spitting on death's breast, on
her spectator shoes,

to distract her.
Trembling in the water,
in the stick of yourself,
you watch the talisman's shadow,
already twisting, diminished against
the tiles, to the pig's-tail stump
of conclusion,

all it ever was.

III.

Stones do not matter.
You are twenty-nine for no reason,
or thirty-seven, your favorite prime.
Perhaps you are precisely that age
when a writer means, finally,
all that he says, a cubed square
of cell after cell containing
all the hounds of childhood,
with their hard buckles and hot
irons, their pins for under
your fingers. Dreams
are of falling
asleep at locked windows,
you are all the stones
that keep missing the glass.

IV.

Nothing stops
for you admiring the hair
that has sprung late
at either shoulder,

for you crushing your face
into the shirts that bloom
like cutaway views of old
lovers from your wall of closet.
It is any morning when the train
rattles over birdsong, the suggestion
of blades coming dry
from the night; brilliantly,
shaft after shaft, the sun passes
over the shit and bone and feather
of yours and other lives on earth,
the canted row-houses, children
in their crippled victory gardens,
throwing knives in the air,

and you tell yourself (already
growing hard again over the train's
crosstown difficulties)
that everything counts:

the correct tie,
the bit of skin between sock
and cuff, the man beside you,
strange and familiar as a tattoo
the hand wakes to and keeps
wanting to touch,
refusing to believe
in that part of the world
where things don't wash off.

A NOTE ON THE AUTHOR

Carl Phillips, born in 1959, received an A.B. from Harvard College and an M.A.T. from the University of Massachusetts. He taught high school Latin for eight years, before returning to Harvard, where he is now a doctoral student in classical philology. The recipient of a fellowship in poetry from the Massachusetts Artists Foundation, his work has appeared in *Agni, Callaloo, Kenyon Review, Paris Review,* and many other journals. He lives in Boston, Massachusetts.

A NOTE ON THE PRIZE

The Samuel French Morse Poetry Prize was established in 1983 by the Northeastern University Department of English in order to honor Professor Morse's distinguished career as teacher, scholar, and poet. The members of the prize committee are Francis C. Blessington, Joseph deRoche, Victor Howes, Ruth Lepson, Stuart Peterfreund, and Guy Rotella.